*Giving in
pleasure
be...*

MISTRESS:
TAKEN BY THE TYCOON

*Three exciting new stories from
three beloved authors*

Coming soon:

VIRGIN
WEDDED BY A BILLIONAIRE

*Three gorgeous heroes, three
glamorous romances*

MISTRESS:
TAKEN BY THE TYCOON

Kristi Gold

Jan Colley

Jessica Bird

All the characters in this book have no existence outside the imagination
of the author, and have no relation whatsoever to anyone bearing the
same name or names. They are not even distantly inspired by any
individual known or unknown to the author, and all the incidents are
pure invention.

MISTRESS: TAKEN BY THE TYCOON
© Harlequin Books S.A. 2010

Through Jenna's Eyes © Kristi Goldberg 2007
Billionaire's Favourite Fantasy © Janet Colley 2008
The Billionaire Next Door © Jessica Bird 2007

ISBN: 978 0 263 87701 4

24-0110

Harlequin Mills & Boon policy is to use papers that are
natural, renewable and recyclable products and made from
wood grown in sustainable forests. The logging and
manufacturing processes conform to the legal environmental
regulations of the country of origin.

Printed and bound in Spain
by Litografia Rosés S.A., Barcelona

THROUGH JENNA'S EYES

Kristi Gold

Kristi Gold admits to having a fondness for watching major league baseball and double-cheese enchiladas and she also enjoys creating dark and somewhat dangerous – albeit honourable – heroes. She considers indulging in all three in the same day as the next best thing to a beach vacation.

She loves to hear from her readers and can be contacted through her website at www.kristigold.com or through snail mail at 6902 Woodway Drive, No. 166, Waco, Texas, USA. (Please include an SAE for response.)

Chapter One

Logan O'Brien had learned long ago the phone always rang at inopportune times. During a shower, which he'd already taken. During sex, which unfortunately wasn't an issue tonight. And in this case, during an extra-inning ball game, which ranked right up there as another worst-case scenario.

After pausing the game with the remote, he grabbed the phone and answered with an irritable, "Yeah."

"Sorry to bother you, boss, but we have a situation."

Good old Bob, Logan's right-hand man. Whenever a problem arose, the retired cop always sounded as if he worked for a Secret Service detail, not as a driver for well-heeled Houston society. "It's late, Bob. I've got the ball game on and I've only been home for an hour. So, unless you're going to tell me that every limo or sedan I own has simultaneously broken down, you handle it."

"We've got an alleged intoxicated female who needs a ride."

Not the first time one of his employees had faced that situation. "And this is supposed to impress me how?"

"It's Jenna Fordyce."

Great. The daughter of his VIP client, Avery Fordyce. Logan's company took care of all the billionaire's corporate and personal transportation needs, not to mention the other clients Fordyce had sent his way. "What about Calvin?"

"He's off tonight. I'd do it, but I'm waiting to take a wedding party to the airport. And I thought since old man Fordyce trusts you, and this is—"

"I know, Bob. His kid." So much for a night of sitting around in his underwear, relaxing. "I'll take care of it. Where is she?"

"At a joint called La Danza. It's on—"

"I know the place." He'd been there before. Several times over the past year, but not in a few weeks. At least the nightclub was less than two miles from his downtown condo. But the Fordyce estate, where Jenna still resided, was located a good thirty minutes away, longer if the Saturday-night traffic happened to be heavy.

"The bouncer called dispatch about five minutes ago," Bob added. "He said he'd wait with her until someone got there. I'm thinking she's in pretty bad shape."

That didn't surprise Logan one bit. The club was known for its high-octane drinks. One or two martinis would do the trick for a lightweight socialite. "Fine. I'm on my way."

After hanging up the phone, Logan sprinted up the stairs to dress in a faded blue T-shirt, jeans and a pair of hiking boots, clothes he would never allow his employees to wear while conducting business. But if the heiress had tied one on, she probably wouldn't notice his attire. Even if she didn't approve, right now he only cared about getting this over with so he could get back to the game.

When he reached the parking garage, Logan opted to take his Hummer instead of the roadster, in case she happened to get sick. God, he hoped she didn't. That would pretty much ruin his night completely.

As he navigated the downtown streets, Logan realized he wasn't sure he'd be able to pick Jenna Fordyce out of a crowd, considering he'd never officially met her. But he had seen her framed high-school graduation photo on Avery's desk—a predictably beautiful, dark haired, dark eyed young woman. Daddy's little princess, just like Logan's ex-fiancée, who had played the pregnancy card until he'd called her bluff, fortunately before he'd been trumped into marriage.

Yeah, he'd had his fill of debutantes. Society babes who couldn't see beyond the fact he had the means and the money to keep them in the lifestyle to which they were accustomed. He doubted Jenna Fordyce was any different from the rest, particularly since she was the only child of a widowed business magnate.

A few minutes later, Logan pulled behind a stretch limo, the only space available beneath the portico of the five-star hotel that housed the popular nightclub. He stepped out into the warm June night and immediately caught sight of a no-neck guy with a clean-shaven head standing a few feet away, his arm around a woman.

The closer he came to the couple, the more certain he became that he'd found Jenna Fordyce—a few years older than depicted in the photo, but still as striking. She was conservatively dressed in a blue sleeveless blouse, a white skirt cut right above the knee and low heels. Her brown hair curled past her shoulders and a pair of sunshades covered her eyes, indicating she'd moved past three to at least four sheets in the wind. She was also pressing a white cloth over her right eyebrow, and Logan wondered if she'd engaged in a catfight. That would definitely make the society page tomorrow.

As he approached the unlikely pair, Logan nodded at the presumed bouncer and addressed the woman at his side. "Ms. Fordyce?"

She inclined her head toward him. "Yes?"

"I'm Logan O'Brien, the owner of your father's transportation service."

When he offered his hand, she ignored the gesture, fumbled in the skirt's pocket and withdrew several bills that she pressed into the bouncer's palm. "This should take care of the bar tab, Johnny, with a little extra for your help. And, if you don't mind, could you tell my friend I'm leaving now? I wouldn't want her to worry."

"What does she look like?" Johnny asked.

"A pretty blonde," she said. "Her name is Candice and she's seated at the bar. I believe she's wearing pink. She always wears pink."

The bouncer regarded Logan, his arm still firmly around his charge. "Someone needs to check out the cut on her head. She had a pretty nasty fall, but she wouldn't let me call the paramedics."

Jenna waved her free hand in dismissal. "It's nothing."

When Logan noticed the red seeping through the cloth, he realized the injury could be serious. "Johnny's right. You're bleeding. You need a doctor."

"Can we discuss this in the car?" she asked.

No discussion required. She could argue all the way to the hospital, but he wasn't about to turn her loose without making sure she was okay. "Let's go."

The bouncer held out her arm to Logan. "She's kind of shaky, so you need to hang on to her."

Usually Logan wouldn't mind wrapping his arm around a sexy woman. But this blue-blooded babe didn't interest him—or shouldn't—for several reasons.

Logan circled his arm around her waist and braced her elbow with one hand. Slowly, he guided her to the SUV, noticing immediately that she was small, maybe five-two, a foot shorter than him. Definitely not his type. He preferred women with more substance, inside and out.

Once they reached the passenger side, Logan opened the door, helped her up into the seat and, in a show of benevolence, buckled her in. So far, so good. She hadn't taken another tumble on the way, even though he suspected she might have if he'd let her go, considering how carefully she'd measured her steps. Whatever she'd had to drink, he assumed it must have been fairly potent. But he didn't detect the smell of alcohol, only the scent of her perfume. Nothing overpowering, just a light fragrance that reminded him of his mother's favorite lavender soap. That was definitely a switch from the women he'd known who bathed in expensive concoctions designed to turn on a man, when it only served to turn him off.

Logan climbed into the driver's seat, flipped on the overhead light and pulled his cell phone from the holder attached to the dash. "Do you want to call your father and let him know what's going on, or should I?"

"Good luck," she said. "He's in Chicago on business until tomorrow. And I gave the staff the night off."

"Anyone else I can call?"

"No."

Figured. That meant she was his sole responsibility for the time being. He shoved the phone back in the holder and released a rough sigh. "Then I guess it's you and me and the E.R."

She frowned. "Just drive me home and I'll be fine."

Not until he had a better look at the cut. When he reached over to remove the cloth, she physically jumped, as if he'd scared her out of her skin with a simple touch. "Relax," he told her as he lifted the makeshift bandage away. "I'm only trying to see how bad this is."

"It's a minor scrape," she said. "I got up close and personal with a wall outside the ladies' room when I tripped."

Obviously she hadn't bothered to check it out in a mirror. "It looks like it might need stitches. The hospital's not that far."

"No hospital." Her voice held an edge of panic. "I don't care for emergency rooms, or doctors."

She could be concerned the medical staff would run a tox screen, and that could pose a problem if the press got wind of an off-the-chart blood-alcohol level. Still, her condition might warrant treatment beyond mending a superficial cut, and right now she was Logan's responsibility. He lifted her hand from her lap and pressed it against the cloth again. "You could have a concussion."

"I'm certain I don't."

"Are you a doctor, Ms. Fordyce?"

"Are you, Mr. O'Brien?"

For the first time in his life, Logan wished he were. Then he could examine her, medically speaking, and take her home. Her home, not his. But medicine hadn't been his calling…and that gave him an idea. "Look, my brother *is* a doctor, and he only lives about ten minutes from here. He could probably check it out."

She mulled that over before saying, "I'll agree to this, but only if you promise to take me home afterward."

Not a problem, since that was his plan. "I'll give him a call and see if he's available."

Logan already knew he was. He'd spoken with Devin earlier in the evening and learned he had a rare day off from his duties as chief resident of trauma, which meant this request could cost him. Big-time.

He retrieved the cell phone again, hit the speed

dial and hoped he didn't wake the whole household, including the baby. Or worse, disturb his brother catching up on lost time between the sheets with his wife.

After two rings, Devin answered with his usual, "Dr. O'Brien."

"Hey, Dev, it's Logan. Sorry to call you so late."

"I'm still up, thanks to a kid who's decided it's playtime, not bedtime. What's going on?"

"I have a client who needs medical attention, but she's not too keen on going to the E.R." He sent Jenna a quick glance to find her staring out the windshield. "She has a cut on her forehead. Mind if I bring her by so you can take a look at it?"

Devin released a low laugh. "A client, huh? Are you charging for stud service these days?"

He was in no mood for his brother's attempt at humor. "I provide *driving* services for her. If you'll do this, I'll let you have my season tickets for the home game of your choice."

"Deal. But if it's something I can't handle in a nonhospital setting, then you're going to have to take her to the E.R."

That could pose a monumental challenge for Logan. But what choice did he have? "Agreed."

"Hang on a minute."

Logan could hear the sounds of muffled voices and realized Devin was consulting his wife. A few moments later, his brother came back to the phone and said, "Stacy's okay with it, on one condition, aside from the tickets. We do this at your condo, and I have to bring Sean with me. Car rides make him sleepy."

"Not a problem. I'll see you in a few minutes." And it wasn't a problem for Logan. He enjoyed being around his fifteen-month-old nephew, as long as he could send him home again. What he knew about taking care of a kid for more than a few hours could best be described with two words—not much. As far as taking Jenna to his place, that meant less of a drive. The faster he got this over with, the quicker he could get her back to the Fordyce mansion.

Logan snapped the phone closed and turned his attention back to Jenna. "He'll meet us at my apartment."

She kept her gaze trained on the dashboard. "Where do you live?"

"Downtown. A couple of miles from here."

"I appreciate this," she said. "I hope I'm not causing too much trouble."

"No trouble at all." And that wasn't exactly true. She could mean big trouble for Logan if he didn't stop noticing things about her, including the fact she had a great body, even if she was short. He needed to remember she was the daughter of a client. An important client who wouldn't appreciate any man having questionable thoughts about his daughter. Especially a man whom he trusted to do the right thing—and the right thing would be for Logan to keep his eyes, and his hands, to himself.

"Do you think I can take this cloth away now?" Jenna asked after he started the ignition. "My arm's getting tired."

"Let me see."

When she lowered the rag, Logan lifted her chin and brought her face toward him.

Okay, so she had soft skin and a really nice mouth. So did a lot of women. She probably had a hefty trust fund and an overblown sense of self-worth, too. Logan refused to head down that sorry road again.

"It's stopped bleeding, so you can take it off," he said as he returned his hands to the steering wheel and his mind back on business, where they belonged.

He drove back to the loft at a sluggish pace behind the weekend traffic and ill-timed lights. During the trip, Jenna kept her sunglasses in place and her gaze centered straight ahead until they pulled into the parking garage. Aside from a muttered, "thanks," when he helped her out of the Hummer and into the elevator, she remained silent. That was okay with Logan. He intended to keep their relationship on a strictly professional level. He also planned to keep his distance, but he didn't feel he could do that until they reached his apartment; the reason why he continued to hold on to her until he had her seated on the club chair in the living room.

"This seems like a nice place," she said, finally breaking the silence.

Searching for much-needed space, Logan dropped down on the sofa across from the chair. "I bought it from my sister and brother-in-law after they moved into their new house."

"Then you have one brother and one sister?"

"Actually, four brothers and a sister."

She smiled. "Wow. I'm an only child, so I can't imagine having such a large family. What are your parents like?"

Small talk was good. He could handle small talk. "They live in west Houston in the same middle-class neighborhood where I grew up." Heavy emphasis on "middle class." Logan wanted Jenna Fordyce to know up front that he hadn't originated from her side of the society divide, even if his financial situation had changed with his success.

When she made no move to take off her sunglasses, he said, "Feel free to get rid of the shades. I've been there before, so I'm not going to judge you."

She wrung her hands together several times. "The light bothers my eyes."

Man, he wouldn't want to be her in the morning. "If you think it's bad now, wait until tomorrow."

"Why's that?"

Obviously she'd never visited hangover central before, whereas, at one time, he'd been a frequent guest. "I take it you don't drink too often."

"No, I don't. I've never cared that much for alcohol. I only have a glass of wine on occasion."

That could explain her current state if she'd had more than a few tonight, but something still didn't quite ring true for Logan. Her speech didn't sound the least bit slurred. In fact, she sounded coherent. Probably one of the lucky ones who could drink and drown and still be able to fake sobriety.

When she grew silent again, Logan considered turning on the TV to watch the baseball game he'd recorded, but decided Ms. Fordyce didn't look like a baseball fan. He suspected tennis was her game, if sports interested her at all. For that reason, he should probably ask what she preferred, and right when he was about to pose the question, the doorbell rang, indicating help had arrived.

Logan pushed off the sofa, strode to the entry and opened the door to his brother who had a duffel bag hanging on one shoulder and a wide-eyed toddler wearing red superhero pajamas braced on one hip.

He stepped aside to let them in. "You made good time."

"The advantage of learning the fastest route when you're on call," Devin said. "Where's the patient?"

"Right down the hall."

When they reached the living room, Logan gestured toward his guest who had yet to acknowledge them. "Devin, this is Jenna Fordyce."

When Devin moved in front of the chair, Jenna offered her hand and a smile, something she hadn't done with Logan back at the bar. "It's a pleasure to meet you, Devin. I hope I'm not wasting your time."

"Not a problem," Devin said as he handed off Sean to Logan before taking Jenna's hand for a brief shake. He pulled up an ottoman in front of the chair and set his bag in his lap. "Now, let's take a look at that cut."

Logan hooked a thumb over his shoulder. "While you're doing that, I'll take the kid into the kitchen and see if I can find him a cookie."

Devin sent him a hard look. "Don't give him more than one. If I bring him home on a sugar high, you and I both are going to have to answer to my wife."

Logan had always considered his sister-in-law to be a reasonable woman, but he didn't want to test her. "I'll keep that in mind."

After he entered the adjacent kitchen, Logan held Sean high above his head, eliciting a laugh from his nephew. "You're getting heavy, bud," he said as he brought him back down and set him on the counter. "I only have a chocolate-chip cookie, so I hope that's okay."

Sean answered with the single word, *cookie*, and a wide grin, indicating Logan was definitely speaking his language.

When he opened the cabinet, withdrew the

cookie from the package and handed it to Sean, the kid squealed. One thing about it, toddlers could be easy to please, unlike several of the women Logan had known. One in particular. He wasn't sure why he kept thinking about his former fiancée tonight. The answer to that was sitting in the next room, undergoing an exam by his brother. But aside from Helena's and Jenna's similar backgrounds, he recognized several differences between the two, at least when it came to the physical aspects. Then again, he didn't plan to explore those differences. Once Devin was done doing his doctor thing, Logan would have Ms. Fordyce back at the family mansion in record time.

Sean finished the last bite of cookie and held out his hand, palm up, and wiggled his fingers. "More."

"Not a good idea, bud." Logan looked around for another form of entertainment and selected a wooden spoon sticking out from the jar holding utensils he rarely used. "How about practicing your batting swing with this? Just don't hit me."

Sean decided the spoon worked better as a drumstick and began pounding the cabinet without the least semblance of rhythm, spewing words that made little sense. But as long as it kept him happy, then that made Logan happy.

Remaining close to his nephew to prevent him from taking a spill, Logan leaned back against the counter and glanced at the pass-through opening that offered a view of the living room. Devin had taped up the cut with thin white strips and right then he was shining a penlight in her eyes. Logan could tell they were discussing something, but he couldn't make out a word with Sean now pounding the metal canisters.

A few minutes later, his nephew grew tired of playing musician and insisted on being held. Logan scooped him up into his arms where Sean rested his cheek on his shoulder. At least Devin could go home and tell Stacy that Uncle Logan had succeeded in wearing the kid out by giving him a spoon.

A few minutes later, Devin walked into the kitchen, sporting a somber expression. "I don't think she has a serious head injury, but someone needs to watch her tonight, in case she does have a slight concussion."

And that proved to be a major problem. "No one's at her house," Logan said. "If you're that worried, maybe she should be admitted to the hospital."

"And maybe you should let her stay in your guest room."

That wasn't in accordance with Logan's plan. "Not a good idea."

Devin frowned. "I've never known you to refuse a good-looking woman in distress."

"A drunk, good-looking woman who happens to be the kid of a billionaire client, and he sure as hell wouldn't appreciate me spending the night with his daughter."

Devin scrubbed a hand over the back of his neck and studied the floor. "She's not drunk, Logan. She's going blind."

Chapter Two

For the past year, Jenna Fordyce had lived in a world of shadows and solitude, and at times excruciating pain, both physically and emotionally. Yet the one night she'd chosen to venture outside her safe haven to celebrate her best friend's thirtieth birthday, she'd landed in a precarious situation—with a cut on her forehead and a possible concussion, being tended by an off-duty doctor in a strange man's apartment.

An exclusive apartment, Jenna had decided the minute she'd walked into the elevator on Logan O'Brien's arm. A very large apartment, she'd realized when they'd crossed the uncarpeted floor and she'd noticed the echo of their footsteps. She'd become skilled at discerning details by relying on other senses aside from sight, particularly sound. Right now she heard the murmur of low voices, and suspected she was most likely the topic of conversation. No doubt the doctor was informing his brother that she was practically blind, not under the influence.

The rapid shuffle of bare feet drew Jenna's complete attention. A child's feet, she decided, and confirmed that when she squinted against the light and saw a small figure standing before her, only a vague image viewed through the hazy film of her failing eyes. She felt the tiny hand resting on her wrist, and experienced the inherent maternal instinct that sent her arms open wide to welcome little Sean.

When he climbed into her lap and rested his cheek against her breast, Jenna laid her cheek on top of his head, inhaled his sweet after-bath scent, absorbed his warmth and turned her thoughts to another baby boy. The one who had recently been little more to her than a voice on the phone, a precious "I love you, Mommy," to carry her through the lonely days and nights. The gift that kept her going. And hoping.

"Nothing like making yourself right at home in the lady's lap, Sean."

Devin O'Brien's voice, Jenna determined. She'd

immediately found an affinity with the caring doctor. The jury was still out on the doctor's hardcase brother. "He's not bothering me, at all, Devin."

"That's because he's finally tired."

When Devin lifted Sean from her lap, Jenna wanted to ask him to wait a few more minutes. To give her a little more time to fill her empty arms and heart. She slid her glasses back into place, this time to hide the threatening tears. "May I go home now?"

"You're going to stay here with me tonight."

Logan's commanding voice made Jenna bristle. "That's not necessary."

"Doctor's orders," Devin added in a more even tone. "Logan told me you'd be spending the night alone, and we'd both feel better if you had some company, in case you have any problems from the injury."

Maybe Devin would feel better, but Jenna doubted Logan shared that opinion. He probably wished she'd never had the bouncer call for a driver. Frankly, she wished she'd called a cab, which she could still do now.

She took a moment to weigh her options, all two of them. She could insist on going home and hope for the best, or stay and know someone would be there if she did suffer latent effects from the fall. She'd fought hard to maintain as much independence as possible, but under the current circumstances, she had no choice but to give up some of that hard-won freedom. The price she had to pay for taking a foolish risk. "Okay, I'll stay."

"Good," Devin said. "And you don't have to worry about Logan. He has a guest room upstairs, and he's a decent guy. Although, I'm much better looking."

"And married, Dev. Now, go home to your wife."

Logan's tone held a touch of amusement, something he evidently reserved for family members only, Jenna decided. He certainly hadn't sounded the least bit amused since the moment he'd become her reluctant escort. "Thanks for everything, Devin."

"You're welcome. Tell Jenna good-night, Sean."

"Night, night," came the childlike voice, followed by a soft baby kiss on her cheek, filling Jenna with more yearning and more memories. "Good night, sweetie. Sleep tight."

She listened with longing to Sean's toddler babble and the brotherly banter as the trio left the room. But when she heard the final goodbyes and the closing door in the distance, she was overcome with a solid case of jitters.

Logan O'Brien made her nervous, and it wasn't due to his imposing height; she was much shorter than most men. It wasn't even the edge in his voice, or his stoic demeanor. His overt, man-in-control attitude made her wary. Many a woman might be drawn to that take-charge aura, but she didn't intend to count herself among them.

"We need to talk."

The deep timbre of Logan's voice startled Jenna, causing her hand to flutter to her throat. "I didn't realize you were back."

She heard the scrape of furniture immediately before Logan came somewhat into view. "I'm right here. Now, explain to me why you didn't tell me you can't see."

Logan O'Brien pulled no punches, and normally Jenna would find that refreshing. But not necessarily in this instance. "I don't usually greet strangers with 'Hi, my name's Jenna Fordyce. I'm as blind as that proverbial bat.'"

"That only accounts for our initial meeting, not for the rest of the time we've been together," he said. "Try again."

She wasn't certain how to explain, aside from handing him the truth. "Tonight was the first time I've been out of the house for months, socially speaking. I wanted to be viewed as normal, and spared the usual pity." At least for a while.

"How long have you been this way?"

"A total recluse or a sassy pants, as my mother used to say?" Before her mother had been taken from her, when Jenna had just turned thirteen.

He released an impatient sigh. "How long have you had problems with your vision?"

Longer than she cared to recall. "I was diagnosed with a form of corneal dystrophy when I was in my early teens. At first, it wasn't too bad, aside from the eye infections, but I've always known it would continue to progress."

"Exactly how much can you see?"

"Not much. It's a little like looking through shattered, cloudy glass. Everything's distorted. I can see shapes, but no real details. Or I can when I'm not wearing sunglasses."

He reached up and pulled the shades away, something Jenna preferred he hadn't done. Since Devin had dimmed the lights earlier, she wasn't too concerned over her photosensitivity. She was worried about how her eyes would appear to him.

"Can you see me better now?" he asked.

"I can tell you're sitting in front of me, but that's about it."

"And there's not one damn procedure in this day and time that will help you?"

He sounded as frustrated as Jenna often felt, and she found that remarkable, coming from a man she'd just met. "A corneal transplant is the only cure."

"And that involves finding a donor," he said.

"Yes. I've been waiting over a year. Of course, if it were up to my father, he'd try to buy a set of corneas. Or at the very least, wield his influence to have me moved up on the list."

"But you won't let him."

She shook her head. "That wouldn't be fair. I've spent a good deal of my life as a sighted person when there are people waiting who've never had that advantage. Some are even children. They should be first in line."

"That's an admirable attitude."

She shifted slightly. "Before you start thinking I'm ready for sainthood, you have to understand that having a transplant isn't something I take lightly. Sometimes it scares me to think about it. But I'm willing to wait." Wait for someone to die in order to see, a fact Jenna tried not to dwell on. If she had only herself to consider, she would accept her limitations and forget the procedure. She'd use her cane all the time and consider finding a guide dog. But she had a three-and-a-half-year-old son counting on her, even if several hundred miles had separated them for the past few months.

"If you have the transplant, your vision will be restored completely?" Logan asked.

"That's what I'm hoping." Although, she would also be facing possible tissue rejection and the chance that the disease could return in a few years' time following the transplant.

"That's got to be tough. I can't imagine not being able to see."

"I've learned to compensate by thinking about what I'll do when I can see again." Being able to care for her child was top priority. "In the meantime, I have to rely on developing mental portraits using other senses. I'll demonstrate, if you'll let me touch you."

"Oh, yeah?" She could hear the smile in his voice.

Jenna released a shaky laugh when she realized how suggestive that sounded. "I meant, I want to touch your face to get a better idea of what you look like, if that's okay."

"What if you're disappointed?"

She shrugged. "Honestly, I've learned that true character has nothing to do with physical attractiveness. I just like to have a frame of reference."

"Then, go ahead," he said. "Touch away."

Jenna was a little unnerved by the provocative quality of his voice, but not enough to discourage her. "My depth perception is nonexistent, so you're going to have to help me. I'll start with your hair and work my way down."

When she held out her hands and closed her eyes, he placed her hands on either side of his temples. She feathered her fingertips through his hair—a nice, thick head of hair. "You're definitely not going bald."

"Not that I've noticed."

"What color is your hair?" she asked.

"Black."

He had the "tall" and "dark" down, and the time had come to verify the "handsome." Jenna began by outlining his forehead with her fingertips before brushing her thumbs over his brows. "What about your eyes?"

"They're blue."

Her artistic nature took over. "Sky-blue? Aqua-blue? Cobalt?"

"I've never thought about it before. I guess, sky-blue." He sounded somewhat self-conscious, and Jenna found that endearing coming from such a macho guy.

"Most people take the details for granted," she said, though she never had. "That's quite a striking contrast, black hair and light-blue eyes."

"My mother's half Armenian, and my father's Irish. I'm a mix of both."

"Interesting." And so was his nose that she now examined. When she contacted a slight indentation on the right side of the bridge, she asked, "What happened here?"

"I jumped out of an airplane and landed on my face."

"Seriously?" she asked around her shock.

He released a low, sexy laugh. "I got hit by a pitch when I was up to bat during a high-school baseball game. I thought the skydiving thing sounded more interesting."

She wasn't surprised he'd been a jock, but she was taken aback by his sudden show of humor. She wasn't surprised by the strength of his jaw, covered by whiskers that lightly abraded her palms, but the creases along his cheeks threw her a bit. "You have dimples."

"Unfortunately, yes."

She smiled. "Unfortunately? Women love dimples. It gives a man a boyish quality."

"If you say so," he said with extreme skepticism.

While she traced his full lips with a fingertip, Jenna put all the finer points together, creating a mental sculpture that probably wouldn't do justice to the real thing. But she'd discerned enough to know that he was definitely attractive.

And absolutely masculine, she realized when she ran her fingers over his prominent Adam's apple and down his corded neck that ended beneath stretchy knit. "You're wearing a T-shirt." She dropped her hands to his thighs. "And jeans." She found his foot with her own foot and gave it a nudge. "Boots, but not the cowboy kind. Hiking boots. You're an outdoorsman. Do you like to hike?"

"Yeah. Hiking and camping. But with the job, I haven't been in a few years."

Her mind wandered back to a better time, a better place, when she'd still had her sight. "I used to hike quite a bit when I was younger."

"How old are you now?"

Although his query was abrupt, and some might say inappropriate, Jenna liked his no-holds-barred attitude. It certainly beat having people view her as too fragile. "I turned thirty last month. And you?"

"Thirty-four."

She hid an unexpected yawn behind her hand. "Now that I've gotten to know you better, I suppose I can comfortably spend the night with you."

"Are you ready to go to bed now?"

She grinned. "I don't know you *that* well."

He cleared his throat. "I meant, are you ready for me to show you to the guest room."

"I'm teasing. I knew what you meant. You go to your bed, I go to mine."

"When you put it that way, it doesn't sound too damn appealing, does it?"

"No, it doesn't."

The sudden onset of silence was heavy, almost stifling. The undeniable tension passing between them required no visual confirmation, only instinct. And Jenna had always had good instincts, even before she'd lost her vision. But as much as she would like to throw caution aside, maybe offer Logan O'Brien a little encouragement, her intuition warned her to back off, before she made another mistake tonight.

When she realized she still had one hand planted on Logan's thigh, she drew it back as if she'd suffered an electrical jolt. In many ways, she had. "Does your guest room happen to have a TV?"

"Just a bed. I don't have many guests."

At least not any guests that required their own bed, Jenna surmised. "Do you have a TV in here?"

"A forty-two-inch plasma. Why?"

Of course he would ask that question. Why would a blind woman be interested in something she couldn't see? "I like to have a TV turned on when I go to bed. The sound helps me sleep."

"I know what you mean. I usually fall asleep watching sports right here in the living room."

"Then the living room it is. Just show me to the sofa and turn on the TV."

He took her hand and helped her to her feet. "I'll make a deal with you. Since I've been instructed by my brother to keep an eye on you, you can have the sofa and I'll sleep in the lounger."

"You really don't have to do that. I'm feeling fine. No nausea. No dizziness." Not exactly true. Knowing he was so close made her a little light-headed.

"Look, Jenna, unless you're going to trust me enough to sleep in the same bed with you, then you're going to have to deal with me staying in the living room so I can watch you."

She wasn't certain she could trust *herself* to sleep in the same bed with him. "Okay, but you don't have to watch me all night."

He ran a fingertip along her cheek. "I have no problem watching you all night."

Jenna experienced a rush of inexplicable heat and a round of regret that she couldn't see him. But she'd felt the softness of his touch, sensed his gaze and, for the first time in a long time, felt like a normal—and desirable—woman.

* * *

Jenna Fordyce was one hell of a stubborn woman, something Logan had discovered when she'd rejected his offer to assist her while she got ready for bed. Right now she was in the downstairs half bath putting on the T-shirt he'd loaned her, while he waited outside the door, hoping she didn't fall again. And that was probably just as well. Watching her dress was a bad idea.

Her earlier exploration had brought about a physical reaction that he couldn't ignore. He also couldn't discard her attitude about her condition, which had been nothing short of amazing. He was having a hard time ignoring her, period.

Still, he didn't particularly like that she'd failed to tell the truth about her vision problems and he couldn't help but wonder what else she might be hiding. He hated deception of any kind, even more so due to his ex-fiancée's betrayal. But after Jenna had explained her reasons for not telling him the truth, he'd understood her motivation on some level. He *didn't* understand why he was so damned attracted to her. Of course, she was a great-looking woman, but that wasn't all. He admired her need for independence and appreciated her insecurities. She might have been robbed of her sight, but she probably saw a lot more than most people who had twenty-twenty vision. She'd definitely seen more in him than most women, without evening knowing what he looked like.

And that pretty much answered his question. Throw all those traits into the mix, and you had a remarkable woman wrapped up in a petite package. Regardless, his post-Helena burn had yet to heal, and the last thing he wanted was another female complication. Jenna Fordyce didn't strike him as a one-night-stand kind of girl, and, lately, that's all that had interested him. No commitments. No promises. Nothing that even remotely resembled a steady relationship.

He also didn't need Jenna hurting herself again, exactly what Logan feared she'd done when a clattering sound filtered through the closed door. He rapped his knuckles on the facing and called, "Are you okay in there?" And if she didn't answer in two seconds, he was going to break down the door.

"I'm fine," she said. "I dropped the toothbrush in the sink and knocked over the toothpaste."

At least she hadn't dropped onto the floor. "Do you need anything?"

"Not unless you happen to have some eye-makeup remover."

He very well could. But he was tempted to deny it in order to avoid having to explain. Then again, if she really needed it, he should give it to her. "Are you decent?"

"That's debatable, but you can come in."

Logan opened the door to find her wearing the threadbare T-shirt that hit her midthigh, standing in front of the mirror and rubbing a washcloth over her face. Ignoring the clothes piled on the marble counter—including a skimpy lace bra—he strode to the vanity, opened the drawer, pulled out the metallic-gold makeup bag and rifled through it. And he'd be damned if he didn't find exactly what she was looking for.

He withdrew the blue bottle and put in her hand. "Here you go. Eye-makeup remover."

She frowned. "Is there something you're not telling me about yourself, Logan?"

"I don't wear makeup, if that's what you're asking. It belongs to someone else."

"You have a girlfriend."

"I have an *ex*-girlfriend."

"I see." She opened the lid and dabbed the washcloth with the clear liquid. "But you've kept a few reminders."

"Yeah. To remind me of one of the many reasons why we're not together anymore. She wore too much makeup."

"Okay."

Logan expected Jenna to question his other reasons, but she concentrated on removing the mascara. He liked that she hadn't grilled him. Liked that she'd let past history remain in the past. He liked her a lot and couldn't remember the last time he'd felt that way about a woman.

She blew out a frustrated sigh. "I should never

have let Candice put makeup on me. It's a pain in the butt, and if I don't get it off, it could cause problems." Then she turned to him and asked, "Is it gone, or am I ready for Halloween four months early?"

"Let me help." He took the cloth from her hand, clasped her chin and wiped at the smudges beneath her lower lids. He was very aware of their close proximity. Aware that she wasn't wearing a bra beneath the shirt, and that particular knowledge was creating major havoc on his body. If he didn't get away now, he was in danger of kissing her.

On that thought, he tossed the rag into the sink and backed up a step. "It's all gone. And you don't need any makeup."

She smiled. "I bet you say that to all the women you rescue from the clutches of evil mascara."

"This is a first. I've never intentionally taken off a woman's makeup."

"I'm sure you're very good at removing lipstick."

"Could be." And if she had any on now, which she didn't, he'd be glad to remove it for her. "Are you finished?"

She pushed her hair back with one hand. "I believe I am. Are you?"

When he realized how close he was coming to making a fatal error, Logan took her by the arm and guided her back into the living room to settle her on the sofa. "Stretch out and I'll cover you up."

After she complied, Logan pulled the blanket up to her chin, concealing her body and giving him some much-needed relief. "Is that okay?"

She worked her arms from underneath the covers. "It's fine. Are you okay?"

"Yeah. Why?"

"I don't know. You sound almost angry."

"I'm not angry." At least not at her.

She stretched her arms above her head before folding them beneath her breasts. "Then you're not going to boot me out on my butt after I fall asleep?"

"You're safe." But if she knew what he was thinking—that he'd like to climb on that couch with her—she might be the one doing the booting.

After grabbing up the remote from the coffee table, Logan switched on the TV. "Any particular show you want to watch?"

"It doesn't matter to me, as long as there's audio. You decide."

A return to his regularly scheduled program might offer a solid distraction. "I recorded the baseball game. They were in extra innings when I left to pick you up."

"I know. I also know the score. I heard some guys talking at the bar."

He set the remote back on the table. "Don't tell me or you'll ruin it."

"I'll let you be surprised, then." She rolled to her side to face him and began twisting the corner of the blanket. "Before you settle in for the night, there's something I need to ask you."

Jenna's tone was so somber, he worried that maybe she wasn't feeling well. Worried that he might have to make a trip to the E.R. after all. But her well-being mattered more than the inconvenience. "What's wrong?"

"Nothing's wrong." She closed her lids, then opened them slowly. "It's been a long time since I've seen myself in the mirror, and I want to know if my eyes—"

"They're as beautiful as the rest of you." And they were—pale brown, round eyes framed by long, dark lashes. No, she didn't need any makeup. She was perfect just the way she was. Maybe even too perfect.

Jenna smiled, but to Logan it looked almost sad. "I bet you say that to all the blind girls who end up on your sofa."

"You're the first, and it's the truth."

When she reached out her hand, he took it without hesitation. "Thanks, Logan. I'm glad we met."

"So am I." And he was, more than he cared to admit. "Now, get some sleep."

He gave her hand a squeeze and took his place in the lounger several feet away. He tried to concentrate on the game, but he was too busy analyzing the woman on his couch. He wondered if she was as real as she seemed. If everything she'd told him was accurate. If he'd misjudged her due to his own bitter experience. He suspected he had, and he wanted more proof.

For Logan O'Brien, the night might have begun with an unwelcome interruption, but it had ended with one huge surprise—Jenna Fordyce.

Chapter Three

"What are you doing?"

At the sound of Logan's distinct and somewhat gruff voice, Jenna turned and leaned back against the kitchen counter. "I was going to make you breakfast to repay you for rescuing me last night. But I've never been much of a cook, even before I lost my sight." She felt behind her for the carton of milk and held it up. "Can I interest you in cold cereal?"

"No thanks."

Jenna detected a hint of irritation in his tone. "Is something wrong?"

"When I didn't find you on the couch after I took my shower, I was worried."

She appreciated his concern, even if it wasn't warranted. "You don't have any reason to worry." She touched the edge of the bandage covering her wound. "My head's a little sore, but I'm fine."

Jenna calculated Logan's approach through the sound of his footsteps, and knew he moved beside her when she caught the trace scent of fresh soap. "As soon as you get dressed, we can leave," he said.

She ran a fast hand down the T-shirt he'd loaned her last night. "This is comfortable. Think I'll just wear it home. I'll have it laundered and back to you next week." Better still, she could deliver it in person.

Not a banner idea. She had no cause to pursue a relationship with a man at this point in her life.

"It looks good on you," he said. "But if you keep it, then you'll have to explain to your father where the shirt came from. And that would lead to telling him you spent the night with me and, in turn, I'll lose his business."

Always seeing things through a business lens, just like her father. "He's not due home until late afternoon, so don't concern yourself with getting caught. Which reminds me. What time is it now?"

"Almost ten."

"I can't believe I slept so late." But then, she hadn't slept all that well last night knowing Logan had been only a few paces away.

"And that's why we need to get a move on," he said. "Before Avery finds out you've been gone all night."

Jenna wouldn't be surprised if her dad had already called home only to connect to the voice mail. "My personal life isn't my father's business, and what happened last night doesn't qualify as questionable. I slept on your couch, and you kept watch over me from a chair."

"I still plan to have you home well before he arrives." He caught her hand and wrapped it firmly in his. "Come on. I'll help you get dressed."

Plainly, he was more than ready to be rid of her. "I can dress myself, thank you."

"I'll hang around, anyway, to make sure you're okay."

"Suit yourself."

Jenna allowed Logan to guide her into the bathroom where she took care of her morning ritual while he played watchdog outside the door. She managed to slide the blouse over her head, but when she attempted to close the skirt's back zipper, it wouldn't budge. At times like these, she wished she had a closet full of shapeless shifts and elastic waistbands, or the return of her sight.

Only one option existed at the moment—swallowing her pride. "I need some help, Logan."

The door creaked open. "What's wrong?"

"Nothing serious," she said, keeping her back to him. "Just a malfunctioning zipper. And if you're like most guys, you've had a lot of practice with women's zippers."

"I'm better at lowering them, but I'll give it a shot."

Though his voice held a touch of amusement, Jenna couldn't quite shake the sudden images his comment evoked as he moved behind her. "If you can't fix it, then I guess I'll have to wear your shirt home, after all."

"I can handle it." Bracing his hand on her hips, he tugged her toward him and went to work.

After only a single attempt, Jenna felt the zipper dislodge, followed by Logan saying, "You're all set."

She turned to thank him, swayed forward and in order to right herself, landed her hands on a wide expanse of powerhouse bare chest. "You're not wearing a shirt." A brilliant observation on her part.

He clasped her waist. "You have my shirt."

Clearly, her brain's command center didn't feel the need to remove her hands. "If that's the only shirt you own, you need to ask my father for more money."

"I own several shirts. I just haven't put one on, yet."

She'd found that out the pleasant way. "I see. Or maybe it's because I don't see. You could be naked, and I'd never know."

"I'm not naked." He shifted closer. "I'm wearing a smile."

Without thought, her hands drifted down his firm sides until she contacted a denim waistband. "Very funny. You really had me fooled for a minute."

"Anything else you need from me?"

She could think of several things, most of which wouldn't be wise. Interesting, yes. Prudent, no. Reluctantly, she dropped her arms to her sides. "I should probably go home now. I need to take a shower."

"I have a shower, and I'd be glad to help."

How simple it would be to take him up on the offer. How very easy to forget why she couldn't acknowledge this overriding chemistry between them. "Believe me, I've showered by myself before. Every morning, in fact."

"Fine, but if you decide on the way home that you'd like my assistance, just let me know."

"Do you know where you're going, Logan?"

Straight into a ditch if he didn't keep his eyes on the road and off of her. "I've been to your place before."

"Really? When was that?"

He glanced at Jenna to find her frowning. "About two years ago, when I first contracted with your dad. He invited me to a dinner party."

"Apparently, I wasn't in attendance at that little soiree."

"No, you weren't there." Without a doubt, he would've remembered if she had been.

"I must have been busy, otherwise I'm sure I would have been playing the perfect hostess to my father's perfect corporate crusader." Her sarcasm was unmistakable.

"You don't sound like you enjoy that scene," he said.

"Not really, but I view it as a favor to my father."

Logan could relate to family loyalty. "What else do you do in your spare time these days, aside from being a hostess?"

"I listen to audio books, mostly nonfiction, although I do enjoy a good legal thriller now and then. I've been learning Braille and several foreign languages, and when Calvin's not carting me to doctor's appointments, he drives me to the library twice a week where I tell stories to preschoolers."

He wasn't all that surprised by the revelation, although he was impressed. "I could tell you like being around kids when I saw you with my nephew."

"Yes, I do." She sighed. "They don't pass judgment or patronize me. Basically they view me as a storyteller who happens to be blind, not the other way around."

He sensed that was important to her—being treated like an average person. As far as Logan was concerned, Jenna Fordyce was anything but average.

"What do you do when you're not working?" she asked.

"I go to sporting events when I have some spare time. And on Sunday, I have lunch with the family."

Although, he'd missed those gatherings several times over the past few months, something that didn't sit well with his mother.

"That means you're going to be late to your lunch because of me," she said.

"It's not going to matter if I'm late." He would receive more grief from his sister for not jumping back into the dating loop, and from his brothers who claimed he'd lost his touch with women. Come to think of it, he could remedy that harassment—at least, temporarily—with one suggestion. "Since Avery won't be back until later, you should come with me. The food's simple, but the company's good."

When she didn't immediately respond, Logan glanced in her direction to find her deep in thought. "Well?" he asked.

"I should stay home in case he arrives early." She sent him an apologetic smile. "Thanks for the offer, but I'll have to pass."

Logan couldn't explain his disappointment, nor did he want to acknowledge it. But he did feel it. "Not a problem."

The conversation waned for the next few miles until Logan approached the estate—a house that looked as if it could hold five families. "We're at the entrance," he said as they pulled into the drive.

Jenna rummaged through her purse and withdrew a remote control, pointed it straight ahead and sent the security gate in motion.

Logan drove through the entry and immediately noticed a man with silver hair dressed in a black business suit, standing on the front porch. The last man he wanted to see at the moment.

Slowing the vehicle to a crawl, he asked, "How well do you and your dad get along?"

She rubbed her forehead, like the question had given her a major headache. "As long as he doesn't try to tell me what to do, we get along fine. He's very overprotective, the consummate doting father. But I love him with all my heart and appreciate all he's done for me since my mother's death. I probably don't tell him that enough."

"Well, now's your chance."

She turned her head toward him, a confused look on her face. "I don't understand."

Maybe not, but she would. And whether Avery Fordyce would understand why his only daughter had been out all night, still remained to be seen. "Looks like your father caught an earlier flight." And right then Avery looked as if he could fly off the porch and put someone in a choke hold.

Jenna tipped her head back against the seat and muttered, "Great," while Logan navigated the circular drive. After stopping underneath the portico, he said, "Let me handle this."

"No. I'll handle it."

Logan had barely left the Hummer and reached the passenger side before Jenna had the door open, one leg dangling out of the vehicle.

After he guided her up the steps, he started to launch into an explanation but lost the opportunity when Avery asked, "Where in God's name have you been, Jenna?"

"She's been with me," Logan said, although Avery didn't look too pleased by the disclosure.

Jenna reached out to find her father's arm, leaned forward and kissed his cheek. "I went out for Candice's birthday and I had a little mishap." She touched the bandage on her forehead. "Logan was kind enough to have his brother, Devin, who happens to be a doctor, take a look at the cut. He fixed me up with a few little strips to hold it together, Logan loaned me his sofa for the night, end of story."

Avery scowled. "That's not the end of the story. Candice called Sasha this morning, and Sasha, in turn, called me. They were both worried sick because you didn't come home and you didn't bother to call."

Jenna lifted her chin in defiance. "I'll explain everything to Candice later, and I told Sasha to take the weekend off."

"My employees are loyal, Jenna." Avery directed a hard look at Logan. "They do as I ask, and I asked her to watch out for you."

"I'm thirty years old, Dad. I don't need a keeper."

"Apparently, you do, daughter."

Logan opted to intervene before all out warfare began between parent and child. "Jenna spending the night at my place was all my idea, Avery. She wanted to come home, but I wouldn't let her."

"And this is supposed to satisfy me?" He topped off the comment with an acid glare.

At this rate, he'd find himself minus an important client. "Devin and I decided she shouldn't be alone, in case she showed signs of a concussion."

"Which I didn't," Jenna added. "Now, let's go inside and let Logan get on with his business."

"Yes, let's go inside," Avery said. "You still have a lot of explaining to do."

Logan witnessed a spark of anger in Jenna's expression. "We can talk later, Dad. I have to have a shower so I can be ready when Logan takes me to his parents' for lunch. What time should I expect you, Logan?"

He couldn't determine who was more shocked—him or Fordyce. "Are you sure you want to go?"

She sent him a bright smile. "Of course. The very accommodating Sasha can look after Dad this afternoon while I'm with you."

Logan recognized pure and simple rebellion, and that he was stuck in the middle of a family battle. He could rescind the offer and insult Jenna, putting himself back in Avery's good graces. Or he could possibly piss off one of his biggest financial benefactors and spend the afternoon with that benfactor's daughter.

He glanced at the sullen Avery before turning his attention to Jenna, who had one of the greatest smiles he'd ever seen on a woman. Business versus pleasure. He chose pleasure. "I'll be back in about an hour."

Without waiting for Avery's response, Logan sprinted to the Hummer and drove off, wondering all the way home what in the hell he was doing.

"Do you know what you're doing, Jenna?"

Although she couldn't see her father's expression, she'd heard the disapproval in his tone. "I'm going to get ready to have lunch with Logan."

As she continued down the hall toward her bedroom, her father moved in front of her, halting her progress. "What do you really know about him?"

The classic fatherly lecture. Despite her limited eyesight, she should have seen it coming. "I know that you trust him. I also know he was very kind to me last night and a perfect gentleman, if that's your concern."

"He's a ladies' man. He's not the kind to settle for only one woman, especially a…"

His words trailed off, but his message came through loud and clear. "A woman like me, Dad? Isn't that what you meant to say?"

"You're special, Jenna."

"I'm going blind, Dad. My eyesight might be

bad, but that doesn't mean I can't enjoy a man's company. Even a 'ladies' man.' And this is only a casual lunch between friends. Logan didn't want me to be alone since I assumed Sasha wouldn't be here, and you wouldn't be home until much later."

"I don't want you to get hurt, sweetheart."

His gentle tone helped ease her resentment. "I'll only get hurt if I let him hurt me, and I won't. Besides, I'm not looking for anything permanent. You should know that by now."

"Yes, I know. Your divorce from David proved that. I wish the two of you would have tried a little harder."

"Don't, Dad. We're not having that discussion again." They'd worn out that territory three years ago.

"I can't talk you out of going to this lunch? We could have a nice afternoon together."

She reached out to pat his cheek. "We can have a nice evening together. You can tell me all about Chicago, and I can tell you how to inquire about the bathroom in Italian and French."

"You're still determined to take that European trip."

"Only after I have the transplants." If she ever had the transplants. "I'd also like to wait until John David's a little older so he can appreciate the culture."

"Have you told Logan about him?"

"The opportunity hasn't arisen yet." She planned to take the opportunity before day's end. "As

I've said, this is only a one-time event, not a prospective-daddy interview. J.D. already has a father."

"Again, I don't want you to—"

"Get hurt. I know, Dad." She drew him into a long embrace. "And I appreciate your concern. But you don't have to worry. I'm a big girl now."

"I know, Jenna, but I still worry about you. I've worried about you since the day you came into our lives."

"And if I'd been able to handpick my parents, I couldn't have chosen any better than you and Mother." Even if she'd often wondered that if they'd known her vision would eventually fail, would they have adopted her?

"And we couldn't have been more blessed to have you," he said, dispelling her doubts, and that earned him another hug.

"I love you, Dad," she said. "And please stop worrying. I can manage Logan O'Brien."

At one time, Logan had been able to manage Avery Fordyce by praising his business acumen, yielding to his demands and leading him to believe he had complete control. But that was before he'd met the man's daughter.

Under normal circumstances, Logan would have expected to be greeted by a member of the household staff. Nothing about this situation remotely re-

sembled normal, the reason why he wasn't surprised when Avery answered the door with a curt,
"Come in."

Logan followed Avery inside the house, hoping
to discover Jenna waiting nearby so they could get
the hell out of there. But the expansive foyer was
deserted, with the exception of a few pieces of
pricey artwork and Fordyce, who turned and said,
"I don't like this, O'Brien."

Logan didn't have to ask what Avery didn't like.
"It's only lunch."

"So you say. Just remember, Jenna means everything to me, son. She's an exceptional young woman. Fragile in many ways. If you mess with her
feelings, you mess with mine. Understood?"

Avery's meaning couldn't be clearer if he'd
carved it into stone—or into Logan's flesh. Still,
Logan had a hard time believing Jenna was as
fragile as her father had claimed. But if he
screwed up with Avery's only child, he'd be out
in the cold when it came to future contracts.
"Understood."

"Now that you know what I expect, you may
wait for Jenna in the study." He pointed to his right
before pivoting around like a drill sergeant and
heading down the lengthy hall.

Logan wandered into the room Avery had indicated, expecting to find a collection of books
stacked on rows of shelves, maybe even an office

setup. Instead, the area held a grouping of casual rattan furniture and plenty of pictures, but not the kind displayed in a trendy gallery. Portraits depicting a dark-haired boy spanned the length of the room. One showed a sleeping newborn lying on a blue blanket; another featured a toothless, smiling infant on his belly in a field of wildflowers, and beside that, a toddler dressed in a red baseball uniform with a miniature wooden bat.

Even if he didn't know the kid's identity, Logan suspected he was someone special. Possibly a member of the extended family—or immediate family.

"His name is John David."

He turned at the sound of the familiar voice to discover Jenna standing in the open doorway wearing a pale yellow, sleeveless dress, her dark hair secured atop her head. The sunshades covering her eyes and the white cane in her hand were the only indications she was anything but a healthy, beautiful woman. In fact, she looked so damn good, for a moment Logan had trouble responding to her comment. "Who took all these pictures?"

"I did. I used to own a small photography studio in northwest Houston before my eyes started giving me grief. I consider these portraits some of my best work."

That explained the quality of the photos, even if it didn't explain Jenna's relationship to the child, although Logan had his suspicions. "You must have really liked this particular subject."

"More than you know." She crossed the room, removed a framed photo from a table before returning and offering it for his inspection. "This one's my favorite."

Logan studied the picture of Jenna turned profile to the boy, their foreheads touching. The perfect depiction of a woman's fondness for a child. Or maybe a mother's love for her son. Then again, he could be mistaken since she hadn't mentioned having a child, nor had her father in the years he'd known him. But when he turned his attention from the photo to Jenna and saw the moisture dampening her cheeks, Logan sensed he was on the right track. And affirmation came when she said, "He's my son."

She raised the glasses and swept a fast hand beneath her eyes before replacing the shades again. "I'm sorry. It's very difficult to talk about him without my emotions going haywire."

Although he was tempted to ask exactly what had happened to the boy, Logan decided not to pressure Jenna for more information than she was willing or able to give. Instead, he said the only thing he could think to say. "He looks like you."

She gave him a tentative smile. "He definitely inherited my brown eyes, but his hair is lighter, like his dad's. Or it was the last time I could see it."

"How long ago was that?"

"He's three and a half now, so that would have been about a year ago, right before my vision took a severe turn for the worse. He went to live with his father not long after that. We share joint custody."

At least Jenna hadn't suffered a traumatic loss of her child, although Logan couldn't imagine how she'd tolerated a year without him. "When will he be back with you?"

She clutched the frame to her breasts, as if she were holding her absent son. "As soon as I have the corneal transplants. Since he's so active, I thought it best he stay with his dad a little longer than the usual six months. But it's been difficult since he's so far away."

"How far?"

"In Tennessee, outside of Memphis. I do talk to him every night, though."

A sorry substitute for physical contact. "I'm surprised Avery never mentioned him to me." Most grandfathers Logan had known doted over the grandchildren, including his own father.

"It's not that Dad doesn't love J.D.," she said. "In fact, he adores him. But he's never accepted the fact that J.D.'s father and I divorced."

Logan could see how that wouldn't go over well with a traditionalist like Avery Fordyce. Or his own parents, who'd had a hard time with his sister's divorce. "How long were you together?"

"I'd known him four years, and we'd been living together for three when I found out I was pregnant. We married five weeks later. Right after J.D. turned six months old, we realized it wasn't going to work. But David's a good father, and that's all that matters."

From the sadness in Jenna's tone, Logan gathered that maybe the divorce hadn't been her idea. He wanted to ask if she'd loved this David and if the guy had treated her well. If he'd accepted her blindness, or if that had been the reason for the split. "I guess marrying for the sake of a child isn't always a good thing." And he'd almost found himself caught in that trap.

She shook her head. "No, it's not. Particularly if two people are less than compatible, something we should have realized in three years. But sometimes you get stuck in a comfort zone with no desire to leave. Unfortunately, accidents happen, although I wouldn't change anything as far as my son's concerned."

Uncomfortable with the course of the conversation, Logan decided to turn the topic to their plans for the day. "Are you ready to go now?"

"Do you still want me to go?"

"Yeah. Any reason why I wouldn't?"

"I could think of several reasons why you might reconsider. Introducing a blind, divorcée with a child to your parents, for one."

"My parents aren't judgmental, Jenna." In fact, they would probably fall in love with her after five minutes in her company—and immediately start jumping to conclusions.

She shifted slightly. "There's also that little issue of my father, who is now in the den, sulking. He's worried you're going to seduce me, and I won't see it coming. Literally."

"I promise I'll behave myself." A promise he hoped he could keep.

Chapter Four

"Do your parents know you're bringing a guest?" When Jenna received no response except the click of a blinker, she reached across the seat and touched Logan's arm. "Are you all right?"

"Yeah. I'm fine."

She had some reservations about that, particularly since he'd been quiet since they'd begun the drive. "Did you hear my question?"

"You said something about my parents."

Evidently his mind was elsewhere. "I asked if they know I'm coming."

"I called my mother and told her I was bringing a friend. She was so glad to hear it, I don't think she'd care if I brought an army of hairy bikers."

Or a blind woman. "When was the last time you brought someone home?"

"It's been a while. I haven't made the Sunday lunches for a few months. Work's been kicking my butt."

Jenna predicted there was much more to his absences aside from work. "Then, you didn't tell her any details about me?"

"What do you mean?"

She wasn't sure if he was being evasive because he had told his mother, or he hadn't. "Did you mention I have a penchant for bumping into walls?"

"Sure. I told them you were a klutz and to secure anything breakable."

His teasing tone brought about Jenna's smile. "Seriously."

"My parents are smart people. They'll figure it out, and it won't matter to them."

Jenna hoped they didn't treat her any differently than they would any guest, and realized she would soon find out when Logan proclaimed, "We're here."

While Logan helped her from the SUV, Jenna gave herself a good mental scolding for her sudden case of nerves. She had no reason to be anxious. After all, following lunch, she would probably never encounter these people again.

With his hand firmly planted at her elbow, he

guided her into the backyard where the scents of charcoal and the hum of jubilant conversation calmed her nerves and buoyed her spirits. Then came the chorus of cheers and applause as the group converged on them. To Jenna, they appeared as a sea of ill-defined figures, but she didn't dare take off her glasses due to the summer sun beating down upon them.

Overwhelmed would best describe her state of mind as, one by one, the O'Briens introduced themselves. The siblings were the first to deliver greetings, beginning with Logan's sister, Mallory, and her husband, Whit, who had their four-month-old twin daughters with them, according to Logan. Then she met Aidan and his wife, Corri, followed by Kieran and his girlfriend, Claire. Devin introduced her to his "better half," Stacy, as little Sean tugged on Jenna's skirt and jabbered on about a puppy, as if they'd become fast friends. Lastly, Logan's parents took their turn.

"Jenna, this is my mother," Logan said as he planted his palm on Jenna's lower back, catching her off guard.

Obviously he was making certain she stayed steady on her feet, despite her cane. "It's nice to meet you, Mrs. O'Brien."

The woman took Jenna's offered hand into hers for a gentle shake. "It's a pleasure to meet you, too, Jenna. And, please, call me Lucy. We don't stand on formality here."

"And you can call me a pain in the arse." The booming voice hinted at an Irish brogue, and the hearty handshake told Jenna that the hulking figure standing before her was a man's man.

"Tell her your proper name, husband," Lucy scolded. "You'll have to excuse him, Jenna. After all the years we've been married, I've never been able to teach him any manners."

"I'm Dermot, Jenny."

"It's Jenna, Dad," Logan corrected.

"To me she will be Jenny. And she is the prettiest girl you've ever brought home to meet your old da."

Jenna's hand automatically went to her neck where a blush threatened. "Thank you, Dermot. I appreciate your hospitality."

She felt a nudge on her arm and recognized Logan's voice when he said, "Let's have a seat at the table before all the food's gone."

"Good advice, Logan," Dermot said. "The boys all eat like they've never seen food before, Jenny. If we're going to fatten you up, we might as well get a head start."

Jenna didn't have the desire to correct Dermot because she liked the fact he'd given her a pet name. She also didn't feel the need to "fatten up"; child-birth had added a few extra pounds she had yet to shed. But she was definitely hungry, for both good company and good food. She'd already received the first and, no doubt, would soon experience the

second, if the delicious scent of barbecue wafting
around her was any indication.

As they mingled with the various family members, Jenna acknowledged that joining Logan for
the family get-together was proving to be a wonderful change of pace. She was glad she'd come,
despite Logan's previous silence, something she
chalked up to his surprise over her revelation.
Amazingly he hadn't run in the opposite direction
when she'd told him about her son. At least, not yet.

Maybe he was simply being a gentleman, and
after today, they would part on good terms with a
permanent goodbye. And that was just as well.
Her life was much too complicated to entertain
any ideas of pursuing a relationship with Logan
O'Brien. Yet she couldn't help imagining what it
would be like to do that very thing. What it would
be like to know him on a much more personal level.
Too many years had passed since she'd experienced
intimacy with a man, and deep down she couldn't
deny she'd missed that aspect of her life. Yet wishing for something that shouldn't be wasn't prudent,
even if the thought was pleasant.

Logan showed her to what appeared to be a picnic table and helped her onto a bench, taking his
place beside her. During the meal of smoked beef
brisket and simple side dishes, everyone treated her
as if she were a part of the family. Although, Lucy
O'Brien had insisted on bringing her a plate of

food—something she did for every guest, Logan assured her—no one had been the least bit condescending or overly concerned. The only indication that anyone even noticed her deficit came when Dermot asked, "What happened to your eyes, Jenny?"

"You're too nosy, old man," Lucy said.

Jenna pushed her plate back and folded her hands before her on the table. "It's okay, Lucy. I have a disease that's clouded my vision. And I hope to have it restored soon with corneal transplants."

"The miracle of modern medicine," Dermot replied. "I look forward to you being able to see what a handsome man I am."

The group shared in a laugh, including Jenna. Yet, it was Logan's laughter that had caught her attention. Logan who had kept her attention. Every now and then, her thigh touched his thigh, and even that simple contact brought about a certain amount of excitement and longing.

She'd sensed him watching her throughout the meal and wondered what he was thinking. If he leaned on the superficial side when it came to women, she would probably be outclassed. But if he preferred a more natural look, she might meet his expectations. Regardless, something about her had captured his notice, she decided, right before he declared, "You have barbecue sauce on your dress."

Great. He'd been analyzing an unsightly stain.

Embarrassed, Jenna lifted the paper napkin and asked, "Where is it?"

"In a place on your anatomy where I'm sure Logan would like to help you remove it."

"Shut up, Devin." Logan's tone was gruff yet hinted at humor. "Come inside with me and I'll take care of it."

"I bet you will, bro."

"That's enough, Kieran."

Jenna determined the time had come to make a quick exit, before the stain set in and Logan had to endure more ribbing. "I'd appreciate your help," she said as he clasped her arm and assisted her from the picnic bench.

"There's some white vinegar in the pantry, Logan," Lucy called while they headed back into the house. "Be sure to dilute it with cold water."

Once in the kitchen, Jenna leaned a hip against the counter while Logan noisily poked around in what she assumed was said pantry.

"I found it," he said, followed by the sound of running water. "Now I'm going to see if I can get this off."

Despite the warning, Jenna had a difficult time ignoring the steady swipes between her breasts, or the acrid scent of vinegar. "Lovely. Now I'm going to smell like a pickle."

"I like pickles." His smile shone through his

voice. "At least the spot looks better. Sorry about the cold water."

If he only knew how warm she'd grown during the stain-removal process. "I appreciate your efforts at eliminating the evidence of my clumsiness. But being blind has one distinct advantage. I can't see people staring at me when I'm wearing my lunch."

"They weren't staring at the stain," he said. "They were too busy looking at your black eye."

"I have a black eye? Sasha never mentioned it when she changed the bandage." Probably to save her from total mortification.

"Just a little bruising. The cut looks better, though."

"Did you tell anyone in your family what happened last night?"

"I told my brothers I picked you up in a bar after you engaged in a hair-pulling fight with a couple of coeds."

Oh, heavens. "You didn't!"

"We're hot-blooded Irishmen. We know all about bar fights."

"But I didn't engage in a bar fight, Logan."

"I'm kidding, Jenna. They didn't ask, and I didn't volunteer any information."

She playfully slapped at his arm. "Good, otherwise I'm sure your family will be glad when I leave, and hope I never come back." Oddly, she wouldn't mind coming back.

"My parents are very impressed with you, Jenna,

particularly my dad, who only gives a nickname to people he likes. The rest of the family is equally impressed. So am I, barbecue stain, black eye and all."

Considering their close proximity, Jenna was impressed she still maintained some semblance of composure. "Speaking of your family, I only counted three brothers. Who's missing?"

"Kevin, and he's probably off somewhere interviewing a high-paid baseball player for the magazine. He's never liked doing the family thing, and he hasn't come around much since Corri and Aidan got married."

"Why is that?"

"It's a long story, but the abbreviated version is Corri was engaged to Kevin first, and she ended up married to Aidan."

A soap-opera scenario was the last thing Jenna had envisioned. "She broke it off with Kevin to be with Aidan?"

"Kevin broke it off with her, and it was for the best. We all knew that, when Aidan kissed Corri in the kitchen before she and Kevin started dating, she'd picked the wrong brother."

"They kissed on the set where she does the cooking show?"

"Not the studio kitchen. This kitchen."

"Right here?" Her voice sounded a little strained.

"Right where we're standing." His voice

sounded much too sexy. "Have you ever been kissed in a kitchen, Jenna?"

"Not that I recall." But she had the strongest feeling she could very well get that kiss, especially when Logan formed his hand to her jaw and feathered his thumb over her cheek. A kiss she had secretly fantasized about since last night. She waited with an eagerness she couldn't contain. She braced herself for the impact of his lips on hers. She resisted the urge to shout "Go away!" when someone cleared their throat, halting any possibility of making her foolish fantasy a reality.

Logan took away his hand and asked, "What do you need, Kieran?" His impatience filtered out in his tone.

"Devin and Stacy are leaving to take Sean home for his nap. Mom thought you might want to say goodbye, if you're not too busy." He chuckled before the click of footsteps indicated his exit.

As much as Jenna wanted to see the couple off, she was in no shape to face anyone right now. "If you'll point me to the powder room, I'll be back outside in a minute."

"I can show you where it is," Logan said.

She raised her cane a few inches from the floor. "My trusty companion can help me find it while you say goodbye to your brother. Just tell me how many door handles and if it's left or right."

Without further protest, he took her by the shoulders and turned her around. "Straight ahead, second door on the right. Watch out for the curio cabinet in the hall to your left."

She greatly appreciated his confidence and trust that she could manage on her own, when so many people in her life insisted on treating her like an invalid. "I should be right out, but if I miss saying goodbye to Devin and Stacy, tell them I've enjoyed getting to know them better."

"I'll do that." She felt his presence immediately behind her and his warm breath at her ear. "And later, we'll work on getting to know each other better."

Fortunately Jenna had her cane to rely on, otherwise she might dissolve into the floor. She walked the hall on rubber legs while counting doorknobs. Using the cane to make certain the path was clear, she analyzed the sensual undertones in his words, and her physical response to them.

When she reached the room Logan had indicated, she found the door ajar and stepped inside. Now she could have a few moments alone to regain her composure and—

"Hi, Jenna."

She immediately recognized Mallory's voice. "I'm so sorry. I didn't realize you were in here."

"It's feeding time for the girls."

"You feed them in the bathroom?"

Mallory laughed softly. "You're not in the bathroom. This is my old bedroom, which has now been converted into a nursery."

Wonderful. Her transformation from bumbling barbecue eater to total idiot was now complete. "Logan told me the bathroom was the second door to the right."

"Logan must have forgotten to count the utility room. That's strange considering he's always been good at math."

Jenna assumed he was good at many things, the least of which was arithmetic. She pointed behind her. "I need to go one more door, then."

"Yes, but Corri's in there now, feeling the effects of morning sickness that continues all day."

"I didn't know Corri was pregnant."

"Oh, yes, and not feeling very well. You can go to the end of the hall and use the master bathroom if you'd like."

Jenna shook her head. "It's no emergency. I wanted to remove all the remnants of barbecue sauce in case it's on my chin as well as my dress." And splash a little water on her face to alleviate some of the heat.

"I don't see one drop anywhere, so keep me company while I nurse the girls. You'll find a chair about four steps in front of you."

Seeing the opportunity to question a woman who probably knew Logan better than most females, Jenna made her way to the chair and took a seat.

The soft suckling sounds sent a surge of longing through her, and the memory of unforgettable moments. "Do you feed both girls at once?"

"Rarely. Lucy's in the crib, playing with a newly discovered toy—her feet. She's the patient one. Madison is the chow hound and demands to eat immediately, or she throws a tantrum. But she falls asleep as soon as her belly's full."

Much the same as John David when he'd been a baby, and she'd still been able to care for him herself. "What do they look like?"

"They're identical. Both have Whit's dark hair and my green eyes."

"I'm sure they're beautiful." She instinctively suspected Mallory was, too, at least according to her husband who'd had no qualms about calling her "beautiful" several times during lunch.

"Would you do me a favor and hold Maddie while I feed Lucy? She's almost asleep."

Little did Mallory know, she was doing Jenna a favor by allowing her to cuddle a baby. "I'd love to."

The creak of a chair signified Mallory's approach right before her cloudy image came into Jenna's view. "I'm putting a burp pad on your shoulder, just in case," she said. "However, Maddie's not one to spit up, unlike Lucy. That's why I always give Lucy's burping duty to Whit."

Jenna smiled. "Husbands do come in handy at times, don't they?"

"Definitely. Whit's handy with a lot of things, which is how I got pregnant in the first place."

Jenna could relate on some level, although in the few months before the divorce, hers and David's lovemaking had been nonexistent. Yet, he had been good with J.D., and that had been her only priority at the time.

"Here she is," Mallory said as she laid the soft bundle in Jenna's arms.

Carefully Jenna lifted the baby to her shoulder and gently patted her back, once more filled with bittersweet recollections of good days gone by— the baby smells, the soft, soft skin, the beat of a tiny heart beneath her palm. "I'd forgotten how wonderful this feels," she said. "It's been a while since I've held a baby this small."

"I'd never held one this small before my nephew was born. I didn't babysit when I was younger, but fortunately Stacy let me practice with Sean."

"I never babysat, either." Aside from having no need to earn extra money, she'd never trusted her weakened eyes enough to take on that responsibility. "But I do have a son."

"Logan didn't mention that to us."

"Logan didn't know until today. John David doesn't live with me at the moment. He's in Tennessee with his father and his new stepmother for the next few months." Longer, if David had his way, even if Jenna did have the transplants.

"How old is he?" Mallory asked.

"Three and a half. He has to be watched closely these days, otherwise he's into something the minute you turn your back."

"Being away from him must be difficult for you. I barely make it through four hours of work before I'm dying to see the girls. Fortunately, my law firm has an on-site daycare and I'm only working part-time."

No one could know how very difficult it had been unless, like Mallory, they'd experienced motherhood. "J.D.'s father and I share joint custody, which was fine until he took the job out of state. Now I have to wait my turn to be with my baby. But I do talk to him every day." She sang him his favorite songs, told him silly stories, yet it still wasn't the same as tucking him into bed and kissing him good-night.

"How do you manage when he's with you?"

Jenna found Mallory's candor refreshing. "It isn't always easy, but it's doable, as long as I make sure there's someone else around." And that also had proven to be difficult, knowing she had to rely on a member of the staff to help her care for her own child.

A brief span of silence passed, interrupted by the steady rasp of the rocker moving back and forth. Jenna shifted little Madison into the cradle of her arms and made the decision to pose a few quetions while the opportunity existed. "What's Logan like?"

"Poor guy. He was hiding under the delivery table when they passed out the looks."

Not at all how she'd pictured him, even though it didn't matter. "I meant what's he like as a person? I've discovered that looks aren't as important as a man's character."

"Oh. First of all, I wasn't serious about the looks thing. In fact, I'd describe him as very handsome, but then I'm biased. As far as his character is concerned, he has a great personality, or he did have until…"

Mallory's faltering words caused Jenna a good deal of apprehension. "Until, what?"

"Until he hooked up with hellacious Helena Brennan, his onetime fiancée."

She recalled Logan mentioning the ex-girlfriend, but not in the context of a previous engagement. The first in what Jenna surmised would be a long list of surprising discoveries. "What happened?"

"Helena had more money than sense, and a devious side. She faked a pregnancy in order to trap him into marriage. Fortunately he discovered the truth on the eve of their wedding, before it was too late."

Jenna questioned whether Logan thought she'd done the same with David. In reality, she'd resisted the marriage until both he and her father had finally worn her down. "How long ago was this?"

"Almost a year. Since then, he's pretty much avoided any serious relationships, even if he hasn't necessarily avoided women. Logan's never been lacking for female companionship."

All the more reason why Jenna found it odd he would want to be with her. "I'm sure it's been hard for him to recover after being burned so badly, especially if he cared for the person doing the burning. I assume Logan did care for her."

"At the time it looked that way." Mallory sighed. "I never knew what he saw in Helena, but that's Logan in a nutshell—always seeing the good in people. He befriended kids in high school who were basically social outcasts and he took the shyest girl to the prom. That's what made him so popular with everyone."

And that could explain why he'd befriended her—poor blind Jenna. "That's a very honorable trait."

"Yes, it is, but if you're thinking that's why he's with you, think again. He might be benevolent, but in your case, he's infatuated."

What a ridiculous thing to assume. "We've known each other less than twenty-four hours. I promise he's not infatuated. He's only being nice to me."

"Yeah, right." When Mallory laughed, Lucy gave a little whine of protest. "Think what you will, Jenna, but I've seen the way he looks at you, like he's just discovered a new Corvette in the driveway. Trust me, he's definitely got a thing for you."

Since she couldn't see how Logan looked at her,

she'd have to take Mallory's word for it, although she had a hard time believing Logan's invitation today had involved anything but kindness. "Believe me, Mallory, Logan and I are only friends. There's nothing serious going on."

"So is this thing between you and Jenna serious?"

Logan continued to stare at the driveway that Devin and Stacy had left a few moments before. "I've just met her."

"Then your answer is no, it's not serious?"

He leveled a hard stare at his brother. "Are you intentionally being dense?"

Kieran grinned. "Nope. I'm just wondering why you looked like you wanted to jump her all during lunch."

"I sure as hell did not." Unfortunately, he sounded defensive enough to keep Kieran making more assumptions.

"Yeah, you did. And maybe you're not looking for a serious relationship, but you're seriously looking to get her into bed."

"Okay. I admit it. The thought's crossed my mind." More than once since he'd met her. "But that doesn't mean a damn thing, and I don't intend to act on it."

Kieran let go a loud laugh. "Sure, Logan. When you succeed in ignoring your animal urges, that'll be the day everyone in Houston carpools."

To hell with it. Kieran was on a tear and nothing Logan could say would change his mind. That meant the time had come for a change in subject. "By the way, where's Cindy?"

"We broke up six months ago."

"I didn't know that."

Kieran patted his back. "You've been too busy hanging out in bars and bedding hot babes to know what's been going on."

He refused to feel guilty over his absence from family dinners, even though he wasn't meeting much success. "Nothing wrong with playing a wide field. And I'm not looking for anything permanent."

"Neither am I, but sometimes things happen when you least expect it."

Logan had learned that hard lesson with Helena. "Just to set the record straight, as soon as I leave here, I'm taking Jenna to her house and saying goodbye. And that's going to be the end of it."

Chapter Five

"Do you have somewhere you have to be right now?"

Jenna looked as surprised by the query as Logan had been when he'd posed it. Regardless of what he'd said to Kieran earlier, he wasn't quite ready to let her go.

"As a matter of fact, I have plans," she said.

He pulled into the circular drive in front of the mansion and turned off the ignition. "With someone special?" Now, why in the hell had he asked that? And why had he sounded so jealous?

She grinned. "I thought I might join an Internet think tank and take a shot at solving global warming. Or maybe paint my nails, which is always challenging."

In spite of his chagrin, Logan couldn't stop his smile. "Good luck."

She shifted to face him. "I could be persuaded to put everything on hold. What do you have in mind?"

Several things, and kissing her topped the list. He'd halt that line of thinking right now if he knew what was good for him. Obviously, he didn't know what was good for him. "Nothing as monumental as the global-warming thing. I thought we could talk for a while."

"What time is it?"

He checked his watch. "Almost seven-thirty."

She frowned. "Darn. My father doesn't go to bed until eleven. I guess we could still go inside and take our chances that he doesn't sit us down and grill us on our day."

"I'm not afraid of Avery." Worried about their business relationship, yes. Afraid, no.

"He's not always gracious when it involves me and the opposite sex, Logan. He's basically inter-viewed every man I've ever been out with. That tends to put a damper on your social life, not that I've had much of one lately."

Logan's social life had been active—and empty. "We could have a drink somewhere."

She unsnapped her seat belt. "I have a better idea. A place I'd like you to see."

He almost asked if she meant her bedroom, but stopped short before the question shot out of his stupid mouth. "Where's that?"

"As soon as I get out of this monstrosity of a vehicle, I'll show you."

Logan barely made it to the passenger side right before Jenna attempted to exit on her own. Her stubborn streak was showing again, something he'd noticed back at his parents' house. Striving for independence seemed important to her, and he'd allowed her to find her own way all afternoon, while keeping an eye on her without her knowledge.

As they walked side by side, Jenna used the cane to navigate the flagstone path that led to the rear of the mansion. "Is the sun still out?" she asked.

"It's setting."

She pushed her shades up to the top of her head. "What color is the sky?"

"Blue."

"You can do better than that."

He had his doubts, but he'd try for her. "It has shades of orange mixed with the blue. And pink."

"See how much better everything looks when you notice the details?"

He'd never given the color of the sky much thought before now. And as far as details were concerned, he preferred to study those that involved her. She had a straight nose, full lips and golden highlights in her brown hair. Even without makeup, she was as beautiful—maybe even more so—than most of the women he'd known, both inside and out.

Damn. Twenty-four hours in her company, and she had him describing the sky and spouting poetry. He needed to hightail it out of there as soon as the opportunity presented itself. But what he wanted to do won out—stay a while longer—proving his common sense was in a headlock.

When they reached an ornate wrought iron gate, Jenna opened it with ease, indicating she'd been there before.

"This is my mother's garden," she said as they walked down a redbrick trail lined with various plants, marble statues and carefully trimmed hedges. "She designed the layout."

"My mom's into gardening, but her garden isn't as elaborate as this one." Just another reminder of their differing backgrounds.

"I've neve had much of a green thumb," Jenna said. "But I love flowers. Are we at the angel fountain, yet?"

Logan surveyed the immediate area and located the concrete landmark. "It's about ten feet ahead to the right."

Jenna picked up the pace, leaving Logan behind, and stopped before a bush covered in flowers.

"These are Gemini roses, although my mother referred to them as 'Jenna's roses' since I'm a Gemini." She bent over to smell one of the blooms. "That means you'll never know which side of me you'll encounter from one moment to the next."

So far, he liked all her sides, including her backside, which had his undivided attention at the moment. "Are you moody?"

She sent him a smile over one shoulder. "I prefer multifaceted to moody. Sometimes I'm into peace and serenity, other times I like adventure. Now, come here and get a closer look at these. They're beautiful."

"I'm really not into flowers."

Jenna carefully snapped one rose from the bush and faced him. "I never gave them much thought, either, before I couldn't see them any longer. There's a lot to be said for that old 'stop and smell the roses' adage." She stepped toward him and held up the flower. "Go ahead and take a whiff."

He swallowed his macho pride, circled her wrist and brought the bud to his nose. "Smells good."

She looked as if he'd presented her with a five-carat diamond. "Told you so."

She also looked like she wanted something else from him. He definitely knew what he wanted from her—the same thing he'd wanted from her back in the Hummer and back in his mother's kitchen, right before Kieran's untimely interruption.

After lowering her hand to his chest, he nudged her closer, trapping the rose between them. Her cane hit the ground with a clank.

He recognized she couldn't see him, but it almost seemed as if she could see right through him. For a brief moment he questioned his judgment and the possible cost of kissing her. But he'd be damned if he could stop when she whispered, "What are you waiting for, Logan?"

Suddenly, the area lit up like a baseball field, causing Jenna to flinch and close her lids against the harsh illumination.

He lowered her sunglasses back over her eyes, questioning if some cosmic force was in play—or her father. "Is this equivalent to your dad turning on the porch light?"

"They're security lights, set to automatically come on at dusk. I've always hated them. I hate them even more now."

After hearing the pain in her voice, he realized he needed to take her out of there. "You should probably go inside now."

"I probably should."

Logan retrieved the cane, placed it in her right hand and hooked her left arm through his. Silently they walked back to the house and stopped on the porch a few paces from the front door, where they remained in the shadows.

"I'm glad you invited me today, Logan."

So was he, more than he cared to express. "Everyone enjoyed having you there."

"I enjoyed them, too. In all honesty, I rarely have the opportunity to socialize these days, which is why I appreciate the invitation. You have a wonderful family."

"Some people find them overbearing." Including Helena, who'd reluctantly attended gatherings only when he'd insisted.

"They're refreshingly real."

He felt the same about her. Even though he couldn't predict where this thing between them might lead, he wanted to find out. "I want to see you again, Jenna."

She shook her head. "That's not a good idea, Logan. After a while, you'd begin to view me as a liability."

"That's bs, Jenna."

"No. It's true. I have a son, I can't see two inches in front of me and my father is your client."

"None of that matters."

"Believe me, it will eventually. I'd rather we part as friends." She held out her hand. "Again, thank you for a lovely afternoon."

Ignoring the gesture, he said, "I don't want to shake your hand."

"What do you want, Logan?"

"You know what I want, Jenna."

"To get into my pants?"

"They wouldn't fit."

"Ha-ha." She transferred her weight from one foot to the other. "I don't need to be rescued."

"I know that and—"

"I don't want a man making overtures because of some misplaced sense of chivalry. I'm not looking for—"

Logan pulled her into his arms and before some force of nature, or an overprotective father intervened, he kissed her—and not an innocent kiss by any definition.

Again her cane dropped to the ground as she draped her arms over his shoulders, while he bracketed her waist. He didn't hold back, didn't waste any time taking it to another level. He wanted to leave a lasting impression. He wanted to change her mind. And when she met the glide of his tongue with her own, he wanted to scoop her up, carry her off the porch and back to his condo.

Jenna pulled away and wrapped her arms tightly around her middle. "We can't do this, Logan."

"We already have and you wanted it as much as I did, Jenna. You asked me to do it in the garden."

"During a moment of weakness, and obviously, I had another of those a second ago."

So had he. "It was one helluva a kiss, and you know it."

She pointed at the ground. "Could you give me my cane, please?"

"That depends. Are you going to beat me over the head with it?"

Finally, she smiled. "No. But I should probably beat myself over the head with it."

"You've had enough head injuries for one weekend." He bent, picked up the cane, put it back in her hand and stroked his thumb across her wrist for good measure. "I'll be out of town on business for the next couple of days, but I'll call you later in the week."

"I'm not going to go out with you again, Logan."

When he heard the minimal conviction in her tone, he sensed that, with a little more effort, he might win this battle yet. "You might change your mind after you've had some time to think about that kiss."

She lifted her chin defiantly. "You've got a tremendous ego, Mr. O'Brien."

"You've got barbecue sauce on your dress, Ms. Fordyce. And the greatest smile, along with an obstinate streak as long as the interstate."

"Look who's talking. That's why it would never work between us."

"Oh, yeah, it would. And after that kiss, you should know how well it would work."

She clasped his hand and gave it a quick shake. "Again, thanks for lunch. Good night and goodbye."

Before he could respond, she'd entered the house and closed the door behind her, leaving him alone on the porch to evaluate the situation.

The blow to his pride had stung, but past experience had taught him when to push, and when to toss in the towel. It looked like it was towel-tossing time where Jenna Fordyce was concerned. Yet pride wasn't the only issue. Truth was, he liked everything about her, and that would be worth the effort to try and change her mind.

"I don't want you seeing him again, Jenna."

Using her cane to tap her way through the foyer, Jenna brushed past her father in search of the study. "We've already had this conversation, Dad. And you don't have to worry. After tonight, it's not going to be an issue."

"From what I witnessed happening between the two of you on the porch, I have reservations about that."

That sent her back around to face him. "You were spying on us?"

"I heard voices and I looked out the window. That doesn't constitute spying."

How she wished he would simply let her be a grown-up. "The only window in the vestibule flanks the door. That means you had to be standing at the door in order to hear the voices."

"What difference does it make?"

She braced both hands on top of the cane. "What I do and who I do it with isn't your concern."

"It concerns me when it involves Logan O'Brien."

His attitude was beyond logical. "For the past few years, I've only heard you say good things about Logan. Great things, in fact. To hear you tell it, he's God's gift to the business community. Highly intelligent, philanthropic, and the list goes on and on." Not to mention he had a very skilled mouth, an attribute she secretly added to the list.

"That was on a professional level, Jenna. This is personal. I've already told you he has a reputation—"

"I know. With women." After that kiss, she certainly could understand why. "And for your information, he treated me with courtesy. He also treated me like a normal person, a lesson a few people around here need to learn."

"I'm cautious because I care about you, sweetheart."

"I know that, Dad. And what happened between Logan and me, well, it was only a kiss."

It was one helluva kiss, and you know it...

She definitely knew it, even if she hadn't wanted to admit it to Logan, or to herself. "I'm going to call John David, then I'm going to bed. It's been a long day. Good night."

She saw the hazy movement before her, followed

by a brief kiss on her cheek. "I love you, sweetheart," he said. "We'll talk about this later."

"I love you, too, Dad. And, no, we won't talk
about it."

With that, she walked into the makeshift photo
gallery and closed the door behind her before taking
her favorite chair in the corner. She groped for the
receiver on the end table and spoke the words "J.D."
to set the dialer in motion. The phone rang three
times before the familiar voice answered with a
short, "Hello."

"Hi, David. It's me. Is John David still awake?"

"Ginger just gave him his bath. Let me see if he's
out yet."

While Jenna waited to speak with her son, she
tried to tamp down the envy over another woman
bathing her baby. Another woman witnessing his
milestones. Yet she'd understood when David had
moved on with his life, even if it had meant bringing
a spare spouse into the mix to serve as J.D.'s surrogate mother.

A clatter rang out in Jenna's ear right before the
endearing voice said, "Hi, Mama."

"Hey, sweetie. Did you have a good bath?"

"Uh-huh. I played with a boat. Guess what,
Mama?"

"What?"

"Daddy and Mommy Ginger are gonna take me
on a boat. A big boat on the ocean."

Jenna swallowed hard around the unexpected news, and the fact he'd called David's new wife "Mommy." "When are you going on this boat, sweetie?"

"In the morning. That's why I gotta go to bed early."

She'd been literally left in the dark. "Do you want me to tell you a bedtime story or sing you our song first?"

"Not now, Mama. Daddy says we have to ride the airplane first to get to the boat so I gotta go to sleep. Can you come on the boat with me?"

If only she could. "Not this time, sweetie, but remember what I've always told you. Even if you can't see me, I'm always where?"

"In my heart."

"That's right, baby."

"I love you as big as the sky, Mama."

His willingness to recite their nightly routine eased her melancholy. "I love you as tall as the trees, sweetie."

"I love you as bright as the stars."

"I love you forever and ever."

"I'll put your picture in my suitcase, Mama. That way you can go on the boat with me."

The same picture she'd shown Logan earlier that day. The last picture they'd taken together.

She closed her eyes for a moment in an effort to fight back the threatening tears. "Have fun on the

boat, sweetie. Now, put your daddy on the phone."
She had a thing or two to say to him.

"Bye, Mama. Here's Daddy."

"I assume he told you about the cruise," David
said.

Her anger crept in again. "Yes, and you should
have told me, first."

"It was a spur of the moment thing, Jen.
Ginger's parents surprised us with the trip for
my birthday. I couldn't very well not accept until
I had your permission."

Jenna wasn't buying his excuses. "Your
birthday's in April, which means you've known
about this for two months. And the least you
could've done is discuss it with me."

"I've been busy."

"I call every night, David. You should have told
me the minute you knew."

"In all honesty, I didn't want you to have a lot of
time to obsess about the trip, which is why I didn't
mention it sooner."

Her anger arrived with the force of a gale. "I
wouldn't have obsessed over it."

"Yes, you would have. You worry about him
too much."

"He's my only child, David." The only child she
would probably ever have. "It's my right as his
mother to be concerned over his well-being and be
informed about his plans."

"You should've seen him, Jen. He was so excited when we told him this afternoon, he started packing immediately. Do you want me to tell him now that he can't go?"

To do so would be selfish on her part. "Of course not. I just worry—"

"I'll make sure he stays away from the railing, and we won't let him out of our sight."

He knew her too well. "Promise?"

"Promise. I have to go now and finish packing."

She wasn't ready to let him off the hook that easily. "How long will you be gone?"

"We fly to Florida in the morning and return next Sunday."

"You'll call me from the ship, right?"

"It's only a few days, Jen. I'll call the minute we return."

She couldn't tolerate not speaking to her child for that many days. "It's the least you can do, David. I only need him to call once. Since I can't be there, I'd like to know he's having a good time."

"He'll have a great time. We'll talk to you Sunday evening and he can tell you all about it then."

As much as she hated David's resistance, she couldn't very well force the issue. "Fine. I'll be waiting to hear from him. Give him a kiss for me, and please take good care of him, David."

"I will. Good night."

After hanging up the phone, Jenna released a litany of mild oaths and a few tears. She admittedly resented David's ability to give their child the adventure of a lifetime, while all she could offer was a nightly phone call. And all of her heart.

At times like these, she hated her deficit with a searing passion. Hated that she would be stuck for a whole week worrying about her son, and going to bed every night without hearing his voice.

She could only hope that, someday soon, she'd have her sight returned so her baby could be with her again. In the meantime, she'd do what she had to do to keep her mind off her troubles, although at the moment, she had no idea how she would fill all those lonely hours.

"How did the meeting in Kansas go, boss?"

Logan looked up from the paperwork he'd been staring at for over an hour to Bob, who was standing in his office doorway. "It went fine."

The man hitched up his pants beneath his big belly, strolled to the desk and pulled up a chair without an invitation. "So are you going to buy the planes?"

That still remained to be seen. He had enough assets to seal the deal, but he could use more capital. After building a successful business, he couldn't help but be ambivalent over letting go of his profits, and that's where his liaison with Avery Fordyce came in—if the man decided to cooperate. "I'll let you know as soon as I decide."

When Bob continued to study him, Logan lost what was left of his patience. "Anything else, Bob?"

"Just wondering what's got you so distracted."

A diminutive brunette. For the past two days, he hadn't been able to get Jenna out of his head, or his fantasies. "I'm not distracted, Bob. I'm tired. It's been a long two days."

"If you ask me, you could use a vacation. I don't remember the last time you've taken even a couple of days off."

Neither could Logan. "Right now that's not a priority."

Bob scrubbed a hand over the sparse hair on his scalp. "You know, boss, I learned a long time ago that you can burn the candle at both ends until you're burnt out."

He wasn't burnt out, at least, not yet. "Thanks for the suggestion. And, unless you have something business related to tell me, we both need to get back to work."

Bob pushed back the chair and stood, looking uncomfortable. "Someone's here to see you, but it's not business. It's personal."

Talking about beating around the bush. "And you're just now telling me that, Bob?"

"You might decide you're too busy for a visit."

Logan compiled a quick list of people he didn't care to see, and came up with two. One happened to be a client who always overstayed his welcome; the other was his former flame, and hell would ice before she'd show up at his office. "Tell me who it is, and I'll let you know if I'm available."

"Ms. Brennan."

The temperature just turned arctic in hell. "What does she want?"

"I didn't ask her, boss. She just said she needed a few minutes of your time and that it's important."

He couldn't imagine what Helena had to say, or if he even wanted to hear it. But he might as well get it over with because, knowing her, she'd force her way into his office. "Send her in, but tell her I only have ten minutes." The sooner he was rid of her, the better.

"Sure thing, Mr. O'Brien."

Before Logan had time to prepare, Helena Brennan strolled through his door, looking much the same as she had the last time he'd encountered her—the night he'd called off their wedding. She was a typical bombshell blonde—tall, long legs, great body and, at one time, he'd known every inch of it intimately. But today she wore a tailored white suit that wasn't up to her usual "got it, flaunt it" standards and her hair pulled back in a bun. In fact, she looked almost matronly.

"Hello, Logan." She paused too survey the

area. "You've redecorated your office." She ran her hand along the edge of the desk. "I like the chrome."

He didn't bother to respond or stand and that would send his mother into orbit. He did gesture toward the chair Bob had occupied a few minutes before. "Sit."

She complied and folded her hands primly in her lap. "I suppose I'm the last person you thought you'd see today."

She was the last person he wanted to see. "Why are you here?"

Helena flinched at his harsh tone. "I have something I need to tell you."

He knew exactly where this was heading. "Look, if you're wanting a reconciliation—"

"I'm here to tell you I'm getting married."

That he hadn't been expecting, and he couldn't deny the blow to his ego. "I would've read about it in the society page."

"It hasn't been officially announced yet, and I wanted you to hear it from me, first. I thought I owed you that much."

As if he really cared what she did or whom she did it with. "Who's the unlucky guy?"

"Randolph Morrison."

Old money uniting with old money. Figured. "Congratulations on the merger."

Anger flared in her blue eyes. "For your information, he loves me, although you might find that impossible to believe."

A year ago, he'd thought he'd been in love with her, too. "I hope the two of you have a long and prosperous life together." Prosperous was a given.

She shifted slightly in her seat. "In the year you and I have been apart, I've realized our relationship was destined to fail, and why."

"Was that before or after you pretended to be pregnant?"

Her gaze momentarily faltered. "I'm sorry for that. You know what they say. Desperate people do desperate things, and I was desperate to keep you. But I've changed, and I have you to thank for that."

He had a hard time believing that. "What do you mean?"

"You've opened my eyes to what I feel is important in a man, and I've found that with Randy. I now understand the reasons it didn't work with us, and it had as much to do with you as it did with me. Would you like to hear my conclusions for future relationship reference?"

He didn't want nor need her opinions. "Is this going to take long? I have a conference call in a few minutes." More like half an hour, but he wanted her out of there and out of his life for good.

She lifted a perfectly arched brow. "Are you afraid of taking a little constructive criticism, Logan?"

Like she had the right to criticize anyone. "If it makes you feel better, go ahead."

"Good." She leaned forward and studied him long and hard. "You're a beautiful man, Logan, and you have a good heart. You're driven to succeed in business, almost too driven, but you're generous when it comes to strangers in need. You're a master at knocking the ground from beneath a woman's feet and getting her flat on her back in your bed using sexy, provocative words. And you also have the talent and skills to back them up. I know that better than anyone."

When she hesitated, Logan recognized the worst of the character assassination were yet to come. "But?"

"You have no idea how to be a friend to a woman."

His frame went rigid. "That sure as hell isn't true."

"Really? Then tell me my favorite color?"

Think fast, O'Brien. "Brown."

"Wrong."

"Is there a point to all of this, Helena?" Aside from citing his shortcomings.

She rose from the chair and clutched her purse in her arms. "The point is that if you ever become seriously involved with another woman, you might want to take her out to dinner a few times and get to know her, before you take her to bed. Ask her questions and let her know you're interested not only in her body, but in her mind, as well. You'd be surprised what a difference that makes."

She was seriously wrong. They'd been to dinner on numerous occasions during their time together. He'd taken her to several business functions, even if he had taken her to bed the first night they'd met. And the only thing on her mind when they'd dated had been the husband hunt…and shopping.

Logan saw no reason to rehash old recriminations. The past belonged in the past. "Your suggestions are duly noted," he said. "Anything else you want to rake me over the coals for?"

"Not at all, because I know that below your tough surface, there's a really great guy just waiting to come out and shine. It's going to take a very special woman to make that happen. I hope you find her soon."

She spun around and swayed out the door, giving Logan a glimpse of the Helena he'd known and had thought he'd loved.

He hated her harsh assessment. Despised that she viewed him as some shallow guy on the make who didn't give a damn about women. Hated that he'd found a measure of truth in her words, mainly when it came to the friendship part.

Fact was, he and Helena had never been friends. They'd had some good times and great sex, but beyond that, they'd shared little in common. She didn't like sports or his brothers. Going a week without a manicure was her idea of roughing it, and walking from the four-car garage into her father's mansion had been the only hiking she cared to do.

He doubted he would find the perfect mix of friendship and passion with a woman…unless he'd already found it in Jenna Fordyce. And that was a problem. Forming more than a casual relationship with her had several strikes against it—her father and that little issue of her refusing to see him again.

Maybe he could convince her to reconsider. Maybe he could prove to himself that he was capable of developing a solid friendship with a woman, even a woman who'd occupied his down and dirty dreams for three solid nights.

He could be setting himself up for failure if she refused to see him again, or even if she didn't. He wasn't sure how this would all come out in the end, but he'd be damned if he wasn't going try.

Chapter Six

When Jenna felt the shake on her shoulder, she pulled the headphones from her ears. "Yes, Sasha?"

"Sorry to be a bother, Miss, but you have a phone call."

For the past two days, she'd been counting the hours until she could reconnect with her son. She prayed David had reconsidered and the wait was finally over. "Is it John David?"

"No ma'am. It's a man."

Jenna's heart took a nosedive. "Does he have a name?"

"He said he's a friend, and that he enjoyed the roses."

She could only think of one man who might fit that description. "I'll take it." If only to hear a friendly voice. Anything to get her mind off her moping.

Sasha placed the phone in her hand and after Jenna heard the study door close, she answered with, "Are you looking for an invitation to see my garden again?"

"Not a bad idea, but it's fairly late."

As far as she was concerned, Logan's timing couldn't have been better. "I'm still wide-awake and probably will be most of the night."

"Why's that?"

"No offense, but I was expecting someone else, and I'm a little disappointed it wasn't him."

"You have another guy waiting in the wings, huh?"

Oddly, he sounded letdown. "Yes. A little guy. I haven't spoken with my son since Sunday. His father and new stepmother have taken him on a cruise."

"And you're missing him."

An accurate assessment from a man she barely knew. "You could say that."

"If you want some company, just say the word and I'll pick you up in a half hour. We could go for a drive or grab some coffee."

His persuasive voice served as an enticement, but good sense told her not to risk making a mistake when she felt so vulnerable. "I appreciate the suggestion, but—"

"Hang on a minute."

The line went silent for a few seconds until Logan came back to the phone. "That's a helluva lot better."

"What were you doing?"

"Undressing."

She had a detailed mental snapshot of that, even if she had no idea if it was accurate. "Do you make it a habit of taking off your clothes while you're on the phone with a woman?"

His laugh was incredibly seductive. "I'm not taking off all my clothes, just this damn noose around my neck and this stiff shirt. I only wear a suit and tie when I have to."

"The outdoorsman has spoken."

"Former outdoorsman. Lately I'm either trapped in my office or an airport."

She could relate to that, only, the house—and her vision loss—had led to her confinement. "I know what you mean. I really miss taking long walks. Fresh air and trees. I love pine trees."

"So do I. And I have an idea that's better than going for coffee tonight. We should go camping this weekend."

Jenna swallowed around her shock. "Are you serious?"

"Yeah. We could both use some time to get away. A trip between friends. There's an Arkansas state park in the Ozarks you'd enjoy."

She couldn't imagine accompanying him out

of state. In truth, she could, even though she shouldn't. "A friendly camping trip, huh?"

"Sure. No expectations. Just good company and conversation."

Jenna was very tempted to say yes but thought better of it. "Arkansas is fairly far way."

"We can leave on Friday and get a head start. If you'll go, I'll make the trip worth your while. I'm an expert camper."

She suspected his expertise went far beyond camping. "I suppose that entails pitching a more than adequate tent."

"Yeah, and with your help, I'll have it up in record time."

She couldn't disregard the suggestion in his tone, or her rather warm response to it. "Nothing like a confident camper. How are you at building fires?"

"Pretty good. I like to start out slowly, then stoke it until it's hot enough to melt steel."

She was veritably hot enough to melt steel. "What's your secret to that?"

"Good wood."

If she didn't stop this provocative conversation now, she'd agree to meet him tonight for a little fire building. Worse, she might agree to go away with him for the weekend. "Are you sure you don't expect more than a friendly trip?"

He sighed. "I'm sure, and I apologize for giving you the impression I expect more."

Quite a switch from the smooth sex talk he'd levied on her a moment before. Yet she wasn't certain she could trust him, or for that matter, trust herself. "Again, this sounds great, but I'm going to have to take a rain check. I need to be available in case John David needs me."

"He's miles away, Jenna, and I'm offering you a distraction."

He was already distracting her and presenting ideas she had no business considering. "With my poor eyesight, you'd have more of a burden with me tagging along than if you went alone." Or with another woman, and she was certain he had more than a few waiting in the proverbial wings.

"Come to think of it, you could be right. You might not enjoy the limited facilities. Not a masseuse or hair dresser within twenty miles. Just me, the wildlife and the fire."

He was wrong about her preferences. Dead wrong. "As I've told you before, I used to hike before my vision gave out on me. I'm very good at all the aforementioned camping aspects, I don't need to be pampered and I can handle a trail blindfolded."

"Then, prove it."

She hesitated a few moments, chastising herself for buckling beneath the power of his intentional baiting. Did she dare spend three days with him? Three days convening with nature, something she hadn't done in a long time. Three days outside the family mansion that had become her personal prison. Three days spent with a man who had seduction down to a science, regardless of his insistence he only wanted friendship.

"Okay. You're on." She only hoped she survived all his proficiency.

"Good. I'll pick you up bright and early Friday morning, and I'll have you home on Sunday in time to talk to your son."

She didn't do mornings very well. "How early?"

"It's a solid day's drive, so I'm thinking 5:00 a.m., unless you can't live without your beauty sleep, princess."

She made a note to put a large Thermos of coffee at the top of her list of things to bring, right beneath the speech she would write about the perils of calling her a princess. "I'll be ready."

"Great. One more thing—" he hesitated a moment "—I'm serious about being your friend, Jenna. I think we could both use that more than anything right now."

He certainly sounded sincere. "Can you really do that, Logan? Be only a friend to a woman without wanting anything else?"

"I'm going to give it my best shot, but I'll need your help."

In other words, she would have to try doubly hard to resist him if he failed to live up to his promise. Or maybe she wouldn't try to resist him. After all, celibacy wasn't what it was cracked up to be. They were both above the age of consent and, should the situation arise, she might decide to simply go for it while she had the chance. "One more thing. Which one of us is going to inform my father?"

"You just worry about packing, and I'll take care of Avery."

"Are you sure you want to do that, Logan?"

"Sure. How bad could it be?"

"If I were you, O'Brien, I'd turn right around and walk back out the door."

Logan had been threatened by fathers before, but none had been business colleagues. He could deal with Avery better if they were seated at a conference table, hammering out a deal not standing in the living room waiting for the man's daughter to appear so he could take her away. Even though Avery was wearing a blue robe instead of his usual silk suit, he looked formidable. He also looked like he could pick up the nearby fireplace poker and impale Logan with it if he didn't comply with his command.

Too bad. He wasn't going anywhere without Jenna. "Look, Avery, it's only for two days."

"Why are you doing this, Logan?"

He'd asked himself that same question several

times. The most important answer—he was on a mission to prove Helena wrong. And he'd been where Jenna was now—isolated from meaningful social interaction—only his isolation had been self-imposed. "Your daughter needs to do something other than sit around, waiting to hear from her kid."

"You don't have a clue what my daughter needs." He pointed at him and scowled. "And if you think I'm going to stand by and let you discard her as you've done countless women, you're sorely mistaken."

Logan should've known better than to frequent the same social events as Avery, a different escort in tow every time. "I don't intend to do that. We're only friends." Something he'd vowed to keep in mind this weekend. Granted, he wouldn't mind knowing her better in every sense, but he'd made the decision to adopt a hands-off policy, even if it might kill him in the process.

"If you truly have her best interests at heart," Avery said, "I see no reason why you can't take her to dinner in Houston instead of carting her thousands of miles away for some camping trip."

For the sake of civility and future business dealings, Logan kept a tight rein on his temper. "We're going to Arkansas, Avery, not Tahiti."

"I vote for Tahiti."

Both Logan and Avery turned at the same time to discover Jenna standing in the doorway, a black nylon bag slung over one shoulder, a cane that resembled a walking stick in her grip and a large black backpack resting at her feet.

"I hear Tahiti's crowded this time of year," Logan said, and then realized it sounded as if he wanted to get her alone—most likely the reason behind Avery's glare. Logan's lengthy appraisal of Jenna's midthigh khaki shorts, white sleeveless blouse and hiking boots probably hadn't helped. But the lethal combination of bare arms and bare legs—toned bare arms and legs for a woman of such small stature— meant only one thing. Big trouble. And if he didn't keep his eyes to himself, it could lead to his own demise—delivered at the hands of her father.

Avery moved to Jenna's side and wrapped his arm around her shoulder. "It's not too late to reconsider, sweetheart."

"I'm going, Dad. End of discussion."

Avery sported a serious frown. "I can't talk you out of this?"

She kissed his cheek. "You tried that last night, and nothing's changed."

He looked resigned. "Then, did you pack your allergy medication?"

"Yes, and my eyedrops, my toothbrush, clean underwear and bear repellant." She snapped her fingers. "Darn, I'm all out of bear repellant."

When Avery looked alarmed, Logan added, "We won't have to worry about that where we're going."

"Speaking of going," Jenna said, "shouldn't we be heading out before the traffic gets heavy?"

"Yeah, we should." Logan crossed the room and took her bags. "I'll meet you at the SUV as soon as I give Avery the contact information."

She smiled. "Sure. I'll expect you as soon as you reassure Mr. Fordyce that we're not running off to Vegas for a quickie wedding, or Tahiti. See you Sunday, Dad."

Cane in hand, she strode out of the room, leaving Logan alone with Avery, who nailed him with another hard glare. "I need to know where you'll be at all times."

With his free hand, Logan fished through his jeans' pocket, withdrew a piece of paper and handed it to Avery. "Here's the number of the campground and my cell phone, which you already have. Feel free to call in case of an emergency."

"Or in case we receive the call that corneas have become available," Avery said. "She'll have a limited window of time to return to Houston."

Logan hadn't stopped to consider the possibility of Jenna being unavailable for the transplant, and he was surprised she hadn't mentioned it. "If you get the call, I'll put her on a plane if I have to."

Avery forked a hand through his silver hair. "You have a lot to learn about Jenna, Logan. If you knew her, at all, you'd know that she hates to fly, particularly alone."

"I'll make note of that." And he would accompany her back to Texas in a chartered plane if necessary. "Speaking of planes, I met with the aviation company in Wichita on Monday. I can take delivery on the jets after the first of the year, if you're still willing to partner with me."

Avery rubbed a hand over his stubbled chin. "That depends. If you bring my daughter home unscathed, I'd be willing to back you financially. As long as you walk away from her afterward."

Logan knew the entrepreneur could be cutthroat, but he didn't realize he'd go to the extreme of using his daughter as a pawn. "We'll discuss it further next week."

"We'll definitely discuss it next week."

He didn't care for Avery's tone, or his suspicions. "You've always trusted me in business, Avery. You can trust me with Jenna."

He refused Logan's offer of a handshake. "My daughter is a very special woman. Remember that."

Avery Fordyce wasn't telling Logan anything he didn't already know.

Shortly after a fast-food lunch, Jenna drifted off to the drone of highway traffic, and had awakened a few moments before to the sound of crunching gravel. She stretched her legs and straightened in the seat. "Where are we?"

"In the Ozark National Forest."

Surely, she hadn't been asleep that long. "What time is it?"

"Almost four. We made it an hour earlier than I'd expected."

She laid her head back against the seat. "That's because we barely stopped since we grabbed the burgers."

"Did you know your lip trembles when you're asleep?"

Undoubtedly he'd been watching her. "I suppose you're going to tell me that I snore or, worse, drool."

"None of the above. But you did look like you were having a good dream."

Jenna didn't remember any dreams, although she did recall thinking about J.D. before she'd fallen asleep. She wondered where he was right now, if he was having a good time on the ship—without her. Of course, that would be her wish, even if she did experience some regret.

She had other things to think about to keep her mind occupied, and a question she'd been meaning to ask Logan. "Out of curiosity, exactly what did my father say to you before we left?"

"Not much, other than I'm supposed to deliver you safe and sound and unharmed on Sunday. In the meantime, I've been ordered to treat you with respect."

"He thinks you want to have sex with me."

Logan cleared his throat. "I'm here to be your friend."

"If I had to judge by the way you kissed me the other evening, and some of our conversation on Wednesday, I'd say you've thought about it."

"Okay, I won't deny that. But I've decided sex can complicate things, Jenna."

"That all depends on your mind-set."

"I guess so, if sex is all both parties want going into the relationship."

Spoken like the consummate player. Oddly, she hadn't viewed him that way since she'd known him, in spite of what her father had said. "If sex is only the primary goal, then it seems you're dealing with two callous people who don't give a damn about each other. And if that's the case, why would they want to have sex in the first place?"

"You just proved my point. You can't have sex with a friend without screwing up the friendship."

"You're saying that, in order for us to remain friends, we should avoid sex."

"Probably so."

Funny, he didn't sound that convinced. "I suppose you could be right." Or not.

"Your father would be glad to hear you say that."

"My father has nothing to do with my decisions, although, he's tried to intervene more than a few times in my life."

"That bad, huh?"

"You have no idea." She tilted her head back and sighed. "You've heard that old expression about running with scissors. He wouldn't let me run with a marshmallow. In fact, he didn't want me to run, at all."

"He only wants to protect you, Jenna."

"I know." She rested her hands loosely on her abdomen. "But he can't protect me from everything. Although, I understand why he's so bent on doing that."

"Like you've said, you're all he has."

"And it took my parents several years of trying to get pregnant before they finally adopted me."

"I didn't realize you were adopted."

Obviously, Logan and her father hadn't shared much when it came to their personal lives. "The adoption was final when I was six months old. Aside from that, I know nothing about my biological parents. It was a private adoption and the records are sealed."

"Have you asked your dad about them?"

"I did, not long after my mom died." That proved to be a disaster in the making. "I think he believed I was looking for a replacement for her. He was so upset, I didn't ask again until I was pregnant with John David. And once more, he was so distressed, I dropped it and haven't mentioned it since."

"But you wanted to know from a health care standpoint."

Another correct assumption. "At first, I wondered if she gave me up because she had the same disease I have. Later, I wanted to know what J.D.'s chances were of contracting it. He'll eventually be tested, but I'd like to be prepared."

"And if he does have it?"

She'd prayed night after night that wouldn't be the case. "Hopefully by the time he's my age, they'll have a cure."

They both fell silent for a few moments before Jenna added, "If my mother did give me up because she couldn't see, I wouldn't blame her at all. I'm sure she felt that it was the most unselfish thing to do."

"But you never considered that when you had your son."

"Not at all." She shifted to face him, wishing she could see enough to gauge his reaction. "I didn't worry about my future problems since John David has a father to help out. And even if I'd been on my own, I'm not sure I could have given him up. Maybe that makes me selfish, but it's hard enough knowing that another woman is practically raising him right now."

"I'm sure that is tough, but he still has you."

If only Jenna could believe she hadn't been replaced. If she could just be with him soon, touch him, hug him, tell him a bedtime story in person, not over the phone.

The conversation suspended for the time being, until Logan announced, "We're here," as he turned the SUV sharply to the right, braked hard and cut off the engine. "I'll be back in a minute."

Jenna didn't particularly like being left behind. "Where are you going?"

"To see what sites are available. The visitor center looks fairly crowded."

In other words, she might get lost among the masses. "Mind rolling down the window so I don't suffocate?"

"Sure."

Before Jenna could issue a protest, the door slammed, indicating Logan had left. She turned her face toward the open window and drew in the scents of pine, relished the warm summer sun and immediately fired off several sneezes.

She felt for the bag at her feet and withdrew her decongestants, along with the eyedrops. As much as she hated relying on medication, she hated runny noses and dry eyes even more.

After downing the pills with a sip of bottled water and applying the drops, she replaced the medicine and groped for the radio's controls. Nothing but static filtered through the speakers, which led her to believe they were far away from civilization, and that suited her fine.

The opening door indicated Logan's return. Or, at least, she hoped it was him and not some stranger.

He confirmed his identity when he said, "The place is packed, so we have two options."

Jenna hoped that turning around and going home wasn't one of them. "I'm listening."

"We can take the only spot left, but it's in the middle of the Falstaff reunion."

"I don't believe I know the Falstaffs."

"I met Billy Joe Falstaff while I was waiting in line. A nice guy. He offered me a beer and a date with his little sister, Liza."

For a second she wondered if Logan might take Billy Joe up on his offer after dealing with her deficits. Pushing the insecurity back where it belonged, she said, "How generous of him. What's the other option?"

"We can take the hiking trail that circles the valley. It's about fourteen miles all the way around, but there's several remote camping spots along the way."

She could live with remote. She preferred remote to a reunion of strangers. "That sounds like a good plan."

"The trail's pretty rough in places. Do you think you can handle it?"

"With your help, I can handle anything."

Chapter Seven

"Is this tether thing tying us together really necessary, Logan?"

As far as he was concerned, yes. "I didn't want you making a misstep when we reached the top of the bluff."

"Please tell me we're at the top of the bluff."

"We are."

"Good, because I feel like a dog and you're my handler."

If she only knew how much he wanted to handle her, she'd probably turn around and head back to Texas.

He regarded Jenna over one shoulder to see her

hair falling out of the band she'd secured at her crown, her cheeks dotted with dirt and a leaf hanging from her ponytail. She looked so damn cute, he wanted to kiss her. But he wasn't going to do it, otherwise he'd be breaking a promise, both to her and himself.

When he pulled up short, Jenna kept going and rammed into his back, face first. He turned and caught her by the shoulders to make sure she remained upright. "Whoa there."

She braced one hand on her hip. "Whoa? Now I've been relegated to pack mule."

Logan couldn't halt the laugh, which earned him a frown. "Stop complaining. I'm carrying a cooler, the tent and a backpack full of supplies."

"I'm not complaining, but I could use a drink and a break."

In reality, so could he. "Fine. We can rest for a few minutes, but we need to get down the hill before dark."

After he unhooked the tether from her belt loop, Jenna dropped her cane to the ground, pulled the backpack from her shoulders and set her other bag down before sitting beside them. She draped her arms on bent knees. "For a minute I thought we were going to walk all night."

He removed his gear, set it aside in a pile and stood above her. "I don't care what you say, you're definitely a princess, princess."

"I am not."

"Oh, yeah? Anyone who considers a foot massager their most prized possession is a princess."

She pulled a bottle of water from the side of the tote and took a swig. "Look who's talking. You're the one who can't live without access to twenty sports stations."

"That makes me a guy."

She picked up a twig and tossed it at his feet. "Shut up, Logan, or I'll short sheet your bed tonight."

"No beds available, just a blanket and the ground." Although he wouldn't mind a bed—with her in it. Naked.

Damn, he was a lost cause. But not yet. Thinking about it wasn't the same thing as acting on it.

After he heard a rustle in the nearby trees, Logan turned toward the sound. And when Jenna began to speak, he told her, "Be quiet and be still."

"If you say there's snake nearby, I'm going to—"

"Not a snake. A whitetail deer."

She came to her feet and brushed off her bottom. "Where is it?"

"In a clearing to your left, about fifty yards or so. It's heading this way."

She knelt, carefully opened the backpack and withdrew a digital camera. "I want a picture."

A photographer he was not. "I'll try, but I make no guarantees on quality."

"I'm going to help you," she said in a whisper.

"Come here and stand behind me. You point and I'll shoot."

He saw no reason to protest. In fact, he'd damn sure enjoy standing behind her. With that in mind, he positioned himself at her back and turned her in the direction of the wildlife. "What do I do now?"

"First of all, describe the deer."

"You've never seen one before?"

"Of course I've seen one. I just want to know what this one looks like."

Logan studied the animal foraging in the grass while inching closer, oblivious to their presence. "It's brown, with a white tail." He saw another flash of tan in the distance. "It's a doe. She has a fawn with her."

"Baby animals make great subjects," she said. "Let's hurry and get a picture before they run away."

Logan moved flush against her and ran his palms down her arms before lifting the camera to his eyes. "It's focused." And he was quickly in danger of forgetting his friendship goal. But he couldn't very well help her with the picture if he didn't touch her.

"Now, keep looking through the lens," she said. "And keep the camera steady. I'll do the rest."

He wasn't sure he could trust himself to keep the camera steady with her so close.

"Are you ready?" she asked.

Oh, yeah. Real ready, but not necessarily in a photography sense. "Shoot."

She set off the shutter in rapid-fire succession right before the deer bolted and took off in the opposite direction.

"They're out of here," Logan said as he gave the camera back to Jenna with one hand while keeping his other resting loosely at her waist. He should back away from her immediately, but his feet didn't want to move, and his hand had developed a will of its own.

"Feel free to let go of me now," she said.

Apparently she could read his mind, and letting her go was the last thing he wanted to do, but he did. Reluctantly.

While he returned to the nylon cooler and crouched to retrieve a sports drink, Jenna wandered to the opposite side of the trail.

"Be careful," he told her as she took a few steps toward the edge of the bluff. "You've got a drop off about fifteen feet in front of you."

"What does the scenery look like?" she asked.

"There's a valley below and a creek. And mountains covered with trees in the distance."

"I'm going to take a few more pictures, then we can be on our way."

"Do you need any help?" He sounded way too eager.

"Not this time. I'm going to rely on my intuition."

Drink in hand, Logan straightened and kept a

close eye on her. So far so good, he thought as she remained in the same spot, snapping pictures nonstop.

But when she started forward, every instinct he owned screamed danger. He tossed aside the bottle and caught her with one arm around her middle, impeding her progress.

As he carried her back to the trail, his chest constricted around his hammering heart. "Dammit, Jenna, I told you to be careful," he said as he set her down without letting her go.

She sent him a sour look. "You said fifteen feet. I only moved two."

Hardheaded woman. "If you'd kept going, you would've walked right over the edge."

"Do you really think I'm that stupid?"

"I think you take chances you don't need to take."

She wrested out of his hold. "Thanks for the vote of confidence, Logan. Are you proud of yourself now?"

"I don't know what in the hell you're talking about."

She draped the camera's strap around her neck. "You've done your good deed for the day, saving a distressed damsel whom you believe doesn't have the sense of a pack mule. Isn't that what this is all about between you and me? Your need to come to the rescue of a helpless, blind woman?"

"You're about as helpless as a fully armed militia."

"And you want to serve as my guardian. I don't need a guardian, Logan."

He only needed one thing from her at the moment, right or wrong. "As far as you and me are concerned, this is what it's all about."

He kissed her hard, and deep, driven by adrenaline and anger. Maybe even some latent fear.

He expected her to pull away and slug him, but so far she hadn't done one thing he'd expected. Instead, she willingly participated in the kiss, and in many ways took the lead. She rubbed her hands up and down his back. He pulled her closer. She executed a full body press against him. He inched his hands beneath the back of her shirt.

He had half a mind to take her down on the dusty ground just to feel her beneath him. The other half of his mind, located below his skull—not his belt—told him that wouldn't be at all comfortable for her.

He had a blanket nearby and a large expanse of grass at his disposal. If she wanted a longer break, he'd be glad to oblige her. If she wanted to know just how badly he wanted her, he'd be more than happy to show her. And if he wanted to retain some honor, he'd stop the thoughts and the mouth action immediately. A tough decision, particularly when she acted as though she didn't want him to stop.

Something brushed Logan's leg, forcing him to break the kiss. He looked to his left to see a patch of black loping away.

"Was that another deer?" Jenna asked.

"I think it was a Labrador retriever."

A whistle sounded, followed by a feminine voice calling, "Get back here, Perry."

So much for being alone. So much for his plans to engage Jenna in a heavy make-out session. And that was just as well. If he'd let his libido do the talking, they wouldn't have made it to the campsite until well after dark—and he might have made a fatal error in judgment. Not a good thing to do if he wanted to befriend her, even if he also wanted to bed her.

After nudging Jenna aside, Logan snatched her cane from the ground and handed it to her. "Time to hit the road again, princess."

"If you don't stop that princess stuff, I will find a way to pay you back."

He leaned close to her ear and said, "You already have. Right now I'm in a helluva lot of pain, thanks to you."

Her mouth gaped open momentarily. The sunglasses prevented him from seeing her eyes, but he figured she had that whole "shooting daggers" thing going on. "Thanks to me? You kissed me first, *friend.*"

Like he'd really forget that. "You didn't stop me, did you?"

She shook her head. "This is ridiculous. I'm not the type to lose control because some guy has a way with his tongue."

"I'm not some guy, Jenna." And she wasn't just any woman, either.

"Whatever." She flipped her hand in dismissal before gathering her equipment from the ground, but he would bet his last limo that she was as unable to ignore their attraction as he was.

Logan had a strong feeling only time would tell how long he could keep his distance before only friendship went the way of the wind.

As they lay side by side on their backs on a blanket, bedrolls supporting their heads, Logan noticed that the fire he'd built earlier had cast Jenna's profile in a golden glow. Since dinner, he'd noticed a lot of things about her, including her ability to avoid certain subjects, namely what had happened on the trail earlier in the day, and the fact that, at some point, they had to climb into the tent together.

Jenna released a satisfied sigh, disturbing the quiet. "Summer's my favorite season. I wouldn't mind if we had hot weather year-round."

He wouldn't mind if someone would douse him with a bucket of ice water, otherwise he could be in for a long, hard night. "That's a good thing since we live in Texas."

"True." She stretched her arms above her head and dropped them at her sides. "When I was little, I used to go outdoors late at night, lie on the ground and watch the stars. Sometimes I'd fall asleep until morning and I'd have to sneak back in before my parents caught me."

"You were daring even as a kid."

"Yes, I was. Fortunately I've never been afraid of the dark, otherwise I'd be in serious trouble now."

Occasionally she would slip in a reminder of her blindness, and Logan didn't know if that was for her benefit, or his. "During the summer, I'd stay up late and play basketball with my brothers until the neighbors complained."

"And your parents didn't object?" She sounded in awe of that concept.

"No. Probably because they were glad to get us out of the house."

"That must have been wonderful, having siblings. I only had myself to talk to at home. After a while, that gets rather boring."

Logan had five siblings he had to talk over in order to get a word in edgewise. "It had its ups and downs, particularly when we'd get into fights."

"You didn't really hurt each other, did you?"

"I suffered a few black eyes in my time. We were more afraid of what my father would do after he broke them up."

"Were you afraid of anything else when you were a child?"

The question took him by surprise. "Not that I can think of."

She touched his arm. "Come on, Logan. Everyone has fears. I promise I won't tell anyone and destroy your rep as a tough guy."

He'd never been into soul baring, but for some strange reason, he didn't feel the need to hold back with Jenna. "For a long time, I used to be afraid of heights before I forced myself to get over it. That started after Aidan pushed me out of the top bunk bed when I was about five and I landed on my face. I had to have stitches."

"Where?"

"On my chin."

She reached out and ran a fingertip along his face, sketching a path beneath his bottom lip. "Right here I feel a scar. Nothing big, but it's there. I'm surprised I missed it before."

He was surprised by his reaction to only a simple touch. "I was lucky I didn't lose any teeth." He would be lucky if he didn't lose his cool when her palm came to rest on his abdomen. "What about you?" he asked. "What were you afraid of when you were a kid?"

"Honestly, not much. Adulthood is another story altogether."

He could think of several fears she might have

and he wanted to know them all. "What are you afraid of now, Jenna?"

"Snakes."

"Seriously."

"I am serious. Oh, and I don't like crowded elevators."

"Is that it?"

She shifted onto her back and broke all contact between them. "I'm afraid my son will forget me."

The abject sadness in her voice cut Logan to the core. He'd never been all that good at consolation, particularly when it involved women. For her, he would try.

After taking her hand, he placed it on his chest. "I doubt your son will ever forget you." He'd never forget her, even if this weekend was all they would ever have.

She worked her way into a sitting position and said, "Enough of that. We're here to have a good time, not to discuss the past or worry about the future."

She'd said it with a good deal of bravado, but Logan surmised she did so only to cover her emotional scars.

When she tried to hide a yawn behind her hand, he said, "Looks like the good times will have to start over in the morning. I have the tent up if you're ready to get some sleep." A tent barely big enough for both of them. A test of his willpower.

She pushed off the blanket and came to her feet. "It's too hot to sleep."

He'd have to agree, especially when she began to unbutton her blouse. "If you want some privacy, I can take a walk."

She slid the blouse away. "I want to go for a swim in the creek and wash the grime off my body."

He wanted to tackle her where she stood. "Did you bring a suit?"

"I don't need one."

Oh, hell. "You're going to go for a midnight swim in a state park, buck naked?"

"What's a little nudity between friends?"

To a man who was really trying to behave, a lot. "We're not the only people around here."

"I haven't seen a soul, but if it makes you feel better, I'll leave my underwear on." She dropped the blouse on his lap, concealing the first signs of an erection that fortunately she couldn't see. "And you're going with me."

He rubbed a hand over the back of his neck and tried to avert his gaze, without success. "It's too dangerous, Jenna."

She looked highly frustrated. "You told me earlier today the creek's not deep at all."

"Me and you swimming together, with you in your underwear. That's dangerous."

"Surely, you've seen a woman dressed only in a bra and panties before, Logan."

He hadn't seen her that way before—until now.

She shimmied out of her shorts, leaving her wearing only a skimpy white bra and skimpy white panties, setting a sufficient trap for Logan's hyped-up hormones. "Are you trying to test me, Jenna?" If so, he was failing.

She pulled the band from the top of her head and shook out her hair. "I'm trying to cool off."

And in the process, heating him up to bonfire intensity. "I didn't bring a suit, either."

"Then feel free to strip down to your drawers. Better still, get totally naked. I'll never know."

Yeah, she would, if he got anywhere near her. "That's probably not a good idea."

"It's a great idea." She hovered above him, one hand fisted on her waist. "Get up, O'Brien."

He already was. "Are you sure you want to do this?"

"Positive."

What the hell? Like she'd said, she couldn't see him, but that didn't change the fact he could see her. A lot of her, from the outline of her breasts to the minimal strip of fabric between her thighs, and all notable parts in between. At least, until they got into the water.

As he tugged the T-shirt over his head and snaked out of his jeans, he made a firm commitment to keep his hands to himself. Maybe he should tie them both behind his back.

* * *

Jenna stepped into the creek and immediately experienced the heady rush of freedom. She curled her toes into the sandy bottom as water lapped at her ankles. Cool water that reminded her of her companion. Although Logan had a firm grip on her hand, he didn't say a word, and she suspected he was literally keeping her at arm's length.

She couldn't exactly fault him. After all, he seemed to be struggling with control, and she had only herself to thank for that. She'd welcomed his kiss earlier in the day. She'd invited him for a swim without the benefit of clothes. And she'd known exactly what she was doing.

All the talk of friendship, of no expectations, had dissolved with every passing moment. With each and every kiss. Some might not understand why she would take such a risk with a man she didn't know that well. Frankly, she didn't care. Didn't care what her father might think or what anyone would think, for that matter. She had a very virile male at her disposal, and she planned to take supreme advantage of the circumstance.

"We're only going to go a little farther," Logan said, breaking into her thoughts.

That remained to be seen, as far as Jenna was concerned, though she recognized he'd been referring to their swim.

After the stream encircled her midriff, Jenna

wrested from Logan's grasp and plunged beneath
the surface, a watery cocoon where she could wash
away the dust and the last of her concerns. The
night sounds gave way to serene silence and complete darkness, yet, she wasn't afraid at all. Not
when a beautiful man waited for her.

After a few moments, Jenna came up for air and
slicked back her hair with both hands. "This feels
wonderful." When she received no response, she
questioned if she'd finally driven him away with her
daring. "Logan?"

"I'm still here."

Of course he was still there. He wasn't the type to
leave her to her own devices; he'd demonstrated
that when she'd gotten to close to the edge of the cliff.
She felt as if she were teetering on another edge right
now, looking for a safe place to land. Her instincts
told her Logan was that safe place, at least, temporarily, as long as she kept her emotional wits about her.

"Where are you?" she asked.

"To your left." He caught her hand beneath the
water and urged her closer.

Her curiosity beckoning, she moved behind
him, using his shoulders for support. His skin was
damp and taut, she realized as she investigated his
back, tracing a line with a fingertip down his spine
until she contacted the rise below his waist. Wisdom warranted she halt the examination, but she
wasn't feeling very wise at the moment. She was

feeling somewhat restless and warm. And she had to know exactly what he was wearing—or not wearing.

Jenna received her answer when she splayed both her palms over the sides of his hips. His bare hips. Aside from a slight tremor, he remained very still as she explored the curve of his well-defined bottom.

"Nice butt, O'Brien."

He clasped her wrists and pulled her around in front of him. "I'm warning you, Jenna." He sounded stern, but not so intimidating that Jenna would veer from her goal.

"Consider me sufficiently warned," she said. And amply excited.

"Do you realize what you're doing?"

"I'm finding out for myself what all the ladies see in you."

"You're stirring up trouble."

"How much trouble?"

He tugged her forward and pressed his pelvis against her. "Does that answer your question?"

Yes, it had. He'd verified he was patently male, and that he had impressive attributes any women would find appealing. Most important, he'd proven that he wanted her, at least, in a physical sense. And she wanted him.

She decided to go for broke. To go for it all. On that thought, Jenna reached behind her, unclasped her bra and tossed it in the direction of the bank. In order to remove her panties, she'd have to rely on Logan's assistance and opted to let him do the honors later.

She slid her hands up his chest and toyed with the fringe of hair at his nape. "Now we're almost even."

She then became the aggressor, and kissed him first.

When he released a feral groan, Jenna recognized she'd sufficiently unleashed something in him, spurring an all-out sensual attack on her mouth. She was mildly aware of a waterfall gurgling in the distance, the hum of locusts and the trill of a bird. She was more aware of Logan's touch on her bottom, then on her breasts.

Too many lonely months had passed since she'd felt so alive, so in tune with her body's need. She craved the intimacy that he could give her, and fought frustration when he took his hands away.

"We've got to stop this," he muttered. "Before I can't stop."

"I've decided to remove *stop* from my vocabulary."

Her attempt at levity fell flat when he said, "I'm serious, Jenna."

"So am I, Logan."

"What about our friendship pact?"

"We'll be really close friends." Yet, she had one serious concern she needed to voice. "When we talked about our fears earlier, there's one I'd failed to mention. Unplanned pregnancy."

"That's only one reason why this isn't a good idea. I didn't bring any condoms."

Major warning bells rang out in her head. "Do you make a habit of not being prepared when you're with a woman?"

"I'm always prepared, just not this time."

Her confidence cracked, sending her back a step. "Then I must have assumed wrong. I thought you wanted me as much as I wanted you."

He brought her back into his arms. "You know damn well I've wanted you since the night we met. I didn't pack condoms because I worried your dad might search my gear. I also didn't want to be tempted to go back on my word."

He'd picked a fine time to be noble. "This definitely presents a problem."

"Yeah, it does." His voice held a world of disappointment, bolstering Jenna's determination.

She saw no reason to end a perfectly good evening on a sour note. "You might not understand this, Logan, but I wake up every morning alone, and I go to bed alone. Sometimes the craving for a human touch is so strong, I ache. Tonight, I'm asking you to give me that much, even if it means we're only going to hold each other."

"It's going to be tough to leave it at that, Jenna."

She brushed a kiss over his cheek. "I know it will

be. But I also know you're strong enough to deal with it."

"I'll try."

"That's all I'm asking of you." At least, for the time being.

Chapter Eight

"**D**id you know that in every square inch of skin, there are over a thousand nerve endings?"

Logan was aware of every one of them at the moment. "No, I didn't know that."

He did know that he was back on the blanket near the fire he'd rekindled, covered only by a thin sheet and a pair of boxers, an incredible, half-naked woman curled against his side—and they'd done nothing more than talk for the past half hour. None of his brothers would believe this. *He* didn't believe it.

Jenna lifted his hand and gave his fingers a flex test. "Did you know that over thirteen hundred nerve endings exist in one fingertip alone?"

And he could think of at least that many reasons why he should put her in the tent while he slept outside tonight. But leaving was the last thing on his mind when he rolled to his side to face her, bringing him up close and personal to her bare breasts. "You must've enjoyed your anatomy classes in college to have retained all that information." And he really didn't need an anatomy lesson. His own anatomy was giving him enough problems as it was.

"I didn't come by the information in college." She flipped her hair back from one shoulder, a feminine form of enticement that Logan recognized immediately. "When I realized it was inevitable that I'd eventually lose my sight, I started studying the optic nerve, which led to the discovery of neurons and receptors, specifically those involving touch. Now, close your eyes and lie back so you can get the full effect of my research."

"I like looking at you." He also worried he might not endure her research without having a lapse in judgment.

"I promise you'll enjoy it."

Exactly what he feared. "Does it mean that much to you?"

"Yes, it does. I want you to experience what I do without the benefit of sight. And don't cheat just because I can't tell whether you have them closed."

"Fine. Be careful or you'll stir up more trouble."

He'd only recently recovered from the effects of their swim and her insistence on remaining topless.

After he shut his eyes and shifted onto his back, Jenna whispered, "I've learned that several areas are very sensitive, such as the face." She kissed him on the forehead, the cheek and the chin. "So are the back of the neck and upper arms." She massaged his nape before raking her nails lightly over the bend of his shoulder and down his biceps. "And the chest." She pressed her lips against his sternum, not once, but twice. "Of course, the area between the legs is very sensitive."

Thankfully, she didn't go there, otherwise he'd be saluting the entire campground. "Interesting."

"There's more."

Logan wasn't certain he could stand much more. "Can you give me hint so I'll be prepared?"

"You'll have to wait and see."

Even with his lids closed, he was all too aware she'd moved partially on top of him and very aware of her breasts rubbing against his chest. As much as he wanted to touch her, he kept his hands balled at his sides and waited for what would come next.

"Receptors known as Krause corpuscles respond to pressure," she said. "They're located in the lips and on the tongue."

She did exactly what he'd expected, and wanted her to do—kissed him. She also demonstrated exactly how much pressure on his tongue it took before he was tempted to turn her over and plunge inside her. Luckily, she pulled away just in time for him to get his grip on the last of his control.

"You'll also find those same receptors a little lower." When she streamed her hand down his abdomen and traced the path of hair below his navel, he opened his eyes and caught her wrist. He brought her hand back to his chest right before she could reach beneath his shorts to discover the rock-hard land of no return. "Don't do it, Jenna. I've been able to handle your little seminar to this point, but if you keep this up, I'm going to lose it."

He couldn't completely make out her expression in the limited light, but he did see a flash of white teeth, indicating she was smiling. "That's the idea."

In one smooth moved, he flipped her over onto her back and raised her arms above her head. "I'm only so strong, Jenna."

"But the only way I can see you is through touch, and I have to see you." She threaded her fingers through his hair and sighed. "It's been so long since I've had any intimacy with a man, Logan. I just want…" She covered her face with her hands. "Maybe I don't know what I want."

But Logan recognized what she needed, and he'd gladly give it to her. "Do you know what I see when I look at you?"

She attempted a half-hearted smile. "A desperate woman?"

He ran his finger down the column of her throat. "A beautiful woman."

"I don't know about that."

He pressed a fingertip against her lips. "Don't speak, Jenna. Just listen."

He guided his palms down her rib cage and back up again, coming closer and closer to her breasts with each stroke. "You have a great body, and right now I want to do things to you that you won't forget."

You're a master at knocking the ground from beneath a woman's feet and getting her flat on her back in your bed using sexy, provocative words....

Ignoring Helena's intrusion into his brain, he outlined Jenna's nipples with a fingertip. "I want to use my hands and my mouth on you."

Her bottom lip trembled. "Where?"

"Everywhere."

...you also have the talent and skills to back them up.

He toyed with the lacy band below her navel. "I want to hear you beg for more, Jenna. And I want to give you more."

...let her know you're interested not only in her body, but in her mind, as well. You'd be surprised what a difference that makes....

Damn Helena for dropping into his mind at an inopportune moment and for making sense.

Logan planted his palms on either side of Jenna

and lowered his head. "And as much as I want to do all those things to you, I can't."

She looked totally dejected. "Why not?"

He straightened and sat beside her, arms draped on his knees. "It has to do with something someone told me."

"Excuse me?"

"Someone I used to know."

"I'm glad you're referring to a real person. For a minute I thought you were hearing voices."

He had heard only one voice—Helena's—and he wished he could shut it up. "She surprised me with a visit."

"She?"

"My former girlfriend."

"You mean your former fiancée, Helena, don't you?"

He centered his gaze on Jenna to find she'd thankfully pulled the sheet over her breasts. "How did you know about her?"

She folded the cotton edge back and forth. "Mallory mentioned her last Sunday. She told me the circumstances behind why you called off the wedding."

Leave it to Mallory to air his business. "And I haven't seen Helena since, until she showed up at my office three days ago."

"I see. You're getting back together with her and I was your last hurrah until your conscience intruded."

He could understand why she might think that, even if it was an erroneous assumption. "She stopped by to tell me she's getting married."

"Oh. That's good." She sounded and looked relieved.

Logan reclaimed his spot beside Jenna, stacked his hands behind his head and stared at the sky. "She also said a few things about me that I didn't particularly like. But she's right."

When Logan turned his head to gauge her reaction, Jenna rolled onto her side and propped her cheek on her palm. "What sort of things?"

As difficult as it was to tell her the truth, she deserved that much. "She told me I have the seduction technique down pat, but I don't know how to be a good friend to a woman."

"And you believe her?"

"I didn't want to, but it's true. I've had my fair share of lovers, but not any female friends to speak of."

"I don't agree." She snuggled up against his side and laid an arm across his chest. "Since the night we met, I've considered you a friend. Someone who was willing to take off my mascara and not my clothes. Someone who took me home only to make sure I was safe. And most important, someone who brought me to this wonderful place where I feel totally liberated for the first time in years."

He grinned. "Someone who still wants to jump your bones."

She returned his smile. "I'm so happy to hear that. I thought perhaps my receptor recitation was a huge turnoff."

"It was sexy as hell." He lifted her hand and kissed it before sitting up again. "But right now we're going to go inside the tent and we're going to sleep together, literally."

"Then, you're saying we're going to keep our relationship strictly platonic?"

"I'm saying we're going to take it slow, for now."

"For as long as we're here?"

"For as long as it takes to know each other better." After wrapping her up in the sheet, Logan stood and pulled her into his arms. "First, you're going to put your clothes on, otherwise I might be tempted to get too friendly."

"Can you handle a little sociable spooning?"

Another test of his will, but something that she needed. For that reason, he'd accommodate her. "You bet. And before we go to bed, I want to let you in on a few things I've learned about you. Good things."

She smiled. "I know a great male butt when I feel it?"

He appreciated her attempt at humor, but what he had to say was serious business, particularly for a man who wasn't always good at expressing himself outside the realm of sex. "You know who you are, you know what you want out of life, and you're determined to get it. You have a killer body, but your strength, Jenna Fordyce, is the most attractive part about you."

She rested her cheek against his shoulder. "I don't always know who I am, Logan, and I'm not always that strong. But I do know I'm thankful that, for the first time in a very long time, I won't have to wake up alone."

The following morning, Jenna awoke to the smell of fresh coffee and a soft kiss on the cheek, delivered by a man who had put honor above all else last night. As much as she'd appreciated his resolve to take it slowly, it still didn't change her decision to have a more intimate relationship with him before the end of the weekend. Before the end of the day, if she had her druthers.

"Did you sleep okay?" Logan asked in a very tempting, very grainy voice.

She stretched her legs and tried to focus on the figure beside her, to no avail. She ached to see him in the light of day, and imagined how he might look. Tousled hair. Unshaven face. Bare chest. Her favorite combination.

Jenna reached for his arm to discover he'd put on a T-shirt, ran her fingers through his thick hair and touched his scratchy chin; her only means of confirmation. "I slept great." And she had, in his arms. "How about you?"

"I was up earlier than I'd planned to be, thanks to Perry. I'm surprised you didn't hear him barking."

"I vaguely remember that, but I was too tired to pay any attention."

"He returned this."

After Logan pressed a ball of damp fabric in her palm, a moment passed before Jenna recognized what she was holding. Lovely. "It's my bra."

"Yeah. He must have found it on the bank where we left it last night."

"Once a retriever, always a retriever."

Logan's ensuing laugh served as morning music to Jenna's ears. "True. After his wake-up call, I couldn't go back to sleep, so I built a fire and made coffee."

An extremely nice memory filtered into her mind. "Speaking of that, I do remember waking up sometime during the night. You had your hand on my breast." And she hadn't bothered to remove it.

"I don't remember that, although it could account for the dream I had."

She'd had a few nice dreams of her own. "Was I in it?"

"What do you think?"

"I hope so." Yet she wanted to be more to him

than just the subject of his dreams. She wanted the reality.

"Take it from me, you were definitely there," he said.

"What were we doing?"

He patted her knee. "A guy's gotta have some secrets."

"Maybe we could have a reenactment tonight."

"Maybe you better get dressed so we can go fishing."

At least he hadn't said no, a positive sign as far as Jenna was concerned. After kicking the sheet away, she groped for her bag she'd left nearby and set it in her lap. "I need to wash up. Looks like it's back to the creek again."

"Not necessary," Logan said. "I hung a tarp between some trees a few feet away to give you some privacy. You'll find a pan of fresh water and a washcloth."

What a wonderful way to start the day—a spit bath. "Guess it will have to do, although I wish you would've packed an inflatable pool."

"The princess will have to manage."

She leaned over and pinched his thigh before rummaging through her bag. "You're asking for it, O'Brien."

"I'm kidding, Jenna. You don't have a spoiled bone in your body."

When she withdrew the travel-sized bottle of

shower gel, he snatched it from her grasp. "Aroma therapy?"

She held out her hand. "I'm willing to make some concessions, but not when it comes to personal hygiene. Now, give it back."

He placed the bottle in the well of her palm and curled her fingers around it. "Have a good time with your avocado and papaya scrub."

"Don't knock it unless you've tried it, Mr. O'Brien. It smells very good."

"Does it taste as good?"

"How should I know? I bathe with it, I don't drink it." She pulled a loofah from the duffel's side pocket. "And I wouldn't advise you taking a swig, either."

"I could always see how it tastes on your skin."

Jenna sensed his honor armor had begun to crack, and it wasn't even noon yet. "Is the 'friends only' thing getting old, already, Logan?"

He cleared his throat. "Not at all. I just momentarily forgot myself."

And. if Jenna had her way, he'd keep forgetting himself all day long.

Jenna stood on the creek bank wearing a pair of low-riding, high-on-the-thigh denim shorts, giving Logan a case of the can't-touch-that blues. Obviously she'd only packed one bra because she wasn't wearing one now, and that was almost too much for a man who'd been struggling to maintain his composure for the past sixteen hours. Not that he was counting the hours. Okay, he was.

If he made it through the day without putting his hands on her unless absolutely necessary, that would be just short of a miracle. But in order to show her how to cast, he'd have to touch her, just as he had with the camera the day before. So far she'd seemed content to chuck rocks in the water, something that would have to stop if they expected to catch anything. Teaching her how to fish in one morning could be challenging, but then they didn't have anything better to do.

In reality, they did, but he still wasn't ready to go there yet. Not until he'd proven he could control himself.

After baiting the line, Logan straightened from the tackle box and approached Jenna from behind. He hesitated a moment just to get a good view of her back and below. Damn, she had great legs and a great butt and if he didn't stop, he'd drop the damn fishing pole and his promise to go slow and steady. Slow and steady sounded about as appetizing as liverwurst for breakfast.

He came up close behind her, but not too close. "Are you ready to do some fishing?"

She glanced back at him. "I've been ready for at least fifteen minutes."

"I wanted to pick out the right lure," he said.

"It took a while. Now I'm going to show you how it's done."

"Oh, really?"

"Yeah, really." He placed the pole in her grasp and put his arms around her. Damn, she smelled good. "First of all, make sure you have a firm grip on the rod at all times, and keep it in the correct position."

She sent him a smile over one shoulder. "You know what they say. A well-positioned rod is hard to find."

He ignored the suggestive comment, even though his body had begun to take the bait. "I've already set the drag, so you won't have to worry about that. When you cast, the trick is to keep your motions smooth. You don't want to create a backlash."

"Let me see if I have this straight. You take the pole in hand, don't jerk it too hard and use a nice, fluid motion." She circled her fingers around the rod and stroked it. "I think I can manage that."

He started sweating like a marathon runner heading for the finishing line. "That's right."

"I do believe I have it."

So did he, and it was making him uncomfortable way down south. "Are you ready to try it?"

Again, she grinned. "Are we still talking about fishing?"

"You're killing me, Jenna."

"I don't mean to do that, at all, Logan." She reached back and patted his cheek. "But just so you know, if I hook a fish, I'm a firm believer in catch and release."

Logan had the catch down; now, if only he could release her. But the area at the back of her neck, exposed because she'd pulled her hair up into a ponytail, was just too damn appealing. Without thought, he lowered his head and kissed the spot, then worked his way around until he had her face in his grasp and his mouth on hers.

She discarded the rod and reel, turned easily into his arms and fitted herself so closely against him that he started calculating the distance to the nearest copse of trees. All the latent sexual energy he'd stored since last night came out in the kiss. All the arguments for avoiding this very thing jogged out of his head the minute she had her hands on his butt and he had his hands up her shirt to confirm she wasn't wearing a bra.

When he touched her breasts, she moaned against his mouth and pressed against his pelvis. His body's reaction was almost volatile and he went for the button on her fly, needing to know if she was as hot as he was. He had her zipper down in a flash and his hand was parting the placket, until a return of good sense—with a little help of voices from somewhere in the vicinity—forced him to reconsider.

He wasn't sure who was more winded, him or Jenna, when he stepped back and quickly readjusted her clothes.

Her disappointment was undeniable when she muttered, "And you thought Tahiti was crowded this time of year."

He had two choices—continue the fishing excursion, or take her back to the tent, away from prying eyes. He should go with fishing for two solid reasons, the first being that unless the condom fairy had left him a few underneath his pillow, he had no way to see this through completely. The second involved the friendship clause that he was in danger of severing if he didn't get his brain out of his jeans.

Jenna tightened her ponytail and picked up the rod, making the decision for him. "Maybe if we're lucky, the fish will still be biting."

Logan grabbed up his own rig and picked a place a few feet away from her. Without further instruction, she began casting like a pro.

"You're a quick study," he told her, in awe that even without her sight, she appeared to master anything she tackled.

"I've fished before, Logan," she said. "Several years ago, my dad and I took a couple of sport fishing trips to Mexico. I actually caught a Marlin once."

Anger set in. Anger that he couldn't quite explain. "You should've told me that before I went into instruction mode."

She continued to cast without missing a beat. "What, and miss all the fun of the post-instruction making out?"

"I'm serious, Jenna. You need to remember one important thing about me. I require total honesty."

She reeled in the line with a vengeance. "That's rich, Logan. You're asking me to be honest with you when you can't be honest with yourself."

"I don't know what you're talking about."

"Yes, you do, even if you can't own up to it."

She was still speaking in riddles. "Care to explain?"

After propping the rod against the rock that also housed her cane, she faced him. "You're hiding behind this whole friendship thing because the truth is, you're afraid of getting too close to a woman. And whether you admit it or not, Helena hurt you badly."

He didn't want to hear this. "She lied to me, Jenna. Sorry if that pisses me off."

She exhaled a slow breath. "I'm not her, Logan. I'm not going to fault you for your imperfections, because God knows I have plenty of my own. And I didn't come here to force you to do anything you don't want to do."

Without hesitation, and without any help from her cane, she walked toward him, stumbling slightly before she strode right up to him. "You might not understand this, but for years I've operated on the assumption that everyone knew what was best for me. Both David and my father treated me like a china doll incapable of functioning in the real world without complete dependency. I fought against it in the beginning, but I gave up to keep the peace."

She circled her arms around his waist. "But you're not like them. You've given me the chance to simply be me. To finally feel like a normal person and a desirable woman."

"You are a desirable woman, Jenna." And she didn't have a clue how much he wanted to fully uncover that side of her.

"That's why I'm going to keep reminding you that this chemistry between us is too powerful to ignore," she said. "My question is, when are you going to stop ignoring it?"

He rested his forehead against hers. "I don't want to hurt you in any way, Jenna."

"You don't want to be hurt again, and I don't want that, either. As long as we know going in that we're here to enjoy each other during the time we have left together, then neither of us will suffer for the decision." She smiled. "I don't want to leave here regretting that I didn't take full advantage of all the opportunities."

Logan found it uncanny how clearly she saw things. How clearly she saw through him, exposing facets of himself that he hadn't wanted to concede.

She'd been right on several counts, including the fact that the raw chemistry between them was too potent to disregard. And this time, he was going to prove that he could be both a lover and a friend. The friendship was already in place.

He kissed her quickly and said, "Pack up your things and let's get out of here."

Disappointment turned her smile into a frown. "You've decided to cut the weekend short."

His decision entailed giving her the best experience of her life. Maybe even his own life. "We're not going home, Jenna. We're going down the hill and we're going to find a cabin with a shower."

Her expression brightened. "Now, Logan, where's your sense of adventure?"

"You'll find that out when we're in bed."

Chapter Nine

After a four-hour trek back to the main camp-ground, Jenna found herself sitting on the edge of a bed in a dark, musty and minimally cool cabin, alone. Logan had left with the directive for her to stay put until he returned in a few minutes. Although she wasn't certain of the time, or where he'd gone, she did know that more than a few minutes had passed. And she didn't want to wait to make good use of the shower.

She located the bag at her feet and withdrew essential toiletries, opting to forgo clothes. If Logan hadn't changed his mind, she wouldn't need them. She prayed he hadn't changed his mind. But if he didn't return soon, she might start believing that he'd left the state without her.

Jenna used her cane to guide her to the bathroom, not a difficult feat because the cabin—according to Logan—consisted of one area that housed the bedroom, a galley kitchen and a small living room.

Finding the walk-in shower wasn't difficult, either, considering it took up half of the tiny bathroom. She set her cane aside and felt along the wall to discover a towel draped on a rack mounted to the wall. Satisfied she had everything she needed, Jenna yanked back the narrow plastic curtain and felt for the metal handles. When she turned on the water, the scent of rust permeated the area and she hoped that her bath didn't result in orange-colored skin. But after she stripped and stepped under the spray, shampoo and shower gel in hand, the metallic smell disappeared and she only experienced the cool tile beneath her feet and blessedly warm, soothing water. Yet she only allowed herself a few minutes to relax before she soaped and shampooed away the grunge; she wanted to be waiting for Logan in bed when he finally came back to her.

After she rinsed and squeezed out her hair, she stepped onto the bath mat, reached for the towel and contacted only a barren metal bar.

"Are you looking for this?"

Jenna felt the slide of terry against her arm before she snatched the towel from Logan's grasp and began drying off—very slowly. "I didn't realize you were back."

"And I didn't realize you didn't understand my instructions." His voice sounded remarkably strained.

"I understood them." She wrapped up in the towel and tucked it between her breasts. "I just didn't see any reason to sit around and do nothing while you were gone. Which reminds me, where did you go?"

"I put the gear back in the Hummer, then I made a trip to the camp store."

"Did you get some things for dinner?"

"Yeah, and a few things for after dinner."

She suspected she knew the identity of those after-dinner "things." "I'm surprised they stock condoms at the camp store."

"They do, but they were out, which leads me to believe the Falstaffs are a wild bunch. I had to drive ten miles to the nearest convenience store."

At least that explained his lengthy absence. "Are you sure you didn't run into Liza Falstaff and have a quickie?"

"Not a chance. And since you didn't wait until we could shower together, it's my turn. I'm feeling pretty dirty right now."

Jenna admittedly felt a little dirty, too, and she was squeaky clean, at least physically. "If you want me to leave while you shower, I will. But if it's okay, I'd rather stay. I promise I won't peek." Oh, that she wished she could.

"You can stay and join me."

Not at all a terrible idea, but she wanted to build the anticipation for a bit longer. "Tell you what. Since the shower is barely big enough for one, much less two people, I'll stay and keep you company."

He tilted her chin up and kissed her gently. "There's plenty of room if you improvise. However, I wouldn't get much bathing done with you in there with me."

Jenna was highly encouraged by his comment. In a matter of minutes, she might finally experience what she'd wanted from him all along. "We'll save the improvising for later. In the meantime, I'll stand by while you wash away. Just leave the curtain open a little so we can talk."

"Not a problem, but I might get the floor wet."

"It's tile and I'm sure it's been wet before."

"Just stay right where you are so you don't slip and fall." He slid his fingertip down the cleft of her breasts. "You know, I can think of certain circumstances when wet is good."

Jenna backed up and reclined against the wall, needing its full support. "So can I. Now, hurry up."

"Yes, ma'am."

Since Logan appeared as an indistinguishable figure standing before her, she would have to rely on her imagination to form a cerebral portrait. She could also rely on him. "What are you doing right now?"

"Taking off my shirt."

She developed a mental picture compiled from her previous explorations of his chest, but she highly doubted it did justice to the real thing. When she heard the rasp of a zipper and the rustle of denim, she realized she didn't have a good frame of reference for how he might look at the moment. But she would soon, if she had any say in the matter.

After she heard the curtain sliding back, followed by the sound of water, she asked, "Are you washing?"

"Yeah, my hair."

"With my shampoo or yours?"

"Mine. Lavender smells a lot better on you than it does on me. And I have my own soap, too. A bar of soap, not gel."

She allowed him a few moments to finish that task before asking, "What are you doing now?"

"Bathing."

"I know that. What part of you are you bathing?" And that had to be the nosiest question she'd ever asked anyone.

"I'm scrubbing my face."

"Where will you go from there?"

"What do you mean?"

"Most people have a routine. For instance, face first, chest, legs and so on."

"I leave the 'so on' for last. Do you want to help me with that phase?"

She was assaulted by both heat and goose bumps simultaneously. "I trust you can handle that yourself."

"Much more fun if you'll handle it."

She resisted the urge to take him up on his offer. "I'll put that on my to do list."

"I'll remind you, just in case."

Closing her eyes, Jenna tipped her head back against the wall and let her fantasies take flight. She could picture him moving the soap over his body, across his broad chest, over his flat belly, down his solid thighs, then on to his perfect bottom. And after that... She wished she could be that bar of soap.

Jenna shifted her weight against the onslaught of damp heat and the rush of excitement. She had never wanted someone so much, specifically her former husband. During the early years together, their lovemaking had been satisfying for the most part, but never so hot that she'd felt as if she would crawl out of her skin if she didn't have him immediately. Right now, her skin was threatening to take a hiatus just thinking about Logan.

The desire he'd unearthed in her was almost frightening in its intensity. Perhaps that intensity resulted from the absence of intimacy in her life or the expectation of a memorable experience. Or maybe it was simply the man himself. A man who had taken time out of his busy schedule to escape with her for a few days, and she could only assume that the best of him was yet to come.

When the water stopped, Jenna's heart accelerated and her respiration sounded strangely labored. And when Logan touched her face, a low, needy sound filtered out of her parted lips.

"Are you okay, Jenna?"

She inhaled deeply. "I don't know. I feel—"

"Aroused?"

"Yes."

He nuzzled his face in the bend of her neck. "Tell me what you need."

His velvet-smooth voice was as effective as a powerful potion, one that left her pleasurably weak. "I need you take me to bed." Before her limbs no longer held her up.

The words had barely left Jenna's mouth before Logan gathered her into his arms and carried her away in every sense of the word. He moved so quickly, she had little time to prepare before he'd deposited her onto the creaky bed. The mattress bent beside her and following a tug, the towel fell open, allowing a cool draft of air to flow over her bare skin. When Logan rolled her onto her side and into his arms, she absorbed the sensory details all at once—the clean smell of him, the welcome feel of him, the taste of him as his mouth covered hers.

His kiss was surprisingly restrained and brief before he pulled back and grazed his lips along her jaw, her neck and finally her ear. "I only have one question to ask you before we go any further."

His tone was so somber, Jenna almost feared that question. "All right."

"What's your favorite color?"

She laughed from relief and utter joy. "Every color in the rainbow."

"I'll remember that," he said as he nudged her onto her back.

The conversation ceased with Logan's next kiss, a thorough yet incredibly gentle kiss. His fingertips skimmed her flesh, light and soothing as he raked them down her throat and over her collarbone. She almost issued a protest when he broke the kiss, but reconsidered when she experienced the warmth of his mouth closing over her breast. The soft workings of his tongue around her nipple urged a soft moan from her lips and his palm gliding down her belly prompted a slight shiver that ran the length of her body.

He turned his attention to her legs, brushing his knuckles back and forth on the tops of her thighs, coming closer and closer to the apex with each pass. She was on sensory overload, not quite knowing where to focus her concentration at the moment— on Logan's skilled mouth or his equally skilled hand.

Definitely his hand, she decided when he divided her thighs with his leg and centered his touch on the source of the ache that had plagued her for days.

"You're hot," he whispered.

She answered with a breathy, "Thanks to you."

"Tell me what else you want, Jenna."

"I want to touch you, too."

He lifted her hand and guided it to his erection. "Touch away."

And she did—with curiosity, with fine strokes as he did with her. She focused on Logan's reaction to her exploration and knew she was pleasing him simply by listening for the catch of his breath when she got a little bolder, yet worried she'd done something wrong when he tugged her hand away. "No more or I'm going to lose it," he said.

Jenna could very well say the same thing to him, if she had the presence of mind to speak, which she didn't since Logan hadn't halted his steady caress. The pressure began to build and build until she could do nothing more than surrender to the sensations. Yet Logan picked that exact moment to stop, eliciting a mild protest from Jenna.

"Not yet," he said.

She heard the sound of tearing paper, keenly aware that soon the wait would be over.

When he came back to her, Logan covered her body with his and said, "Now," as he lifted her hips and pushed inside her.

The climax hit her immediately with overwhelming authority, a release that completely consumed her and went on much longer than she'd expected. Only after the effects began to fade did she focus on the powerful thrust of Logan's body as she slid her hands down his back to his buttocks, delighting in the play of muscle against her palm. How much she'd missed this. How very, very much. More important, she was sorely reminded of her lack of vision and what that meant to their lovemaking.

"I wish I could see you," she said, and with all her heart, she did.

He stilled, raised her hands and kissed both palms before bringing them to his face, providing the means for her to observe his current state as best she could. "You feel so damn good," he said.

Even those few words seemed to cause him a great deal of effort, yet they moved Jenna more than she could express. And so did the heartfelt kiss he gave her immediately before he again gave in to his body's demands. As he drove deeper, harder, she continued to touch his face, wanting so badly to see the concentration in his expression, to witness the instant he was stripped of control. Instead, she relied on the rapid beat of his heart against her breasts and the tension in his frame that let her know the moment was close at hand. He climaxed with a hard thrust, shuddered and collapsed against her.

As Jenna rubbed his back and listened as his breathing slowed to a normal rhythm, she felt as if she had entered a place of peace that she never wanted to leave. A place where she could stay for a long, long time.

"What are you thinking?" she asked when Logan failed to move or speak.

"That was too rushed."

"That was pretty incredible."

"It could be better."

Any better and she might not have lived to tell the tale. "I don't agree, and it was definitely worth the wait." When he shifted slightly, she tightened her hold. "Don't go yet."

"I'm not going anywhere, and the wait is why it was too rushed."

She frowned. "We've known each other, for what, a whole seven days?" Oddly, she felt as if she'd known him much longer. "But then I suppose most women don't make you wait that long."

"Believe me, Jenna. You're nothing like most women."

The wooden headboard felt like a cement block against his back, but Logan didn't dare move or he risked ruining the moment.

After a light dinner consisting of cold sandwiches, he and Jenna had settled back into bed to talk. But somewhere along the way, while he'd been explaining to her about adding charter planes to his business plan, she'd fallen asleep, her head tucked in the crook of his arm, her hand resting loosely on his chest, her features slack. And that's where she'd been for over an hour, looking innocent and peaceful. For the past few minutes, he'd watched her eyes twitch behind closed lids and wondered what she was dreaming. If in those dreams she could see again.

He'd begun to realize she was a contradiction— fiercely independent and at times almost vulnerable, although, she tried to hide it behind her strong will. He could relate. No one wanted their weaknesses bared, especially not him. But he'd be damned if she hadn't chipped away some of his steel shell and made him care about something aside from business and temporary escapes in the beds of women he barely knew. She'd made him *feel* for the first time in a year—and that scared the hell out of him.

When Jenna turned away, Logan eased his arm from beneath her and carefully climbed out of bed. He slipped on a pair of shorts and walked to the refrigerator to find something to wet his dry mouth, craving a beer and settling for a bottle of soda—and some distance.

After sitting in the lone chair next to the aged plaid sofa, he set the drink aside, leaned his head back and closed his eyes. But he wasn't the least bit tired even though it was nearing midnight. In fact, he was too keyed up to sleep. And it was too bad the cabin didn't come equipped with a TV so he could find some ball game to occupy his mind. He could go for a walk, but he didn't want to leave Jenna alone. Or he could crawl back into bed, wake her up and expend some energy.

That thought alone brought his body back to life, but the sudden distressed cry brought his eyes wide-open to find Jenna sitting up in the bed, a frantic look on her face. He bolted from the chair and practically sprinted to the bed to hold her.

He rocked her back and forth until she seemed to calm. "It's okay, babe."

She pulled away, her expression a mask of confusion. "Logan?"

"Yeah, I'm here. You must've had a bad dream."

She streaked both her hands over her face, as if trying to erase the images. "It was a nightmare."

A really bad one, if the fear in her brown eyes was any indication. "Want to tell me about it?"

"It didn't make a lot of sense."

"Most dreams don't."

"I know, but this one was so strange and frightening." She inhaled a short breath and blew it out slowly. "I was in a small boat on the creek by myself and I saw J.D. on the bank. He looked exactly as he did the last time I could see him. I kept calling to him and when he saw me, he ran away into the woods. The next thing I knew I was chasing him and I couldn't find him. I had this horrible sense that something had happened to him and I couldn't protect him."

Logan realized that her subconscious was playing havoc with her fears. "Have you had this dream before?"

She shook her head. "Not exactly, but I've had a few that were similar. I'm hoping it's not some premonition, although I've never believed in that sort of thing before."

He kissed her forehead and held her tighter. "I'm sure he's fine. He's probably in bed asleep, which is where you and I need to be if we're going to get on the road early in the morning." With that thought, he reclined on the bed, taking her with him.

"I don't know if I can sleep until I'm certain John David's okay," she said. "And that won't happen until tomorrow night, if David even bothers to call me."

"Why wouldn't he?"

"Just to prove a point, which is typical of the Leedstone family."

Logan had to think a minute before he realized where he'd heard the name before. "As in Leedstone Electronics?"

"That's the one. He's in Memphis overseeing the opening of another phase of the dynasty."

Another instance of money marrying money. "Did you take your maiden name back after the divorce?"

"I never changed my name when we married. John David's last name is hyphenated."

Logan rubbed his chin. "John David Fordyce-Leedstone. Has a nice ring to it, but it'll never fit on a baseball jersey."

Finally, she smiled. A tentative one, but still a smile. "Anyway, David says I obsess too much over J.D. and that I tend to overreact. He's a fine one to talk considering how he treated me when we were married."

Alarm bells rang out in Logan's head. "Did he hurt you?"

"Only in the sense that I couldn't lift a finger without him questioning why I didn't ask for help, and that was when I could still see okay. He hired a nanny because he didn't trust I could take care of our child. But I did take care of him and I did it well."

The bastard. "I'm sure you did. My mother always said that maternal instinct is the strongest instinct in the world."

"Your mother is a very wise woman." She felt for his face and touched his lips with a fingertip, then with her own lips. "And she has a very special son."

He grinned. "Devin is a good guy."

She punched him in the arm, hard. "Stop pretending you're not worthy of a compliment, because you are."

Another one of his mother's lesson's intruded into his brain—accept praise graciously. "Thanks. You're kind of special, too." Kind of special? That was one hell of an understatement.

She linked her hand with his. "In some ways, I wish we didn't have to go tomorrow. But in others—and don't take this wrong—I'm looking forward to being home in time to talk with J.D."

Leaving the campground and leaving her, were the last things Logan wanted to consider at the moment. If it wasn't for the all-important communication with her son and Avery's insistence he bring her home tomorrow, he wouldn't mind extending the trip a few days. Then they could make the call to her son from his cell phone. He could ignore Avery's threats. Or they could…

Nah. That was a crazy plan. Insane. Impractical. But doable.

"Did you fall asleep on me, Logan?"

He rubbed her arm. "I'm still awake. I'm just thinking."

"About what?"

"About a phone call I need to make. The cell phone's on the charger in the car." He pushed out of the bed and tugged on his jeans. "I'll be back in a few minutes, so don't go anywhere."

She rolled to her side and played peekaboo with the sheet. "Maybe this will convince you to make it quick."

He leaned over and kissed her. "I'm convinced, and hold that thought."

She went one better and kicked the sheet entirely away. "A little added incentive."

The sight of her lying naked in a provocative pose made him hard as a steel beam. "You are one wicked woman."

"A lack of sight means a lack of inhibition, so get used to it, O'Brien."

Oh, yeah, he could definitely get used to it. He could also climb all over her, but first things first. "I'm leaving now," he said as he backed to the door. "Don't move."

"I promise I won't, if you'll hurry back."

He sprinted down the porch steps and hiked to the Hummer parked several yards away. He slid into the cab, detached the phone from the charger and hit the speed dial.

When Bob answered with a gruff, "Hello," Logan didn't bother to return the greeting. "I need you to do something for me, Bob."

"Where are you, boss?"

"Still in Arkansas. Go to your computer and look up David Leedstone's address and phone number in or around Memphis, Tennessee."

"That could take a while, boss, especially if the number's unlisted."

"Do what you have to do, but have it for me first thing in the morning."

"What's this all about?"

None of Bob's business. "Just get the address. And clear my schedule Monday. I probably won't be in until Tuesday morning."

"I see a big problem with that, Mr. O'Brien. You have a two o'clock meeting monday that we can't move again without losing a prospective client. You also have a meeting with Mr. Fordyce."

"I don't recall scheduling a meeting with him."

"You didn't. He did."

Great. "I'll be in on Monday afternoon, and I'll give Fordyce call."

And he would tomorrow, as soon as they were well on their way to Tennessee.

Chapter Ten

"How much longer before we're there, Logan?"

"My best guess is about five minutes."

Although the sun wasn't as bright as it had been when they'd left the park, Jenna sensed it wasn't all that late in the day. "What time is it now?"

"Almost six."

"I know we haven't been on the road for ten hours because we didn't leave until midmorning."

"Hey, our delayed departure wasn't my fault. You were the one who wanted to sleep in."

She felt an annoying blush coming on. "You didn't let me sleep."

"And I don't recall you complaining. Moaning, but not complaining."

She couldn't deny that, nor could she deny her continued confusion. "If my calculations are correct, we still have at least three hours to go before we reach Houston, not five minutes."

"I didn't say we were almost in Houston. I said we were almost there."

"Where exactly is *there?*"

"Hang on a minute. I need to concentrate." Logan braked and muttered, "Damn. I missed it," before he threw the Hummer in Reverse.

"Missed what?"

"The place we're going."

Jenna was growing increasingly frustrated with Logan's secrecy. "What place?"

"It's a surprise. You'll find out in a minute."

Occasionally, she liked surprises, but she had one vital issue on her mind. "If you're intent on stopping, I'll need to call J.D. from wherever we are."

"You're going to talk to your son tonight, Jenna. I promise."

All day long, she'd thought of little else aside from speaking with John David, when she wasn't thinking about Logan and what they'd shared over the past few days. Right now she wanted to give him a good tongue-lashing for being so mysterious.

When Logan took a sharp left, Jenna wondered if he'd found a notable restaurant. Maybe a hotel.

No, he'd said he'd planned to drive straight through. But straight through to where?

"We're here," Logan said, followed by the metallic clank of a releasing seat belt.

Jenna decided not to move until he provided some answers. "Could you please give me a little hint?"

"Okay. We're about to go inside a house and see some people about something."

She rolled her eyes. "That's not very specific, Logan. You should win an award for evasion."

He had the nerve to laugh. "Tell you what, if you're not happy with what I have planned, then you can tie me up later."

Somehow she didn't see that as adequate punishment. "You'd probably enjoy it."

"Could be. We'll discuss that later."

After Logan helped Jenna from the car, she heard the sound of dogs barking and children playing in the distance. She detected the scent of wisteria as they navigated what appeared to be a walkway.

"There's two steps up to the porch," Logan said.

After Jenna managed those without incident, she heard the chime of a doorbell—and an all too familiar voice saying, "It's good to see you, Jen," with little enthusiasm.

For a split second she'd thought her ears had betrayed her until Logan replied, "Thanks for having us on short notice, David."

"It's a little inconvenient, but come on in."

As they stepped over the threshold, Jenna's shock finally subsided and she regained her ability to speak. "What's going on?"

Logan caught her free hand and gave it a squeeze. "I promised you'd talk to your son, didn't I?"

Only then did Jenna allow herself to believe that Logan had granted her an incredible gift. She was going to be with John David, hold him, kiss him. She'd kiss Logan right now if her ex wasn't nearby.

"Where is he?" Jenna asked as she lowered her glasses from her head to cover her eyes against the harsh light in the foyer.

"He's in his room," a feminine voice answered. "Hi, Jenna. I'm Ginger."

Jenna found herself in the presence of the woman who'd entered J.D.'s life less than a year ago. A woman she'd never met nor seen before. The same woman who hadn't accompanied her new husband when he'd come to Texas to retrieve his son. "It's nice to finally meet you, Ginger."

"It's my pleasure," Ginger said as she took Jenna's hand for a brief shake. "But I'm afraid John David's rather tired from the trip right now. He's not in a very good mood."

Jenna knew how to remedy that. "Just point the way and I'll cheer him up."

"I'll see if he'll join us in the parlor," Ginger said.

"That's probably better, Jen," David chimed in. "He'll be more comfortable if we're with him."

If they were with him? For all intents and purposes, *they* were treating her like a stranger. "Fine, but I'd like a few minutes alone with him while I'm here."

"We'll see how it goes, Jen."

She wanted to tell David to quit shortening her name. At one time it hadn't bothered her, but now it grated on her already frayed nerves. "I'm sure he'll be fine once he sees me, David."

"I'll go get him," Ginger said. "In the meantime, make yourselves comfortable."

"A place to sit sounds good," Logan said. "It's been a long day."

"Right this way." David's tone reeked with forced politeness, and Jenna suspected he'd already begun to wonder about her relationship with Logan. As if that were any of his business.

Logan guided her to a sofa where she sat as stiff as a post and kept her opinions to herself. She couldn't let her anger get the best of her, not when she had the chance to be with her son.

Jenna's excitement increased when heard the endearing voice of the wonderful little boy she'd given birth to. The child she had loved, and still loved, without limits. And that precious son who'd always eagerly answered her phone calls suddenly cried out, "I don't know that lady!"

When she heard the rapid footsteps heading away, Jenna's heart began to break one fissure at a time. Her greatest fear had been realized—John David had forgotten her.

She couldn't bear knowing that her own child had rejected her when she'd come all this way to see him. She couldn't bear his distress, knowing she was causing it. Right then, she only wanted to get away.

As calmly as possible, she pushed off the sofa with the help of her cane. "This probably wasn't a good idea. Let's go, Logan."

Logan clasped her hand and tugged her back down on the couch. "Just give him a few minutes and let Ginger settle him down. Then you can go tell him a bedtime story."

"Jen's right, Logan," David said. "It isn't a good idea, and that's what I told you on the phone earlier."

"I don't give a damn what you told me." Logan's voice was even, but to Jenna it still sounded menacing. "She deserves some time with J.D., and once he understands it's really her, he'll be fine."

"I'm sorry, Jenna," Ginger said. "He refuses to come out of his room. Right now he's very upset. Maybe you should come back some other time."

Some other time. Ginger acted as though that were something Jenna could manage on any given day. "Thank you for making the effort, and tell John David I love him."

Again she stood and before Logan could stop her, she headed in what she hoped was the direction of the door, tapping her cane along the walls. The cloying scent of potpourri and polished wood caused her stomach to roil, along with the horrible notion that she'd lost the only thing that meant more to her than anything in the world, even her sight.

When she reached out and contacted the latch, a hand came out and stopped her before she could open the door. "Don't leave, Jenna. And don't listen to them."

Tears began to stream down her face despite her effort to hold them at bay. "He doesn't want to see me, Logan. He doesn't even know me."

Logan took her by the shoulders and turned her around. "He didn't get a good look at you. He'll only recognize you if you talk to him."

She swiped the back of her hand over her cheeks. "What if he doesn't?"

Logan brought her into his arms. "He'll remember you, Jenna. You only have to give him the chance to remember."

Jenna didn't know what to do. If she left now, she might regret it, or the same could apply if she stayed. But she had no idea when she would have this opportunity again.

"I'm sorry, Logan. You've gone to all this trouble for me, and the least I can do is make it worth your while."

"You need to make it worth your while, and it hasn't been any trouble at all. It might be if I lose my cool and punch your ex."

She clasped his hand and smiled. "You'd have to stand in line behind me. And if David does call the police, do you know a good bail bondsman in Tennessee?"

"He's not going to do that, and if he does, I'll take care of it."

For once Jenna didn't mind relying on someone for support. But Logan O'Brien wasn't just anyone, a fact that had become all too apparent in the past few days. "I guess, I could try."

"That's all you can do. And I'll be right there if you need me."

After they returned to the living room, David released a long-suffering sigh. "I thought the two of you had already left."

He was hoping they'd left, Jenna decided. "There's been a change in plans, David. Where's J.D.'s bedroom?"

"I thought we'd determined this was a bad idea."

Jenna was losing her tenuous hold on her patience. "I want to visit with my son tonight. If he sees me, he'll know it's me."

"I don't have to agree to this, Jen."

"You need to consider what's best for J.D.," Logan said. "And that's a visit with his mother."

"I am considering him, O'Brien, and right now he doesn't want to see either of you."

Jenna sensed movement in front of her right before Ginger said, "I understand how distressing this must be, Jenna, but I really don't think you want to upset John David further."

Jenna was on the verge of surrendering again until Logan asked, "How far along are you, Ginger?"

"Almost four months."

Setting aside her momentary astonishment and unreasonable bite of envy, Jenna decided to run with information Logan had provided. "How would you like it if someone kept you from your baby, Ginger?"

"I wouldn't."

"Then, let me have the chance to speak with my son. If he becomes too upset, I promise I'll leave."

"She's right, David," Ginger said. "She should have the opportunity to at least try."

"I don't like this one damn bit," David muttered.

Logan's grip tightened on Jenna's hand. "This isn't about you, Leedstone. Now, tell us where his bedroom is or I'll find it myself."

Jenna loved Logan for his concern. She loved that he'd given her this opportunity, no matter what the outcome might be. She loved…him? Now was not the time to examine that random thought.

"At the top of the stairs, second door to the left,"

David conceded. "But if he refuses, I want both of you back down here immediately."

Keeping her fury in check, Jenna gathered all the benevolence she could muster and said, "Thank you so much for *allowing* me to see my own child."

Logan took her by the hand and escorted her back through the corridor before he paused. "We're at the staircase. The steps are about two feet deep with about ten leading up the first landing and probably as many after that. Think you can make it on your own?"

Yes, she could, but she didn't care to. "Will you come with me?"

"If that's what you want."

"That's what I want." It's what she needed.

They ascended the stairs and traveled down a hallway before he paused and said, "We're at his bedroom. But let me go in first and talk to him."

"He doesn't know you, Logan." Jenna wasn't sure he would know her even after he got a good look at her.

"True, but I have a plan. Trust me on this, Jenna."

Somehow, she did. "Okay."

"I'll leave the door open so you can hear what I'm saying, but stay out of sight, for now."

When Logan left her, Jenna leaned a shoulder against the wall and listened.

"Hey, J.D."

"Who are you?"

He sounded wary and Jenna wanted to go to him now, hold him tightly, yet she held her impatience in check while Logan implemented his plan.

"My name is Logan, and I'm a friend of your mom's."

"Mommy Ginger?"

Jenna covered her mouth with her hand and squeezed her eyes shut against the tears.

"No. Your mom, Jenna."

"Oh. My *mama*," he said, bolstering Jenna's confidence that he hadn't completely forgotten her.

"That's right. What's your bear's name?"

"Pookie Bear," Jenna mouthed at the same time as John David. The fluffy blue bear dressed in the sailor suit that she'd given him on his first birthday. The one he'd taken to bed every night since that time. At least that much hadn't changed.

"I used to have a brown bear that looked just like him," Logan said. "His name was Buzz."

Jenna couldn't imagine Logan with a stuffed animal. Tough guy Logan, the expert camper. The expert lover—and friend.

A span of silence passed before Logan asked, "Is this your mom in the picture?"

"Uh-huh. She's in Texas."

"She's right outside the door, buddy, and she wants to see you."

"She can't see me. Her eyes don't work."

She'd never kept that fact from him, but hearing

him say it, with such grown-up authority, stung something awful.

"But you can see your mom, bud, and she really wants to visit with you. Do you want me to go get her?"

"'Kay."

She heard approaching footsteps and felt Logan's touch on her arm. "He's sitting in the bed, which is against the far wall straight ahead when you enter the room. There's a chair on the left. The lamp's on the nightstand between the two, and I turned off the overhead light so you can take off your glasses."

Amazingly he'd thought of everything. "I appreciate that."

"I'm going to give you some time alone with him."

Jenna stood on tiptoe and kissed him lightly on the lips. "I owe you so much, Logan."

"You don't owe me anything. After all, that's what friends are for."

She smiled at the pride in his voice, although she realized she was dangerously close to wanting more than only his friendship. "Will you be right here?"

"I'll be back, but first I'm going to see if Ginger will make some coffee. We have a long night of driving ahead of us."

Jenna had assumed that maybe they'd find a place to spend the night and she could visit with J.D. tomorrow. But that was too much to ask. Logan had already taken a good deal of time away from his business to cater to her whims. "I'll see you in a bit, then."

"I'll be waiting. And take your time."

When she heard Logan sprint down the stairs, Jenna pulled off her sunglasses and pocketed them, smoothed a hand over her hair and drew in a fortifying breath. With cane in hand and a return of her courage, she walked into the room.

"How's my big boy?"

"Mama?"

"Yes, sweetie. It's me." She located the chair and perched on the edge. "I came a long, long way to see you tonight."

"Texas?"

She didn't feel the need to explain that she'd come by way of Arkansas. "That's right. Your dad told me you've grown a whole two inches this year."

"Uh-huh. I'm this big."

The bed creaked and she saw his hazy form not far away. "Can I have a hug?" She prayed for a yes and prepared for a no.

Her prayers were answered when John David crawled into her lap. And when his little arms came around her, she didn't want to let him go, although she did. Yet she was pleasantly surprised when he remained in the chair even after she released him.

She feathered his hair with her fingertips. "Did you have a good time on your vacation?"

He straightened and clapped his hands together. "I did!"

"Well, tell me all about it, then."

Jenna listened intently as he talked nonstop about the trip, the cartoon characters on board, the ocean and the beach. Through his childlike joy, she could imagine how wonderful the sights had been, how free he must have felt.

Following a lull in his enthusiastic recounting of the details, J.D. laid his head on her shoulder and yawned. He grew so still, Jenna assumed he'd fallen asleep in her arms, as he had so many nights not so long ago.

"Mama?"

Apparently she'd thought wrong. "Yes, sweetie?"

"Is my bed in Texas?"

"You have a nice bed in Texas, in a room with lots of toys at your Grandpa Avery's house. Do you remember him?"

"Nope."

She would have laughed over his cowboylike response, had she not been so distraught over how much he'd forgotten. "Anyway, it's a big house with a swimming pool. And someday soon, you can come to live with us again."

"When?"

"After I have my eyes fixed."

He traced a line below her lids. "You get new eyes?"

This time, she did laugh. "Only the parts that don't work."

He mulled that over for a time before he said, "Daddy told me I don't live in Texas anymore. I'm gonna go to school here and Mommy Ginger's going to give me a baby brother. But Daddy says you can come see me and my baby."

David had relegated her to visitor status, a phantom voice on the phone, a person who'd been in John David's life but wasn't any longer. Not in any real sense. And she would have something to say about that, but not now. Not when she had only a limited amount of time to enjoy these special moments.

Jenna swallowed around the tightening in her throat and gave him a squeeze. "How about I tell you a bedtime story?"

"'Kay. Then I go to sleep."

"Then you can go to sleep." She tucked away her sorrow and focused on the way he felt in her arms—so soft and warm and sweet. She would forget for a while that David and Ginger could give him things that she couldn't—a two-parent home, trips on big boats, a baby brother.

And as Jenna prepared to recite her son's favorite tale of wood sprites and fantastic creatures, she made a conscious effort to store this moment in her memory and house it with those she'd gathered throughout his young life. Because deep in her soul, she feared this could very well be the last time she would have the opportunity to hold her child.

"Where is my daughter, O'Brien?"

Thankfully Logan had stepped outside when the call had come in. "She's with me, and she's fine."

"Then why is she not answering her cell phone?"

Come to think of it, Logan hadn't seen her cell phone. "The battery could be dead." Or she could be avoiding her father.

"How long before you arrive in Houston?"

"We still have a few hours to go because we're in Tennessee." Logan tipped the phone away from his ear in preparation for a minor explosion.

"What in the hell are you doing in Tennessee?"

Make that a major explosion. "I'm doing what you should have done a long time ago, letting her visit with your grandson."

"And why wasn't I notified of your change in plans?"

"I'm notifying you now. We'll be home in the morning. But you might want to reschedule our meeting in case I get stuck in traffic."

"The meeting is off, O'Brien. And so is the deal."

No real surprise to Logan. He'd known what he was risking when he'd chosen to take the detour on the way to Texas. "Not a problem, Avery. Jenna's more important than your financial backing."

"Exactly how important is she to you?" he asked suspiciously.

"She's my friend, Avery, and that's all." The words sounded false to Logan, in part because they weren't exactly true. "I have to go so we can get on the road."

"I don't like the thought of you driving all night."

"I've driven all hours of the night before without incident." Or they could get a hotel room, which would mean setting aside work for a little more pleasure and possibly losing more business in the process.

"I want my daughter home as soon as possible, Logan. And I'm holding you personally responsibile for her safety."

"I'll have her call you when we're in Houston."

Before he had to endure any more of Avery's reprimands, Logan flipped the phone closed and shoved it into the holder attached to his belt loop. The ten-hour drive was going to be tough, but after a few cups of coffee from the pot Ginger was making, he should be good to go. But he wasn't looking forward to tearing Jenna away from her child.

He also wasn't looking forward to confronting David Leedstone who'd suddenly appeared on the porch. He wore a go-to-hell expression as he leaned a shoulder against a column and shoved his hands into his pockets. "Tell me something, O'Brien.

How long has this thing with you and Jenna been going on?"

The man sounded a little too interested to Logan. "Jenna's a friend."

"Are you two sleeping together?"

"That's none of your damn business, Leedstone."

"That's what I thought."

Logan was tempted to wipe the smirk off the bastard's face. "Think what you will. Your opinion doesn't matter to me or to Jenna."

"I've seen the way you look at her, O'Brien. I know because I used to look at her that way, too. She's the kind of woman who gets under your skin. You want to protect her, but she won't let you. And if you get too close to her, she pushes you away because she automatically believes you're trying to run her life."

"I figure that's exactly what you did, Dave. Ran her life until you ran her off."

"It's David, not Dave. And did she tell you that?"

"She didn't have to, *Dave*. I saw a prime example of that tonight. You're a control freak and you hate the fact that she can survive without you. In fact, my guess is you're still in love with her."

David's face turned stone-cold. "You're wrong. I got over her the minute I met Ginger. And mark my words, if you're not in love with her now, you will be before it's all over."

Logan saw no reason to respond to the conjecture, even if it did bug him on some level. "I'm going to have some coffee, and then we're getting the hell out of here. I'd like to say it's been nice to meet you, but I'd be lying like a dog."

Before Logan could get through the door, David said, "I hope you are her friend, because she's going to need one in the next few weeks."

Logan turned around and glared. "What do you mean?"

"I'm putting you on notice that I'm filing for full custody of J.D. Jenna has no way of knowing when she'll receive the transplants, and our son needs to be in a stable environment."

Logan fisted his hands at his side, realizing he needed to leave now before the situation digressed any further. "Jenna needs to be with J.D., and I'll see you in hell before I let you take that from her."

Before Logan made it through the door, David called him back. "You're right about one thing, O'Brien. I did love Jenna at one time, and a part of me always will love her because she gave me J.D. And I'm not as unreasonable as you might think. I'm not doing this to hurt her. I only want what's best for my son."

Leedstone's admission only added fuel to the fire burning in Logan's gut. "If you cared about her, at all, then you wouldn't even consider keeping J.D. away from her."

Without waiting for a response, Logan tore into

the house and up the stairs at breakneck speed. He paused outside the bedroom and harnessed his anger before opening the door.

The scene playing out before him only cemented Logan's concern for Jenna. With her eyes closed and J.D. asleep in her arms, she looked serene, totally unaware of what the future might hold. And the worst part was, she had no clue that, if David Leedstone had his way, this could be the last time she'd hold her child until the custody war had been won—or lost.

No matter what he'd said to Leedstone a few minutes before, this wasn't his fight, and he couldn't do a damn thing about it. Not unless Jenna invited him into the battle.

Chapter Eleven

Jenna had slept on and off most of the journey, and when she'd been awake, she'd been unusually quiet. But then, so had Logan.

For ten hours straight, his mind had reeled with the knowledge he held, and whether to share it with Jenna. He felt certain she was still oblivious to Leedstone's plans. Nothing had been said aside from forced goodbyes when they'd left. And now Logan was charged with telling her the sorry news, as hard as that would be on her. No one knew bitter betrayal better than him.

When they reached the city limits, the stop-and-go Monday-morning traffic bought Logan a little more time before he dropped her off at the estate and provided the opportunity to make the revelation he didn't want to make. But she deserved the truth.

He glanced at Jenna to find she'd put on her shades to protect against the rising sun. But he could tell she was awake from the way she thrummed her nails on the console.

He reached over and clasped her hand not only to still her movements, but also to provide some support. "Your ex-husband's an ass."

She smiled. "He's not really that bad most of the time. In fact, he used to be very charming. I'm not sure why he acted the way he did last night."

"He has a guilty conscience."

"Why would you say that?"

Damn, he hated doing this to her, but he didn't have a choice. "He told me he's going to file for full custody of J.D." He expected an angry response, maybe even tears, yet she only continued to stare out the windshield. "Did you hear what I said?"

"My ears are working fine. I'm just not surprised. John David basically told me the same thing."

No wonder she'd been so sullen on the drive. "He told you about the custody issue?"

She released a humorless laugh. "He's smart, Logan, and very articulate for a three-and-a-half-year-old. But he's not quite that smart. David told him he lived in Tennessee now, not Texas, and that

I could visit. He also said in so many words that he doesn't want to live with me."

Damn Leedstone to hell. "And that doesn't bother you?"

"Of course it bothers me. It tore my heart out. But David might be right."

Logan hadn't anticipated the defeat in her tone, and hearing it made him sick inside. "He's wrong, Jenna. J.D. belongs with you."

"I'm not sure he does. Visual impairment and a child is a terrible combination, which is probably why my biological mother gave me up for adoption."

"You don't know that your mother was blind."

"No, I don't know for certain. But my instincts tell me she was and she made the decision based on what she thought was best for me."

"I'm not going to let you give up, Jenna."

She swept her hair back with one hand. "It's not your decision to make, Logan. And honestly, I'm too tired to discuss it."

He decided to let it go, for now. "You'll be home in fifteen minutes, then you can sleep the rest of the day."

"I'd rather go to your place."

Logan could foresee one major problem with that. "Your dad's already royally pissed off. If he learns that you—"

"I'll call him, unless you don't want me to come home with you."

If he said he didn't, he'd be lying to her and to himself. "My condo it is."

Jenna rifled through the bag at her feet, withdrew her cell phone and spoke the simple word *home*.

"Hi, Dad. We're in Houston, but I won't be there for a while. I'm going to cook breakfast for Logan at his place and I'll let you know when I'm heading home. Bye." She slapped the phone closed and dropped it into the bag.

"It didn't sound like you gave him a chance to say anything."

She shrugged. "I didn't. And since I can't make toast without cremating it, I seriously doubt he bought the breakfast thing. But I certainly couldn't tell him the truth."

"What is the truth, Jenna?"

She leaned over and laid her hand on his thigh. "The truth is I don't want to be in my bed. I want to be in yours until it's time for me to go."

Logan got the feeling she could be on the verge of ending their involvement before the day was done, right when he was contemplating the possibilities. He'd just have to work hard to prevent that from happening, and he had several ways to do that. For the next few hours, he planned to try every one.

When they pulled into the parking garage a few minutes later, Logan left most of the gear in the SUV while Jenna slung her smaller bag over her

shoulder, leaving her cane behind. They entered
the elevator with a group of people and stood side
by side in silence until the only remaining couple
exited on the fourth floor. As soon as the doors slid
shut, Logan couldn't stand it any longer. He kissed
her all the way to the ninth floor and only let her go
long enough to unlock and open the door. And when
they stepped inside, he kissed her some more.

In the interest of saving time, Logan lifted Jenna
into his arms and carried her up the stairs—stairs that
he always took two at a time, a routine act he'd taken
for granted. Since he'd met Jenna, he'd begun to
recognize all the challenges she faced on a daily
basis, and that had only reinforced his appreciation
of her.

He definitely appreciated her sexy smile after he
set her down on her feet in his bedroom. "Where's
the shower?" she asked.

"Right behind you." Logan pushed her hair back
and kissed her neck. "We're going to take one together this time."

"Definitely."

After he backed her into the bathroom, they undressed as if competing in a race to see who could
finish first and, remarkably, Jenna won, while Logan balanced on losing control.

Even in light of his exhaustion, he honestly believed he could drop to the ceramic-tiled floor and
do a hundred push-ups—or take her on the floor

right where they stood. He chalked that up to pure adrenaline. To Jenna.

With what strength he had left, he led her into the shower where he opted for limited foreplay. Just enough to taunt her while they bathed, before he pulled out all the stops. But she wasn't making it easy when she did some pretty creative things with her hands. In fact, she was making it extremely hard. And he returned the favor until he had her digging her nails into his back.

"The bedroom," he told her before things got too out of hand.

"Good idea," she said, and gave him a quick pinch on his bare butt.

They barely dried off, didn't bother with clothes and hit the bed without turning down the covers. As they faced each other, no words passed between them and it wasn't because they had a hard time talking to each other; they'd had several good conversations over the course of the weekend. Logan had plenty to say to her, just not now.

He didn't need words. He needed to hear the sound of her sighs when he touched her and the rapid rhythm of her breathing when he kissed his way from her neck to her breasts and then down her belly. Using his mouth, he brought her to the brink, then let up until he knew she couldn't take any more. He had her precisely where he wanted her—completely under his influence and in a place she wouldn't soon forget. Or so he thought until she nudged him onto his back and levied a little persuasion of her own.

He gritted his teeth and hissed out a breath when she did to him what he'd done to her. She didn't hold anything back, didn't miss an inch of his skin with her deadly kisses, and by the time she shimmied up his body, he was ready to wave a white flag.

He rolled away from her to retrieve a condom from his nightstand and after he tore open the packet, she held out her hand and said, "Let me."

Yeah, she was definitely the one in command, and that became even more obvious as she straddled his body, taking him inside her.

She began to move, and Logan detected a hint of desperation. But then he felt a little desperate, too. Desperate to understand why she affected him in ways no woman ever had.

He couldn't consider that now. He couldn't consider anything except Jenna hovering above him, her hair hanging down in damp strands around her face, her lips slightly parted, her eyes closed tight. She drove him to the edge with the rise and fall of her hips. Her smile indicated she knew exactly what she was doing and where she planned to take them both. Her lack of inhibition, her determination, her periodic kisses, hurled them to that destination quickly. The pulse of her climax brought on his own, a force that ripped through Logan and drove every lucid thought from his brain.

As Jenna buckled against him, his arms came around her, and as he continued to hold her, he couldn't shake the guilt over what he'd done the past twelve months. Although he'd been discriminating when it had come to his lovers, he'd also been a jerk, no better than his youngest brother who'd made sex a sport. And among the half-dozen women Logan had taken to bed, he'd never been sorry to see one of them go.

But today, as he started to drift off to sleep with Jenna's body curled into his, he never wanted her to leave.

Jenna awoke with a start when she heard an annoying buzz. She shook Logan's arm and whispered his name, yet he didn't respond. She wasn't all that surprised. He'd been on the road all night and his exhaustion had finally gotten the best of him. Their lovemaking had also been a contributing factor. Even so, if she had her way, she'd ask him to do it all again, at least one more time before she left for good.

The buzzer sounded again, sending Jenna from the bed to follow the noise originating from the hall outside the bedroom. She felt along the wall until she located the intercom. After depressing the button, she said, "Yes?"

"Miss Fordyce?"

The man sounded as surprised to hear her as she was to hear her name. "That's me."

"Uh, there's a man down here named Calvin. He says he's supposed to take you home."

Clearly, her father had called out the guard. "Tell him I'll be down in about five minutes."

And that was just as well. This little bit of paradise with Logan was almost over. It had to be. She had too much going on in her life and not enough confidence to believe that she could be the woman he needed—even if she'd tried to fool herself into thinking that was possible. He deserved a woman who was whole, both physically and emotionally.

After she located her bag and dressed in the last of her clean clothes, a blanket of depression settled over her. Tonight, she would again go to bed alone and wake tomorrow alone. But the decision weighing heavily on her mind was one she had to make by herself. The most difficult decision she would ever have to make—relinquishing custody of her child.

After one more futile attempt to wake Logan, she left the room and carefully descended the stairs. She relied on her learned ability to mentally chart a course of places she had been before, the steps she had taken, in order to find the front door. As she waited for the elevator, she chastised herself for leaving Logan without any explanation. But she couldn't very well write him a note; her handwriting was barely legible these days. And knowing him, which she did—better than she ever dreamed she would know him—he would call her later and demand an explanation. Yet she wasn't certain she could explain her feelings to him because she didn't know how she felt, aside from confused. She did know that in the limited time she'd spent with him, she'd never been so happy. So liberated. So close to falling in love.

"Were you going to leave without saying goodbye?"

Jenna turned to the sound of his voice, as if he had some magnetic hold over her. "I didn't want to wake you up." She didn't want to say goodbye, either. "Dad sent Calvin for me. He's waiting downstairs."

"I can drive you home on the way to my office."

She shook her head. "That's not necessary, Logan."

"Fine. I'll call you later."

"That's not necessary, either."

"I know that, but I want to."

When he circled his arms around her waist, she wanted to ask him not to touch, otherwise she would never be able to do what she had to do. Yet she couldn't force herself to pull away from him.

"We can go out to dinner tomorrow night. Or I can take you to the baseball game. I have good seats. I'll nab a fly ball for you as a souvenir."

He simply didn't get it, and that couldn't be more

apparent to Jenna at the moment. "I couldn't see a fly ball coming at me, Logan. I couldn't even see any of the action."

"I'll give you a play-by-play."

Gathering her strength, she wrested out of his grasp. "We've had a great few days together, but now it's back to the real world. And my reality isn't very pretty."

"What the hell are you saying?"

"You were absolutely right. Lovemaking complicates everything. It's better we end it now before someone starts caring too much."

"It's too damn late for that, Jenna. You've already made me care, like it or not."

She prayed the elevator would hurry and arrive, before she completely broke down. "I'm a mess, Logan. My life's a mess. I may lose my child. I may never regain my sight."

"You don't have to go through this alone. I'm willing to be there for you."

He'd proved that to her yesterday, but still… "It's my problem, Logan. You don't need the hassle."

"Don't presume to tell me what I need. But I'm going to tell you something and you need to listen carefully." His tone reflected anger yet contrasted with the gentle way he touched her face. "After Helena and I broke it off, I spent a year trying to convince myself that I could survive by moving from one woman to the next. But it didn't do anything to cure my loneliness. In fact, it made it worse. And then I met this sexy, determined, hardheaded beautiful woman and I didn't feel alone, anymore."

She closed her eyes and willed away the tears, at least for the time being. "Please stop, Logan. You're only making this more difficult."

"This whole thing's difficult, Jenna, and I didn't plan on it happening. But whether you meant to or not, you made me feel something for the first time in a long time and I'm not willing to blow that off."

The elevator chimed, providing her with the out she so desperately needed. "I'm sorry, Logan," she said as she backed up a step, "I can't do this. I don't know what else to say."

"You don't have to say anything else. I get it now. We had a great time, it was a nice diversion, and that's it. At least for you."

If he only knew how wrong he was. "It wasn't only a diversion, Logan. It was—"

"Don't try to come up with something to make me feel better, because I'm still going to feel like hell. Have a nice life, princess. And good luck."

Jenna entered the elevator not knowing if Logan was still there, or if he'd already left. Her eyes were so clouded with tears that she couldn't detect the boldest movement or the darkest shadow. She felt along the bank of buttons and, using her Braille, found the one that indicated the lobby.

She had learned to manage her life as best she could. She had worked hard to maintain some normalcy as an unsighted woman in a visual world. Yet she couldn't help but wonder if by walking away from Logan, she was blind to what could be the best thing that had happened to her in years.

He found her tending to her garden, as he knew he would. Lucine Kabakian O'Brien always spent every morning from March through August pruning her plants with the same commitment she'd shown to her family.

From a very early age, the O'Brien boys had learned to seek out their father for guidance on sex and their mother for counsel on affairs of the heart. Logan needed that counsel now more than any time in his adult life.

She kept her back to him, still totally unaware he'd entered the yard. And when he walked toward her, bent down and popped a kiss on her cheek, she spun around and gasped.

"Heavens, Logan. Don't you know better than to startle a woman with pruning shears? That's a good way to lose all hope of fathering children."

He slid his hands into his pockets and sent her a sheepish smile. "Sorry, Mom. I didn't mean to scare you."

"You're forgiven, dear." She tossed the tool into the nearby cart and worked the gardening gloves from her hand. "Your father is always sneaking up on me. I thought you were him."

"He told me to tell you he's reading the morning paper."

She sent him a skeptical look. "He's in the lounger, taking his morning nap."

Logan grinned. "Yeah, he is. And before I left the living room, he started snoring as loud as a turbo-charged engine."

"Nothing new there." She gestured toward the patio with a glove. "While he's occupied, let's have a nice chat. Just the two of us."

She hooked her arm through his and after they were seated in two chairs opposite each other at the small table, Logan leaned forward and clasped his hands together on the metal surface. "I wanted to apologize for not being here the past two Sundays for lunch and for not calling."

She studied him with concern. "It's more than that, Logan. Something is terribly wrong."

He wasn't surprised by her ability to read him. She'd owned that talent for as long as he could remember. "I'm having a tough time right now." Tougher than he'd expected since he'd said good-bye to Jenna. He'd been doing a good impression of a lovesick idiot and he didn't know why. Maybe it was only wounded pride. After all, he was usually the one to call things off with a woman, not the other way around.

"I distinctly remember the last time you surprised me with a morning visit," Lucy said, breaking into his thoughts. "You told me you were planning to marry Helena and you wanted suggestions on how to propose."

That was a sorry subject he'd rather avoid. "And it turned out to be a huge mistake."

Lucy laid her palm on his arm, garnering his attention. "This little visit doesn't involve another woman, does it? Perhaps a pretty, down-to-earth young woman whom we met and fell in love with two weeks ago?"

Jenna had predictably received the O'Brien family stamp of approval. "Yeah, it does."

He launched into a summary of the camping trip, the visit to Tennessee and ended with Jenna's insistence she didn't need anyone to support her through the custody battle. "Anyway, I haven't talked to her since."

"You haven't even tried to call her?" His mother sounded astounded and a little disappointed.

Truth was, he'd picked up the phone every day for almost two weeks, sometimes two or three times a day, and he'd hung up before the first ring every time. "I don't want to push her."

"There's a difference between pushing, Logan, and letting her know you care. And I suspect you care much more than you're willing to admit."

She'd hit that nail straight on the head. He afforded her a quick glance before lowering his gaze to the table, something he hadn't done since his early teens, when he'd awaited punishment for toilet papering the principal's front lawn. "When did you know you wanted to spend the rest of your life with Dad?"

"You're asking me to think back to a time when George Washington was still wearing knickers?"

Logan laughed over her use of one of his father's favorite phrases. "I guess, I assumed that was something you wouldn't forget."

She smiled. "No, I've never forgotten. I was a very shy girl in school and I didn't know any boys at all. Then out of the blue, your father asked me to the senior dance. Funny thing was, he didn't even know how to dance, but that didn't stop him from trying. I suffered a few sore toes that night, but I also fell in love with him. A tough, loud Irishman who was willing to risk embarrassing himself in order to make me happy. We married three months later, I became pregnant with Devin three months after that, and he's been making me happy ever since."

That was a story Logan had never heard, but he'd never thought to ask before he'd met Jenna. "Only three months before you two married?"

"Yes, and I would have married him the day after the dance if he'd asked me." Her expression turned serious. "Love doesn't stop to consider how long you've known a person, Logan. Sometimes it never arrives. Sometimes it doesn't come about for years. Other times it hits you immediately. And that was much the case with me and your father. Is that what's happened with you and Jenna?"

Logan still had a hard time wrapping his mind around that concept. "I don't know, Mom."

"Tell me something. Are you finding you can't sleep? Do the things you like to do no longer give you joy? Are you having trouble concentrating at work?"

She had a surplus of insight for such a small woman. "All of the above."

"Did you find yourself watching her while she was sleeping?"

"I never said I slept with her."

It was his mother's turn to laugh. "My dear child, all my sons are genetically predisposed to uncontrollable passion when it comes to women, thanks to your father."

He damn sure didn't want to get into this. "It's not about sex, Mom. It's more." Okay, he'd said it, and the house behind him didn't cave in.

"Then, you are most likely in love with her."

"I didn't intend to be anything but her friend."

Lucy clasped his joined hands. "Be her friend, honey. Give her a little more time, but not too much time, then pay her a visit and let her know you want to be there for her. What's the worst that could happen?"

He knew the answer to that. She'd tell him to get the hell out of her life.

But as it had been with building a successful business, nothing worth having had ever come easily. And Jenna was worth one more try.

He'd give her some time, and then he was going to give her something he'd never given to another woman, not even Helena—his heart.

Chapter Twelve

"I'm worried about you, sweetheart."

The same song and dance from her father she'd endured myriad times over the past two weeks. "I'm going to be all right, Dad. You don't have to worry."

"You're not all right, Jenna. You barely eat. You haven't been out in days."

"I went to the eye doctor on Thursday."

"But you didn't go to the library to tell the children stories. And I want to know right now what Logan O'Brien did to you to cause you this much distress."

She leaned her head back in the chair and groaned. "My current state of mind doesn't have anything to do with Logan." And that wasn't completely true. She'd had no idea she could miss someone so much—someone she'd known such a brief time.

"You were fine before you went on that trip. If you hadn't gone—"

"Then I would have been surprised when the custody documents showed up on the doorstep. At least I was prepared." Or as prepared as she could have been in light of the situation.

"But you haven't signed them yet."

She pinched the bridge of her nose between her thumb and forefinger. "No, I haven't signed them." Giving up the right to raise a child was no small task. She had to be certain she was willing to go that far in order to ensure her son's well-being, although the way things stood, she didn't feel she had an alternative. David had more to offer, and J.D. preferred David over her.

"You need to focus on the good news. We've waited so long for you to move to the top of the donor list."

And that was something else she'd thought about incessantly. Another decision that had weighed her down. "I'm considering being removed from the list."

"You can't be serious."

The alarm in her father's voice came as no surprise. "Yes, I am."

"But if you don't go through with the surgery, you have little chance to retain custody of J.D."

"I don't feel I have much of a chance now." She didn't feel as if she had any hope left. "Besides, being at the top of the list doesn't guarantee I'll have the transplant immediately. It could be years from now."

"It could be tomorrow."

"I realize that, but it's not likely. And the thought that, someday, someone will suffer a tragic accident or irreversible brain damage so I can see again, isn't pleasant."

"I don't understand your attitude, Jenna. You've always been a fighter, and now you're giving up."

She could understand why he would view it that way. She wasn't giving up; she was simply resigned to her future. A future without sight, without more children. She could still have a good life. She could still visit J.D. twice a year, maybe more. But would that ever be enough to maintain a relationship with him? "I'm tired, Dad. I want to go to my room and finish an audio book I've been listening to."

"More Italian lessons?"

She hadn't seen any need for more of those lessons. The European trip seemed as improbable as having J.D. living with her again. "It's a true-crime novel."

"Are you going to call John David?"

Oh, how she longed to do that very thing. "No, Dad, I'm not. If he wants to speak with me, he'll call."

"He's three and a half years old, Jenna. He doesn't know how to make a long-distance call."

How well Jenna knew that. But when she'd attempted to call the past few nights, all she'd received was voice mail. David had already set the wheels in motion to effectively drive her child out of her life.

Too weary for anger or more revelations, Jenna slid her chair away from the table and hoisted herself up with the cane. "Have a nice night, Dad."

"I knew when I allowed you to go on that trip with Logan, something like this would happen. I knew he would get what he wanted from you and then toss you aside. He doesn't realize how special you are and he's beaten you down. That's why you're so depressed."

Suddenly she wasn't so tired that she couldn't get mad. "You don't know what you're talking about, Dad. Logan was absolutely wonderful during our trip. He gave me space and let me be me the whole time. He knew how much I missed John David and he took me to see him. He's done nothing wrong."

"Except for breaking off all ties with you."

She tightened her grip on the cane. "He didn't break it off. I did. He's a good man, Dad. He's a great man. And he doesn't deserve to get caught up in my chaotic life."

When her father failed to respond, for a moment she'd thought he'd left the room and she wished he had when he said, "You're in love with him."

Unfortunately, that was true. "It doesn't matter how I feel about him. It's over between us, and there's no going back."

If she had the opportunity, she might take it all back. If she'd known how it was going to turn out, she might have never said yes to the lunch at his parents, the walk in the garden. The camping trip.

But that wasn't accurate. Regardless that their relationship had been severed, and with good reason, she'd never take back one moment of their time together. And she'd never stop wondering what might have been.

Logan had waited long enough to tell her how he felt about her, but that was about to end. After grabbing the receiver, he pounded out the number he'd dialed numerous times—only, today, he wasn't about to hang up.

"Fordyce residence."

Logan recognized the woman's Eastern European accent from the last time he'd called. "I need to speak to Jenna." His mother's lesson on the importance of manners came into play. "Please."

"May I ask who is calling?"

He considered withholding that information, then decided honesty was the best policy in this case. Even if it meant Jenna refusing to talk to him. If that happened, he'd keep calling until she finally caved. "Logan O'Brien."

"One moment, please."

He waited for what seemed like an eternity before someone finally answered—and that someone wasn't Jenna.

"My daughter doesn't want to speak with you, O'Brien."

Apparently, Avery didn't, either. Fordyce hadn't contacted him since their conversation in Tennessee. Fortunately, he hadn't severed the business ties, either. Not yet, anyway. "Did you ask her if she'd take my call?"

"I don't have to ask her. She told me last night that the two of you are finished with whatever was going on between you. But, while I have you on the phone, I have something I have to ask you."

Logan had expected as much. He'd let Avery have his say, hang up and try Jenna's cell phone. "Fire away."

"What in God's name did you say to her to convince her she didn't need the corneal transplants?"

That he hadn't seen coming. "I don't know what in the hell you're talking about, Avery."

"At her doctor's appointment this afternoon, she claims she's going to request to be taken off the list.

And don't try to tell me you had nothing to do with that decision."

"Believe me, Avery. That's the last thing I would tell her to do."

"Well, someone wielded some influence. I can't believe, after all the waiting, she would decide on her own to halt the process."

Logan couldn't believe it, either, or he wouldn't have two weeks ago. But he had a theory on what had changed her mind. "Did she mention her ex-husband's plan to get full custody of J.D.?"

"Of course she did. The documents came two days ago. If she signs them, it's a done deal. If she doesn't, she'll face a court battle. And if she refuses to correct her vision, she might not win."

One other key to Jenna's attitude switch had yet to be broached, and now was a good time for him to bring it up. "If anyone's partially at fault for Jenna changing her mind, it's you, Avery."

"You have a lot of nerve saying that to me."

He had a lot of nerve making accusations about Jenna and him that he couldn't prove. "Whether you mean to be a contributing factor or not, you are through your refusal to tell her about her biological mother."

"I don't see how that's relevant or any of your business."

Logan tightened his grip on the phone and silently rehearsed several oaths. "Jenna has it in her head that her mother gave her up because she had the same disease. She firmly believes that the unselfish thing to do would be to give up J.D. for the same reasons. On some level, I get why she might feel that way, but only if she had no chance to regain her sight."

Avery sighed. "The transplants carry a risk of rejection and the disease could return in a matter of years, even if the surgery is successful. She could require another transplant if that happens."

At least some of this was beginning to make sense. "I also suspect she has some heavy-duty guilt over possibly passing the disease on to J.D."

"According to the eye specialists, we have no way of knowing unless we have an extensive family history."

"And that brings me back to my point. You've got the money and the means to track down Jenna's mother. Why haven't you attempted it?"

"I did several years ago, only to learn she died long before Jenna started having trouble with her vision."

"Then you know who she is."

"According to the agency, she was a strung out runaway who lived on the streets of Atlanta. She had no idea who Jenna's father was and, to this day, that remains a mystery. But I also know she wasn't blind. She was a lost cause, and that led to her death two years after Jenna was born."

Avery's motivation behind concealing the information was much more evident to Logan, and understandable, even if he didn't agree with his reasoning. "You were trying to protect her."

"Yes, I was, and I realize now that was probably a mistake."

"You could rectify that mistake by telling her the facts, before it's too late to matter."

"I'm not sure she can handle more bad news."

Logan would have argued that point the day he met her, but not now. "You can at least assure her that her mother wasn't blind without getting into all the ugly stuff."

"I might have a solution to everything. When we brought Jenna home, the agency sent a letter from her mother with her. It's not pretty, but it does explain why she chose to put Jenna up for adoption and that she'd wanted to keep her, but couldn't."

Unbelievable. "She's never read it?"

"No. I almost gave it to her several times, but I couldn't bring myself to do it. I didn't want to hurt her."

Logan wanted to yell at Avery for not seeing what his daughter needed. "You might hurt her more in the long run if you don't tell her the truth now."

"I know. And you might not understand this, Logan, but everything I've done for Jenna, I've done because I love her, wise or not."

Logan understood it more than Avery realized.

In fact, what he planned to do was a direct result of his love for her—a love he'd tried to deny until his mother's wisdom had forced him to own up to it. "Where is Jenna now?"

"The place she goes every time she wants to think. Her mother's garden."

With the sun on the rise in the midmorning sky, she knew she should go back inside before the rays became intolerable. Yet Jenna continued to sit on the wrought iron bench, immersed in the fragrance of roses and memories of the woman she'd called "Mama." A woman who may not have given her life, but had provided her with an abundance of love.

Jenna recalled the times she would come to the garden with her mother to play hide-and-seek, a tradition she'd continued with John David not long after he'd learned to walk, while she'd still been able to watch him. Now, more than ever, she longed for her mother's shoulder to cry on to help alleviate the unshakable loneliness and confusion. Her father was trying, she'd give him that, but it simply wasn't the same. Although his heart was in the right place, he didn't understand he couldn't protect her from everything and that only she could decide what was best for all involved.

The echo of footsteps brought Jenna's musings to a standstill. Heavy footsteps that led her to be-

lieve the approaching party was male with an unknown identity. Her father had surely left for work
and the yard crew never came on Tuesdays. Still,
Jenna doubted some dangerous intruder had infil-
trated the high-tech security system surrounding
the estate. "Who's there?"

"Logan."

Even if he hadn't identified himself by name, she
would have begun to sense him as he moved closer.

"Mind if I sit down."

Jenna probably should mind, but she didn't.
She probably should ask him to leave, but she
couldn't. "Be my guest. You can tell me why
you're here."

He settled in beside her, an obscure image in her
ever-failing field of vision. Yet his presence was
somehow comforting. "I need to talk to you about
something."

"You could have called." In spite of what she'd
told him when they'd parted, she'd longed for that
call, that last little attempt to win her over.

"It's hard to reach someone by phone when you
have a father running interference."

"You called me?"

"This morning. Turns out that after your dad insisted you didn't have anything to say to me, we
had a long conversation, at which time he informed me you're not going through with the
transplants."

Now she understood. He was here because her father had recruited him. "I see. The resident white knight has come to talk me into having a surgery I'm not sure I want to have. There are worse things than being blind, Logan."

"I agree, particularly if you can't see the good because you're too focused on the bad."

"I only see my life as this series of decisions I can't seem to make."

"Then you're not altogether sure you're going to cancel the surgery."

She shook her head. "I'm not sure of much of anything, these days." Aside from the fact that she'd ached for him day and night. Ached for him even now.

"Just so you know, I didn't come here to talk you out of anything, Jenna, because it's not my place to do that, or Avery's. But I did come here to read you something."

"Excuse me?"

"It's a letter your father should have given you a long time ago."

He'd done nothing to this point to lessen her confusion. "I don't understand."

"It's from your biological mother."

When Jenna realized that he was about to provide a piece to the puzzle of her past, she ran the emotional gamut—anger, shock, sadness.

Perhaps even fear. But she had to know what she'd yearned to know for years. "Go ahead. I'm listening."

"Dear, baby girl,

Today, I'm going to do the hardest thing I've ever done. I'm going to give you to strangers. I can't keep you because I'm only seventeen and I don't have a job. Your dad is a nice boy, but he went back to his home to Kansas. I can't go home because I've never really had one.

I hear your new parents have a lot of money. That's good, but I hope they give you a lot of love since that's the most important thing. I know because I've never really had that, either..."

Logan paused to clear his throat, letting Jenna know he wasn't unaffected by the content, either.

"...I also know that every day of my life, I'm going to hate myself for not having the guts to try harder. But I promise I'll think about you all the time and I'll always love you, no matter what.

Please forgive me.

Your real mom,

Carol Anne."

She now had a name to go with the face of a mother she'd only imagined—Carol Anne.

The onslaught of tears prevented Jenna from speaking. Tears for the mother she'd never known, a woman who'd barely been a child when she'd given birth to her. A woman who, for some reason, had never known love.

Logan held her close to his side, providing that much-needed crying shoulder. And as she began to regain some composure, more questions rolled around Jenna's murky mind. "Why now, Logan? Why not ten years ago when I first asked him about her? Or four years ago when I was pregnant with J.D.?"

"Avery didn't want you to know that your biological mother was a child from an abusive family who ran away from several group homes. Her life was a mess, Jenna, until the day she died from a drug overdose, two years after your birth."

Jenna had wrongly believed that she could not suffer any more shock today. "I'll never have the chance to meet her and I have no way of knowing if she had the disease, or if she was only a carrier."

"You do know she didn't give you up because she was blind," Logan said. "You also know that, had she lived, she would have regretted the decision. Do you really want to risk doing the same thing if you let David have full custody of your son?"

Jenna could see quite clearly where this was heading. "None of this changes my situation with J.D., Logan. David can still give him things that I can't."

"He can't love him more than you do, Jenna. And Ginger can't replace you as his mother, even if you're thinking that's what your adopted mother did. The difference is, you never knew your biological mother. J.D. knows you, and I don't care what you say, he hasn't forgotten you. And he won't unless you take yourself out of his life."

It all sounded so logical coming from Logan. "David's the one who's bent on taking me out of his life."

"Then fight him, dammit. Fight for your son."

Logan's adamant tone, along with the prospect of missing more of J.D.'s milestones and years of possible regret, fueled Jenna's determination and prompted a decision she should never have had to make. "You're right. I'm going to fight him on this. I want to be there when my child grows up." Yet she still foresaw one problem. "But let's face it Logan, if it goes to court, he has the best argument—a two-parent home."

"We could give him that."

Her shock meter was now off the scale. "What are you saying?"

He took both her hands into his. "I'm saying I want to marry you."

His proposal was totally outlandish, and so was her urge to say yes. But reason didn't always take precedence when the human heart was involved. "You and I both agree that you don't marry for the sake of a child."

"What if we do it for our sakes?"

"Do we really know each other well enough to jump into matrimony?"

"Look, we were both in long-term relationships that didn't pan out. Commitment might be a crapshoot, but we're not. I know in my gut it's going to work with us."

"How do you know that, Logan? How can you be so sure?"

He sighed. "After my experience with Helena, I'd pretty much given up on marriage. I didn't think I'd ever fall in love, either. But here I am, more than ready to get married and long overdue in telling you that I love you."

He'd said it with such heartfelt sincerity, she almost believed him. "How could you possibly know that when you still know so little about me?"

"I know that you burn toast. I know that your lip quivers when you sleep. I know your politics, where you went to school, what makes you afraid. I know your preference for taking up more than half the bed at night, your taste in food and your love of flowery shower gel. I know what you really, really like when we make love and I also know that you are the most headstrong, independent, sexy woman I've ever known. Do you want me to go on?"

She laughed through a few latent tears. "Please, stop. At times you make me sound as appealing as a rush hour traffic jam."

"But there's still one thing I don't know, Jenna."

She smoothed a hand over his face to discover his expression matched his suddenly somber tone. "What's that?"

"I don't know how you feel about me."

She brushed a kiss across his lips. "I know you're as stubborn as I am and that you're the one who takes up more than half the bed. I know the same little tidbits about your personal history and I know exactly what's going to happen when you make that really low, animal sound while we're making love. I also know that you love and respect your mother, which is saying a lot. More important, I knew I loved you the minute you took off my makeup."

"Oh, yeah?"

"Oh, yeah."

"Then we definitely need to get married so we can fill in any missing gaps."

Now it was Jenna's turn to be serious. "We can't rush into this, Logan."

"I'm not saying we should do it tomorrow, or next month, for that matter."

"Good, because I'd like to wait until after I

have the transplants, so I can see the man I'm marrying."

"You already see more in him than anyone else ever has, Jenna."

They kissed a long time then, seated in the garden where he'd almost kissed her the first time, until the lights had interrupted them. And now the sun was responsible for doing that very thing.

Reluctantly, Jenna pulled back. "This light is—"

"Hurting your eyes. I should've realized that. You need to go into the house, anyway, and pack a bag for our trip."

He was certainly full of surprises. "What trip?"

"The one we're going to take together as soon as you're packed."

"If you don't tell me where we're going, I won't know how to pack. Should I bring my hiking boots?"

"Nope, because we're not going camping and we're not driving, either. We're going on a plane."

Just the word *plane* made her anxious. "I hate to fly, Logan. I have since my vision became so poor. I don't like crowds and those narrow aisles and—"

"We're taking a chartered jet and I'll hold your hand the whole time. It'll just be me, you and the open skies. And a crew of two experienced pilots in the cockpit. It also has a nice fold-out sofa in case we get bored on the way."

Jenna felt a serious bout of boredom coming on. "How do you know all of this about a plane?"

"I'm in the transportation business, babe. And I also own the plane, or half of it, I should say. Your father owns the other half."

Having the two most important men in her life working together again couldn't have pleased Jenna more. "So you and my father have finally made amends?"

"We're getting there."

"Speaking of getting there, exactly where are we going?" She pointed at him. "And don't tell me it's a surprise."

"When Avery gave me the letter, we also looked over the terms of your divorce. According to the joint custody clause, David's several months overdue in giving J.D. back to you, even if you originally agreed that he'd stay until you had the transplants. We're going to see if what David told me is true— that he's a reasonable man—by telling him you're ready to bring J.D. home, surgery or no surgery."

As much as she wanted that, she still had reservations. "What if John David doesn't want to come with us?"

"Look, Jenna, he was impressed with a ship. How do you think he's going to feel about a plane he can fly in anytime he wants? Not to mention what he'll have on that plane."

"A widescreen TV with access to every sport channel known to God and little boys of all ages?"

"His mother."

If Jenna had ever had any doubts over whether Logan honestly loved her, they'd all been dispelled. "You're an amazing man, Logan O'Brien."

"You are one helluva woman, Jenna Fordyce."

She didn't have the words to express how much he meant to her, so she settled for the three that meant the most. "I love you."

"I love you, too. And I only have one small condition I haven't covered. If you don't have the surgery in three months' time, we're going to get married, anyway."

"Why is that?"

"Take my word for it. In my family, three months is a lucky number."

Epilogue

Three months later

For the past five minutes, Jenna could only stare at the man standing next to the banquet table in the hotel ballroom. The beautiful man whom she'd married a few hours ago in her mother's garden, surrounded by family and close friends. The first face she'd seen when she'd undergone the corneal transplants nine weeks before. The second had been her child's, who now happily lived in the house she and Logan had purchased the previous month. A lovely two-story home with a large backyard, many trees and myriad flowers.

Though her vision wasn't perfect, the new contacts allowed Jenna to see clearly enough to recognize her image of Logan hadn't come close to the real thing. His eyes were bluer than the early morning sky she'd always cherished, his hair as black as the night she'd once dreaded before she'd met him. And his smile was the kind that had women struggling to find something funny to say so he would reveal those gorgeous dimples. But she'd learned how to do that with only a special look, and she gave that to him now when he met her gaze.

When he held out his hand to her, she crossed the room, her steps steady as she joined the man she'd grown to love more each passing day.

He wrapped one arm around her and kissed her cheek. "Where've you been?"

"Talking with Kevin who I mistakenly thought was Kieran. I don't know how you tell them apart." After you've been around a while, you'll figure it out. Kieran's the one who'll offer sound advice. Kevin will offer to take you out if you get tired of me."

She elbowed his side. "I'll never get tired of you, and Kevin can't be that bad. In fact, he was very cordial and charming."

Logan looked beyond her and grinned. "And it looks like he's charming your friend Candice. You might want to warn her."

"Candice can take care of herself," Jenna said as

she spotted Dermot at the front of the room, standing on a chair that looked as if it might not hold him. "I believe your father's trying to get everyone's attention."

Logan grinned. "Brace yourself, babe. He's about to toast us."

John David chose that moment to burst through the masses and hurl himself at Jenna's legs. "Can I have more cake, Mama?"

She bent down and rubbed the spot of chocolate from the corner of his mouth, the same chocolate that now dotted the front of his miniature tuxedo and the skirt of her satin wedding gown. Obviously, he'd inherited her tendency to wear his food. "We'll see about that as soon as your Grandpa Dermot gives his toast."

J.D. frowned. "I don't want toast. I want cake."

Logan laughed. "Come here and I'll put you on my shoulders so you can see better, bud."

Without hesitatin, John David complied, demonstrating the solid relationship that had formed between her son and her new husband. Jenna had acknowledged that Logan could never replace David, nor would he try, but he would serve as an integral part of the mix of their blended family.

After Logan hoisted J.D. into position, the new family of three turned toward Dermot who had let go a shrill whistle loud enough to wake every hound in Houston.

After Lucy brought Logan and Jenna their own glasses of champagne, she took her place on Jenna's other side and slid an arm around her waist. "I apologize in advance for anything my husband might say."

Jenna wasn't sure what to expect from Dermot, although, she firmly believed it would be interesting.

"Ladies and gents," Dermot began. "We are gathered here today to welcome a new lassie into our family and a new grandpup, too. And on this blessed occasion, I have a wee bit to say to the happy couple."

"Let's hope this doesn't take all night," Logan muttered, earning him a quelling look from his mother.

Dermot raised his glass to Jenna and Logan. "To my middle boy, Logan. You have honored us by choosing a woman who is not only fair on the outside, but just as fair on the inside. And to lovely Jenny, I am glad you have finally seen in Logan what his family has seen all along—a good man with a strong heart and his da's good taste in women. And I'm especially tickled that you can finally see what a handsome man I am."

Following a spattering of laughter, Dermot tapped his glass again and took on a somber expression. "And now I'll be repeatin' the blessing passed onto me from my Irish forefathers. Jenny, Logan and little Johnny, may you be poor in misfortune, rich in blessings, slow to make enemies and quick to make friends. And may you know nothing but happiness from this day forward."

The crowd shouted "Here, here," and in response to the applause, Dermot took a bow. As the band began to play a romantic ballad, Logan set J.D. back on his feet, gave their champagne glasses to his mother and took Jenna's hand. But before they made it to the dance floor, her father intercepted them.

"I'd like to have this dance with my daughter, Logan, if that's all right with you."

Logan regarded Jenna. "It's fine by me."

Jenna smile at the remembrance of other dances she'd shared with her dad. "Of course, as long as you don't expect me to stand on your feet like I did when I was five."

Avery grinned. "Not with you wearing high heels."

After Logan handed her off, Jenna followed Avery onto the floor and took a moment to survey his face—an endearing face she had missed during her time of darkness but had never forgotten. "You're looking rather dapper tonight, Dad."

He set her back and twirled her around before taking her into his arms. "And you're a vision, Jenna. I wish your mother were here to see what a remarkable woman you've become."

She swallowed hard when she noted the slight tremor in his voice. "I know how much you miss her, Dad. And I know how difficult it's going to be for you now that I'm no longer at home. But I expect you to visit us often."

"I'll be fine sweetheart, as long as I know you're happy."

She couldn't begin to express the depths of her joy. "I am. Logan's a good man and he loves me."

"I know. And I want to apologize…"

She pressed a finger against his lips. "You don't have to apologize for anything. But I want to thank you for being the most incredible father a girl could ever hope for."

He bent and kissed her cheek. "I love you, sweetheart."

"I love you, too, Daddy."

After giving her a long embrace, Avery guided her back to Logan. "Take care of her, son. She's a gift."

"You can count on it, Avery."

When Logan and Jenna returned to the dance floor, he held her closely and whispered, "Are you ready to get out of here?"

She was definitely moving in that direction. "Maybe we should wait a bit longer."

He looked decidedly disappointed. "I'm in a hurry to get you in bed."

"We still have a long drive to Arkansas." Some brides might take exception to a honeymoon camping trip, but not Jenna. She found it fitting to start their new life in a place where they'd laid the groundwork for a solid friendship and the start of an exciting future.

"We're not going to Arkansas tonight," Logan said. "I reserved a room upstairs."

That was her Logan, always full of surprises. "I left my bags in the Hummer."

"You're not going to need any clothes."

"True, but unless you have your luggage, then you're going to have to make a stop at the gift shop or risk getting me pregnant." She smoothed a hand over his lapel. "Or we could just not worry about it and make a baby."

Finally, she'd sufficiently surprised him. "I didn't think—"

"That I wanted to have another child? I changed my mind when the geneticist explained that our children have almost no chance of contracting the disease and neither does J.D. When Logan simply stared at her without responding, she added, "Of course, if you've decided you don't want—"

He kissed her gently and smiled. "I can't think of anything I'd like more than to give you a baby, and J.D. a brother or sister, which he's already mentioned he wanted at least five times. And nothing would make me happier than to give my parents the next grandchild before someone beats us to it."

Jenna nodded toward her right at the couple who'd joined them on the dance floor. "I think Devin and Stacy have already beaten us to it."

Logan glanced at his borther and sister-in-law before returning his attention to her. "Do you know something I don't know?"

She shrugged. "I heard a rumor, but don't repeat it since it's not official yet."

He frowned. "If we'd married right after I'd proposed, you'd be pregnant by now."

"Possibly, but I wouldn't have wanted to miss seeing your face when we exchanged vows." Or finally seeing the love in his eyes that she'd sensed all along. "Now, let's hope these transplants hold up so I can continue to see you and our children."

Logan paused and settled his gaze on hers. "If, God forbid, something happens with the transplants, just remember, I'll be your eyes for however long it takes."

Jenna could trust that he would, and she also trusted that, no matter what the future held, his love would always be a constant. She knew she would never wake up alone again, or go to bed alone again. And she vowed never to lose sight of what mattered most—friendship, family and the love of an exceptional man who held her close, but not so close that she couldn't be herself.

She'd found all of that in Logan O'Brien, and so much more.

* * * * *

BILLIONAIRE'S FAVOURITE FANTASY

Jan Colley

Jan Colley lives in Christchurch, New Zealand, with Les and a couple of cats. She has travelled extensively, is a jack of all trades and master of none and still does not know what she wants to be when she grows up – as long as it's a writer. She loves rugby, family, friends, writing, sunshine, talking about writing, and cats, although not necessarily in that order. E-mail her at vagabond232@yahoo. com or check out her website at www.jancolley.com.

One

"It is with great pleasure that I introduce Madeline Holland, our new chief operating officer, based in Sydney."

As the smattering of polite applause died away, the acting chair peered over his specs down the table at her. "Please tell us a little about yourself, my dear. I know you spent many years with Global Hospitality…"

Madeline returned his smile, smoothed the skirt of her smart burgundy skirt and started to rise.

Suddenly the door flew open and banged against its stop with a crack. All eyes swiveled to assess the intrusion. Beside her, Madeline felt her best friend, Kay, tense and prepare to rise. Kay was regional manager of the three Premier Hotels here in Queenstown, New Zealand, so security came under her domain.

A tall, lean, impeccably dressed man stood framed by the doorway, holding a stack of glossy files. Half standing, half crouching, Madeline glanced at his face and her throat snapped shut. Dear God, it was him! Her fantasy lover of the night before.

The punch of adrenaline rocked her all the way to her heels. Her smile froze as she stared at his longish dark-blond hair, the model stubble along his jaw, his aquiline nose and sharply cut upper lip. She closed her eyes, remembering mesmerizing sea-green eyes, hazed over with passion but now thankfully hidden by sunglasses.

No, no, no...

Her breath came back in a strangled gasp and she eased herself back down in her seat, praying the floor would open up and swallow her. Had he known who she was? As she'd writhed in his strong arms during the night, had he, even then, been thinking about crashing this closed meeting today?

She shrank in her seat.

The man gave a cursory all-inclusive glance around the boardroom table and moved forward into the room. "Good afternoon, ladies and gentlemen. My name is Lewis Goode." He commenced handing out files while Madeline kept her eyes resolutely lowered. Would he acknowledge her? Would he smile, smug in the knowledge that he'd seen her sans clothing, inhibitions, coherence? Her heart pounded against her rib cage.

His hands now empty, he strode to the front and offered his hand to the acting chair, who smiled broadly, and took a seat at the side of the table.

Lewis Goode took off his sunglasses, slipping them into his inside pocket, raised his head and surveyed the table. "Some of you here will know me."

He gave a brief smile at the six places on both sides closest to him, made up mostly of the directors of the board. Then he lifted his head to take in the rest of the Executive Committee.

Madeline hunched even lower, her fingers gripping the table edge lest she lose her nerve and bolt. She shouldn't even be here since she was not a member of the Executive Committee. Neither was Kay, but as she'd organized the annual conference here in Queenstown, she had asked for permission to attend and bring Madeline along to be introduced as the newest member of the team.

"For those who don't know me," the man said, "I am now the majority shareholder and new chief executive of Premier Hotel Group."

A collective gasp rose up from Madeline's half of the table, but most of the directors up front did not look surprised. Madeline, however, fought against covering her mouth lest she groan out loud.

She had slept with her new boss.

"Yesterday morning," Lewis continued, "the Australian Securities and Investments Commission approved the corporate takeover I initiated a year ago. For those of you on the board who supported me, I thank you. For those who didn't—" he paused ominously as the assembled guests cast surreptitious glances toward the top of the table "—there is nothing I admire more than loyalty—to me. If you cannot commit to that, then you only have to make your position known and I will see that you get a fair termination package."

All eyes scrutinized the implacable faces of the directors of the board.

"As with any corporate takeover, we are embarking on a settling-in period," Lewis Goode continued. "There will be reviews, and all executives will be required to reapply for their jobs."

Her friend Kay turned to her, a look of dismay and apology on her face. Kay didn't realize it but she had more to apologize for than persuading Madeline to give up a perfectly good job to apply for the Premier Hotels position. She had also unwittingly provided the magical setting for Madeline's indiscretion last night.

But at the time, it had felt so uncannily right…

"Except," Lewis went on, "for the man I've replaced, Jacques de Vries, whose contract is terminated immediately." Again a gasp went around most of the table. Jacques de Vries was iconic, the founder of this massive global hotel company. "And—" Lewis paused and looked straight at Madeline, sending her nerves jangling in panic "—Madeline Holland, who will take up her position as COO, Australia and New Zealand division, as planned."

Madeline's breath huffed out and she tore her eyes from his face. Kay's somber expression lightened considerably, her relief evident that she hadn't persuaded Madeline to return to the Southern Hemisphere after twelve years away, only to be made redundant.

Madeline envied her friend her ignorance. How, she wondered, agonizingly close to tears, could she ever live this down?

Her gut jumped again as she realized Lewis Goode's eyes still bored into her face. Get me out of here, she prayed.

Lewis smiled thinly, as if he could clearly see the path of her thoughts. "Your reputation in operations and administration precedes you, Ms. Holland. Your first job will be to relocate the head office of Premier from Singapore to Sydney. I look forward to working closely with you on that."

Kay nudged her, smiling, but Madeline was still reeling from the force of his gaze and his smile; the inflection he placed on the word *closely*—and from the fact that he had just given himself away. *Your reputation precedes you...* So he had known exactly who she was last night.

Somehow she pasted a semblance of a smile onto her mouth and held it there, but confusion and a slow-burning anger nipped at the heels of her panic.

Finally Lewis took his eyes off her hot face. "I look forward to getting to know all of you over the next few days while we enjoy the annual Premier conference in this beautiful part of New Zealand's South Island. But now, I would like to talk to the board of directors, so if everyone else would kindly excuse us."

A flurry of chairs scraping and excited whispers ensued while everyone not at the head of the table rose and collected papers and briefcases. Madeline kept her head down and forced herself not to push as she made for the door. Thankfully, once outside, Kay was diverted by several colleagues, giving Madeline a chance to regroup and compose herself.

The delegates huddled around Kay. "Did you know about this?"

Kay shook her head. "I've heard rumors but I don't think anyone expected it so soon."

Madeline leaned against the wall, the conversation largely washing over her. Everyone wanted to know how this could have happened or, more important, how the powerful Jacques de Vries could have allowed it to happen.

Madeline couldn't care less about the former CEO. She wanted to know what the new CEO had been thinking of when he'd whisked her to bed last night. Unbidden, her mind bombarded her with myriad images of well-honed muscle and sinew over tanned skin, the feel of him wedged deep inside her body, his lips pulled back in a grimace of ecstasy.

She pressed against the wall, her nipples tingling with the memory. Twenty-eight years old and she hugged a wall, feeling ashamed and insignificant. She was transported back twelve years to another episode of her own making, the one that instigated her decision to leave her mother, friends and home town. Madeline had worked tirelessly to erase the insecure, inhibited girl she'd been. And she thought she'd been successful.

Oh, why had she let Lewis Goode seduce her last night?

Kay broke away from the group and turned to her. "I could use a drink," she muttered. "My office or the bar?"

Madeline pushed away from the wall. "Office." Anywhere, she thought, away from people.

"I'm sorry, hon. I didn't see this coming." Kay stopped at her secretary's desk and looked at Madeline. "Is chardonnay okay?"

Madeline nodded and Kay requested a bottle and two glasses be brought up from the bar.

They continued on into Kay's office.

"I should have warned you this was a possibility."

Madeline shrugged. How could she be anything but grateful to old school friend? While she'd been relentlessly climbing the corporate ladder, it was Kay who'd kept an eye on her mother, who notified her of the old woman's slide into Alzheimer's disease, who'd persuaded Madeline to apply for a job closer to home. She'd even organized her mother's move into the retirement village.

Kay plopped down behind her desk, gesturing for Madeline to sit. "I honestly thought—we all did—that Jacques was way too strong to let something like this happen. He started this company, you know." Kay raised her cell phone and began to text expertly. "Obviously the board of directors thought differently."

Madeline had never met the former CEO, but his name was legend in the hotel industry. Premier Hotel Group was largely Australasian but there were a smattering of hotels in the United States, where her old company, Global Hospitality, was based.

Kay's face brightened. "You must be relieved not to have to reapply. I wonder if that applies to regional managers."

"Your guess is as good as mine," Madeline murmured distractedly. "Tell me about Lewis Goode." After all, she only knew the little stuff, like the naked desire in his eyes as he'd slowly undressed her, the heat of his skin when she touched him. His clever hands and mouth… "I've heard his name, I think—" Not last night, she hadn't… "—but I didn't realize he had anything to do with the hotel industry."

"He doesn't, to my knowledge." Kay waved her fingers vaguely at the coffee table behind Madeline, where she kept her stash of business magazines. Madeline riffled through a couple.

Her heartbeat kicked up when Lewis Goode's

handsome, somber face stared up at her from the second magazine. She obviously read the wrong business publications. The face was unforgettable.

"He owns a lot of companies, notably Pacific Star Airlines," her friend went on. "Bought it for a song about five years ago, and now it's the second biggest airline in the Pacific."

Madeline stopped poring over the photo and flicked to the article, justifying her ignorance by acknowledging the geographical distance. After all, she'd been based in the States and came home rarely. And she'd only applied for the Premier job less than a month ago.

How did he know who she was? And why didn't he disclose his identity? Never mind that in the surreal ambiance of the Alpine Fantasy Retreat, the scene of last night's unexpected rendezvous, they'd playfully decided not to divulge any personal details to each other, including their names. What was he hoping to gain, apart from a cheap thrill? Madeline wasn't in a position to assist with the corporate takeover.

She was, however, in an unenviable situation. "Hopefully he'll play with his planes and leave the hotel business to those who know it."

"From what I've heard, he's sharp—a hands-on boss," Kay commented.

Oh, if only you knew, Madeline thought.

"It's me who should be worried," Kay said grimly. "Just between us—and since you're my new boss,

I'm trusting you, here—we're really struggling. Pray for a fantastic ski season."

Madeline stopped wallowing in self-pity long enough to take in her friend's words. Both women had started at the bottom and, over the years, worked their way up through the ranks, studying in their free time to get ahead. Madeline advanced her career with a different hotel chain, travelling, taking the postings no one else wanted, to reach a level of success she could only have dreamed about. Kay made regional manager last year after a decade in the trade, barring a year off when her twins were born.

"Even if things aren't great," Madeline reasoned, "he wouldn't be a very savvy CEO if he pulled Premier from the number-one tourist destination in New Zealand."

Queenstown's reputation as an adventure playground and ski resort gave it the happy dilemma that it didn't have an off season. There were literally hundreds of accommodation options to choose from in the tiny town. Premier, with its Waterfront, Lakeside and Mountainview Hotels, held prime positions in the town. In fact, when she and Kay started in the business, the three Premier Hotels were the single largest employer in town.

The door opened and Kay's secretary entered, carrying a tray with a bottle and two glasses. "There is a Mr. Lewis Goode outside to see you. He doesn't have an appointment."

Madeline's head rose so sharply, she heard her neck click. Here? She hurriedly rose, looking for a means of escape.

Kay exhaled noisily, raising her brows at Madeline. "Okay. Another glass, Felicity."

Please, please, let the earth swallow me now.

Lewis walked straight to Kay's desk, his hand outstretched and a semi-smile on his lips. Madeline hovered to the side, pressing her damp palms down her hips.

"I thought we should meet before the conference starts," Lewis said to Kay. "I understand you are the event organiser this year."

"Yes." Kay sounded almost relaxed. "Just one of my many talents. Have you officially met Madeline Holland?"

Lewis turned to Madeline and her heart leapt with velocity into her throat. His green eyes were cool and assessing, as opposed to hot and wanting. His mouth curved on one side in what she perceived to be a wolfish amusement.

"Not officially, no." He held out his hand. "Madeline."

She took his hand briefly, aware that hers probably felt like a damp squib. His was warm, dry and came with a businesslike squeeze, but when he released her, she felt the pressure remain as if he hadn't let go.

"You were at Global Hospitality for ten years, yes?"

Madeline nodded, afraid that to speak would be to squeak.

"What brought you to Premier?" he asked.

"I—" Madeline tried to swallow the lump of nerves lodged in her throat "—wanted to be closer to home."

He arched a brow. "Home?"

"My mother is in a retirement village here."

"Madeline and I grew up together," Kay put in helpfully. "In fact, we both started right here in the Premier Waterfront as part-time housemaids when we were sixteen."

Both his pale brows rose as he still looked down on Madeline's face. "I didn't know that."

The door behind them opened, and Kay's secretary entered, carrying another wineglass.

"You'll join us, I hope." Kay said. "We're having a welcome-home drink for Madeline."

For a few agonizingly hopeful seconds, Madeline thought he would decline. But then he turned to Kay, a smile warming his face. "If you're sure I'm not intruding."

"Not at all." She picked up the bottle and began to pour while Madeline focused on the amber liquid slipping into the bowl of the glass. Anything not to dwell on the widening smile on his face. She wondered if wolves, like cats, liked to play with their prey before delivering the killing blow.

"And are you enjoying your visit home so far, Madeline?" Lewis asked politely. To her it seemed his voice was full of intent, stroking over the syllables of her name, rendering it exotic, seductive, while she'd always considered it stuffy and old-fashioned.

But then his words sunk into her brain and she knew what he meant. *Did you enjoy last night, Madeline?*

Lewis Goode was going to milk this for all he was worth. She inhaled carefully and inclined her head on a neck that felt like a pole of steel.

Kay passed a glass of wine to each of them, her eyes lingering on Madeline's with a loaded look confirming her stuffed-dummy impression. She wrapped her fingers around her glass tightly, trying to erase the feel of his hand on hers.

Kay coughed. "Will you be staying for the conference, Mr. Goode?"

Smiling, Lewis turned away from Madeline. "It's Lewis. And yes, for a few days."

"Queenstown is the adrenaline capital of the world," Kay prattled on heroically. "I've organized some pretty wild activities, my way of getting some revenge on all you executives."

Lewis smiled. "We should enjoy that, shouldn't we, Madeline?"

Her head rose. "I'm on holiday at the moment." Her eyes slid away from the relentless green gaze and she sipped her wine. "I start on the first of next month."

Lewis's smile was polite, but she heard the steel in his voice. "Not too busy for the annual conference, I hope."

She bit down on a retort, but her heart sank. While Kay and her new boss chatted, she stood silently, ruminating on irony. All her hopes of reaching the pinnacle of success, a triumphant homecoming, dashed. If this got out—and it would get out—how could she face the people of Queenstown, her mother or her new staff in Sydney?

Lewis sipped his wine and enjoyed Madeline's discomfort, listening with one ear to Kay's prattling.

Madeline Holland was a world-class actress, he'd give her that. Even in the throes of indescribable passion, she'd given no indication she knew who he was. Jacques had chosen his seductress well.

But that was Jacques de Vries to a T. Always one step ahead of everyone else—until this morning.

Lewis took another satisfying draught of wine. Today was the culmination of two years of planning and hard work. He'd gotten most of the directors onboard months ago, but had been forced to cool his impatient heels while the government's business watchdog completed its investigation and agreed that the deal was sound and of full disclosure.

Jacques's apoplectic face swam before his eyes, and he almost smiled. Lewis wasn't a cruel man, but in this case, vengeance was sweet. Jacques had believed himself so strong, so untouchable that no one could harm him. He'd learned today that no one was bulletproof, especially those who surrounded themselves with toadies and people accustomed to jumping on the backs of the strong in order to feather their nests.

"You mistook their loathing for fear and respect, Jacques," he'd told the old man earlier, before ordering him out of his presidential suite and the hotel. "The directors were easy to sway."

He glanced at the uncomfortable woman standing two feet away, unwilling to meet his eyes. When he'd left her this morning, he'd forced her from his mind because there was work to be done. Now he indulged in a moment of reflection.

Her lashes and brows were dark, her hair a mane of silky gold, although it was pulled back into a neat knot now. An unusual beauty spot accentuated her high cheekbones and perfect honeyed skin. Lewis had pressed his lips to it while she slept when he'd left her this morning. He inhaled, all his senses remembering and warming to her elegant fragrance. Her thick brows knit together in perplexity, and she kept her cobalt-blue eyes directed at her feet.

Yes, Madeline Holland was memorable. He'd intended to keep her on after reading her file because of her reputation in the industry and the fact that she would have no loyalty to the old regime and would be easy to mould. Sleeping with her was a most unexpected and welcome bonus.

Lewis had known chemistry before, but Madeline's pull on his senses was easily the most intense of his life. He'd gone to the Alpine Fantasy Retreat to keep a low profile until today's meeting. When the Kiwi beauty sneaked into his private space, he'd played along with Jacques's silly ploy to send in his spy. He took his fill of her charms, again and again, and now had staked his claim for the company she worked for.

Satisfied beyond measure, Lewis widened his smile to include her. She'd earned her bonus and then some, although her panicked expression when he walked into the boardroom earlier had elicited a pang of sympathy from him. How was he supposed to know she'd be at the meeting? She wasn't listed on the Executive Committee.

Lewis realized Kay was waiting for him to answer a question and took his eyes off Madeline. "Sorry?"

Kay asked if he intended to utilize the speech time Jacques de Vries had been allocated at the Gala Opening the following night.

"Of course," he affirmed, "though I doubt I will be quite so long-winded." He checked his watch and set his half-empty glass down on the desk. Dusk bathed the lake outside Kay's office window in an eerie purple bruise. He knew the roads iced up early and it was a forty-minute drive to the Retreat. "Kay, I'd like to move into the top floor tomorrow. I hear the presidential suite is vacant." He ignored Madeline's sharp inhalation, but it confirmed his suspicions that she was probably accommodated in the hotel. "And I'd like you to find some time in your busy schedule over the next few days to discuss your operation here."

Lewis thanked her for the drink and said goodbye, saying he'd see them at the Gala Ball to open the conference tomorrow night.

Madeline's mumbled comment that she wasn't sure if she was going elicited a sound of dismay from Kay, but Lewis only nodded at both of them.

"I'll see you both there," he said firmly.

Two

The next night Madeline laid her knife and fork down and gazed around the ballroom of the Premier Waterfront Hotel. Kay's inspired midwinter Christmas theme dazzled, complete with a massive, sumptuously decorated tree. Large circular tables accommodated the five hundred delegates in front of a mezzanine stage. It was a visual masterpiece with stars overhead, a digitally generated cornucopia of ever-changing Christmas themes dancing around the walls, and columns of silver mesh lights hanging from the eight-meter ceiling.

Each of the ten-place, linen-clothed tables had a small Christmas tree as the centerpiece and gaily wrapped gifts at every place-setting. Kay had outdone herself, Madeline thought admiringly, watching her friend on the stage welcoming the guests as the formal part of the evening commenced. The banquet impressed everyone at her table, and the wines were top of the range.

Madeline looked around at the beautiful dresses and tuxedos of the high-powered executives from all over the world and knew she could never have organized such a glittering event. "She's wasted in hotels," she murmured to John, Kay's proud husband, seated beside her. "Event management is her forte."

She glanced over to the head table where Lewis Goode sat with the board of directors, waiting for Kay to introduce him. The rumors about the new CEO's plans for the town's hotels had already begun. Would he give her friend a fair hearing or had he made up his mind already about the reportedly unprofitable Queenstown hotels? She set her mouth grimly. He would have her to answer to if he tried to get rid of Kay.

The subject of her thoughts strode up onto the stage and shook Kay's hand warmly.

"Most events of this size," he began, "take an Olympic-size team of event coordinators to do what Kay has achieved with her small band of hotel staff. It is testament to the regard in which she is held in this community that she has been able to put everything together with such vision and style."

Beaming, Kay left the stage and took her place next to her husband and Madeline. For the first time, Lewis Goode faced most of the executives of his multinational corporation.

Madeline watched him captivate the crowd so intently for the next twenty minutes, you might have heard a pin drop in the huge ballroom. Despite her conflicted feelings, she couldn't help admiring his supremely confident bearing and impressive business knowledge. No one hearing him could doubt that he was a man with high expectations, who knew exactly where he was going. He urged everyone to work together with him to bring Premier once again to the forefront of the world-wide hotel industry.

"For too long," he said, "this company has been hamstrung by a few at the top living it up to the detriment of everyone. In the past few years, expansion has stalled, maintenance neglected, recruitment and training ignored. Join me in welcoming the winds of change." Judging by the applause this missive received, clearly most of the international delegates agreed with his assessment. Madeline wondered whether the local population would be so enthused with all this talk of change.

He left the stage to a rousing ovation, words like *charisma* and *magnetism* whispered enthusiastically around the tables.

"Wow!" Kay turned to her, rolling her eyes. "I'd follow him into battle any day."

Reluctantly Madeline agreed. How could she tell her friend she'd been burned with the same charisma and magnetism, but in a much more personal venue? Her shameful secret weighed like an anchor on her chest and she longed to share, but Kay had enough on her plate with the conference plus the threat of Lewis inspecting the hotels under her jurisdiction in the next day or two.

"Speaking of wow," Kay continued, pointing to Madeline's cocktail dress. "Would your mother approve of that dress, Madeline the Good?" They laughed at the high school nickname that had dogged her for years.

Madeline's mother owned the dubious distinction of being the town kook, dubbed the "Bible Lady" for her habit of standing on street corners haranguing people about the evils of liquor and sex. Madeline grew up being either ridiculed or pitied by her peers. Friends were discouraged, her school uniform draped her like a sack, and her mother cut her hair. As for makeup, her mother called that the devil's pride. The older she got, the more excruciating the teasing, but her mother seemed oblivious.

Madeline smoothed down the charcoal-satin cocktail dress, tugging at the bubble hem that stopped just above her knees. "You chose it," she grumbled, reminding Kay of their shopping trip last month when she'd come to Sydney to offer moral support for Madeline's interview.

"Relax. You look great," her friend said as Madeline fidgeted with the bodice that enhanced her modest cleavage. There was no sense regretting the purchase. Her belongings were en route from her last posting to the Darling Harbour Premier Hotel in Sydney, her bolthole until she found an apartment. She had nothing else suitable for a function like this.

Kay turned to speak to someone at the neighboring table. A strange prickle of unease skittered up Madeline's spine, as though someone was watching her. Involuntarily, her eyes drifted over to where Lewis sat with high-ranking members of the board of directors. His eyes raked her even as he bent his head toward one of his cronies and appeared to be listening intently.

Madeline looked away hurriedly and wondered how she could have made such a huge blunder. She *was* a good girl, who'd never escaped the inhibitions imprinted on her by her straitlaced mother. Her love life was a joke. Over the years, she'd worked insane hours to study for the qualifications she needed to win her impressive cache of promotions. Her professionalism kept temptation at bay in the office, and since work was her life, there were few other opportunities. Sexual encounters were rare, on vacation, away from any semblance of the familiar and anyone she may know. Sweet, short, and most of all secret.

Okay, technically she had been on holiday at the Alpine Fantasy Retreat, but to sleep with a stranger after knowing him only a few hours, with her home town just a few miles away, was stupid in the extreme.

Madeline was nothing like the woman Lewis Goode thought she was.

A band struck up on the stage, the lights dimmed, and the atmosphere changed from business to pleasure. Beside her, Kay and John conversed quietly. Madeline idly tapped the lip of her champagne flute against her mouth, looking around at her new colleagues, none of whom she knew. Perhaps she might slip away soon. She'd had little enough sleep at the retreat two nights ago, and her dreams last night were peppered with ominous images.

"Bored, Ms. Holland?"

Lewis Goode eased his long frame into the empty chair beside her, his presence instigating a flurry of nerves. She focused on steadying her hand as she set her glass down. "Not at all," she said with a sideways glance at Kay, who was still deep in conversation with her husband. "I was about to leave, actually."

Lewis frowned and glanced at his watch. "Before dessert and not even ten o'clock. Do we want to give the impression that the new COO is a lightweight?"

Her shoulders lifted—until she remembered the cleavage perpetuated by this dress. "I didn't intend staying long." Forcing her eyes up above his throat, she met his gaze.

His eyes crinkled at the corners. "It would be a shame to take that dress home without at least one twirl around the dance floor." He stood up and put his hand out.

Madeline closed her eyes briefly, wishing she was anywhere else in the world. His presence alone was enough to remind her of her lack of judgment. Spending one second in his arms with everyone watching would be torture.

But Lewis stood smiling easily, somehow knowing she wasn't the type to make a scene.

With a petulant sigh for his ears only, she stood and slid her arm through his, ignoring his hand. They walked stiffly to the dance floor.

As he turned her toward him and slid a hand around her waist, she successfully absorbed the wild palpitations in her chest at his touch, enough, she hoped, not to raise any eyebrows.

"Why are you doing this?" she asked quietly, focusing over his shoulder.

Lewis tilted his head toward her and she had to physically check herself from ducking back as a delicious wave of sexy male scent, familiar but forbidden, washed over her.

"Dancing with my COO?" he asked lightly. "We're the newbies here. Best we stick together."

Madeline listened carefully for some sardonic inflection or twist to his words but couldn't identify it.

"You have quite a reputation in this small town," he continued, his lips only centimeters from her ear.

Her heart took a dive. So he'd heard of her teenage

disgrace, the reason she'd left. Perhaps that was why he'd made a play for her at the retreat: a woman of loose morals and one he held a position of power over. Or possibly, he'd just heard about her mother's eccentricities.

"Everywhere I turn," Lewis said in a low voice, "people are saying 'little Miss Holland, hasn't she done well?'"

Madeline knew that most of them would have tacked "considering" onto the end of that, but a smile still ghosted over her lips. She'd kept away for years, wondering if she'd ever be accepted here. Landing the job based in Sydney, Australia, seemed like the best option. She could keep her distance, but still be close enough to rush home if her mother's health deteriorated.

Lewis leaned back slightly so he could look down into her face. "You're a little uptight tonight. Let's indulge in some party talk. Seen any good movies lately?"

Not fair! His sly reference to their first meeting at the Alpine Fantasy Retreat's private movie theatre, churned up a ripe pique that had her pressing her lips together.

Her vain hope that he may be as embarrassed as she about their sordid little fling was dashed. Lewis Goode did not believe in gallantry, obviously. Just like a man, she thought savagely. He clearly did not share her view that acting on something as primal as pure lust diminished both of them, not just her.

"Did you know who I was when you seduced me at the retreat?" she clipped out as he twirled her around.

Lewis's eyes warmed. "I seduced you? Hmm. I rather thought it was a mutual decision."

"Did you know?" she demanded in a fierce whisper.

He inclined his head. "I'd seen the executives files. You made a charming spy."

"What do you mean, spy?"

A steely glint flashed in his eye. "Come, Ms. Holland. Jacques put you there at the lodge to keep an eye on me."

Madeline somehow managed to keep moving, albeit stiffly. There was no way she wanted their colleagues to suspect there was anything more than a working relationship going on. But the bitter realization that he thought she was nothing more than Jacques de Vries's prostitute, lashed hard. "For your information, Mr. Goode, I never even met Jacques de Vries. The retreat was a welcome-home present from Kay. Ask her, if you don't believe me." Madeline arched slightly away from him, her stilted steps a lame excuse for dancing. How abhorrent that he thought she would sleep with him because her boss asked her to. She kept her eyes down, trying to swallow righteous anger and calm her breathing.

Lewis's grip on her fingers tightened and then his thigh nudged hers, blanking her mind with a speedy flush of sexual energy that seemed to flow from her to him and back again. Not now, she thought despairingly, when she needed her wits about her like never before.

He pulled her closer. "Dance," he muttered.

Somehow, she forced her feet to move, her spine to loosen, but she couldn't do much about the burn of hot blood to her cheeks.

Lewis inhaled deeply, his chest rising. "You must appreciate the coincidence," he said quietly, close to her ear. "No one knew I was in town. I planned to keep a low profile until the meeting, and there you were."

"My key…" she whispered heatedly, but what was the point? He knew she'd left her key on the seat in the theatre and that is what led to their portentous meeting.

While she strove for composure, he ducked his head and looked into her eyes for several moments. Then he straightened, sighing. "All right, in the interests of forging an amicable working relationship with my right-hand man, as it were, I'll give you the benefit of the doubt." He shrugged nonchalantly. "Consider it forgotten."

"Forgotten?" If only! "Forgotten that you had me at a disadvantage by knowing my identity while not revealing yours?"

His arm tightened around her waist again, bringing his body so close, she felt the muscles shift and ripple in his upper thighs.

"No names, remember?" He smiled tightly. "I believe that was your idea."

Madeline blinked. He was right. In a mind splintered by reckless sexual attraction, she'd suggested they play along with the magical spell the place cast and not divulge identities or personal details. The only direct question she'd asked was if he lived in Queenstown. He was obviously Australian and he told her he was here on business.

That was all she'd wanted to know. What he did, who his loved ones were, what consequences there might be of a coupling based on lust only, did not interest her. She knew within minutes of meeting him that they would finish the day in her big four-poster bed. They'd walked, talked, eaten dinner and drunk wine. It was five hours before he kissed her the first time. Shortly after that, she drowned in passion.

It sounded tawdry, but it hadn't been that way, not one minute of it. Not at the time. "Are you—are you going to tell?"

He raised his brows. "Kiss and tell, you mean?" His eyes drifted to her mouth and lingered there. "You must admit, it gives me some leverage, and I could use an ally."

Madeline blanched and tried to tug her hand away, but Lewis tightened his grip, indicating the other dancers with his chin.

"If idle gossip distresses you, I suggest you stop making a scene and make this dance look slightly more as if we are newly acquainted business colleagues."

Madeline stilled, hating the fact that he spoke sense. Breathe, she ordered herself. Move.

"That's better," he murmured, still not looking at her.

She willed her body to relax, and it obeyed and flowed in the direction he took them. Lewis was a good dancer, but she already knew that from the other night. They'd danced to a different tune then, a slow-moving soul number that brought sultriness into a cabin deep in snow-covered mountains. The memory of it, coupled with the heat of his hand around her waist, his thigh nudging hers, made her tingle and burn.

How was she ever to work with this man when his every look and touch reminded her of what they'd done? Overwhelmed by his magnetism, she hated herself for wanting him as she did.

"This isn't going to work," she muttered, not caring whether he heard or not.

Lewis smiled grimly. "You're better than that, Madeline. You didn't get to where you are by being lily-livered."

Maybe not, but she'd never felt an attraction of this magnitude before.

"Besides," he went on, lowering his head so his mouth brushed her ear, sending a shiver through her. "I think I have self-control enough to keep my hands to myself in the office. And if I can't, then we'll just have to alter your job description."

Bastard!

She injected some steel into her spine, knowing if she didn't stand up for herself now, she didn't have a hope of having a career in his company. And she wanted that, more than anything—didn't she? "My position is confirmed, Mr. Goode. You said so yourself."

"As I recall, you can be quite flexible when it comes to your—position."

Something in her died. There was no respect here. There never would be. Madeline stepped back, dragging her hand from his. Who cared what their colleagues thought? His colleagues, she amended silently. "This really isn't going to work. You will have my resignation in the morning."

She turned abruptly and strode away from him as fast as she could in three-inch heels, pausing only long enough to snatch her purse off her table and give a terse nod at a surprised-looking Kay.

She stalked from the ballroom, but seeing Kay brought the realization home of what she was giving up. What had she done? Her dream job, the prize for which she'd worked so hard. How could she be so stupid, so spineless, to let him goad her into resigning?

It surprised her that he could be so callous. They'd talked, too, at that Alpine retreat, it wasn't just sex. Only in the most general terms: what they wanted, what was stopping them, likes and dislikes. How could he listen to her hopes and dreams and make love to her with such absorbing intensity, and now treat her like a plaything?

Her heels clicked sharply on the marble floor of the hotel foyer as she made for the bank of elevators. She clutched her evening purse in a death grip, imagining her fingers around his neck, squeezing hard. But really, her anger and humiliation were directed at herself. What man would turn down a willing partner in a no-strings fling? And even now, blinded by dismay and disappointment, she still wanted him, wanted him to want her.

The elevator doors swished open and she stepped inside, desperate to be alone. But suddenly, Lewis was there, his broad shoulders taking up all the space, squeezing through the closing doors and looming purposefully over her. Making her dizzy with shock and excitement.

"Oh, no, you don't," he muttered. "You don't walk away from me. And don't even *think* about resigning. I won't have it."

Shocked at his audacity, she could only stare and try not to quail at the storm in his eyes.

"The people of this town will suffer—your friend Kay will suffer—if you do anything stupid like resigning."

Her mouth dropped open. "Wh-what? How?"

His tone was grim. "You think I care about a few run-down hotels at the bottom of the world? I will close these three hotels like that!" He snapped his fingers under her nose.

Behind him the elevator doors closed and silence descended, except for the sound of her heart pounding. Since neither had pressed the buttons, this car was going nowhere. Just like her career.

"You wouldn't." She hardly recognized her own voice, thin and thready.

"That's where you're wrong," he grated. "Premier's name in this town is a standing joke. We'd be better off cutting our losses."

Madeline knew she had to clear her head, take stock, think! Or else her friend would really have something to worry about. But his proximity in the confined space set her heart thundering in excitement.

"What do you want?" she whispered.

"What do I want?" His voice softened considerably by the end of the short sentence. The light in his eyes changed to something even more dangerous than his threats to close the hotels. More dangerous because she'd seen it before, just before he kissed her for the first time.

As if to underscore the point, his hand lifted to brush her cheek, telling her what she'd just finished admitting to herself.

"You've already had that," she whispered hoarsely, praying she'd be able to resist.

"Did you really think that one night was ever going to be enough?" The tip of his tongue flicked out to lick his bottom lip while he stared at her mouth hungrily.

"You despised me when you thought I was Jacques's prostitute," she told him, holding on to her control, the last vestige of anger by a thread. "Now you want me to be your exclusive prostitute?"

"Strange, isn't it?" He stepped forward, breaching

her last defense. "I keep thinking walk away, but then I see you, get close enough to touch and smell…"

Her heart pitched to the ceiling, then settled back down as an ominous fatalism told her she wouldn't—couldn't—resist. Not when he was this close, taking her air, her power of thought and reason. It was as if she was his to command.

Surely she was above this?

Then the elevator lurched, pitching her toward him. Her arm bumped his side and her nose nearly ended up in the middle of his chest. Fizzy excitement imploded in her chest, and her hands rose involuntarily to ward him off, somehow found his hands, and felt her fingers lace through his. Cool against warm, large against slender, firm against soft.

"And I think," he continued softly, "just one more touch, one more kiss…"

His lips were just millimeters away now, his breath wafting over her face. The pulse in her throat skittered violently. Her eyes and thought blurred as his face descended, but she was aware enough to know she lifted her chin to meet him. Parted her lips slightly to meet his, just like before.

And when they touched, it was as exhilarating as she remembered, maybe more so because of the absolute taboo of it. Her boss, the public arena, the air of entitlement that emanated from every pore in his body.

He took her lips hard, greedily. Her eyelids fluttered closed and her fingers curled more firmly around his, tugging him closer.

His mouth devoured hers and the heat of his body surged through him into her. She kissed back, absorbing the shock to her system, accepting the danger. The warm slick taste of him exploded through her, mingled with the wine, her want, his primal need. Helplessly trapped in mindless lust, his arms were the only place she wanted to be.

His tongue slid across hers, erotic and intoxicating. She pressed against him, tugging her hand out of his grasp so she could touch him, run her hands up his long, broad back and up over strong shoulders to the skin above his collar.

He slapped one palm on the wall beside her head and leaned into her, pressing all the way down her body. Then his free hand plunged into her hair, tugging at the comb that held it back. She heard a tinny clink as it fell, felt the cool sweep of her hair on her bare shoulders before he bundled up a huge handful of it in his fist and gently coaxed her head back to expose her throat. Then his hot mouth moved down, burning her skin as it tracked her throat, sucking on the frenzied thump-thump of her pulse, lower to the crease between her breasts, where he stilled and inhaled deeply for a moment.

His hands stroked firmly down her back to her bottom. He spread his fingers wide and dug his fingers in, rendering her as weak as a kitten as he pressed her firmly against him. His eyes fierce and hot, he captured her mouth again, and she met him, tongues thrusting, hips grinding and hands tangling in hair.

Just like the first time, she met him all the way.

The elevator dinged.

Three

Reality returned with a crash. In the hum and downward pressure of the car braking, Madeline pulled back jerkily, wrenching her eyes away from him. Unfortunately, as she moved to maneuver around him, she caught the whole grotesque thing on the mirrored wall of the elevator. Lipstick smeared, hair tangled. Somehow the skirt of her cocktail dress seemed hitched high up on thighs that visibly trembled.

Self-disgust and fear of being caught kept her moving. She hurriedly pushed her dress down and then ran a hand through her hair, dragging it down in the forlorn hope that it may look as if it started that way. Lewis bent and retrieved the comb from the floor and handed it to her. She couldn't look at him.

Out of the fry pan and into the fire! She was never going to be able to work with him, precisely because she was never going to be able to resist him. Every time he clicked his fingers, she'd come running.

The door opened on her floor and a young couple got in. Madeline shoved past them, rummaging in her purse for her key. When she heard a step behind her, her heart plummeted even lower. This was his floor, too, since he was staying in the Presidential Suite just down the hall.

She felt him come up behind her, and the keycard wobbled in her hands. She dropped it and had the ignominy for a second time of seeing Lewis Goode retrieving something of hers. *Pick up my fallen pride while you're there,* she thought despairingly.

She held out her hand for the card. Lewis leaned against the wall, looking amused. "Aren't you going to invite me in?"

Wordlessly she shook her head, her arm still stretched out for the keycard. She'd met women who'd fallen from grace in the workplace. They were sad cases, reduced to positions well below their ability because of a lack of respect. Men got away with it, but sleeping around was the death knell for a woman's ambition. And sleeping with the boss was a sure-fire way to get any other female executives in the organization off-side, not just the men.

Lewis lifted his arm, his eyes darkening to forest green with what could be disappointment, and swiped her card through the lock. "I meant what I said. If you resign from Premier at this stage, there will be consequences. The future of these hotels rests on your shoulders."

Madeline put a steadying hand on the door so that it opened a mere inch. "I don't see how we're going to get past this."

Lewis pushed away from the wall and handed her the card. "What we do or don't get up to in private is no one's business but our own. I need you onboard to teach me the hotel industry. From what I've seen and heard, the operation in this town is in trouble. You can attempt to persuade me otherwise, or your friend and ex-neighbors can look for another employer. Closing these three unprofitable hotels would free up a lot of cash to put towards the new head office in Sydney."

"Sleep with you or everyone gets the chop? Is that it?"

"No. Sleeping with me is optional and should be done because you want to. Resign and everyone gets the chop."

The elevator dinged again, and Madeline pushed the heavy door to her suite open and rushed in. She sagged against the door, breathing heavily. He'd laid it on the line. The choice was hers. And what a choice.

* * *

The next morning she had a headache for real as a consequence of how little sleep she'd had in days. As galling as it was, she peeked through the peephole before exiting her room and took the stairs instead of the lift. The memory of herself in the mirrored wall of the elevator was a great motivator for exercise.

Her mother liked to nap in the afternoons, so Madeline generally visited during the mornings and evenings. Often she found her watching television, something Madeline was rarely allowed to do when growing up for fear of being corrupted. The Alzheimer's disease had taken years to set in, but now it seemed that with every visit, her mother was less cognizant and often did not recognize her.

Today she patted Madeline's sleeve, sniffing about her "fancy threads."

"Plain cooking, plain clothes, plain hard work," was an oft-repeated phrase in the Holland house. Tasteless food and drab, shapeless clothes colored Madeline's recollections. But it hadn't always been like that.

"You used to have a dress this color." She took her mother's leathery hand and placed it on the arm of her midnight-blue sweater. "I remember you and Dad took me somewhere, and how pretty you looked."

Her mother's face smoothed out a little in wistful remembrance. "We went to a wedding dance. The Robinsons'. You were five."

"You and Dad danced."

Her mother blinked several times, a faraway look glistening in her rheumy old eyes. Madeline's heart swelled and she felt a girlish certainty that she hadn't dreamed the good times. She'd been the apple of her parents' eyes until her father had died.

"They divorced, you know," her mother muttered, her face lapsing into its customary censure, thin lips pressed together. "Who didn't see that coming? Their wedding was the only time they ever entered the house of God."

Madeline sighed. It hadn't been all bad, but the reminiscences were few and far between—and of short duration.

"Get me my spinning wheel, Nurse," Mrs. Holland ordered, peering at her tetchily. "Idle hands…"

She had a nasty cold, and soon succumbed to a violent coughing fit that racked her small frame, and Madeline sat her up, patting her on the back. For the first time, her mother seemed fragile. Had she lost weight?

"Has the doctor been today?" she asked the nurse after half an hour of unsuccessfully persuading her mother to have a cup of tea. "She doesn't look good at all."

"The doctor does his rounds tomorrow," the nurse told her. "We'll keep a close eye on her, and if her temperature rises or there is any change, we'll call the doctor."

"And me," Madeline said firmly, checking that they had her cell phone number.

Next she drove out to her family farm on the outskirts of town. She had finally chosen a real estate agent to market the property. A lot of the big stuff had been disposed of last weekend in a garage sale. Now she had to finish packing her mother's clothes and personal effects and clean the place from top to bottom before it could officially go on the market.

Clearly, from the state of the house and the grounds, her mother had not been coping for some time to keep on top of the maintenance. Feeling uncharacteristically nostalgic, Madeline wandered the house and the surrounding outbuildings. Much of the land had been sold off when her father died over twenty years ago, the victim of a freakish farm accident.

Her poor mother, out here all alone while the house crumbled around her. What sort of a daughter was she? She sat on the window sill of her old room, looking out at one of the most stunning vistas she had ever seen, and she had seen a few.

Madeline was a late child, her parents well into their forties when she was born. If only she'd been a boy, or had the slightest interest in taking over the running of the farm that had been passed down from her great-grandfather.

But after her father died, her mother's pious disapproval of and disappointment in her daughter seeped into every corner of the house. Madeline dreamed of escape and freedom from the time she hit puberty.

Her cell phone rang and she answered it on the first ring, thinking of her mother and her poor cough.

"Madeline?" the deep male voice said while she tried to identify the number. "Lewis. Kay gave me your number. Where are you?"

The peace and nostalgia she'd gathered shattered. "At my mother's house."

"There is a workshop I want you to attend in Meeting Room Three in twenty minutes. Be here."

He hung up.

Madeline slid off the window sill, cursing softly. Who the devil did he think he was? She was on holiday, dammit. Checking her watch, she ran out to the car, muttering about his peremptory tone and unfair expectations, but years of professionalism triumphed. She'd changed from her jeans and walked into that meeting only one minute late.

Lewis's head rose and he tracked her all the way to her seat. Ignoring him, she looked at the information screen at the front of the room.

A symposium on eco-waste in the hotel industry? Concealing her irritation, she compressed her lips together and hoped she wouldn't doze off. It was bad enough she was here when she hadn't even officially started work yet, but he could have chosen something a little more scintillating.

For the next hour she listened, fuming inwardly. But suddenly Lewis turned to her. "Madeline, our COO, has managed many hotels overseas. Perhaps she could enlighten us on how other countries manage their waste."

Her heart skipped a beat, but she somehow managed to cover her dismay. "I have nothing prepared."

"Wing it," he suggested.

Madeline pursed her lips, trying to see past the benign gaze to what lurked in his mind. Was he testing her? Perhaps he wanted her to fail.

Madeline would not let him win. She rose, cleared her throat, and spoke for ten minutes, and it wasn't until she took her seat again, to a smattering of polite applause, that she felt the sweat cooling on her back.

At the end of the session, she rose to follow the others out of the room, but Lewis raised his head and his brows, halting her. She reluctantly slid back down into her seat.

"Well done," he said simply when they were alone.

Madeline exhaled, thinking she deserved more than that. "Was that a test?"

He shrugged. "A test?" His lips pursed thoughtfully. "Or punishment for bunking off today?" Then he rested his chin on his hands and looked at her intently. "Or maybe I was just bored and wanted something nice to look at."

Madeline swallowed her swelling temper. "As you know, I'm not due to start till the first of next month.

I need to be excused from the conference to make arrangements for my move to Sydney."

Lewis turned away from her as if he was bored and snibbed his briefcase. "There are four more days of conference left and as my COO, I expect you to attend all relevant workshops and activities. You will still have two weeks to make your arrangements when the conference closes."

She inhaled carefully. Anger nibbled at the edges of her control, but she could do this. She'd earned her position and was the consummate professional. He wanted a reaction? She wouldn't give him the satisfaction.

If Lewis was disappointed with her lack of response, he didn't show it. He glanced at his watch and stood.

"Come on, we don't want to miss the—" he peered at the program in his hand "—Things Get Personnel lecture in the auditorium."

"I have an appointment this afternoon." She was supposed to meet the real estate agent at the farm in an hour.

"Reschedule," he told her and then he smiled at her. The warmth of it hit her right in the solar plexus. Pure pleasure curled her toes, and her own lips twitched. She remembered that smile from their illicit night together. He hadn't been so stingy with his smiles that night.

"I love HR people, don't you?" he asked, still grinning. "Things Get Personnel…" He walked out ahead of her, chuckling, while she gathered her things and followed, hiding her own reluctant smile.

The next three days passed in a blur as Lewis insisted she attend every workshop, meeting and cocktail function going, as well as the team-bonding activities Kay had organized. Madeline may have been brought up here, but she'd never tried any of the myriad adventure activities on offer, although she had learned to ski passably in Europe.

They jet-boated the Shotover River, twisting and turning through frighteningly narrow canyons. There was skiing and luging and one crazy moment where she mentally said goodbye to the world as she was strapped into a flimsy chest and seat harness and swung out over a gaping canyon a hundred meters up, screaming her head off at 150 kilometers an hour.

She accepted every dare, every challenge because that's what she'd learned you had to do to get ahead. She may not have been the most proficient skier or the fastest on the luge, but she would die rather than let her colleagues see her back down. Especially Lewis. Perhaps because of the way they started, she wanted his respect, first and foremost.

And darn it, it was fun!

But all this activity was exhausting. She spent her evenings rushing from cocktail functions to visits with her mother, who was still bedridden with a cold, and to the farm to pack and clean. To save time, or perhaps to avoid running into Lewis outside conference activities, she spent some nights at the farm in her old room, but retained her hotel suite.

Finally the last day of the conference dawned. She dressed warmly for the programmed tandem skydiving, but Lewis announced that he would treat four volunteers to a helicopter ride to the West Coast for a spot of underground caving.

Madeline was pretty sure she'd prefer the wide-open sky to crawling around in dank, dark caves. But Lewis's eyes swiveled straight to her while several other executives vied for the opportunity. The challenge glowed in his eyes and so, against her better judgment, she joined the group.

It started off so well. The helicopter ride was fantastic, and the 130-meter abseil down into the cave presented no problems. Once underground, they used wire ladders to access rifts and waterfalls, but after only half an hour, Madeline felt a deathly fear looming up on her in the darkness. She didn't think anything could surpass the fear of the canyon swing yesterday, but she was wrong.

She began to sweat, a cold sweat that trickled down her back and slicked the chin strap of her helmet. Her chest constricted like a crushing weight. Every step was torture and she began to lag, just a few steps behind the others, but not far enough that she couldn't see them. What was happening to her? The walls of the cave and the dark pressed in on her until her vision diminished to a tiny white spot ahead of her.

She couldn't lose it now, could she? Fighting down a numbing panic, she concentrated on just putting one foot in front of the other, as they squeezed through tiny spaces, navigated waterfalls. It was a nightmare Madeline could not wake up from. She was drenched in cold clammy breath-stealing panic.

Suddenly Lewis's voice filtered through her, calm and reassuring. "You're all right. Take some deep breaths." He loosened her chin strap.

She tried to breathe, but sweat poured down her face, and she felt a scream start to wind its way up from her chest.

Lewis slipped his arm around her shoulder and gave her a brief hug. "I'll get you out. Wait here just a minute." He jogged ahead and spoke briefly to the guide. Madeline felt so afraid and so sick that she wasn't even embarrassed at showing herself up. Then Lewis was back, guiding her out of the loathsome hole, holding her hands when space allowed, all the while talking in low, soothing tones.

Finally they were out in the fresh air and Madeline tore her helmet off and turned her face up to the weak winter sun. Lewis pulled her down to the ground and pushed her head down between her knees, ordering her to breathe.

Furious, but relieved that her breathing was finally calming and a little color returned to her deathly pale face, Lewis kept pushing her head down between her drawn-up knees.

"What did you tell the guide and the others?" she asked, wiping her face.

"I said you'd sprained your ankle," he said tersely. "Why the hell didn't you say you were afraid? Christ, are you so concerned with your precious reputation, you'd risk your life just so no one will think you're scared?"

Madeline blinked at him. "I didn't know. I've never been caving before."

Lewis hesitated, remembering she had admitted as much in the helicopter. "Well, what is it then? Are you afraid of the dark? Confined spaces?"

She shook her head, looking confused. "No, but I can't remember ever being in both at the same time." She covered her face, still trembling. "Please, Lewis, I'm sorry I ruined your trip, just go back and leave me alone. I'm fine now."

"You're not fine," Lewis said gruffly. "Look at you, shaking like a leaf, drenched in sweat."

And yet, still so appealing, he thought wryly. What a sicko he was.

She fumbled with the domes of her overalls. Lewis reached forward and tapped her hands away, popping the domes himself. "The guide said there's a first-aid kit in the truck. I suppose I'd better bandage you up, since you'd die if anyone knew you're not perfect."

He went to the car for the kit, leaving her to scramble

out of the overalls. Why had he pushed her so hard? He knew she was competitive, would never back down from a challenge. Hell, he'd known that from day one.

Madeline sat stiffly while he bandaged her fake sprained ankle for the benefit of her pride. She was pale and subdued on the flight back to Queenstown. Did she really think Lewis gave a damn about one small phobia? That anyone would give a damn? She was flesh and blood, not a superwoman.

"Meet me at ten tomorrow outside the Waterfront."

She halted on her way across the car park, dark shadows under her eyes. "The conference is over. Aren't you going home?"

"I have one last job for you." A job that would test her loyalty. At least, that was the excuse he gave himself. But wasn't it really because he just wanted to spend more time with her?

Lewis was relieved to see she looked fully recovered from her ordeal the next morning, and as vibrant and beautiful as ever.

"Get in," he said, opening the door of his rental. "We're touring the Mountain View and Lakefront Hotels."

Madeline stared at him over the roof of the car. "Is Kay coming?"

Lewis shook his head and got into the car.

"Shouldn't we at least inform her?" she asked, worry tinting her voice.

"I'm meeting with her at one to go over the financial situation." Lewis pulled out of the car park. "I want to see the hotels through your experienced eyes. Are they a quick fix or a hopeless cause?"

"Can't I at least warn her? I feel disloyal, both as her COO and as her friend."

Lewis parked at the Premier Mountainview Hotel, shut off the ignition and faced her. "You are about to take over the running of 150 hotels," he told her sternly. "Have you got what it takes, Madeline?"

Her head rose sharply and she turned in her seat to face him. "Yes," she said firmly.

He thought so, too. "Good enough." He snapped off a nod, pleased with her. "Shall we get started?"

Lewis had been so busy enjoying himself, watching her rise to anything he could throw at her, he'd neglected his responsibilities. Yes, he probably was breaking with etiquette not pre-warning the regional manager of an inspection, but he wanted to see where his COO's loyalty and responsibility lay. His knowledge of the business was sketchy enough without wondering if he could trust her.

They spent an hour at the Premier Mountainview Hotel. By the time they left, his mood was as grey as the flaking paint on the wall that ran around the building. The hotel had worryingly low occupancy, worn facilities and a cleanliness issue, although the building was so poorly maintained that it was difficult to define dirt on the cracked and crumbling surfaces. He had a spirited conversation with the manager about the elevators' expired warrant of fitness. As they left, a backpacker bus pulled up and people began alighting.

"About all it's good for," Lewis snarled.

They drove on to the Lakefront. "We'll lunch there," he decided. "I don't know that I have the stomach for any more substandard rooms and bathrooms."

"You have to remember," Madeline cajoled as they studied an uninspiring menu, "Kay only took over fourteen months ago, and her first job was to completely overhaul the Waterfront—a necessity because the conference had been awarded there."

"Premier is four star and above," Lewis told her. "No way in hell either of these qualify." He stared around at the nearly empty restaurant.

"We're early for lunch," she said, following his gaze.

"Or everyone knows something we don't." He leaned back and fixed the waitress with a stare. "May we have some water, please?"

Madeline raised her brows.

"We sat down seven minutes ago," he told her curtly, looking at his watch. "What do you think of the menu?"

She skimmed the cheaply laminated card, grimacing as her finger wiped over something sticky. "A little—tired."

"Bloody comatose."

"Lewis, you referred to mismanagement on a grand scale at the Gala Ball." Madeline leaned forward earnestly. "Kay's predecessor blew his entire maintenance budget on schmoozing important people in the bid for the annual conference, and then splashed out on a whole new troop of courtesy vehicles."

"I'm also aware," Lewis interrupted, "that Kay was manager of the Waterfront at the time. She should have reported it."

Madeline's smile was loaded with cynicism. "I never met Jacques, but I do know the hotel industry. It's the old-boy network, nothing to do with talent or accountability. Reporting him would have killed Kay's career stone dead."

The waitress arrived with water and took their orders.

"Kay had to make a decision," Madeline continued when she'd gone. "She had no choice about the conference, it had already been awarded. So she threw what little she had left into refurbishing the Waterfront."

Lewis had some sympathy. He liked Kay and he was impressed with the Waterfront. Rooms, restaurants, service and conference facilities were world class. But then, he was a novice in the hotel industry.

The food came and, as he expected, it was mediocre in the extreme.

"You have a good rep in this industry," he told her. "Tough, but fair, capable, motivating. We have a lot of work to do because change has to start from the top."

He picked up his fork, looked at his plate and put his fork down again.

"What do you think?" he asked Madeline.

She pushed some limp salad around her plate. "Not great."

Lewis called the waitress over again. "Would you take us to meet the chef, please?"

Twenty minutes later they were back in the car and heading for the Waterfront Hotel. He'd had a few choice words for the chef, who looked as if he would enjoy taking a meat cleaver to Lewis's head, but Madeline had smoothed things over, telling the man she'd gone to school with his daughter.

It took quite a lot to rattle Madeline Holland, he thought admiringly. In fact, he'd only seen her truly rattled once—apart from the caving incident. And he blamed himself there for pushing her too hard.

Whereas rattling her in the elevator had been all pleasure.

They walked into the lobby, and Madeline turned toward Kay's office, but Lewis led her to the elevator.

"One last little job," he said as the doors closed behind them. "The Presidential Suite here. Have you seen it?"

She shook her head.

"It's supposed to be the best there is in all of Premier's suites."

"I'm sure it is," Madeline murmured. "Everything Kay's done here at the Waterfront has been top quality."

"Nevertheless, I'd like your professional assessment."

She nodded and Lewis pressed the button for the top floor. "I have very fond memories of this elevator," he commented lightly as they began to move.

Madeline pursed her lips and looked at him coolly. But then somehow their eyes tangled in memory of hot mouths and busy hands and the silky feel of the skin on her bare arms. He watched her swallow, careful and controlled, almost imperceptible. They carried on in silence, but neither of them looked away.

Lewis unlocked his door, stood back and gestured for her to precede him. But he stopped her in the doorway, dropping his hands lightly on her shoulders. "First impressions?" he murmured, watching his breath lift a strand of her hair.

She jerked forward a step or two. "Uh, light and airy. Spacious." She walked fully into the living area, seemingly gathering threads of composure as she settled into her work.

"The drapery is nice, rich but understated, furnishings elegant and fresh." She turned, looking at the small kitchenette. "First-class appliances—clean. Well-stocked mini-bar. The freezer could use some attention." She walked around the suite, ticking off boxes in her head, dragging it out until there was nothing left, but to go through to the bedroom.

Lewis was hardly listening, standing back and

watching her lips move, but too steeped in admiration to take note. And anyway, he already knew that the suite was impressive.

She was impressive. These last few days, she'd filled all the spaces of his mind, every waking moment. Her skin was like cocoa butter, rich and creamy with a golden luminescence. Ever since the skiing trip a couple of days ago, when she'd worn a pure-white ski jacket, he'd had this burning desire to see her in white again, the contrast between that and her golden skin and intense blue eyes.

"Bathroom?" She turned, jolting him back to the present.

"Through the bedroom."

Lewis wondered five minutes later how long one could wax lyrical about a bathroom's finer points, but he sensed a reluctance for her to move on to the bedroom.

That feeling was certainly not reciprocated. Every cell in his body was on high alert. Enclosed in this suite, he wanted her with more intensity than he'd ever experienced. He'd sorely neglected his love life lately, but the instant he laid eyes on Madeline Holland, his love life had re-established itself in his mind rather insistently. Their one night together had only intensified the ache of desire.

She turned and almost ran into him as he crowded the doorway. Lewis stepped back to let her pass, and their eyes met and hers skittered away, but not before he saw the awareness in their blue depths, the tension in her smooth jaw.

"The bedroom," Madeline sighed.

Furniture…Manchester…wardrobe…check, check, check. She rattled off the amenities like a shopping list and at a gallop, and he smiled because he knew he could affect her this way.

"You know, these are some of the best refurbishments I've seen anywhere," she gabbled, moving toward the door. She paused. "Wow, great entertainment center."

Lewis chuckled. "I never could understand the need for television in bed. I'm either asleep or—I'm not."

Madeline blushed but raised her chin and looked him straight in the eye. "Won't you be late for your appointment with Kay?"

He saw her out and came to a decision that had been skirting around his mind for days. He would have Madeline Holland again or he'd never get her out of his system. He had to know if that one perfect night was a one-off or if they could recreate it. One last night, he reasoned, to prove it was just sex, and then they could both get on with their jobs and their lives.

Four

It seemed every time she ventured into town, someone recognized her and stopped to talk. Madeline had just decided she didn't know the woman in front of her in the supermarket queue, but then she turned and smiled. It was her English teacher from high school.

The woman asked after her mother and then suggested Madeline give a talk to the pupils on career paths. "It's always nice to see one of ours doing so well for herself."

Madeline's heart squeezed in pleasure. That was the second invitation this week. The president of the Queenstown Women in Business Association had called a few days ago to ask her to speak at their next meeting on how to succeed in the corporate world. Madeline had a sneaking suspicion Kay might have put her up to it, but she couldn't help being pleased.

Motivational speaking was something she enjoyed immensely and was lucky enough to be asked to do, two or three times a year. These small overtures warmed her heart, given they were made by people who hadn't seen her in years and probably never thought she would amount to much.

"What do you think of your new boss?"

Madeline smiled. The million-dollar question.

That was another thing the people of this town seemed obsessed by. Lewis had ruffled quite a few feathers with all his talk of change and impromptu hotel inspections. "I haven't had a lot to do with him so far," she told her ex-teacher. "I don't actually take up the position for a few weeks."

"People say he doesn't have the best interests of the town at heart."

Kay had mentioned the hotel-staff tearooms were abuzz with rumors about the threat of closures and redundancies. It seemed everyone knew someone or had a relative working at one or the other of the hotels. It would be a pity if the locals felt the same reserve toward her just because of who she worked for.

She said her goodbyes and was loading her groceries into the car when her cell phone rang.

It was the man himself, asking her to meet him at the new Ice Bar in town. She decided to walk, grumbling to herself that the conference was over and he had no right to any more of her time. But her step quickened, as did her pulse at the thought of seeing him again.

An attendant handed her a fur-hooded parka and gloves, told her there was a time limit of thirty minutes and a drink limit of three cocktails, the first of which was complimentary in the price of the entry fee.

The bar itself took her breath away, and not only because of the freezing temperature. She walked into a huge cavern where everything was made of ice. Walls, the bar, high tables and stools, even a sofa made of ice and covered in animal skins. Candles and a stunning ice chandelier supplied the lighting. At three in the afternoon, it was surprisingly low-key, but because everyone wore the same ice garb, it took a minute to track Lewis down. He sat in a corner, contemplating the wall while tapping a pen on the icy counter top.

Madeline held back for a moment before he registered her presence. She sipped her cocktail through a straw and wondered what he was thinking about. Her primary concern was his meeting with Kay, but beneath the layers of cold air and the clean taste of the vodka warming her belly, a hollow feeling stirred. This may be the last time she'd see him until she arrived at the Sydney office.

Something inside her wanted more than that, even just a final acknowledgment of the night they'd shared. Since then, he'd infuriated her, tested her, and for the last few days, showed signs that he respected her. But maybe their night together meant little to him. Another night, another executive warming his bed.

Lewis looked up and saw her and she stepped forward, putting all her fanciful thoughts to the back of her mind. "Only you would hold a business meeting in minus five degrees."

He raised his chin and met her gaze. "The conference is over. You and I are on holiday."

Madeline decided not to remind him she was supposed to have been on holiday the whole of the last week.

She slid onto the stool beside him. "How was your meeting with Kay?"

"Ominous," he said, folding his arms. "But I didn't ask you here to talk business."

"You didn't?" Suddenly nervous, she shifted and the glass nearly dropped out of her gloved hand. She righted it, but when she glanced at Lewis's face, she nearly spilled it again. She was at the sharp end of a gaze spiked with intensity and began to feel far too warm in the current environment.

"I want you, Madeline," he told her gravely. "Tonight. One last night."

She gaped at him and through a rising swell of excitement and dismay, she didn't even try to interpret his words any other way than as he meant them.

Correction. Than she *thought* he meant them.

He continued to watch her steadily, making no apology or argument for or against his preposterous proposition.

An age passed, but her vocal chords seem to have blanked out in shock. All she managed was a matter-of-fact-sounding "Oh."

Oh. That's nice. Or, *Oh, thanks but no.* Or even *Oh, okay then.* Think, Madeline! How did she feel about this? Excited. Afraid. Scandalized. And yet, hadn't she dreamed of this every single night since the first perfect night?

It was out of the question. He was her boss. "I don't think that's a good idea."

His gaze didn't waver. "Trust me, it's a good idea."

"Why?"

"Because we want to," he said simply.

She repeated his words soundlessly, as if the feel of them on her lips would bring some reality to the situation.

They didn't.

"One last night," he continued, "at the Alpine Fantasy Retreat."

Shoot him down right now, her pragmatic self huffed. Tell him she didn't do interoffice relationships, especially with the boss. What he proposed was crazy, immoral even.

So why wasn't she stalking out of there?

Because she wanted it, too, Madeline realized. One night, just the two of them, that magical setting, and completely secret.

"Did I mention I'm leaving first thing in the morning?"

His smoothly spoken footnote dealt another blow to her resistance. Two whole weeks to worry about how to deal with seeing him again.

How to face her new colleagues if anyone ever found out… "I don't think I can do it," she blurted.

"You did, beautifully, the other night."

"I didn't know who you were, or I would never…Lewis, I've worked hard to get where I am. If this ever got out, I couldn't bear it. I need respect, it's all I've got."

And wasn't that the truth? Madeline lived to work. Without work, and without respect, she was nothing.

"You have my respect and my admiration," Lewis declared without hesitation.

"Tell me this is a test."

He shook his head. "I'm not asking as your boss, I'm asking as a man. And if you say no, I will never hold it against you, I will never mention it again. Although—" his mouth softened "—I won't promise never to hit on you again."

She blew out a long breath, and steam fogged the air between them. "And what if—what if we want more," she asked, "afterward?"

He might be addictive. Imagine if she fell in love! Madeline had never had a broken heart and it wasn't something she thought she would try.

"Do you want more?" he asked politely.

She nearly laughed out loud at his tone. "No," she said politely back.

"Neither do I."

Good. That was settled then. Except she wrestled with a fleeting disappointment that they'd both discounted the notion out of hand, so carelessly and immediately.

"Can you honestly say that you're not tempted?"

She gazed at him, a million thoughts tumbling around her head. Of course she was tempted. That was the whole problem. Who wouldn't be? No strings, no recriminations. No future.

"One night, Madeline. One night to play out all our fantasies and put them to bed forever."

The bleak thought of never touching him again dampened her leaping nerves. She longed to be considering this somewhere in private, away from his knowing eyes.

And did someone mention fantasy?

An illicit night with her wildest fantasy. She picked up her drink with both hands and took a careful sip, buying time. If this was a virtual program with all the choices in the world, she asked herself, what would she choose? A night—no, a week with him at the villa in Greece she'd stayed at two or three times?

She placed the glass carefully back on the counter, knowing there was nothing she'd rather have than what he was offering: a night of passion with Lewis Goode, in a log cabin with a fire, champagne and a big bath.

Madeline teetered on the side of giving in. "You intimated earlier that I was strong," she said, desperate to give herself every reason to turn him down. "If I was, I should be able to reject this—this madness—out of hand."

To Lewis's everlasting credit, no triumph glittered in the depths of his eyes. If there had been, she told herself, she would have walked.

"Isn't it weak to give in to something as trivial as desire when it can only get in the way of our working relationship?"

"Only if we let it." He leaned forward, frowning. "And I reject that what we had last week was trivial. It was much too intense for that."

Madeline almost apologized at his dangerously glinting eyes. She agreed wholeheartedly, and he'd now given her the acknowledgment she'd wished for when she first walked in the door.

Madeline wanted what Lewis wanted, only she was too much of a good girl to say it out loud, to his face.

Then Lewis unwittingly gave Madeline what she wanted. He rose and looked down at her with some seriously nice lights in his eyes, and took one of her gloved hands in his. "I will be at the Alpine Fantasy

Retreat from 6:00 p.m. If you decide not to come, I will look forward to welcoming you to Head Office in two weeks." Then he leaned forward, brushed her cold cheek with his cold mouth and left the bar.

It was Madeline's turn to sit by herself and contemplate the wall of ice in front of her. She was twenty-eight years old. Single. She worked hard, took far too few holidays and lived in hotel rooms. Didn't she deserve the odd departure from her reality?

And the reality was, she was lonely, inhibited, stilted socially and felt rootless. She lacked friends because all her time went on the job, and her success meant that almost everyone she knew looked upon her as their boss.

One night, not long enough to fall in love. Secret, just as she liked it. Of course she was tempted.

And if you say no, I will never mention it again.

Did she trust him on that? Yes, but she could not say exactly why, only that he seemed to be a man of his word. And she'd already trusted him with her body, which was huge for her.

The barman tapped her on the shoulder. "Would you like another drink, ma'am? Your thirty minutes are almost up."

Madeline checked her watch, only three-thirty. What the heck was she going to do until she absolutely couldn't put off the decision any longer?

Six o'clock until "first thing"; maybe twelve hours of illicit sex.

* * *

The text came through when she was on her way to the retreat. *"Cabin 3,"* it said.

Madeline's stomach gurgled uneasily. She had gone to Kay's office, longing to talk, dreading it at the same time. She wanted her friend to say, "Don't be bloody stupid!" And then she could feel justified in sniping that if it hadn't been for Kay's welcome-home-congrats-on-getting-the-job gift of two nights' stay at the Alpine Fantasy Retreat, she wouldn't be flipping out.

But Kay's husband arrived at Kay's office with the twins. Perhaps that forced the decision. Two adorable girls crawling all over her elegant and capable friend, who somehow morphed into a doe-eyed, face-pulling, raspberry-blowing mother, while the girls wreaked havoc on her tidy desk and clothes. Faced with such domestic bliss, Madeline hoped she might recoil from the thought of hours of illicit sex, but the opposite happened. She came away knowing that she unequivocally did not believe her body harbored a biological clock. She was ambitious, wanted the life Lewis did as CEO of a huge company. Like her mother, she did not have a maternal bone in her body.

Madeline was damned if she would throw away twelve years of hard work and study just because she was touched by how chubby and sticky the little girls fingers were on their mother's face and clothes, how soft her friend's eyes were when she looked at her little treasures.

That life wasn't for her. She found a lingerie store and gave her credit card something to worry about, then rushed to her suite and lavished herself in expensive shower creams and lotions.

Now she stood at the door of the cabin, trying not to think about movies she'd seen where the prostitute arrives at a hotel room and knocks on the door. Madeline took a deep breath, opened the door and walked in.

Like last time, colored candles in little glasses sat winking on many surfaces. A cheery fire crackled in the grate and the heavy velvet drapes were drawn. Fresh flowers on a table scented the air, and music played softly on the stereo.

Madeline set her overnight bag down softly on the floor. No sign of Lewis. Was he already in bed? Perhaps drawing a bath?

Turning, she locked the door then started for the bedroom, just as he appeared at the door.

Madeline stopped, barely breathing. Lewis stopped, too, and leaned against the doorjamb, looking as relaxed as she was tense. His eyes washed over her slowly, glinting in the dim candlelight. His hair was slightly damp and swept up over his forehead. The slight cleft in his square chin was accentuated by being clean-shaven. Like their last night together, he wore jeans and a black T-shirt, and no shoes or socks.

He gave a small smile. "My first fantasy fulfilled," he murmured. "You came."

"Did you think I wouldn't?"

"You're no coward." He pushed away from the wall. "Can I take your coat?"

She turned toward the fire, unbuttoning the long camel-colored woolen coat, and handed it to him.

"Champagne?"

Madeline nodded, thinking the bubbles could hold hands with the squillions of bubbles of nerves in her system right now.

Lewis put her coat away, poured two heavy flutes from a bottle in an ice bucket by the table, and came to stand beside her in front of the fire. He held out his glass and touched it gently to hers. "Did you bring a fantasy?"

The pitch of the crystal reverberated through her chest.

Madeline took her time glancing around the room. "It's all here."

Her breath hitched when he reached for her free hand and laced their fingers together. She remembered the little things he did that first night to make her feel liked, respected, a little calmer. Like now, as he kissed the tips of her fingers.

"Would you care to eat in the restaurant tonight?"

She shook her head. They could do room service if necessary, like last time. Now that she'd made the decision, she didn't want to waste a minute on other people, and staying in lessened the chances of anyone she knew seeing them.

Lewis squeezed her hand. "Nervous?"

She inclined her head. "Maybe a little."

"More than last time?"

Madeline nodded again. Now he was her boss and she would have to see him again, maybe on a regular basis. He could make or break her career with one word or sly insinuation. But as she searched his eyes, soaked up the reassurance she saw there, her world became aligned on an axis of peace. It was right to be here.

"What's your fantasy?" she asked breathlessly.

His eyes slid to her lips and he bent his head and closed the distance between them. "I have a few," he whispered, and brushed her mouth with his. "But they all start the same way."

His tongue traced the seam of her lips, coaxing her to open for him, and she closed her eyes. Other than his mouth and his hand holding hers, he didn't touch her. All her focus centered on the silky slide of his lips, the practiced stroke of his tongue, his breath melting into her mouth. So different from the greedy assault in the elevator. All feeling, patient, a leisurely entrée to entice and prepare her for more substantial fare.

A minute later, without thinking, she stretched out her hand to set her glass down somewhere, anywhere, so that she could touch him. Lewis pulled back, took her glass and put both of them on the mantel.

Madeline pressed both hands flat on to his chest, but he circled her wrists and held them away.

"You can't touch," he whispered and bent his head toward her again.

"But I want to…" She gazed hungrily at the tight T-shirt that moulded to smooth muscle, his biceps bulging with tight, smooth skin. She wanted to touch very much, to feel all that tanned, smooth skin under her fingers.

Lewis smiled lazily. "My first fantasy involves me sitting over there—" he jutted his chin toward a chair placed well back in the shadows "—and you right here, taking your clothes off, one piece at a time.

Madeline laughed shakily. "Really? That's it? A peep show?"

His teeth flashed in the dimly lit room. "Oh, that's just the start of it."

He waited while she assimilated that, stroking her cheek with his thumb. Madeline captured the tip of his thumb in her mouth, swirling her tongue over it before releasing it, and watched his eyes darken with desire. "Will you be giving instructions?"

"Most definitely," he said, the hoarse tone of his voice turning her knees to water. Then he walked away to his chair, and when he sat, she couldn't make out his features at all, only his knuckles resting on his knees.

Nervous laughter bubbled dangerously close to the surface. Could she do this, be the woman he thought she was? If Madeline had been told a week ago that she would meet a sexy stranger while on holiday and spend the night making love to him, she might just have believed it. But if anyone said she would knowingly go to a secluded cabin with the express purpose of having sex with her boss, and end up doing a striptease for his gratification, she would have laughed until she cried.

She took a long draught of champagne, pleased about the blow-out on the lingerie. The music he'd chosen was slow and seductive and although she didn't recognize the group, she liked the sound and stood for a minute, learning the beat. Think of it as a test, she counseled herself. But her hand still trembled as she put down her glass. Then she turned to her faceless stranger, put a hand to her blouse and pushed the first tiny mother-of-pearl button through the hole.

Five

"Slowly," Lewis murmured as she stripped the blouse off, revealing an oyster-colored bra that looked luminous in the flickering light. She covered her nerves well, just a slight breathing irregularity, but he already knew that Madeline Holland thrived on challenge and prided herself on her composure.

His eyes drifted over her from top to bottom and his heart gave a thump as it had when she walked in tonight. She'd worn knee-high white boots with killer heels. He couldn't imagine anything hotter.

Her breasts were pert and beautiful, barely dipping when she released the front-opening bra, their rose-tips pointed and aroused. The sight forced him to wet his lips and he pressed down in his seat to stop himself from going to her, filling his hands and his mouth with her. Not yet.

Her hips swayed almost imperceptibly as if the slow beat of the music came from inside her. He watched, mesmerized as she unzipped her skirt and pushed it down, shimmying a little to help its slide. A curse stuck in his throat. A delicate strip of lace hugged her hips with thin straps reaching down to attach to a pair of shimmering stockings. Lewis let his breath whistle out through his lips, trying to recall if he'd ever been with a woman who wore stockings. If he had, she hadn't looked like this.

She reached out with the toe of her boot and nudged the skirt away. The stockings were sheer, paler than the bands of soft golden skin above them. Her long lithe legs glowed in the gossamer sheen of something so wispy and perfect, he could have looked at her all night. Then her hands went to one of the clasps at the top of her leg and he leaned forward abruptly. "No!"

Her head jerked up and she narrowed her eyes in his direction, framed by the light behind her.

"Leave them for now," Lewis murmured, reclining back into the shadows. He wasn't ready to dispense with the most pleasure he'd had in looking at a woman just yet. A sip of champagne to ease his parched throat and he acknowledged the many pleasurable sensations pulsing through his body, his fingertips, nipples, the skin over his kidneys, and his crotch, especially there.

Madeline peered into the air around him then bent to unzip her boots. Again he stopped her. "Not yet."

She straightened, her elegant fingers dropping to her sides. "What now?" she asked, her voice not quite steady.

Lewis leaned forward, his elbows on his knees. "Now I want to look."

Her breasts rose a little as she stood straight, tall, achingly beautiful, a vision in white and creamy lace. He couldn't take his eyes off her. "Tell me you've got nothing on under that—" he waved vaguely toward her "—that lacy thing."

Madeline smiled and brought her hands down to caress the outside of the lacy thing. "Garter belt."

His mouth dried when she slid her index fingers an inch inside the lacy confection and lifted it to reveal a strip of smooth, shimmering satin.

"I'm wearing a thong."

He almost missed her reply, intent on the ripple of her fingers sliding under the fabric. Damn.

"But it's a special thong."

Lewis's eyes shot to her face almost as fast as his heart leapt into his throat.

"It unties," Madeline murmured, "at the sides."

"Does it?" His voice cracked in the middle of the two small words.

Madeline stilled her fingers and wet her lips. "Would you like me to take it off?"

He was a dead man. "That would be—nice."

He sat back into the shadows, squirming to accommodate all the extra flesh and blood straining the seam of his jeans. A deft flick of her wrist here, a flash of silky ribbon there, a firm slide and then her smile as she held aloft a prize to surpass any trophy he had ever desired.

She was killing him. That scrap of material was his to keep if he had to wrestle her for it then drive into town to buy her a replacement.

"I've had a vision of you in my mind for days," he said, rising, tiring suddenly of the distance between them, "but I didn't know then that this—" he opened his palm "—was exactly what I wanted."

Bending, he picked up the bag from a prestigious brand shop that he'd put by his chair, and walked toward her. "Close your eyes."

"Oh, my," she whispered shakily.

"Don't be nervous, it won't hurt a bit."

Madeline obeyed after an apprehensive look at the bag in his hands. Lewis shook out the long snow-white faux-fur coat from the bag, took her hand and placed it on the fabric. Her pink-tipped fingers flexed and then sank into the fur.

She opened her eyes and gasped. Lewis put the coat around her bare shoulders and pulled the portrait collar up so her face was framed in white fur.

"Lewis, it's…"

"Faux fur," he murmured, pulling the sides together at her throat. "I almost wish I'd made reservations at the restaurant, just for the pleasure of watching you wearing this with exactly what you have on underneath."

Madeline looked down at the coat in wonder. "Where did you get it?"

"One of the big hotel shops in town. I didn't have much time, but I knew it was you the moment I saw it."

"You bought this for me?" Her lovely eyes searched his.

Lewis stepped back, holding her hand, and gave her a thorough, smiling inspection.

"Well, for you and for me, I think."

He moved in a couple of steps and bent to kiss her, closing his eyes at the first touch of her lips. His fingers combed through her soft hair, brushing it away from the back of her neck as he pulled her in for a much deeper kiss.

Deeper and deeper, they kissed until they were both breathless, until little claws of impatience raked him, and Lewis needed patience to carry out the rest of his fantasy. Sliding the coat off her shoulders, he laid it on the floor in front of the fire and coaxed her down to lie on top of the fur.

He eased himself down beside her, raised up on one elbow, and looked down the length of her body. Her nipples peaked visibly and he nearly groaned out loud. But not yet, they had all night and he wanted to indulge both of them.

He took her lips again, clamping down on a desire so fierce, he called on all the finesse he could muster. Her response was all and more than he could take. Their tongues tangled in a mating dance until he thought he might embarrass himself on the spot.

He lifted his head, breathing hard. Her lips were plump and moist, but his mouth needed to disperse the pleasure and his hands were growing restless. With his index finger, he traced her chin, circled the hollow of her throat and pressed his lips down gently on her erratic pulse. Down in between her lovely breasts, skirting under and around, squeezing gently as she arched up and into his hands.

Lewis couldn't help it, he just had to taste her again. But as his mouth closed around one taut bud, Madeline's hands sank into his hair.

He raised his head. "No touching."

She inhaled sharply. "But I want…"

"No touching," he repeated. "We're still on my fantasy."

Composure, Ms. Holland. He wanted her screaming by the end of this. She narrowed her eyes but subsided. He watched until her hands fell to her sides, fingers spread wide with the white fur rippling between them.

Lewis bent his head to her breast again. She kept her side of the bargain technically, but there was touching in the way she angled her body up under his caresses and kisses. He lavished his attention on her breasts and the soft flesh of her inner arms, the sensitive dip of her waist. He returned, time and again, to tease her lips. Her body arched high and rubbed against his chest. "Cheat," he murmured and felt her lips curve against his. And he knew he'd never enjoyed a woman so much.

He'd taken her last time without knowing who she was inside. Now he knew some of her, a quick intuitive mind, loyalty, how much she cared about doing a good job. He derived great satisfaction in accepting the trust she brought to their lovemaking tonight. It couldn't have been an easy decision, but trust was probably the thing that swayed it.

He was primed and set to go. His fingers throbbed with pleasure as they slid over her lustrous flesh, her hair, glimmering with shades of honey and cream and gold and spilling over snow-white fur. He tried to focus on the little things before the big picture went up in flames. The sounds she made in her throat when he suckled her, the serrated edge of the straps that joined the lacy confection on her hips to those gossamer stockings, and the lovely band of skin above the stockings, much darker, but just as silky.

He came up again and the scent of her, excited, heated, wanting, washed over him. And all Lewis's good intentions went up in flames when he remembered that there was nothing between him and paradise.

* * *

Minutes hazed into a long block of time that she had no way of measuring because she had nothing to do but succumb to the bliss of his touch. It weighed heavy on her, that she got to just lie there, enjoying herself without responsibility or reciprocation. What had she learned in her meager experience that would persuade him to allow her to touch and give pleasure also.

It blew her mind that he wanted nothing for himself. He wielded his mouth and hands so expertly, building layer after layer of pleasure until she was nearly incoherent with need. Her consciousness cleaved in two, one large part of her taut and trembling and searching for release; the other languid and floating in rapture so warm and safe, she never wanted him to stop. Sex had never been like this before.

It was a balancing act—give in to an aching desire for release or continue to float. She doubted she could have made the decision. He made it for her. A long, slow, gradual pressure, building and layering until his hand, his mouth stopped teasing, showed her he meant business.

His hands and mouth firmed gloriously, his fingers slid unerringly inside to a sweet spot she hadn't known she possessed. Muscles shaking, inside and out, she succumbed to a double whammy of sensation that went on so long the trembling lasted for minutes, that the sound torn from her throat keened in her ears, that her fingers cramped on the soft faux fur of his fantasy, and she wouldn't have been surprised if she'd ripped great clumps of it out.

While she was still only barely conscious, he prized her fingers from the coat, linked hands, slid over her and inside her, and the pleasure was mirrored in his eyes as he looked into her face and sipped at her lips. She still couldn't touch him because her hands were imprisoned in his, but she felt his restraint in the rigid weight of his still-clothed body barely brushing hers, in the fierce grip of his fingers and the taut, veined line of his throat.

He moved slowly, deeply, completely inside her, his thighs pressing the clasps of the stockings she still wore into her flesh. They dug in even more when she lifted her legs to wrap around him, to keep him there. In response, she dug her stiletto heels into the flesh of his back and buttocks. He groaned and lost his smooth rhythm, and Madeline smiled to know she had at least participated to some extent in shattering his control. My, but was she going to get him back!

Later, when she could think straight.

She lifted and angled her hips, in invitation, in demand, and he stilled for a moment. She felt him heavy, pulsing, revving, and then he looked at her again—pure challenge—and they went mad, plunging into each other as though their lives depended on it. They hurtled toward the peak so incredibly fast, the pressure bearing down and overtaking her, roaring, and she crashed over the edge at the precise moment he did. They collapsed in a sweaty, shaking, breath-defying heap.

The sound of their panting drowned out the logs shifting in the fireplace and the low thrumming music from the stereo. Lewis moved the bulk of his weight off her while still managing to be mostly on top. He gently brought her hands down, curled her fingers in his and pressed them to his chest.

It was a long time before either moved. Madeline felt so replete, so heavy with delicious, sated exhaustion, she thought about drifting off, probably did. His weight pressed her into soft fur, caressing her skin in luxury.

She smiled. No man, barring her father, had ever bought her a gift, not a special intimate gift. She'd had a few funny desk calendars from subordinates, but nothing remotely personal, just for her.

Think about that. That was sad.

She shifted. "This probably isn't very good for the coat." *My coat,* even though he'd said it was for both of them.

Lewis grunted.

The CD whirred and shut off. The fire had burned low to sullen embers. It was so quiet, silence coated the air. She turned her head, wondering.

"Listen," she said.

Lewis opened one groggy eye. She smiled at him.

"I think it's snowing."

"You can hear snow?" he mumbled.

"Of course!" She wriggled out from under him and sat up, looking toward the windows. Madeline loved snow. The snows of her childhood were like a gift, at least while her father was alive. They tobogganed down the slope at the back of the house on a sled made of an old car door. An army of two, they pelted her mother when she came out to watch. Later, after he'd gone, she mostly sat inside to watch, but the memories were all good.

She stood and walked to the window, pulling the heavy drapes back. There was an old street lamp across the drive. It was perfect. The flakes drifted down, illuminated in the light, like millions of stars. Her car was lightly coated. She turned around and walked back to the supine man lying on a bed of fur. "Look."

Lewis sat up, still with his T-shirt on and pants down to his knees. He squinted past her out the window. "Is this going to be a serious storm?"

She kneeled in front of him and tugged his jeans the rest of the way down, then turned and sat with her back pressed into his front and he put his arms around her and they watched the snow fall.

"Are you worried about your flight?" she asked. While she would be perfectly content to stay here for as long as it took, she remembered he had an early departure.

She felt his shrug. "I've been snowed in once before."

Madeline leaned back into him and nestled her head in his neck. "Where?"

"Switzerland," he said dourly. "What was supposed to be a dirty weekend turned into four days."

Madeline wouldn't mind four days. "You don't sound as if you particularly enjoyed the experience."

She felt his shoulders rise and fall behind her.

"It was the company, not the snow."

A sharp pang of insecurity bit her. Was it someone in his organization? Was Madeline one day to be gossiped about as a bad dirty weekend, in another cabin with another woman?

"Even CEOs make bad judgment calls sometimes," she said slowly, pushing her maudlin thoughts away. Recriminations were for tomorrow.

"The call wasn't mine," he said shortly. "I was manipulated into the whole thing."

"Do tell." That surprised her, that he would allow himself to be manipulated. Lewis was one of the sharpest men she'd ever met.

Lewis clicked his tongue, rubbing his finger over a small red mark on her upper thigh, a mark made by the clasp of the stockings she still wore. "Her ancient husband was supposed to be there, that's what the invite said. She wanted something, me preferably, or a place for her husband on my board."

"Everyone wants something," Madeline murmured.

"They do," Lewis agreed gravely. "I seem to meet a lot of people, especially women, who want something for nothing."

Her breath hitched. She squirmed around to look at his face. "Lewis, you don't think I…"

"No." He put his finger to her lips. "I asked you, remember?"

Right. Of course he did. "Sounds like you don't have a very high opinion of women," she said, trying to keep it light.

"Present company excepted." He dropped a kiss on the tip of her nose. She turned around again and faced the window, snuggling into his front.

"The needy and greedy seem to gravitate toward me like a magnet," he commented, putting both of his hands down to play with the lacy bands at the tops of her stockings. "That's why I like strong, independent women like you."

She was both—but tonight wasn't about the future. As long as she kept reminding herself of that, she could enjoy the rest of the night and look forward.

The touch of his hands stroking over and under the lip of her stockings reminded her that this was her one night, her perfect fantasy, and it was going to have to keep her warm on all the long lonely nights ahead.

"Lewis." She flexed her legs so that his hands slid up a precious inch or two.

He stilled.

Madeline covered his hands with hers, lacing their

fingers, pressing them into the soft flesh at the top of her inner thighs. "I want something."

She felt his mouth move in a smile on her hair. And an interesting pressure on her lower back. It was her turn, and if she wasn't mistaken, her fantasy was very much up for it.

She twisted around to face him, placing her legs either side of him, and leaned in for a hot wet kiss. Mouths locked, she took the hem of his T-shirt and worked it up, breaking the kiss long enough to whisk it over his head.

He was so beautifully toned, she thought admiringly, finally getting her hands on his smooth, broad chest. She ran her hands over his chest and back and leaned forward to nibble under his ear and down his throat. Lewis scooted forward and she gasped at the ridge of hot steel pressed against her. But when he raised his hands to cup her breasts, she took his wrists firmly and placed them by his sides. "No touching," she said sternly, and a smile turned up the corners of his mouth. "It's my turn now."

She moved down to lave his nipples with her tongue. His breathing became ragged and eyes filled with dark desire. Moving back slightly, she ran her hands down his abdomen and cupped him, watching his chest rise and his eyes glaze over.

"It's my turn," she whispered, rubbing gently, feeling his leap of response all the way to her core. "And now," she said, pushing him slowly until he was on his back and she was straddling him, "you get to just lie there and take it. You're not the boss now, Mr. Goode." To emphasize the point, she filled her hands with him. "I have you in the palm of my hand."

Madeline awoke feeling fantastic, despite having only slept three hours. How was it possible to feel so good on such a miserly amount of sleep?

And then she remembered. This was the Alpine Fantasy Retreat. Again.

She dragged the pillow out from under her head and put it over her face, suddenly hot with adolescent pleasure. What a glorious night. How could she even have contemplated saying no?

If possible, last night was even more perfect than the first. The beautiful coat and all the other things that had made it so special, like chocolate-dipped strawberries and more champagne, and the unexpected snow.

Madeline stretched luxuriously, thinking that if she never lay with another man again as long as she lived, she wouldn't feel cheated.

After another dreamy minute of X-rated reminiscences, she got up and went to face the mess in the bathroom. She knew it was a mess because it had survived a shower and a spell of lovemaking in the spa bath. Madeline the Good tidied up.

Later, making up, she brushed blusher over her cheekbones and the feel of it evoked a vision: Lewis dressed, looking down at her as she lay in bed. She'd heard birdsong, but the room was dark. She'd snuggled lazily down into the feather duvet, her eyes drifting closed, and then she felt the faintest touch of something on her cheek. His hand? His lips? It was probably a dream.

When she stepped out of the bedroom, she saw the white faux-fur coat hanging on the back of the door. She stroked its pristine softness and folded her overcoat up and put it into the shopping bag he'd brought the white coat in. How decadent was that, sneaking out of this den of discretion wearing her lover's fantasy?

Nothing could dim the light in her eyes. She forgot to be tired. She felt so buoyant that not a pang of worry about how she would feel the next time she saw him permeated her rosy glow. The night had delivered total absorption in pleasuring each other, and somehow she knew that it was special to him also and he would never disrespect her or use this against her.

Now it was holiday time. She would spend lots of time with her mother, sort out the farm and house once and for all, maybe even talk Kay into a trip up to Christchurch to see an opera or something.

A great new job, new friends and challenges, the biggest of which would be working with Lewis. And she looked forward to that, too, even knowing how demanding he could be. She would never die of boredom with him at the helm.

Life was great! She turned into the driveway of the farm, smiled at the fog-shrouded trees lining the drive. It was such a beautiful spot, even if it was run-down. Madeline wondered if the real estate agent she'd hired had received any interest yet. There was no rush. She could easily afford her mother's expenses for the time being.

The phone rang as she stepped into the kitchen and tossed her bag down on the table. "What good is a cell phone when you don't have it on?" Kay's voice said.

Madeline sighed guiltily. There was no reception at the cabin so she'd turned the phone off last night. "Sorry."

"Are you alone?"

Foreboding stirred in her gut at her friend's grim tone. "Yes."

Before she could draw breath, Kay went on. "Is your car in the garage?"

"No." Madeline frowned out the window. "Why?"

"I need you to put it in the garage, lock the door and don't answer it to anyone, okay? I'll be there in under an hour."

Madeline sank down onto a chair. "Why? What's happened?"

"And don't answer the phone, either."

"Oh God, is it Mum?"

"No, no," her friend said hastily. Madeline slumped in a chair and heard Kay sigh heavily.

"I don't know how to tell you this, so I'm just going to come out with it."

A sickening pall smothered Madeline's sunny mood.

"I am so sorry, Madeline. Someone from the hotel sold a security tape of you and Lewis in the elevator here on the night of the Gala Ball. You're on the national news."

Six

Madeline swayed in her chair. Someone from the hotel had sold a tape? "Oh my God," she breathed. "Who? Why?"

"I know who," Kay said grimly. "He's sitting outside my office right now, waiting to be given his marching orders."

Madeline closed her eyes. How could this be happening? "Why?"

"My guess is it's a knee-jerk reaction to all Lewis's talk about change." Kay sighed. "People are feeling threatened."

"We didn't even talk about it last night," she realized,

thinking out loud. She'd asked about his meeting with Kay, but he didn't want to talk about business.

"You saw him last night? He checked out of here yesterday."

Her mind churned up with horrible images—she and Lewis groping each other, *that* look on her mother's face…

The person sitting outside Kay's office right this minute… Because of her lusty appetites, someone was going to lose their job. "Yes," she said heavily. "I was with him last night."

She imagined her friend's face in the long, pregnant silence that followed.

"With him," Kay said, adorning her words with the same inflection. "At the farm?"

"At the Alpine Fantasy Retreat," Madeline said. "Where we met last week."

Another five-second pause, then a loud exhalation. "Oh, Christ, Madeline. Another hotel? Did anyone see you?"

"I don't think so."

"Stay there, don't answer the phone or the door, it'll be reporters. Where is Lewis, by the way?"

"Probably in Christchurch, about to leave for Sydney."

"Lucky old Lewis," Kay said dryly. "I'll be out in an hour. Do you need any supplies?"

Madeline was under siege.

* * *

Lewis surprised himself by falling asleep on the plane after an hour's delay in Queenstown while they cleared snow off the runway. He did not wake until the pilot announced their impending arrival into Christchurch Airport. Damn it! He'd missed his connection to Sydney.

Lewis hated changes to plans, but all he could think was—it was worth it. Thirty-four years old and he'd just discovered you could improve on perfection. He thought their first night had surpassed every sexual expectation. He was wrong.

Forget his promises about a strictly working relationship from now on. Lewis was old enough to know that chemistry of this kind was super-rare. Madeline would resist at first. He smiled, knowing what store she put on her professional reputation. Just one of the many things he admired about his new COO.

He disembarked and made his way straight through to the first-class departures counter.

"The next flight to Sydney departs at four-thirty."

Lewis groaned. "What about indirectly?"

"Via Melbourne? In three hours."

There was nothing to do but wait in the Pacific Star VIP lounge. The worst of it was, he could have had another hour in bed with her. As he walked away from the counter, he recalled her face as she slept this morning. He'd stooped and dropped a kiss right on her beauty spot, just like last time. She probably wouldn't even remember.

"Can you make sure I am called in two hours, please?" he asked the hostess on the door of the VIP lounge. "I may try for some shut-eye."

He looked around approvingly. The lounge was very quiet. Helping himself to some juice from the buffet, he chose a comfortable lounger next to a sun-drenched window.

For the first time in his life, he allowed his mind to consider something more than someone to warm his bed occasionally. He pictured Madeline in his old villa in Double Bay. Waking in his bed. Smiling as she ate breakfast on his deck overlooking the ocean. Sitting on his bed rolling gossamer-sheer stockings up her endless, beautiful legs—or better—rolling them down.

They could go into work together…

Whoa, boy! No sense getting ahead of himself. She hadn't even started yet, but one thing was for sure, one or two nights was never going to be enough.

He sat up, suddenly not in the least tired. Things were going to change. It was time he took something for himself now. He would have his COO and her sweet body, too.

Someone tapped his shoulder. "Do you mind if I put the television on?" The man indicated the TV remote on the table beside Lewis. He handed it over, but his inner plasma screen replayed Madeline riding him, still in her garter belt, stockings and boots.

He was going to embarrass himself in public at this rate.

A few feet away, the television chattered quietly, some breakfast TV. He picked up his juice and then heard the word "Queenstown" spoken, saw the light dusting of snow, and then a shot of the Premier Waterfront Hotel.

It was amazing how fond he'd become of the little tourist mecca after only a week....

How would she ever show her face in town again?

With a heart full of trepidation, Madeline turned the television on, knowing she shouldn't, but it was better than restlessly prowling the house while she waited for Kay.

It was worse than she feared. The Alpine Fantasy Retreat had joined the fray now, although the breakfast show host did not mention the name. "An unnamed source has suggested that a top Premier Hotel Group executive and the new CEO, Australian entrepreneur Lewis Goode, have spent more than one night together at a plush Queenstown resort."

Her poor mother. Madeline had put off calling her, hoping that Kay's arrival might bolster her courage. But it was obvious that this story was on the rise.

She called the retirement village and asked to be put through to Mrs. Holland. The manager came on the phone and told her they'd had a couple of calls from reporters and even one from the local TV station wanting to interview her mother. "Adele hasn't had the television on yet. She's taking a nap."

That was unusual, Madeline thought, checking her watch. "Can I rely on your discretion not to talk to any media?"

The manager reassured her. "Of course you can, and we'll make sure no reporter gets near your mother, although I'm afraid we can't stop her watching TV."

Her mother had mellowed a lot over the years, but there were bound to be newshounds in town who remembered her regular tirades. The Bible Lady in full strident flight would make great copy, especially as it would be the second time she'd railed publicly about her daughter.

TV, radio talkback, newspapers—it was everywhere. The Internet had posted the whole shameful tape from the elevator. The camera sat high in the corner and the images were grainy but infinitely recognizable. Her hair hung down her back, her boobs from that angle looking like they were spilling over the low-cut bodice and practically waving at the camera. Lewis's hand had lifted one of her legs so that her skirt rode high and you could almost believe they were doing it. At one part of the show, he appeared to suckle her breast, and she knew he hadn't done that, it was just the angle. But these were the shots the papers would blow up and publish. Worst of all were the two close-up inserts of their faces as they devoured each other, slack-mouthed in lust, their tongues so very obviously tickling each other's tonsils.

She wanted to die. When Kay got there, Madeline threw herself into her arms in a rare foray into self-pity.

"*How* is this news?" she demanded of her friend.

Kay stroked her hair. "Lewis is always big news in Australia, and he's big news here right now because of the perceived threat to the town's economy if he closes the hotels."

"My poor mother," Madeline moaned against her friend's chest as she held her. "It'll be the last nail in my coffin, as far as she and I are concerned."

"It won't. She'll give you hell for an hour and have forgotten it by teatime. You know, if this video was taken in an elevator in Sydney, the whole thing would have blown over by tomorrow. But in your home town, with your history and your mother and the worry about the hotels, they're going to get some mileage out of it."

Madeline wiped her eyes. "I suppose I can forget the Women in Business meeting, and don't even think about the high school."

Kay squeezed her hands sympathetically. "Jeez, Madeline, I've never seen you cry."

Madeline couldn't remember crying, ever.

Their eyes drifted to the front page of the local paper. "You would have to go for a man with his surname." Both she and Madeline laughed shakily at the headline: Madeline the Good has Goode Time in Queenstown.

Kay sobered and fixed her with her best school-marm look. "Do you like him?"

Madeline looked down at the picture in the paper, at the tilt of his head as he kissed her. "It doesn't matter. It happened and it's over and even this morning, I was looking forward to working with him." She wrapped her arms around herself, remembering the warmth and softness of the coat. "Good old-fashioned lust, that's all." She looked up at her friend's face. "It was your fault. We met at that retreat hotel last week. In fact, it was all so perfect, I even wondered at the time whether he was part of the package."

Kay grinned and got up to bring the coffeepot to the table. "I do give the best presents," she said smugly, topping up Madeline's cup. "Tell me everything. I probably can't help, but it will give me a licentious thrill."

Madeline wondered why she hadn't told her before, and if she should be telling her subordinate—Lewis's subordinate. But it wasn't like she ran to her with every failed love affair. There hadn't been any failed love affairs to talk about.

"Have you been there? There is a tiny theatre where guests can book to watch their favorite movie, and they have someone on the door to see you're not disturbed. Around lunchtime on the second day, I watched *Out of Africa...*" Kay nodded approvingly, as they'd both seen it many times.

"Afterward I went for a long walk, then I realized I'd left my cabin key in the theatre. I went back and there was a movie on, but no usher at the door. I peeked in and saw a man sitting in front of the seat I'd used. I figured I could grab my key without bothering him," she explained. It had seemed entirely plausible at the time.

"What was he watching?" Kay asked.

Madeline shrugged. "Some old war flick. Anyway, I'd just put my hand on the key when he turned and grabbed me like that." She shot her arm out and grasped Kay's wrist firmly. "I got such a shock, I yelled out, and then the lights came on and the attendant rushed in, apologizing over and over. But—" she shook her head in wonder "—all I know is, we couldn't stop looking at each other."

Looking into Lewis's face that first time was like being tied to the tracks in front of a runaway train. "I knew I should run, but I just couldn't."

Kay sat back and exhaled, her eyes thoughtful. "And neither of you knew who the other was?"

Madeline shook her head. That still rankled a little, although Lewis had explained that he had no idea she was going to be at that meeting, which seemed plausible since she wasn't on the Executive Committee. "He told me at the ball that he thought Jacques had sent me there."

"He told you at the ball?" Kay frowned. "Not before?" Her face cleared. "So you ran out and he followed and he kissed you in the lift and then you carried on where you'd left off?"

"No, not that night. I was so angry with him I sent him away."

Kay gave a forthright look at the photo in the paper.

Madeline sighed. "Okay, I kissed him, but then I came to my senses."

"And last night?"

Last night…it seemed so right at the time and she realized that even now, with all this upset, she still couldn't regret that.

"I couldn't resist," she said simply. "One last night to see if it lived up to the first." She laughed and there was a tinge of bitterness in it. "A virgin until I was twenty-two—do you think I'm making up for lost time?"

Kay smiled grimly. "I just hope the memory will keep you going beyond the crap that's about to descend."

The home phone rang solidly for an hour before she took it off the hook, cursing her mother for not having an answer machine. Kay had urged her not to talk to anyone in the press, hoping the fuss would die down in a couple of days. So when she heard a car pull up and stop outside, she peeped through her bedroom window, and as she couldn't identify the person, she didn't answer the door. That happened three times during the afternoon.

The real estate agent called midafternoon to say he had an offer on the property to present to her. Reluctantly she agreed to see him, even though she felt too ashamed to see anyone. But she couldn't let a serious offer slide, especially now when all she wanted to do was slink out of town, under cover of darkness preferably, just like twelve years ago.

The agent didn't refuse her polite offer of coffee. Madeline had interviewed several candidates before settling on this young man, liking his friendly and genuine manner. Now, whether it was there or not, she imagined an insolent twist to his mouth and sly muddy eyes. Her cheeks burned during the whole encounter.

"It's a very good offer, Ms. Holland," he told her while she tried to concentrate on the paperwork. "A clean contract like this should go through without any problems, although of course you can counter."

The prospective buyer was a development company. Madeline knew what that meant. The old house and farm buildings would be razed and a hotel or maybe some swanky apartments put up.

Her father was born in this house…

The agent smiled smugly, reminding her that these were small-town people with small-town minds. She bent and signed the contract in the places he indicated and hustled him out the door before he'd finished his coffee.

Tonight she would go and make peace with her mother. Please, God, she wasn't having one of her rare lapses of coherence and lucidity. The house was pretty well packed up and she could get a cleaning company to do what she hadn't been able to yet. And then she could slip off to Sydney quietly and in relative anonymity.

Someone banged on the door and she retreated to her bedroom again to check through the window, castigating herself for being so pathetic. All the years of hard work and hard-earned respect for nothing.

The door knocker hammered again.

"Madeline! For Christ's sake! I know you're in there."

Lewis's frustrated voice filtered through her shame. But—he was supposed to be in Sydney, wasn't he?

"I've been knocking for ten minutes," he muttered as she opened the front door a crack.

He pushed past her, looking grim.

"I thought you'd be in Australia by now."

"I saw the news when I got to Christchurch. Jesus, it's freezing in here." He walked to the old coal range stove and opened the door.

The creases on his suit were sharp, making her aware of how rumpled she was in ancient jeans, over-size jersey and woolly socks. She hurriedly ran a hand through her hair. "Why are you here?"

Lewis turned. "Are you all right?"

Madeline turned away and started to fill the kettle, but then banged it down and leaned on the bench. Her throat had filled up.

Lewis came up behind her and put his hands on her shoulders, squeezing firmly. Making her tension ten times worse.

"It's not so bad, is it?" He gently turned her to face him and smiled crookedly. "It's not the first time my name has been linked with a beautiful woman."

"Is that supposed to make me feel better?"

He pulled her over to the table and sat her down. "Sweetheart, it's not the end of the world. When you get to the top, there are always people who want to pull you down. You must know that."

She shook her head. He wasn't the least upset, but he was a man, after all! "You think I make a habit of this sort of thing?" She paused. "It's just another conquest to you, isn't it? How do you expect me to hold my head up here in my home town, face my mother?"

Lewis frowned. "Why do you care so much? You don't live here, haven't for years." His tone softened a little. "As far as your mother's concerned, it's a little embarrassing, perhaps, but the virginal histrionics are a bit over the top. You're a grown woman."

Madeline stood up, twisting her hands together. "You don't know my mother," she said feelingly, and moved back to the bench with no clear purpose, just to get out from under his gaze.

Lewis rested his elbow on the table, staring out the window as if giving her a chance to compose herself.

After a minute he stood up. "You got anything against me putting a match to that fire?"

Madeline sighed distractedly. "I've had reporters knocking all day, I don't want anyone to know I'm here."

He stood up, took his jacket off and rolled up his sleeves. "I don't know about you, but I got no sleep at all last night. How about some coffee, and then you can tell me why a little indiscretion has suddenly catapulted you into Public Enemy Number One."

Madeline did as he asked, relieved in some way after all these hours floundering in self-pity, to be given orders. Strange when she was much more used to giving them.

Could she make him understand why the salacious publicity was ten times worse because of what happened when she was sixteen? Even Kay said she should forget the shame, that no one judged her on it anymore. But that was before she was splashed all over the media now.

They sat down with coffee and the biscuits Kay had brought out.

"My mother's—difficult," she began, "and very well-known around here." If she wanted to make him understand, it was necessary to tell him some of her mother's more endearing traits, like her public tirades, and practically insisting Madeline parade through the town wearing sackcloth and ashes after the church incident. "She wasn't—isn't—cruel, but she didn't care that as a teenager I was embarrassed by her, especially when many of my friends and most of their parents came in for her tongue-lashings at regular intervals."

"You say she has Alzheimer's now? Maybe she won't even take it in."

"I'll go and see her later," Madeline said listlessly.

"Is that why you left home, Queenstown?" he asked, loosening his tie. She gazed at him, wishing she could recapture the mind-and-body-consuming passion they'd shared. What a sad end to what could have been a stupendous memory.

But her selfish pleasure was what had gotten her into trouble in the first place.

"I left home because I burned the old church down."

Lewis munched on a chocolate chip biscuit, his eyes steady on her face.

"Kay and I worked part-time as housemaids at the Premier Waterfront. We were sixteen, both still at school, but years apart socially. I was very sheltered." Try completely socially stunted, she thought ruefully.

But she did have a normal teenager's curiosity and hormones. So when Kay told her that some of the staff were having a party down by the old church, and that Jeff Drury, one of the houseboys, was going to be there, she couldn't stop thinking about it. She had a huge crush on Jeff even though he was four years her senior.

"On the night, I sneaked out of my bedroom window and met Kay at the end of the drive." They'd spent a few minutes in the car putting makeup on in the rearview mirror. Kay had brought some clothes for Madeline to wear since the clothes her mother made on the old foot-pedal sewing machine were hardly the height of fashion. "I'd never tasted alcohol before. I had two rum and cokes and felt great at first. Everyone sort of paired off. The boy, Jeff, started kissing me and somehow we ended up inside the church, alone. And then I suppose the alcohol kicked in and I began to feel sick. There was kissing and touching, but after a while, I didn't want his hands on me anymore and I pulled away and he ripped my blouse—Kay's blouse."

She was so ashamed; the blouse was new and she'd ruined it. Everything began to overwhelm her. The alcohol she'd drunk, desperation to get away from him and guilt at behaving like this in a church with her mother's stance on morality and religion. "I started to struggle and we must have knocked over the candles we'd lit and put on the pulpit. There was this beautiful big tapestry, very old, draped over the pulpit. But we didn't notice at first. He wouldn't let me go."

Panic added to the mix. Jeff had his hand firmly planted in the crotch of her jeans even while she was hitting and pushing at him. "By the time we smelled the smoke, the pulpit leaning against the wall was well alight. There was so much smoke." She looked at Lewis, still surprised by it. "It was terrifying. You don't expect it to be so black. I mean it was dark, but I thought the flames would light everything up.

"I couldn't see a thing. I kept running into walls and falling over and I couldn't breathe. By the time I made it outside, I was nearly hysterical."

She'd thrown up until there was nothing left, to the sound of the church windows breaking and the roaring of the flames. Madeline just knew she was going straight to hell.

"Jeff and the other kids took off. I don't know why I stayed. It wasn't like I could do anything. Even the fire brigade couldn't save it. But I couldn't leave, I was too guilty. Kay stayed, too."

The church was the pride of the town at that time. It was a small, very old wooden church, set in the most picturesque location imaginable on the edge of Lake Wakatipu. It featured in many postcards of the region, and tourists came from everywhere to be married or photographed there.

The townspeople were appalled, but that was nothing compared to her mother's wrath. "We were lucky not to be charged. I think when the cops dropped me off home, in Kay's torn clothes, covered in smoke, stinking of alcohol and vomit, they probably thought I'd be punished enough." She smiled wryly. "They called her the Bible Lady back then."

Lewis leaned forward. "What happened to the other kids?"

Madeline shrugged. "I think most people knew what happened, but the cops dropped it."

Lewis opened the door of the range and shoveled

some more coal in. "I guess that explains what happened in the cave the other day," he said, and walked to the sink to rinse his hands. "Dark confined spaces."

She nodded, considering. "Maybe." It was a pity she hadn't thought about confined spaces in the elevator last week.

He sat back down, drying his hands on a tea towel. "Did she throw you out or did you go voluntarily?"

She smiled. "I couldn't wait to go. She was unbearable." The shame might have faded a lot faster if her mother hadn't insisted on preaching about the error of her own daughter's ways to anyone who would listen. "I'd saved enough to get me to Australia. And that was that."

"Is this the first time you've been home?"

She shook her head. "No, I come home every year or so for a quick visit, but I don't think she's ever forgiven me. She got a lot softer in her old age, but then the Alzheimer's set in."

A sad laugh bubbled up. "You'll think this is funny. I always thought that one day, I'd ride into town and be the golden girl. The triumphant return of the prodigal daughter. I'd make them all sit up and say, 'Well, she started out bad, but look what she's made of herself.'" She sighed. "And now look what I've done."

Lewis made an impatient noise. "Come on, Madeline. So we had a kiss in an elevator. Hell, let's just hope the Alpine Fantasy Retreat doesn't have cameras in the rooms."

She looked at him sharply. "Don't! I can't believe they told. That place is famous for being discreet."

"I gave the manager a piece of my mind, believe me," Lewis told her grimly. "He phoned today to apologize and said he'd see the culprit never works in the hotel business in this town again."

Another person burned by their total absorption in the pursuit of pleasure, Madeline thought. Another person in this town she'd successfully alienated.

Lewis rubbed his eyes wearily. "It'll pass. Get back out there, hold your head high and show them you don't give a damn. That's what I'm going to do."

Madeline wrapped her arms around her middle. "I *do* give a damn." She wondered if he'd been caught with his pants down—figuratively speaking—before.

And that led her to wonder what interest, if any, there was in Australia about this matter. "Have you heard from anyone over there?" she asked, a hollow feeling squirming in her gut. "Has this made the news?"

"Who cares? Madeline, I'm always in the news."

Knowing that didn't help. "I care. I haven't even thought about that." She closed her eyes in anguish. "How am I going to face my new team?"

How could she expect to be taken seriously once that tape was bandied around? She was starting a new job as chief of operations for a multinational company, and she would start with no credibility at all.

"You will," Lewis said firmly. "Because you're better than that."

Easy for him to say. He was a man. Another notch on the bedpost was no skin off his nose. "Respect is paramount to me, probably because of what I've just told you. I'll be a laughingstock."

Lewis sighed impatiently. "There's no room for weakness at the level you're at. They'll chew you up and spit you out."

"I've seen it time and time again," Madeline argued. "It doesn't matter what I achieve in the board-room, or if I survive this humiliation at first. This will be bandied about every time I do something. Every time I get a promotion or apply for a new job or have to make cutbacks. The snide comments behind my back or veiled references to my face. I got there because I screwed the boss and got caught on camera."

Lewis pushed himself up from the chair abruptly. "Toughen up, Madeline," he said sharply. "Get your ass to Sydney or you'll have more than snide comments to worry about. Remember, the fate of the Queenstown hotels rests on your shoulders."

Her mouth dropped open and she stared at him, stunned. That he could still hold this over her, on top of everything else, cut deeply.

He picked up the overcoat he'd tossed on a chair and put it on. Now she had yet another choice to make. If she took up the position in Sydney, she would start with no credibility at all. If she stayed and survived the innuendo and humiliation by the towns-folk, not to mention her mother, she could then be responsible for the axing of many jobs, including her best friend's.

That would kill any chance she might ever have of being accepted in her home town again.

Lewis shoved his hands into his pockets and stared sternly down at her. "I have an appointment. Meet me for dinner in town later."

"No." She shook her head. "Lewis, I…I couldn't face it."

He leaned down until his face was two inches from hers. "You can't face the town and your mother. You can't face your staff in Sydney. Make up your mind, Madeline, because you can't have it both ways." He straightened. "Seven-thirty at the Waterfront in the restaurant."

Lewis checked into the Presidential Suite at the Waterfront, ignoring the stares of the staff. He had an hour to kill before his appointment and spent most of it trying to push Madeline's strained face to the back of his mind.

He refused to let her throw away a stellar career because of some negative and embarrassing publicity and he'd already put a contingency plan into place to that end. But as he showered to shake off the effects of too little sleep, he kept hearing that old familiar voice whispering in his ear.

I could help her, he thought. I could make things better.

He'd always thought that—until two years ago when revenge became his prime motivator. He'd spent his whole life fixing people up and trying to protect them, and he wasn't going there again. That's why Madeline was such a refreshing change, why he wanted her in Sydney. Not to teach him the ropes of the hotel business; he could hire someone for that. But because she didn't want anything from him. She had it together, ruled with her head not her heart.

And then he had come along and kissed her in an elevator. Lewis was responsible for the unhappiness on her face today.

The suite phone rang.

"Mr. Goode, it's the *Queenstown Daily* here. We heard you were back in town."

The small-town grapevine was alive and kicking, he thought savagely. "What do you want?"

"Do you have any comment to make on the story we broke this morning? Did you see it? I could have a copy…"

Lewis cut him off. "Why would I make a comment to you?"

"Well, sir, sometimes it's helpful to put your perspective across in these matters. You're not the most popular man in this part of the country. We can humanize you."

"You don't have a story," Lewis snarled. "You have a photo and that's it, and you want to drag someone's name through the mud."

"We've tried to get hold of Ms. Holland to put her side, but she doesn't seem disposed to take our calls."

Leave her alone! He wanted to yell, but that might make things worse for her. Damn it! He wanted to make things better.

So he wasn't the most popular man in town, hey? Perhaps the reason the security tape ended up at the local rag was down to him. He'd come into this town trumpeting change, hinting at redundancies, ordering reviews, making surprise inspections. These things could probably be absorbed in big cities, but with a big percentage of the town's population working under the Premier umbrella, maybe he should have reined it in a little.

"Perhaps if I met you downstairs for a drink," the man said, "we could chat about your business interests here. That might take the heat off the lady a bit."

Lewis took a deep breath, wondering if he could actually sit across a bar without planting his fist in the man's face.

He was certain Madeline could handle the office gossip, even if she herself wouldn't agree today. But could he do something to help restore her tarnished reputation here and smooth things over with her mother?

Seething about suddenly finding himself in the role of protector for the one woman he admired for her strength, Lewis told the man he'd see him in the bar in five minutes.

Much later, after his appointment in town, he

returned to the bar at the Waterfront to wait for Madeline. Seven-thirty passed, and he felt the first stirring of disappointment and anger that she might not show. Fifteen minutes after that, he was ropable. After what he'd done for her today, against his better judgment, was she about to show her true colors? Not strong enough to be a worthy prize.

He called her cell phone. She picked up immediately.

"You're late," he ground out, not wanting excuses.

"Oh, Lewis."

She sounded like she was surprised to hear from him.

"I'm at the retirement village. My mother is missing."

Seven

Lewis raced to the retirement village and picked out Madeline standing by the entrance, talking to a couple of police. In the distance her face was a pale smudge, abruptly cut off by the dark-colored beanie she wore. Kay stood by her side, clapping her gloved hands together. All eyes swiveled to him as he stepped out of the throng toward them.

The worry in Madeline's eyes arrowed straight through him, but in light of the day's events, he thought it prudent not to take her in her arms.

"She was last seen eating dinner in her room two hours ago," Kay told him. "She wasn't there when they came back to collect her dishes."

"They've checked her clothes," Madeline said in a voice that sounded like the ache of unshed tears. "She only has her nightie and a pair of slippers on."

Lewis cleared his throat to cover the shiver that rattled his bones in the chill winter air. Remnants of last night's snow still lay on the ground.

"Is there anywhere you can think of she might go?" one of the policemen asked. "A friend? A special favorite place?"

Madeline bit her lip and shook her head sadly.

"The farm." An elderly man in a dark hooded oilskin and thick gloves stepped forward. "She might try to go home." The man put out his hand and patted Madeline on the arm. "Hello, love. I haven't seen you since you were a little-un."

Madeline peered at his face. "I'm sorry, I…"

"You won't know me, Brian Cornelius. I'm a longtime friend of your mum's."

A woman dressed in a white uniform nodded briskly. "Brian visits Adele often."

Mr. Cornelius ducked his head. "Well, I visit everyone. Passes the time on a Sunday since my wife passed away."

"What makes you think she'd go back to the farm?" Madeline whispered.

The old man shuffled about, looking embarrassed at being the center of attention. "She missed her home, the view. Missed her daughter and husband." He coughed self-consciously. "Not all of the time, you understand."

"Perhaps you should go back to the farm," Lewis said to Madeline.

She shook her head. "No, I...I feel I should be here."

Even though she hadn't said it, everyone's thoughts turned to just how far the old lady would get in two hours in the freezing night air, barely dressed.

"I'll go," Mr. Cornelius said.

"Would you?" Madeline grasped his hand. "Thank you so much. The key is under the mat, go inside and keep warm. I'll call the home phone if there is any news."

Everyone split up and fanned out all over town. Apparently, Adele Holland had lived here all her life and enjoyed reasonable physical health until the last few days. Lewis felt a pang of guilt for monopolizing all of Madeline's time over the last week when her mother was clearly unwell.

It seemed the whole town turned out to search, and the still night air resonated with calls of Adele Holland's name. But as the hours passed, Madeline's head dropped. Lewis asked her repeatedly if she wouldn't rather go home and wait at the farm, but she told him she'd go mad if she just had to sit and wait.

"So much for being outcast because of a little kiss," he whispered in her ear, staring at what must be a hundred searchers.

She chewed on her bottom lip, looking stricken. "Lewis, I can't get it out of my head. What if...what if she saw us, on TV?"

Damn! He knew what she was going to say, had wondered himself. He grabbed her hands, squeezing tightly. "She's got Alzheimer's disease," he told her firmly. "Anything could have triggered her confusion."

She didn't look convinced. A deep elemental need to comfort her welled up. Lewis didn't care who saw what or that they were the stars of the current society pages. He began to tug her toward him to comfort and warm her. But someone approached and Madeline snatched her hands away, leaving him standing there with his arms outstretched and feeling foolish.

She wouldn't want his comfort, he realized, letting his arms drop to his sides. Madeline would hate to be seen accepting comfort in full public view, especially by the man who'd shown her up to be human.

They searched for three hours in zero degrees and complete darkness before a shout went up and the news spread like wildfire. Adele Holland was safe. She'd been found on one of the freezing back roads that led out of town. Her old friend was right; she was heading for home. If it wasn't for the many searchers that covered every street, every park and every foot of the waterfront, the consequences would have been too terrible to contemplate.

They rushed to the hospital to find she was uninjured but suffering from hypothermia and a suspected chest infection. Kay and Lewis stayed while Madeline sat with her mother in the emergency department, but the old lady did not recognize her or even acknowledge her adventure and soon went to sleep.

It was one in the morning when Lewis took Madeline back to the farm. Adele Holland's old gentleman friend had left after the call to say the search was over, but had lit the range in the kitchen, which took the edge off the chill. Madeline stood in the middle of the kitchen, as tired and emotional as she could ever remember feeling.

"Have you got anything to eat?" Lewis asked, opening a few cupboards.

She shrugged, too tired to be interested in food. Then she glanced guiltily at Lewis, who looked as weary as she felt, only better dressed. He probably hadn't eaten, himself, since she'd stood him up for dinner.

His peremptory command had angered her this afternoon, even through her shame. Madeline had done all he'd asked of her during the conference. She'd attended workshops, balls, even allowed herself to be flung off a cliff into a canyon. To imply that the future of the hotels still rested on her shoulders if she didn't do what he said was the last straw.

While she'd been standing aimlessly in the middle of the kitchen daydreaming, Lewis had left the room. Now he came back in, took her hand and led her into the lounge. He'd lit the fire and now he pushed her down onto the couch. "I'll fix us something to eat."

Relieved to be alone for a minute, Madeline

stared into the fire, so grateful to her old friends and neighbors for their support tonight. Despite everything, it seemed her mother was very fondly regarded in the community.

Touched by their rallying around, Madeline wondered for the first time whether she was doing the right thing by leaving. Not one person had mentioned the scandal tonight, to her face, anyway, but many had said how proud they were of what she'd achieved, and when was she coming home for good, and even how right it was that a Holland was still on the old Holland farm.

Their reserve toward Lewis was evident, but no one actually challenged him, either about the elevator business or his intentions toward the hotels.

Too tired to think straight, she wondered what the legal ramifications of cancelling the deal on the farm were. Maybe she'd call the guy tomorrow. Madeline yawned and leaned back on the couch, the fire warming her face.

Lewis walked in with a plateful of hot buttered toast. "It's only instant soup," he said, setting down the plate and a couple of spoons, "but it'll warm you up."

Madeline watched him walk back into the kitchen, touched at his fussing. See, she told herself, sometimes he could be nice. He'd certainly been a rock of support tonight. How she wanted to know him. Had he ever been married, been in love? Why did he work so hard and what gave him pleasure?

Madeline curled up on the couch, feeling warmer than the fire should get credit for, knowing exactly what gave him pleasure. Had it ever been like that for him before? she wondered dreamily. No one had ever made her feel like he did. Wouldn't it be nice if she'd touched something in this man that no one else had?

Next thing she knew, she was in his arms and he was taking her somewhere cold. She knew it was Lewis; she remembered his smell and the longish hair tickling her face. But this was way too cold to be the Alpine Fantasy Retreat. She tightened her arms around his neck, glad that he was here to warm her up.

He carried her down the hallway and she groggily told him the way. The bedroom was cold. Boxes containing everything she'd loved and left lined one wall. Still holding her, he walked to the single bed and tugged the covers back. Madeline nosed her face into the skin of his neck and inhaled, strangely embarrassed that he was here in her childhood bedroom, nowhere near the luxury he was used to.

His arms tightened and he even brushed her cheek with his lips very briefly as he lowered her to the bed. With fuzzy surprise, she thought she hadn't equated tenderness before from Lewis.

She supposed she hadn't needed to.

Lewis sat on the edge of the bed beside her. "Lift your arms."

She complied and he whisked the jersey she wore over her head, leaving her in a long-sleeved tee. She flopped back onto the bed and he turned and began easing her Ugg boots off.

"I could get to like this gentle side of you," she murmured, not realizing until too late that she'd spoken aloud.

Lewis gave a tight smile and set her boots on the floor. "I've had plenty of practice."

Madeline knotted her brows. "Practice?"

He lifted up momentarily and pulled the covers up to her chin. "My mother was an alcoholic," he said. "I've put her to bed hundreds of times."

Wow! A personal detail. He wasn't big on revealing them. Mind you, neither was she. So his mother was an alcoholic. Questions whispered through her tired mind, but then got stuck on the word *mother*. Lewis's personal history retreated while her mind and heart filled slowly with sadness and relief.

"Lewis, I don't think I can leave my mother," she whispered, snuggling down under the covers and closing her eyes.

He took so long to answer that her thoughts wandered to the dream she'd had where he'd leaned down and kissed her cheek. Sometime, somewhere, long ago. A muted longing for him to do just that drifted in and out of her mind.

"I think you're too tired and emotional to make any decisions now," he murmured as if in her dream. "Get some sleep."

Fine by me, she thought, sighing, *if you're not going to kiss me.*

"Can you tell me where I can find a blanket or two? I'll park up on the couch."

Madeline moved her head vaguely. "Next room," she mumbled. "Boxes."

She was asleep by the time he left the room.

Madeline slept for nine hours.

She walked into the lounge to find blankets neatly folded on the end of the couch, the curtains drawn and no sign of Lewis's car on the drive.

Her mother was comfortable and on the ward, she was told when she called the hospital, but they wanted to keep her in for another day to monitor her chest infection.

Relieved, Madeline unrolled the newspaper Lewis must have brought in from the step with only a little reluctance. Somehow the scandal had taken a backseat in light of yesterday's events.

Lewis and Our Madeline Are an Item! the headlines read. The pragmatic side of her sighed at the fact that this sort of gossip passed as news in the only supposedly serious daily paper in the region.

The personally involved woman in her took a deep breath and read the article.

Mr. Lewis Goode of Pacific Star Airlines and new CEO of Premier Hotel Group has broken his silence on the kiss in the elevator affair, run by this newspaper yesterday.

"Madeline Holland and I are in a relationship of some duration," he says. He had asked the high-ranking corporate executive to move to Australia to be closer to him. He denies knowing that she had applied for and landed the top Chief of Operations position in Premier at the time he concluded his corporate takeover of the massive company here in Queenstown last week. Ms. Holland could not be contacted last night for comment.

In news the local population will be relieved to hear, Mr. Goode intimated that Ms. Holland has personally persuaded him to reconsider his plans to close the three Premier hotels in the town.

Madeline took the article and her coffee to the step to reread it in the sun. "'Madeline Holland and I are in a relationship of some duration.'"

What had prompted him to do that? Could Lewis have feelings for her? The possibilities zinged about her brain. Did he want a relationship "of some duration" with her? Probably he just felt sorry for her about her mother going walkabout—no, he'd have had to put the statement out before that to get it in the morning papers.

Madeline was touched. He'd said it because he

wanted to make her feel better. He knew how ashamed she was about the grotesque tape splashed over the news. She had to admit, it would certainly make her feel better and may even appease her mother.

Her buoyancy lasted all of three minutes. The fact was, there were no facts. It was a great big lie, and that made her uneasy. Lies had to be sustained. Lies had a habit of coming out. The paper—or if not this one, another—would continue to try to contact her for comment. They would ask questions, Where did you meet? How long ago? Questions she had no answers to. What on earth could she say that had a ring of truth to it?

The phone rang and, to her surprise, it was the president of the Women in Business Association, confirming her invitation to speak tomorrow night. Feeling lighter than she had in the last day and a half, she called the real estate agent about the status of the contract she'd signed.

"It's with the lawyers at the moment."

"Say, hypothetically, I change my mind about selling. How would that work?"

The agent told her that only the purchaser could crash the deal at this time. "There would be substantial penalties if you renege on a signed purchase agreement." His voice had a tinge of annoyance about it.

"It was just a query," Madeline said and hung up, her brow furrowing. Damn. She hadn't made a final decision on her future yet, but it was nice to have options. Could she consider staying in Queenstown and not living at the farm?

She raised her head and drank in the glistening lake and bristling mountains above. She didn't think so.

She would just have to pay the penalties, then. She could afford it, if and when she made the decision.

Her mother was at her strident best that afternoon, running everyone ragged.

"Thank the Lord you're here," she said when Madeline walked into the ward. "You have to take me home."

Madeline had already spoken to the staff nurse on duty. Her mother had a fever and they were worried about her cough. She was allergic to strong antibiotics, just another thing Madeline hadn't known about her.

She took her mother's hands and sat down beside the bed. "Mum, you have to stop playing up. You have a chest infection. They need to keep you in here just a little longer and keep you warm."

Her mother seemed comforted by her presence for once. They talked of the farm and dogs they used to have. Madeline thought how old her mother looked. She was old, she supposed, but for the first time she seemed frail. And that was the last word Madeline would ever have used to describe her mother.

"Madeline?" her mother suddenly said in a perfectly calm, lucid tone—a rare occurrence these days. "I have something very important to say to you."

She started guiltily, knowing she was about to get

a right royal telling off, and if she knew her mother, everyone on the ward would hear. So her mother *had* seen the news yesterday.

Madeline was wrong. In fact, she discovered she'd been wrong most of her life:

Her mother had indulged in an affair that spanned several years, but the day she broke it off, realizing that she loved her husband and daughter too much to go on, was the day Madeline's father was killed.

Everyone thought after John Holland died that her mother changed and became the righteous zealot she was out of grief. But it was much more than that.

"Don't you see?" her mother cried. "I never got his forgiveness. That's why I've been so horrible and pushed you away all these years. I was the biggest sinner in God's Kingdom and so I punished everyone else, most of all you."

Madeline reeled with the revelations. When was this emotional roller coaster going to stop? She shushed and tried to placate her poor mother who was beside herself with guilt and shame, apologizing over and over for pushing her own daughter away.

When Madeline finally left the hospital hours later, she could not shake an ominous feeling that they didn't have much time left to forgive each other. For wasn't Madeline as much to blame for letting her mother get away with punishing her? She'd just accepted that that's the way things were and had abandoned her poor mother, when perhaps with a bit of love and understanding they could have forged a closer relationship and her mother could have forgiven herself.

She pulled up the driveway of the farm and saw the lights on, smoke curling out of the chimney. And her decision was made.

Madeline was home.

Eight

Lewis gave up trying to pretend anymore.

Madeline sat opposite him at the kitchen table, disinterestedly pushing the steak and stir-fry he'd made around her plate. She'd just recounted the details of her visit to the hospital and she looked done in. And he'd stopped pretending he didn't want to help anymore.

Lewis knew all about how the actions of a parent impacted a child, shaped their lives. If he was lucky enough to have kids, he would make damn sure any mistakes were owned up to and compensated for at the time, not left until the children were scarred by it.

"Rough day, huh?"

She smiled sadly. "Rough couple of days."

He'd not had a good day himself. The statement he'd given the paper had caused a bit of a fuss amongst the board of directors. From the calls he'd taken, no one had a problem with him sleeping with the newly appointed COO. They did, however, have doubts about a potential conflict of interests. Had Madeline known about the proposed corporate takeover? And how much, if any, influence had Lewis had over her appointment?

With Kay's help, he'd spent the day organizing a telephone conference call with all of the board for tomorrow. Most were en route back to their countries of residence. Only two of the directors lived in New Zealand and he was picking them up from the airport in the morning. There were several in Australia, and some as far afield as Paris and the United States, so time zones had to be considered. He'd finally nailed them down to midday tomorrow. He expected to be hauled over the coals for his actions, but he wasn't sorry. Madeline was blameless. She'd gotten the job on her own merit. No conflict of interest as far as he was concerned.

She finally pushed her plate aside, put her elbows on the table and steepled her fingers. "About the statement you made…"

He didn't regret sticking his neck out for her on this. If they kept to the same tune, he was sure he could sway the directors. "It should, I hope, ease some of your embarrassment here."

"It does, and I'm grateful." She paused. "But it's not true."

"It doesn't obligate you in any way," Lewis said quickly. "It's just a united front until the fuss dies down."

She inhaled. "It obligates me into perpetuating the lie."

Lewis steepled his fingers, mimicking her. "It sounds a bit better than what everyone thinks, that we had a couple too many drinks and decided to have a quickie in a public elevator."

She blinked. "As I said, I am grateful. It was—nice, what you did. But these things have a habit of coming out. People are going to want to know the whens and the wheres. We're digging a hole for ourselves."

But we're in it together, he thought. "Well, I think it will blow over quickly now. And when you get to work and people see you in action…"

She chewed on her bottom lip. "Perhaps my position in the company might be compromised."

Lewis should have known she'd realize how the corporate mind worked. He shrugged. "I've organized a conference call with the board of directors tomorrow, but don't worry about it. I think I can shoot down their concerns."

Her brows arched.

"Conflict-of-interest issue. How much you knew

about the takeover and so on." Something stopped him from citing one of the directors who suggested that perhaps she wasn't COO material. "Leave it to me. There's nothing to worry about, so long as we're on the same page."

"Same page?" she asked.

Lewis sighed patiently. "If anyone asks, we met overseas, I asked you to move to Australia. You knew nothing of the takeover bid, since you'd lived overseas for years and we didn't waste our precious time talking business."

Her brows lifted even higher.

"You kept the Premier job news a secret and came over here to attend the conference and sort out some personal stuff. We'll say it was as much a shock to me to see you in the Executive Committee meeting as it was to you when I walked in." He smiled wryly. "That, at least, is the truth."

Madeline held his gaze steadily. "Sounds like we need a scriptwriter for all that."

That ticked him off. He'd thought he was helping.

"The newspapers are after me to make a comment," Madeline said. "That's an awful lot to lie about. What if they ask for dates and places, where we met, when?"

"Say no comment. They'll get bored soon enough and I'll handle the directors, don't worry about that," he said confidently.

"You wouldn't have to handle the directors if you'd discussed it with me first," she said quietly.

Lewis sat back in his chair and put his hands behind his head. "You've got a lot on your mind."

"It's my mother," she said, looking away from him. "I don't know how much time she has left."

"What do the doctors say?"

"It's not what the doctors say. It's me. I feel I should be here for her now."

Lewis exhaled. "Well, take some leave. A couple of weeks, and then, when she seems stable…"

"I want to make it up to her so at least she doesn't have me on her conscience, as well."

She'd spoken almost over the top of him, as if she hadn't heard him. Now she picked up her utensils and began scraping her leftovers onto his plate.

"Leave that," he snapped. "Take some time…"

"My priorities have changed," she began.

Why was he even bothering? "Use your head, Madeline. What the hell would you do here? You're a businesswoman, not some small-town girl."

She picked up both plates and stood. "I thought so, but…" She turned and walked to the sink.

"Don't you think you're being a bit emotional about this?" he asked.

The plates banged down on the bench with a crack. "She's my mother, for God's sake! I'm allowed to be emotional." Her back bristled with tension and she just stood there at the sink not facing him.

Lewis lost the battle with his patience. "There are

retirement homes in Sydney. I'll get my assistant to send you some information."

Madeline whirled around, eyes flashing. "This is her home. She's lived her whole life here."

Something had changed; he could see that. He'd done his best to needle her throughout the conference, but it was "steady as she goes," all the way.

Not anymore. He took a deep breath. "She has Alzheimer's disease, Madeline. Most of the time she won't know or care where the hell she is."

She jerked as if he'd slapped her. Her eyes filled with disappointment and then slid away from his, leaving him feeling hollow, cutting him to the bone. She stalked into the lounge.

Hell, he hadn't meant to be callous.

But no one walked away from him. He headed after her, stopped when he saw her sitting on the couch leaning forward with her head in her hands.

His formidable chief of operations? His sexy responsive lover? Which? The lines had suddenly blurred and he didn't know which was more important to him. All he knew was, he wanted her in Sydney to find out.

She looked up and saw him watching her. "You have no heart," she said, and Lewis knew that if he didn't give her something, something of himself, he'd lose her.

He sat down beside her, and she watched him, that same dark disappointment in her eyes. Her hands twisted in her lap. "What made you so hard?" she whispered.

"I've had to be."

Jacques de Vries was Lewis's whole reason for living for the past two years. Now that he'd vanquished that septic thorn in his side, the sensible thing to do was to set some more goals, purge the revenge he'd supped on for two years.

Or else, with too much time on his hands, he was in danger of falling for a beautiful blonde with summer-blue eyes.

Lewis had never told another soul about his checkered childhood. He shied away from why he felt compelled to tell Madeline now. He wanted to take his time with her, and for that, she'd need to be in Sydney, so he'd better start making up for hurting her just now.

She arched one dark brow, waiting for him to speak, to lay bare his past.

"Jacques de Vries killed my father."

She exhaled slowly, her lips parting.

"Not what you expected?" he asked lightly. "I discovered that charming piece of news a couple of years ago, while identifying the body of my brother, whose death Jacques also had a hand in."

Madeline drew her legs up under her and leaned back in her seat, her eyes on his all the while.

Start at the beginning, he thought. "My father and Jacques were business partners in the early eighties. They ran a transport company taking aid throughout the African continent. We, my parents and I, lived just outside Nairobi."

It was a great life for a boy. Kenya was so colorful, the people warm. Lewis and his parents weren't rich by any stretch, but comfortable enough to have a great old house on the outskirts of town, with a housekeeper and cook. Lewis attended a school in Nairobi and spent every other minute having adventures.

"But one day, when I was seven, the police came for my father and threw him in jail, charged him with stealing the aid supplies and selling them on the black market. Jacques was in France, visiting his wife. My mother tried to get some help, some answers, but no one helped. After a week or so, she took me out of school and back to Australia."

Lewis had fought long and hard to be able to stay, wanting to be close to his beloved father. He never even got to say goodbye.

"She dumped me at my grandparents' house in Sydney, and that was the last I saw of her for months. She went back to see what she could do to get him out."

It was the worst time of his life. His grandparents were dour people who'd never approved of his father. They thought taking his young wife and child to Africa was irresponsible in the extreme. They enrolled Lewis in school and refused to let him speak of his father. He hated their deathly quiet house with the big ticking grandfather clock and all the surfaces gleaming, stinking of polish.

"When my mother finally came home, she was pregnant and deeply depressed. She hadn't been able to get my father released and had to trust that Jacques would pull off some miracle. She tried to prepare me for the worst. At the rate justice moved in Africa, it could be years before we saw him again."

All their money was tied up in the company. As much as both he and his mother hated staying with her disapproving parents, they were destitute. He'd never stopped nagging her to leave, felt bad about that now, but he hated living there so much. His mother knew, as he did not, the practicalities of being on her own with one child and another on the way.

"When Ed—my brother—was a couple of years old, Mum went on a benefit and we moved into a small flat. I think the grandparents were glad to be rid of us by then."

His mother never emerged from the depression and as soon as they moved away from her parents, she began drinking. Many days, Lewis bunked school to keep an eye on the toddler because his mother was trawling the town for money for drink, or passed out in bed. But he had to be careful. The grandparents were suspicious and he knew they would bring in the authorities if there was any question she wasn't looking after the boys properly.

"My father died of cholera, but we didn't find out

for a long time. He was still in jail with charges pending, but no conviction. It was like everyone just forgot about him. Poor Ed never even knew his dad.

"The next few years were hard, moneywise. Mum stuck Ed in child care and did a bit of cleaning. I had a paper round, but a lot of the money went on drink. And Ed was growing up wild." He smiled fondly. "He was trouble from the day he was born, always wanted what he couldn't have. When he started school, he'd just take things from the other kids if he wanted them. I had permanently bruised knuckles from keeping the school bullies away."

Madeline's leg moved out casually and her sock-covered foot nudged his thigh. He looked down and rubbed his knuckles. "Everyone said he was weird looking. He had this round head…" Lewis was too ashamed to tell her the truth. The bullies said Ed stank. He stank because he wet the bed every night of his life, and at thirteen or fourteen, Lewis didn't have the common sense to insist he shower before going to school.

"Ed inherited Mum's depression, I reckon," he said slowly, not keen to go into too many details. He recalled one day finding his brother drunk on the dregs of a bottle of whiskey his mother hadn't finished the day before. The little boy was only seven or eight years old.

When Lewis did go to school, he never knew what he would find when he got home. Sometimes there was a man, as drunk as his mother. Often he found her facedown in her own vomit. He and Ed would drag her down the hallway into her room, then Lewis would clean her up, put a pillow under her head and blankets over her and leave her to sleep it off on the floor. Once he got bigger, of course, he was able to wrestle her into bed himself.

He looked up to find her watching him closely. "I looked after them, I suppose. No one else was going to.

"I left school at sixteen and got a job as a storeman for a courier company, but with me out of the house all day, Ed hardly went to school and Mum didn't bother working anymore. But things picked up. With some help from my boss, I started my own business at eighteen, a courier franchise. We just kept speculating, and pretty soon the money was pouring in. I'd made my first million by the time I turned twenty-three."

No matter how good things were, his mother was still a drunk—just a better-dressed drunk with a better address. "But Ed," he said sadly, "he got away on me. He abused drugs for all of his teens."

The nights he cruised Kings Cross in the city looking for his younger brother would have numbered in the hundreds. There was no question of his leaving home—who would keep an eye on the other two? That put a dampener on his love life for all of his twenties. Since Lewis never knew what he'd find when he got home from work, there was no way he'd bring a girlfriend into the mix.

Then things looked up for a while. "Ed suddenly decided when he turned twenty he'd had enough of the drugs. He was a whiz with IT so I gave him all the encouragement I could.

"I finally got my own place at the ripe old age of thirty. Mum still drank but she went to AA meetings and she met a fellow drunk. They're still together, still drinking, but they have each other and a nice house to get blotto in."

Madeline smiled bleakly. Lewis bet she was thinking how different her straitlaced childhood was compared to his. How could two families be so very different and yet both dysfunctional in the extreme?

"And then a couple of years ago, I got a call from the cops, or Interpol or something, saying I had to go to Singapore to identify Ed's body. It was a drug overdose. I couldn't believe it. He'd been clean for three years."

He felt her foot pressing his thigh again and absently dropped his hand onto it and left it there. He wouldn't bother telling her about the horror of it all. Being classified as guilty by association and enduring strip searches in both Singapore and when he came back to Australia. He wouldn't tell her how much of a failure he felt as he stood over his little brother's white, lifeless body in a morgue far from home.

Her foot moved under his hand, pressed against his leg. "Why?" she whispered.

He shrugged. "I couldn't make sense of it at the

time. It took weeks getting through the formalities, bringing the body home, dealing with the cops there and in Australia."

"Your poor mother," Madeline said quietly. "Poor you."

Grief and guilt had consumed him, but he'd had to be strong for his mother, who went absolutely blotto. At one point, he seriously considered having her committed or put in rehab or something.

"A woman—Natasha—turned up at the funeral, said she was a friend of Ed's. I...got to know her."

Lewis wasn't proud of himself for the way he'd behaved. Natasha was French, beautiful, wild. After the stress of the last few weeks, he surrendered to a crazy lust. She was exotic and intense and they spent a week in bed before he started to wonder if she really was crazy, or worse, on drugs like Ed.

"She wanted to meet my mother, so one day I took her there, and suddenly she was screaming at Mum, she attacked her, slapped her, I had to haul her off. Ed wasn't my father's kid at all. He was Jacques's. She was Ed's half sister."

"After I'd thrown Natasha out, my mother confessed all. Jacques was kind, the only person in Nairobi who tried to help her make the authorities understand that her husband wasn't a crook. But nothing happened. Day after day, she visited the prison, pleaded with every authority she could think of. Jacques told her bribery was the only way, so she did that, too. The lawyers didn't want to touch the case. Nothing happened, everyone just kept saying come back tomorrow, maybe something will happen tomorrow."

Madeline shook her head with a sad smile. "That's exactly how some countries work, and not just in Africa." She shifted to lean her back against him with her feet up on the other end of the couch.

"Finally my mother snapped, I suppose." And Jacques de Vries was there to pick up the pieces, he thought bitterly. "Jacques 'comforted' her. But the moment she told him she was pregnant, he threw her out. He didn't want an affair with his jailed business partner's wife. He went back to his wife and child in France. Mum had nowhere to go but home. He gave her a few thousand, nothing like her share of the business, and she gave up, came home and tried to cope best she could."

"No wonder she was depressed," Madeline murmured. "What happened to Natasha?"

"She was heading back to Singapore when I caught up with her. She said she had proof that it was Jacques, not my father, who'd been responsible for ripping off millions of dollars worth of aid. She couldn't prove it, but suspected he'd bribed police and insurance officials. But she did have documents showing he'd received a vast insurance payout for the company when it folded. He went back to France, divorced his wife and set up his hotel corporation with the proceeds of the transport company, plus, I suppose what he got from his Black Market dealing. Silly bugger left a lot of the paperwork in the family home, which is how Natasha got hold of it."

"Can you prove it? Clear your father's name?"

The million-dollar question and, for a long time, his greatest desire. His poor father rotting in jail for years while his best friend and partner lived it up. No family to support him… Lewis inhaled deeply. If there was any way he could achieve that now, he'd be a happy man.

"It's—complicated. I hired some investigators. Their findings and some of the documents Natasha came up with would have made a pretty good case against Jacques, if I wanted to bankroll it, which I did. But some of the documents had my mother's signature on them. She swears she knows nothing of the fraud, but she had signed things, with Jacques's supervision. She thought they were gift certificates he told her would help pave the way for Dad's release. She certainly didn't profit from the insurance payout or after the company was wound up. Jacques told her he'd lost everything, too. I'd like nothing better than to see him behind bars." He gave a short, sharp laugh. "Actually I'd like nothing better than to see his eyes bulging with the pressure of my hands around his neck."

It had taken superhuman control the day of the Executive Committee meeting not to do that very thing when he went to see the man before publicly ousting him.

"But I can't be absolutely sure that the authorities wouldn't go after my mother."

Madeline snuggled in closer and he heard her yawn. "So you went after his company instead."

His arms tightened around her. "*My* company," he growled. "Born of the destruction of my family."

They sat quietly for a few minutes and Lewis wondered if she'd dropped off to sleep. The fire was toasty and he felt tired himself. He hadn't been counting, but he reckoned he was on the debit side of hours of sleep since he'd arrived in Queenstown and met Madeline Holland.

She suddenly heaved a great sigh while he rested his chin on her hair. "But I still don't understand why Ed did what he did."

Her hair smelled like apricots. "Who knows? Natasha contacted him by e-mail and said she knew who his real father was, and to meet her in Singapore. She told him Jacques's name. That's all I know for sure. I think he confronted Jacques and things went badly, leaving Ed so distraught he took some bad drugs. That's my personal view, but there could be any number of things. Jacques denies meeting him in person though admits Ed contacted him by phone. Whatever the chain of events, something led to Ed taking a massive dose of heroin, a dose he must have known, with his experience, would kill him."

"Well, what did Jacques say when you told him you knew about him?"

A fist of hate squeezed his heart but he was too tired to pander to it. "Laughed in my face and said good luck proving it."

"What about blackmail—" a yawn caught her unawares "—can't he be persuaded with the proof you have?"

"Really, Ms. Holland." Lewis chuckled. "The way your mind works." He'd spent months weighing up his options before settling on taking the man's company. "Jacques believed he was untouchable, but he's quite capable of taking everyone, my mother included, down with him. My way took a long time, but that's all right. I won."

A log shifted in the grate, sending a shower of sparks up the chimney. Lewis's hands were clasped around her middle, and now Madeline covered them with her own, stroking slowly.

"Am I forgiven," he murmured into her fragrant hair, "for being heartless before about your mother?"

Her hands stilled. He heard her long breath in and the rasp of his chin on her hair as she nodded.

"You're forgiven," she said simply.

Nine

Madeline woke to find herself spooned by a warm body, an arm lying heavily around her waist. It took a second to understand where she was—the couch in the farm's living room. As to why, the facts took their time seeping into her languorous brain.

She remembered most of the life story he'd told. Weird how his mother's guilt and shame shaped her children's lives, with striking similarity to her own. She understood better now Lewis's need for revenge, his ruthlessness when something distracted him from his goal, his scathing lack of sympathy for weakness.

Such a responsibility for one so young: hiding his home life from the world; eking out a living to save his family from Social Services, the poor house; death's embrace due to drink and drugs.

His hand moved, shredding her thoughts. The fingers spread slowly and it was impossible not to flinch in response to a heartbeat suddenly gone from a walk in the park to a canter, in one second flat.

They'd snuggled down together in the chill of a dying fire and he'd finished his story. She couldn't think of anything useful to say so had just leaned into him, giving him her warmth, hopefully her comfort. They must have fallen asleep. The last thing she recalled was the perplexed tone of his voice saying that he'd never told a soul what he'd told her tonight.

Lewis gave a beefy sigh behind her, arching so that the length of his body settled warmly against her back. His spread fingers curled into her diaphragm, cool even over her clothes. At some stage, he must have grabbed the blanket he'd used the night before on the end of the couch and spread it over them. But Madeline wasn't feeling the cold at the moment. She sucked her gut in, not to get away, but to contain the feeling of him holding her there, just below breasts that were suddenly wide awake.

It was a strange feeling waking up with a man beside her—well, technically behind her. Not something she'd done more than three times in her life.

She didn't want to move.

Lewis's lower body stretched and hunched into the dip under her buttocks, sending an eruption of unaccustomed early-morning desire welling up. Her nipples hardened, pushing against her bra and sweater.

Don't even think about it! They'd had their final night. How much perfection could a man and a woman want? It was batting against average to try for three perfect nights in a row.

"Good morning," Lewis mumbled into her ear.

Madeline squeezed her eyes shut and pulled a face to stop herself from groaning. Her ear turned out to be another erotic zone of hers, she'd discovered when she discovered Lewis. She tried, she really did, not to respond, to pretend she was asleep. Anything not to give in to something she already knew would be sensational.

He hummed deep in his throat, a sound of pleasure, contentment. That's all it was, she told herself. You can't sound contented if you're excited. Unless you were going "Mmmm" rather than humming. Like her, he was only half awake, warm, comfortable. Not aroused.

Except there was no point denying that she could feel his arousal. Especially since she couldn't resist pressing her behind up against it.

Just checking.

Lewis continued his gentle wake-up assault on her senses, and she pretended she was dreaming, a hot, sweaty dream that necessitated his plundering under her clothes and palming her breasts while she tried her best to grind him into the back of the couch with her backside.

It was like a dream come true when he finally began stroking her intimately, and then when she felt him hot and heavy between thighs that were mysteriously bereft of clothes, gliding back and forth, leaving her shuddering in jerky uncoordinated ecstasy so quickly, it made her head spin.

The only thing that could improve on the dream was when he was inside her, pressing her down; miraculously finding him inside her, snug, on an angle she hadn't felt before, liking it, moving with it, loving it—until they fell off the couch and hit the floor with a whump. And she couldn't pretend anymore that his weight on top of her hadn't caused a stampede of breath from her lungs, and then that she was laughing out loud, great gasps of it as she dug his elbow out of her stomach and fought with the trousers shackling her legs.

Couldn't pretend that she didn't see the fun in his eyes change to awareness and then, shockingly, to tenderness that made her heart bleed as he linked their fingers and slid over her, inside her again. Stilled, all fun gone in a slow lingering kiss, and then began to move, slow, deep, deeper.

She wished she was dreaming because she didn't want to see what she saw in his eyes. She saw all the things she felt; tenderness, liking, respect, safety. Wanting to support him, needing his…

Needing just a bit faster to stroke that pleasure point there, there and again there. Oh! Don't think, just feel, don't stop, and she spun out as he lifted her and crushed her to him, wrapping her up tightly, and came himself with a gusty sigh of pleasure and relief.

She lay there listening to his heartbeat, knowing she didn't want to look into his eyes again, she had to pull back, keep something in reserve or she would lose her heart.

She had lost her heart.

She knew it because of the pain that arrowed there when he disengaged himself, when his body left hers and she knew, without a doubt, that this was the last time, even though the other night had been the last time. Just as exquisite as all the other times, but with the added dimension of real caring, real feeling. Real heartache.

Lewis leaned back, smiling a little. Madeline ducked her head. She had to because her eyes were filling and there was no way in the world she would cry in front of him. But he was quick to call her on it. He moved his head sharply to put it in her line of vision. "Don't do that. Don't ever regret this."

She shook her head, looking down. "It's too late for regrets," she mumbled, knowing he wouldn't have a clue what she was talking about. How could he know that with their lovemaking today, she had fallen in love for the first time in her life.

She was too vulnerable, too needy to be with him now. She would not become one of his projects, his fixer-uppers. Maybe one day, she'd get off this emotional roller coaster that had kidnapped her lately and be the strong, competent, pragmatic woman she knew she was. But for now she was a puddle of emotions, and Lewis needed strength.

Then his phone was ringing and he was rising in a swathe of blankets and mismatched clothes, leaving her exposed and feeling silly. She let him have the bathroom first because the New Zealand-based directors had just hit town and wanted to re-schedule the conference call earlier and meet with him beforehand.

At least, she thought as she sat waiting for the coffee to drip, he'd have the comfort of familiarity. Soon he'd go home to his apartment, his city, his office. He'd call up whatever woman he was squiring around for a date. He'd visit his mother.

Whereas Madeline was starting from scratch. Floundering. She'd left a great job, was about to turn down an even greater job, been made a laughing-stock, discovered her mother was not only fallible, but scarily mortal. And now she had the memory of making love to Lewis on this couch, in front of this fire. And the thing that terrified her the most was the possibility that she wouldn't even be left with those cherished memories if she couldn't extricate herself from the contract of sale.

Lewis came into the kitchen looking gorgeous and clean, and swallowed half a cup of coffee. "Lewis, about this conference call…" Madeline began. There was no point in him going through with this thing with her when she would never be part of the team.

"Not now," he said quickly, banging his cup down. "I'm going to that conference call and I'll come back with the desired result, and then we'll talk, all right?"

As if she had much choice, with him already halfway out the door.

But then he stopped, came back, lifted her out of the chair with one arm around her waist, kissed her soundly on the lips and plopped her back down again.

"We'll talk," he repeated, his eyes serious. "Keep your phone on."

Maybe, Madeline thought, still breathless from that kiss. They'd talk of her mother, and why Madeline was having second thoughts about the opportunity of a lifetime to reach the very top echelon of the corporate world in Australasia. They'd talk about how good the sex was and how she'd never be happy as a small-town girl. But they wouldn't talk of the real issue.

She had to stay; he had to go. His businesses, his life, were there. And Lewis had spent his life looking after the needy, and, ashamed as she was to admit it, she was needy right now. Her life was out of control and she couldn't be the strong, competent woman he needed and wanted.

And that hurt like hell because the only other thing she knew for sure in this helter-skelter life of hers was that she was in love with him.

Her phone rang. It was the reporter for the local paper. He wanted to "give Madeline a chance to put her side of the story" and to comment on Lewis's statement about their relationship.

She was so not ready for this.

It was the moment of truth.

A sudden realization of what might happen if she refuted his statement, told the truth, trickled through her thought processes. Lewis would be angry. He would hate that she'd slapped his attempt to help down and that she'd rebuked him in public. He'd be pissed that he'd gone to bat for her with the directors for nothing. He wouldn't want her for his COO anymore. He wouldn't want her.

She haltingly agreed to meet the reporter later that day at an Internet café in town.

"Sorry, Ms. Holland." The real estate agent put his phone down with an apologetic look. "The lawyer says it's all confirmed. There's nothing you can do."

Madeline stared at him blankly. "But...I only signed the papers yesterday." Or was it the day before? So much had happened in the last day or two, she couldn't be sure. "How can it have gone through so quickly?"

"The sale and purchase agreement you signed accepted the purchaser's offer and their conditions. It's a binding contract. As I said before, the only one who can break the deal at this stage is the purchaser, and only then if he can't meet the conditions you accepted on the contract." He picked up some papers and straightened them, avoiding her eyes.

Madeline knew when she was being politely dismissed.

"Can't I talk to someone? To the manager of the development company?"

He looked down at the contract in front of him. "The signatory is an agent designated by the development company, PacAsia Enterprises. He probably isn't even part of the company. You can look PacAsia up in the company register, if you like." He stood up. Clearly the conversation was at an end. "But I warn you, big pieces of prime real estate don't come up here very often. Frankly, a development company would be crazy to let that go."

Madeline got the same story at the lawyer's. "What if I offer the purchaser a sweetener to crash the contract?"

The lawyer pursed his lips. "That's your prerogative. But if they don't accept, then there is nothing you can do."

Madeline was being naive. She also realized that the real estate agent or the lawyer were hardly likely to assist her to do away with their fees.

With a heavy heart, she wandered the streets until she found herself outside the Internet café where she was supposed to meet the reporter. She was an hour early, but got herself a coffee, logged into a computer and then keyed in the name of the development company.

Frustrated beyond measure, she drummed her fingers as the register took its sweet time loading. Now, when she had finally made the decision to stay in Queenstown, it seemed everything was conspiring against her. Where would she live? She knew it would break her heart to leave her family home.

PacAsia Enterprises Ltd. finally came up on the screen.

Madeline wrote down the registered address. No phone number, three directors, she scrolled down to the share parcels and saw that one company held all the shares. She read the name, checked, and read it again.

PacAsia Enterprises shares were all owned by one company, Pacific Star Enterprises.

Madeline read it again, very slowly, just to make sure, then, with icy expectation, she raised her eyes to the directors listed.

"Goode, Lewis Jay."

The hum of chatter around her faded as her heart sank somewhere close to her ankles.

Lewis Goode had stolen her farm.

The two New-Zealand-based directors sat at the boardroom table with Lewis. The conference call had been rescheduled a number of times, but finally they were underway. Lewis prepared to receive a grilling.

The directors were concerned about the conflict-of-interest angle—how much did Madeline Holland know about Lewis's corporate takeover bid at the time she applied for the job? His explanation was pretty much what he'd outlined to Madeline last night.

Most of the directors seemed amenable. The New Zealand directors had flown down as a show of support because they knew of the opposition he would face from at least two of Jacques's old cronies. These two directors spoke up now, offering the view that Madeline was not COO material for allowing herself to get into this position.

"Oh, for Christ's sake," Lewis growled. "There were two of us in the elevator. How come my morals haven't come into question?"

Suddenly the door flew open with a bang, and Madeline stalked in.

"You bastard!" she said in a breathy exhalation, her eyes blazing.

Quick as a flash, Lewis hit the mute switch.

"You won't get away with it."

Lewis stood with a quick glance at the two men around the table. "Please, excuse me." Then he was on his feet, striding purposefully toward her, his lips flatlining. Every muscle vibrated with anger. He grasped her above the elbow, turning her smoothly, and whisked her outside.

Hardly pausing as he pulled the door closed behind, his relentless momentum took them to the wall opposite and then, when she had nowhere to go and no room to move, slapped his hands on the wall at both sides of her head.

Her eyes spit sparks of blue, and she opened her mouth but Lewis intended giving her not a second's grace. He could not recall when he'd last been so angry. Probably not since the night he discovered Jacques de Vries's part in his father's and brother's deaths.

"I will *not* be interrupted, do you hear?" He delivered the forceful missive in a deadly low voice that surprised even him.

Madeline's eyes were wide, but he could see she was determined and not the least intimidated.

"You. Bought. My. Farm." The words left her mouth equally forcefully like four quick smart slaps to his ears.

Shit!

"You do not interrupt me," he gritted, "in an important meeting like this when my balls are being nailed to the floor because I am standing up for your integrity."

Madeline blinked. For one fraction of a second, he saw the slightest hesitation, then it was gone. Doubt smoothed away, replaced by cold and composed anger. "Don't do me any favors, *Mr.* Goode. I want my property back, and you are going to assure me of that right now."

She was good. In spite of the tension, Lewis was once again awash with admiration. Madeline

Holland was his chief of operations and he was damned pleased about it.

Not that he was going to let her know that right now. "I will discuss this *private* matter with you at a more opportune time, Madeline." He stretched the syllables of her name out, reminding her that he was the boss and she the subordinate.

She opened her mouth to protest but he was quicker. "Go home and I will see you there later." He pushed away from the wall and stood glowering at her, waiting for her to make her move. He would call security before he allowed her to burst in on him again.

Madeline drew herself up to her full impressive height. He'd never wanted to kiss her quite as much as he did at this moment, but he carefully concealed it.

"You won't get away with this, Lewis," she said, her chin rising. "You are going to cancel that contract and you are going to do it today."

Lewis looked down his nose at her. "We'll see. Don't you ever interrupt me like that again."

They glared at each other for a moment more, battle lines drawn, then she nodded briskly, turned on her heel and strode off down the hall, the tight A-line skirt hinting at a femininity that even her brisk, angry, businesslike stride couldn't hide.

And Lewis watched her all the way, not because he was afraid she would return once his back was turned and burst in on them again. He watched her because his blood was pumping, most of it in a southward direction. If it was not imperative that he get back to his very important conference call, he would have gone after her and taken her up against the wall.

The interlude did more to help his case than anything he'd come up with before. He came back into the room fired with admiration and so adamant that Madeline Holland would turn out to be the best COO Premier ever had the privilege to employ. The directors were convinced. And the meeting concluded soon afterward.

Now he just had to convince Madeline herself.

He'd bought the farm on the day the story about him and Madeline in the elevator broke. He intended nothing to get in the way of her coming to Sydney, certainly not a bit of scandal. And hey, the place was on the market, it was fair game. Over the last day he'd congratulated himself on his decision, especially when she began to vacillate about staying here with her mother. Taking the farm off her hands, and for a very fair price, was just one more reason for her to pack up and go.

Perhaps he should have told her, especially before making love to her this morning. That wasn't a meeting of strangers, nor a planned last fantasy romp before they knuckled down and got on with the job. This morning had a whole Pandora's box of feelings about it. Something had changed. It went deeper than wanting her or professional admiration.

This morning he'd felt warmed by her. He'd gone to sleep with her on his mind and woken the same way. And he wasn't afraid to have it happen that way again. And again.

Naturally, once he'd started loving her, he could hardly spoil the moment by telling her he'd bought her farm out from under her.

He called her as soon as the two men left the room. Now that his task had been finalized to a satisfactory conclusion, it was time to start eating humble pie. Madeline was going to Sydney with a clean slate, a bit of office gossip aside, which he knew she'd deal with easily. So what need did she have for the farm? Her mother certainly wouldn't be using it.

He dialed her number, but she was either on the line or the thing was turned off. Lewis decided against leaving a voice mail and chose to go and have a celebratory lunch in the hotel restaurant. Just as he finished, someone approached.

"Are you trying to catch us out?" Kay smiled brightly and pulled out the chair opposite.

Lewis pushed his empty plate aside and smiled at her. "The Akaroa salmon was excellent. Will you join me for dessert?"

"I've eaten." Kay signaled the waitress. "I will have a coffee if you don't mind."

They chatted for a few minutes and then Lewis asked if Kay had seen Madeline. "I've been calling for an hour, but no luck."

Kay looked away, her eyes on the approaching waitress. After they'd given their order, Kay cleared her throat. "She came to see me after she'd...surprised you in the boardroom," she finished judiciously.

Lewis nodded, smiling pleasantly. "I trust she won't make a habit of surprising me in boardrooms. Any idea where she is now?"

"Well, she had an appointment with a reporter, but that was an hour or so ago."

He gave her a sharp look. "What the hell is she talking to a reporter for?"

"In case you hadn't noticed," Kay murmured, "you two are all the rage at the moment. He contacted her. I believe his reasoning was that the media have had a say, you have had a say, it was time Madeline put her side of the story across."

Lewis folded his arms and studied Kay thoughtfully, careful to conceal the little bit of unease that skittered through him. He knew Madeline wasn't happy about lying.

What if she told the truth, that there was no relationship and the security tape and reports of passionate liaisons in plush resorts were the real deal. Lust, pure and simple.

That would certainly put a fly in his ointment.

"Don't worry," Kay said soothingly. "Madeline's the soul of discretion, even if she may not be that happy with you at the moment."

And Lewis stopped worrying because this was Kay, Madeline's oldest and dearest friend. And she didn't look worried.

Ten

Three hours later, Lewis walked off the flight from Queenstown and stepped into Christchurch Airport, ninety minutes before his flight to Sydney.

This time there was no smile for the hostess in the Pacific Star lounge. He didn't bother with the buffet. He stood by the window, looking out at the tarmac, wondering how it had all gone so horribly wrong.

The reek of betrayal clung to his nostrils. He'd never felt the need to share his personal history until last night. Some misguided notion that he wanted Madeline to understand him, and wanted to distract her from the emotion and distress of the last couple of days.

Lewis had only just started thinking about relationships when he'd moved into his own place, finally believing that his brother and mother were safe. A scant year wining and dining and fighting off the gold diggers, and then Ed up and died. From then on, he lived and breathed revenge.

He wasn't looking when he arrived in Queenstown, and then he found her, wanted her, and now—well, fool that he was—he might just be in love with her.

Darkness gathered on the tarmac, as grey as the doubt flirting with his mind. What if he was wrong, what if it wasn't her? Surely he hadn't confused tough and capable with cruel and calculating?

Of course it was her. He'd bought her farm. She'd told him, in front of his colleagues that he wouldn't get away with it. And then she went off to have a cozy tête-à-tête with the reporter.

It was unbelievable how quickly everything had unfolded. The reporter and the Sydney police broke all records, but wasn't that the way when a public persona was involved? He'd assumed, when he saw his mother's number come up on his phone, she was calling about the scandalous reports in the media.

In fact, she'd called to tell him she'd been arrested on historical insurance-fraud charges, and all because of her son's pillow talk. He really had to stop sleeping with women. They weren't good for his mother's health. She'd endured a verbal and physical assault by Natasha and now Madeline's actions had her sitting in a police cell.

How quickly Madeline had wound her way into his heart. It was a short, sharp reminder that looking out for number one was the only way to go.

His boarding call came and Lewis took his phone out to turn it off just as it rang.

"Where are you?" Madeline asked, her voice cool.

"Christchurch Airport." He waited, tapping his passport and boarding card on his leg.

"Christchurch? I don't understand."

Again he grappled with doubt. Was it just wishful thinking to wonder if Natasha could be the culprit? But as much as she hated her father for abandoning her mother, she'd begged Lewis to be discreet about his revenge. Could Jacques himself have had an attack of conscience?

Lewis rejected that out of hand. Madeline was the only possibility.

"Lewis? I thought you were coming out tonight. Only, I have to go out now, the Women in Business thing."

"Did you enjoy your little talk with the reporter?" he asked acidly.

Another pause, longer this time. He pictured her lovely heart-shaped face, shadowed with guilt.

"Nothing left to say?"

"Lewis…" Her voice was barely audible. "I'm sorry. I did what I had to do. The truth always comes out in the end."

Lewis laughed harshly. "In this case, the fantasy was better than the truth."

He heard her indrawn breath and it tore at him, but now that she'd confirmed her betrayal, he would excise her from his life as if she'd never existed. "I have a scoop for you, Ms. Holland. You're fired." He paused, waiting for a sign that she cared about that. "The Waterfront will be sold and the other two hotels torn down as soon as I can get a buyer for the land." A clear sound of distress came down the line but he ignored it. "And…" He paused one last time, just for the hell of it. "You have one month to get off my farm!"

Madeline slid down to the floor in a daze, still holding the phone. His words could not have slashed her deeper.

In the space of a couple of minutes, righteous anger had turned into confusion and then fear, heartbreak, letdown. Her guilt about publicly refuting Lewis's statement faded. His reaction was way over the top, undeserved.

Madeline had lost everything. Her job. The respect of her peers, who would now hate her for losing their jobs. Her home. And her love.

Her throat constricted and tears prickled at the backs of her eyelids, but she wouldn't cry, couldn't. In half an hour, she'd be standing in front of a gathering of up-and-coming businesswomen, telling them how to have it all.

When she'd lost it all.

Things in Madeline Holland's world could not get any worse—or could they?

Two days later she heard the door knocker and watched Kay wend her way through the throng of people in her living room at the farmhouse. Another plate of scones to go onto the already laden table. Well-wishers from all over town and country bustled around talking quietly, while she stood like a dummy, fortified by their kindness and affection.

Her mother had lost the fight against a sudden and savage bout of pneumonia. Lucky, as it turned out, when the chest X-rays showed a pair of lungs covered in tumors. Big, inoperable tumors.

Who were all these people? She'd had more hugs and kind words today than she'd accumulated in twenty-eight years. So much for thinking she didn't have a home. Home was here—not the farm, sadly—but this town, these people whom she, and her parents before her, had grown up with. They stood in the hall, fussed around the table, sat on the couch that she and Lewis had— But she wouldn't think of that now.

"No, sadly," she said to old Mrs. Lucan, who lived down the road. "I won't be able to stay here, but I will be staying in Queenstown."

"The farm is too big for you on your own." The old lady nodded understandingly.

"I sold it when I thought I was leaving, then I tried to stop the sale, but it's too late now."

Someone touched her arm, and she turned to find Brian Cornelius, her mother's friend.

Her mother had told her that her lover's name was Brian. The nurse said he visited Adele every Sunday. Suddenly it all fell into place.

Madeline wanted to thank him for visiting her mother regularly, for sticking with her and trying to show her she was not a bad person, even though she was sure Adele would have saved her choicest missives for the man who'd toppled the Bible Lady from grace.

She put her arms around him and kissed his cheek. "Perhaps one Sunday, you could come out and we could scatter Mum's ashes together."

Brian squeezed her hands, unable to speak for long moments. A gentle smile creased his face. "I'd like that," he said. "Very much."

She squeezed his hands back. "I think she would, too."

Kay pushed through the crowd, holding out the phone. "It's Lewis," she whispered close to Madeline's ear. "Want me to tell him to get lost?"

Madeline closed her eyes for a long second. There had been little time to dwell on the heartache. She had heard via Kay that apparently Lewis's mother had been arrested on suspicion of insurance fraud. She'd felt for him and wished his poor mother strength to survive. But thoughts of his mother only brought back thoughts of hers.

She took the phone. "Hello, Lewis."

"Madeline?"

At least he didn't sound hateful and cold like he had last time she'd heard his voice.

"Sounds like you have a houseful."

Was he ringing to gloat or to offer commiserations?

"Madeline, I'm—sorry. Truly sorry."

That didn't sound like gloating. Thankfully, Kay must have told him. Madeline hadn't quite worked out how to say it, how best to get her tongue around it. My mother has died, has passed away, is no longer with us...

"Thank you, Lewis. How is your mother?"

Lewis cleared his throat. "It's been tough, but she'll be all right, as long as the Scotch holds out."

Madeline smiled. "Look after her. You never know..." Her voice hitched and she took a couple of steps away from her neighbor, battling for control.

"Madeline, those things I said, I'm just...I don't know how to make it up to you."

She didn't know, either. And she didn't want to even think about it right now. Her system was overloaded.

"Bye bye, dear," one of the well-wishers said, pecking her on the cheek.

"Thank you for coming," Madeline said, hugging her back. "I'll see you Wednesday."

"Yes," Lewis said. "I'll be there Wednesday. I can't leave until I've got Mum's lawyers sorted out."

"*You're* coming on Wednesday?" Madeline asked, bemused. "For the funeral?" It was nice to get the sympathy call, but she hadn't expected that.

There was a long silence. "Lewis?" she asked, thinking she'd lost the connection.

"Funeral? Your mother's funeral?" he asked quietly.

"Yes," she said, noting another carload of well-wishers coming up the driveway. "I have to go, Lewis. Thank you for calling."

"To the Holland funeral," Lewis clipped out, sliding into the back of the airport cab.

"You're late," the taxi driver commented, pulling smartly away from the curb.

Late. Too damned late to recognize that he loved Madeline Holland.

Lewis had no idea what her reaction to his presence at her mother's funeral would be. He hadn't spoken to her since the day her mother died. For all he knew she would order him from the church.

Trying to clear the mess Jacques de Vries had left in his sudden and unexpected attack of conscience had taken forever. He couldn't leave his mother to battle the legal stuff while she was in such a state. The insurance company had not opposed bail as long as she handed in her passport. It wasn't over, but finally he could leave her with her boyfriend to drink away the horrors of the past week.

The church overflowed out into a pretty little courtyard, so he stood in the drizzle like a hundred other mourners and listened to the last of the service through a tinny intercom system.

Then the church organ started and the crowd in front of him sidled back to let those inside out. Lewis stood firm, his head well above most of the crowd, copping his share of curious looks.

They would be even more curious if Madeline ignored him or gave him his marching orders. No more than he deserved for his appalling behavior.

Then she was there, walking slowly toward him, looking as if a puff of wind would blow her over, except Kay had a tight hold of one arm. Her long black overcoat almost dwarfed her and contrasted sharply with the pale skin of her face. The freezing drizzle drifted down onto her shining, golden bare head.

She looked so sad. Lewis hoped she'd had time to make her peace with her mother before she died.

Then her face raised and she looked full at him and held his gaze. Her step faltered for a second, and he wondered if she'd turn from him, or be vague and polite like the other day on the phone. If he knew her at all, she would hold strong, and certainly wouldn't countenance any public display of emotion.

But she didn't stop, and she didn't stop looking at

him. In fact, as the crowd parted before her, she kept on coming and walked straight into his arms.

Lewis wrapped her up and held her tight, resting his chin on her head. She stood quietly, her face hidden in his shoulder, and slid her arms around his waist. He never wanted to let go.

He accompanied her to the graveside, along with the whole town, it seemed, even in the freezing grey drizzle. He stood by her side at the community hall, where ladies bustled around making hundreds of cups of tea and setting out plate after plate of food. And when most people had left and Kay asked if Madeline wanted to stay with her tonight, she shook her head. "I want to go home."

The rain had stopped and a watery sun broke through the clouds as the cab turned into the long driveway of the farm.

"Going to be a nice sunset," the driver commented before they alighted.

Lewis set about lighting the fire in the lounge and the coal range in the kitchen. He had no idea what he was doing here, if she wanted him to stay, if she wanted to talk.

Madeline came out of her bedroom. She'd changed into jeans, a black high-necked jersey and a white cardigan over it. They stared at each other for a moment.

Holding his gaze, she smiled at him tremulously. "Thank you, Lewis."

He raised his brow. For what? Accusing her of doing something she wasn't capable of? For not listening and going behind her back? Or for not telling her how he felt about her after making love with her on the couch? Who would have thought a crummy couch and a patch of floor could totally overshadow the much grander fantasies of the past?

"If you don't mind," Madeline said, her eyes drifting out to the veranda, "I'd like to sit outside for a while, watch the sun go down."

He stepped toward his coat, but she held up her hand. "Alone, if that's all right. I have a goodbye to make."

He nodded, but picked up his coat anyway and slipped it over her shoulders, wanting to be close to her in some small way. "I'll bring you out a drink."

"Thanks. A glass of wine would be lovely."

He took the wine out to her, then went back inside, poured himself a glass and pulled a kitchen chair up to the old coal range. But his eyes kept wandering out to where she sat, with her back to him, on a rocking chair on the veranda. The chair moved slowly. She faced the turbulent sky as the sun slid slowly down behind the Remarkables mountain range.

She was saying goodbye as the sun went down on her mother's life. Although he badly wanted to be with her, comfort her, he knew she needed some time and space to say her goodbyes in private.

* * *

Madeline pulled Lewis's coat up around her neck and ears, inhaling him, rocking slowly on the creaky old chair. The ache of unshed tears was almost painful.

"You did us proud, Mum," she said, knowing her mother would have been delighted at the unprecedented turnout. Adele Holland loved a crowd. "Just think how many sinners you could have lambasted today." She ticked off a few names on her hands, only feeling a little silly.

The lowering sun arced through the clouds and sent a ray of yellow from the step to her feet. "Goodbye, Mum," Madeline whispered, feeling the tears back up, her throat swelling. "I love you and I'm sorry, and thank you for telling me you were sorry. Perhaps now we can be friends."

She kept her eyes on the last streak of orange in the sky, focused on it until her eyes nearly crossed and there was nothing but dusky grey black.

Gone. All gone…she wrapped her arms around herself and finally gave in to the tears.

The door opened and then Lewis was in front of her crouching down, his hands on her knees. "Just let me hold you."

Without waiting for her reply, he slid his hands under her, lifted her up, then turned and sat with her in his arms.

The unaccustomed slide of tears down her face, the unfamiliar feeling of being wrapped up in security and strength, only made her cry more. Maybe she was entitled. She snuggled into his warm chest and cried all the tears she'd never been able to cry. All the times she'd missed home, missed her parents, wondered why she was so terrible that her mother didn't seem to love her at all. She'd thought she had time to mend bridges but she'd run out of time. She cried for the longest time, and Lewis held on tight and rocked her slowly and said nothing, which was just as she wanted it.

A long time later they went back inside and he refilled their glasses while Madeline mopped at her face with tissues.

"Sorry about that," she said as he settled down beside her.

"What, for being human?"

A niggly little headache squeezed behind her eyes. "I'm sure that's the last thing you needed after the few days you've had."

He'd borne her tears well, she thought, but that was the very reason they couldn't be together. Lewis needed strength and reliability and Madeline was fresh out.

She tossed the tissue on the fire. "How's your mother?"

"The police are satisfied there was no intent to defraud. It's up to the insurance company if they want to take it further."

"But how is *she?*"

Lewis gave her a crooked smile. "Relieved. Old."

She smiled into the fire.

"Who would have thought," Lewis commented, "that old Jacques would get an attack of conscience at this stage of his life?"

"Jacques?"

"He turned himself in," Lewis told her. "I don't suppose you've had much time to read the papers."

She shook her head. "So he turned himself in for bribing the officials to keep your dad in prison?"

"That, the insurance fraud, bankrupting the company, selling on the black market." Lewis frowned. "Why do you think I blamed you for Mum's arrest? I never, in my wildest dreams imagined he would come clean to the authorities. I thought you'd told that reporter everything."

Madeline turned to face him. "You thought I dobbed your mother in?"

He spread his hands wide. "You were the only one who knew the whole story, except Natasha, and I couldn't see her telling after all these years." He shook his head. "And you hated me, remember, for buying the farm?"

Madeline gave a resigned laugh. "And here I was thinking you were angry because I'd told the reporter the truth about our relationship." With her mother's death and then the funeral arrangements and constant visitors, she wasn't even positive that her comments had made the papers.

It all seemed rather silly now, anyway.

Madeline took a deep breath. "Lewis, I want you to sell the farm back to me."

"I bought it because I wanted you in Sydney."

She'd worked that out for herself when she calmed down.

"Is that what you really want?" Lewis asked, tucking a strand of hair behind her ears.

"Yes." She nodded emphatically.

He gazed at her for a long time and she didn't look away, even though she knew she must look disgusting. Puffy eyes and blotchy skin, if the rumors were true about crying.

There was no disgust in his eyes, only serious contemplation.

She'd appreciated his support today. She appreciated all the support he'd offered in their short acquaintance. As he'd told her once, he'd had plenty of practice.

"Confirmation is tomorrow," he told her. "I won't confirm. The contract will be cancelled."

"Thank you." Her voice was thick with relief. Now she knew she could bear anything.

"Is there no hope?" he asked. "Of you coming to Sydney? The things I said were just heat of the moment. You're not fired. I won't be closing the hotels."

Madeline stared into the flames and finally felt a lick of that old familiar confidence and assurance that she'd worked so hard to attain. "But I don't want to be an executive anymore," she said brightly, delighted that she had found it. "I know, it must seem like a waste, but I'm tired of being rootless. Of living in hotels. Tired of making decisions, big important decisions that affect hundreds of people, when I don't make any decisions in my own life, my personal life."

She squeezed his hand because he looked bereft and she wanted to show him that she was happy. "I want to stay here, start something. Maybe a homestay or a boutique hotel…I don't know exactly. A weekend retreat of some kind, become a life coach maybe—don't laugh!" How utterly ridiculous after the mess she'd made of her own life.

"I'm smiling," Lewis said, "because it sounds perfect for you. Remember our first night at the retreat? You told me then you wanted to teach, but not children."

Her eyes shone. "Did I?" She hadn't remembered many details except the physical ones! "I want to get to know people, maybe have a garden, gossip amongst the neighbors. Live amongst these people who loved my mother, no matter what." She sighed. "You know, I might put some money toward rebuilding that old church."

Madeline was so excited with her new plans, so relieved that she had her farm, her home back, it took her a while to notice how pensive Lewis looked. Her brow furrowed. There were plenty of corporate executives out there. He'd have no problem finding someone to run his hotels.

"Do I have any place in this?" he asked finally, and reached out to take her hand.

She lifted his hand in hers and linked their fingers. "Life's been so crazy lately. I only know two things. One is that, for now, this is home. I don't know if it will be forever, but for now, I need to be here." She kissed his fingertips and then gave him a sidelong look. "Of course, you could visit. I happen to know this great place in the mountains."

He dragged her hand over to his and repeated her actions, kissing her fingertips, one by one. A sultry slide in her stomach told her that he was thinking about four-poster beds and candlelight and probably garter belts.

"That would get the town's tongues wagging," he smiled. Then he sobered. "What's the second thing you know?"

Oh, damn. Why had that slipped out? How could she tell him she loved him with all her heart when they couldn't possibly be together? Not seriously, not in any other than as long-distance lovers, who would eventually tire of the distance and find someone to build a future with.

She and Lewis dealt in fantasy and they were good at it. There was no harm in giving in to fantasy once in a while, although she wrote a mental memo to use a bit of discretion next time. But Madeline wanted reality now, even if it hurt.

"Ahh." She held his gaze, biting her lip. Diving into the unknown. "Just that I love you." Something shifted in his eyes, like someone had pressed the alert button. "Don't worry," she said quickly. "It doesn't obligate you to anything."

Lewis sighed heavily and she took that as an admonishment.

"Must you always try to beat me at everything?" he asked, squeezing her fingers. "The ski field, the luge…"

She grinned, glad the awkward moment had passed. "I never beat you at anything."

His smile faded slowly. "You would have made a great COO."

"Thanks." She would have, but that wasn't who she was anymore.

He shook her hand gently to get her attention. "Would you marry me?"

Her head jerked up and she was shocked to see that his face was perfectly serious. "What?"

His eyes bored into hers. "Well, you beat me to what I was about to say—that I'm in love with you—so I thought I'd get in first with the proposal."

"Before I…beat you…" she stammered, her heart suddenly rapping on her rib cage. "You love me?"

"Absolutely," Lewis said with typical directness. "When I saw you at that retreat, I thought you were the most beautiful thing I'd ever clapped eyes on. It truly felt like we'd stumbled upon a real-life fantasy, you, the surroundings, the way we met—and the sex was out of this world. It was the whole deal." He smiled. "Like a dream, it could not have been improved upon."

Madeline smiled, nodding. That was pretty much her take on that night.

"But one night of bliss was never going to be enough. I watched you work, I saw you in pain, we comforted each other. I fell in love, but events tore us apart and I'm so sorry I left without getting the facts, giving you a chance. I don't want to spend another minute apart."

Madeline's eyes filled quickly with tears again. This crying jag was getting out of control. She never cried. "I'm not one of your projects, am I? Something to fix up because I'm having—was having—a hard time lately?"

He shook his head slowly and she recognized the same look in his eyes as the other morning, when she'd finally admitted to herself that she loved him. They'd crossed the finishing line together, it seemed. "I've just felt so low with everything that's happened, and I couldn't bear it if you saw me as a burden. I'm normally a very strong capable person—and I will be again…"

"Madeline, you have all the qualifications for the job." He kissed her fingers again. "Say yes, and we'll stay here and fix your place, *this* place up, into anything you want."

Her heart had already overflowed at his declaration of love and his proposal. But to think he wanted to stay here on the farm with her… The tears spilled over and she brought their hands up to her cheek, held them there. This really was the best fantasy she could ever have dreamed up.

"How can we stay here? Your businesses?"

"Modern communications being what they are, I can run most things from here. We'll work it out." He brushed the tears from her cheeks. "I own an airline so the commute won't be a problem."

"You've made me the happiest person in the world," she murmured, cupping his cheek and leaning in for a tear-glazed kiss. Then she pulled him to his feet and they walked to the window and looked out at a near-full moon glistening on the lake, throwing the jagged edges of the mountains beyond into blurred, sullen shadows.

"That's a billion-dollar view," Lewis said, pulling her close.

"It's more than that," Madeline said softly. "It's where fantasy meets reality."

* * * * *

THE BILLIONAIRE
NEXT DOOR

Jessica Bird

Jessica Bird graduated from college with a double major in history and art history, concentrating in the medieval period, which meant she was great at discussing anything that happened before the sixteenth century, but not all that employable in the real world. In order to support herself, she went to law school and worked in Boston in health care administration for years. She now lives in the South with her husband and her beloved golden retriever. Visit her website at www.JessicaBird.com and e-mail her at Jessica@JessicaBird.com

Chapter One

"No, really, I heard he was coming tonight."

The young investment banker looked at his buddy, Freddie Wilcox. "O'Banyon? Are you crazy? He's in the middle of the Condi-Foods merger."

"I asked his assistant." Freddie tweaked his Hermès tie. "It's on his calendar."

"He must never sleep."

"Gods don't have to, Andrew."

"Well, then, where is he?"

From their vantage point in a corner of the Waldorf-Astoria's ballroom, they sifted through the crowd of Manhattan highfliers, looking for the man they called The Idol.

Sean O'Banyon was their boss's boss and, at thirty-six, one of Wall Street's big dogs. He ran the mergers-and-acquisitions arm of Sterling Rochester, and was capable of leveraging billions of dollars at the drop of a hat or killing a mega deal because he didn't like the numbers. Since arriving on the Street, he'd engineered one perfectly executed corporate acquisition after another. No one had his track record or his instincts.

Or his reputation for eating hard-core financiers for lunch.

Man, folks would have called him SOB even if those hadn't been his initials.

He was indeed a god, but he was also a thorn in the side of the I-banking world's old-school types. O'Banyon was from South Boston, not Greenwich. Drove a Maserati not a Mercedes. Didn't care about people's *Mayflower* roots or European pedigrees. With no family money to speak of, he'd gone to Harvard undergrad on scholarship, got his start at JP Morgan then put himself through Harvard Business School while doing deals as a consultant.

Word had it that when he lost his temper, his Southie accent came back.

So, yes, the white-shoe, country-club set couldn't stand him…at least not until they needed him to find financing for their corporations' expansion plans or share buy-backs. O'Banyon was the master at drumming up money. In addition to all the bank funds at his disposal, he had ins with some serious private sources like the great Nick Farrell or the now-governor of Massachusetts, Jack Walker.

O'Banyon was who everyone wanted to be. A rebel

with immense power. An iconoclast with guts and glory. The Idol.

"Oh…my God, it's him."

Andrew whipped his head around.

Sean O'Banyon walked into the ballroom as if he owned the place. And not just the Waldorf, all of New York City. Dressed in a spectacular pin-striped black suit and wearing a screaming red tie, he was sporting a cynical half grin. As per usual.

"He's wearing all Gucci. Must have cost him five grand before tailoring."

"Couch change. I heard he spent a quarter million dollars on a watch last year."

"It was a half million. I checked at Tourneau."

O'Banyon's hair was as dark as his suit and his face was nothing but hard-ass angles and arched eyebrows. And his build matched his attitude. He topped out at six-four and it wasn't padding that filled out his shoulders. Rumor had it he did triathlons for kicks and giggles.

As the crowd caught sight of him, a swarm condensed and closed in, people pumping his hand, clapping him on the shoulder, smiling. He kept walking, the powerbrokers and A-listers forming his wake.

"He's coming over here," Andrew hissed.

"Oh God, is my tie okay?"

"Yeah. Is mine—"

"Fine."

"I think I'm going to crap in my pants."

Lizzie Bond stared at the stripped hospital bed and thought of the man who'd lain in it these last six days.

The heart monitor he'd been on and the IV that he'd needed and the oxygen feed were all gone. So too the cardiac crash cart that had failed to revive him forty-two minutes ago.

Eddie O'Banyon was dead at the age of sixty-four. And he had died alone.

She shifted her eyes to a window that overlooked Boston's Charles River.

As a nurse, she was accustomed to being in patient rooms, used to the tangy smell of disinfectant and the bland walls and the air of quiet desperation. But she had come to this room as a friend, not as a health-care professional, so she was seeing things through different eyes.

Like how empty and quiet it was.

She glanced back to the bed. She hated that Mr. O'Banyon had died alone.

She'd wanted to be at his side, had promised him she would be, but when the final myocardial infarction had occurred, she'd been working at the health clinic in Roxbury all the way across town. So she had missed saying goodbye. And he had dealt with whatever pain that had come to claim him by himself.

When the call that he had passed came through to her, she'd left her day job immediately and screamed through traffic to get here. Even though the dead had no schedules to keep and he would never know if she'd hadn't rushed, it had seemed right to hurry.

"Lizzie?"

Lizzie turned around. The nurse standing in the doorway was someone she knew and liked. "Hi, Teresa."

"I have his things from when he came in. They were still in the ED."

"Thanks for bringing them up."

Lizzie accepted her friend's personal effects with a sad smile. The plastic bag was transparent, so she could see the well-worn robe and the plaid pajamas Mr. O'Banyon had had on when he'd been admitted around 1:00 a.m. last Sunday.

What a horrible night that had been, the beginning of the end. He'd called her around twelve with chest pains and she'd run up the duplex's stairs to his apartment. Though he'd been her landlord for two years, he was also a friend and she'd had to call on all her professional training to keep sharp and make the right decision about what to do for him. In the end, she'd called 911 over his objections and not let herself be swayed. The paramedics had come quickly and she'd insisted on riding in the ambulance with Mr. O'Banyon even though he'd tried to tell her he didn't need the help.

Which had been so like him. Always irascible, always a loner. But he had needed her. His eyes had watered from fear the whole trip from South Boston to Mass General in Beacon Hill and he'd held on to her hand until her fingers had gone numb. It was as if he'd known he wouldn't be going back out into the world again.

"I know you were the emergency contact," Teresa said, "but does he have any next of kin?"

"A son. He wouldn't let me call him though. Said only if something happened." And something certainly had.

"You'll get in touch with the son, then? Because unless you're going to claim the body…"

"I'll make the call."

Teresa came over and squeezed Lizzie's shoulder. "Are you okay?"

"I should have been here."

"You were. In spirit." When she started to shake her head, Teresa cut in, "There was no way you could have known."

"I just… He was alone. I didn't want him to be alone."

"Lizzie, you always take such good care of everybody. Remember in nursing school when I fell apart three weeks before graduation? I never would have made it without you."

Lizzie smiled a little. "You would have been fine."

"Don't underestimate how much you helped me." Teresa went back to the door. "Listen, let me or one of the other girls know if you or that son of his need anything, okay?"

"Will do. Thanks, Teresa."

After the other nurse left, Lizzie put the plastic bag on the bare mattress and rifled around until she found a battered wallet. As she opened the leather billfold, she told herself that she wasn't invading Mr. O'Banyon's privacy. But it still didn't feel right.

The piece of paper she eventually took out was folded four times and as flat as a pressed leaf, as if it had been in there for quite a while. There was one name on it and a number with a 212 area code.

Guess his son lived in Manhattan.

Lizzie sat down on the bed and took her cell phone out of her purse.

Except she couldn't call just yet. She had to stitch herself back together a little. At the moment, she felt like a stuffed animal whose side had been torn open and whose padding was leaking.

She glanced back at the bag and was overcome with grief.

Over the past two years, Mr. O'Banyon had become a kind of surrogate father to her. Gruff, prickly and standoffish in the beginning, he'd stayed that way…but only on the surface. As time had passed and his health had declined, he'd gotten as attached to her as she was to him, always asking her when she was coming back to see him, always worried about her driving after dark, always keeping up with how her day went or what she was thinking about. As his heart had grown weaker and weaker, their ties had grown stronger and stronger. Gradually, she'd done more things for him, buying groceries, doing errands, cleaning up, helping him keep all his doctor's appointments straight.

She'd liked being responsible for him. With no husband or children of her own, and a mother who was too fey to really connect with, Lizzie's caretaking nature had needed an outlet beyond her job. Mr. O'Banyon had been it.

Clear as day, she pictured him sitting in his Barcalounger in front of his TV, a crossword puzzle balanced on the arm of the chair, his reading glasses down on his nose. He had been so sad and lonely, not that he'd ever shown that outright. It was just…well, Lizzie was a little sad and lonely, too, so she'd recognized the shadows in his eyes as exactly what she saw in her own mirror.

And now he was gone.

She stared down at her cell phone and the piece of paper she'd taken out of his wallet. His son's name was Sean, evidently.

She started to dial, but then stopped, picked up the bag of Mr. O'Banyon's things and headed out.

When she talked to the man's son, she was going to need some fresh air.

Standing in the Waldorf's ballroom, Sean O'Banyon smiled at Marshall Williamson III and thought about how the guy had tried to blackball him at the Congress Club. Hadn't worked, but good old Williamson had given it his best shot.

"You're the pinnacle," Williamson was saying. "Without peer. You are the man I want on this merger."

Sean smiled and figured that given the amount of groveling that was going on, Williamson was remembering the blackball thing, too.

"Thanks, Marshall. You call my assistant. She'll get you in to see me."

"Thank *you*, Sean. After all you did for Trolly Construction, I know you—"

"Call my assistant." Sean clapped Marshall on the shoulder to cut him off because getting stroked was boring. Especially when the sucking up was insincere and business motivated. "I'm going to get a drink. I'll see you sometime next week."

As he turned away, he was still smiling. Watching men who'd cut him down eat their pride made up for the social slights he had to deal with. Thing was, there was one and only one golden rule on Wall Street: He who had the gold, or could get it, made the rules. And in spite of his nothing-doing background, Sean was a mine for that shiny yellow stuff.

While he headed for the bar, he looked around the ballroom and saw the crowd for exactly what they were. He was under no illusions that any of these people were his friends. They were his allies or his enemies and sometimes both at the same time. Or they were acquaintances who wanted to have their pictures taken with him. Or they were women who'd been his lovers.

But there was no one here he was particularly close to. And he liked it that way.

"Hello, Sean."

He glanced to his left and thought, ah, yes, a bridal barracuda. "Hello, Candace."

The blonde sidled up to him, all pouty lips and big, insincere eyes. She was dressed in a black gown that was so low cut you could almost see her belly button, and her surgically enhanced assets were displayed as if they were up for sale. Which he supposed they were. For the right engagement ring and a generous prenup, Candace would walk down the aisle with a bridge troll.

Her voice was slightly breathless as she spoke. Possibly because of all the silicone on top of her lungs. "I heard you were out in the Hamptons last weekend. You didn't call."

"Busy. Sorry."

She pressed herself against him. "You need to call me when you're there. Actually, you just need to call me."

He disengaged himself as if he were peeling free of a coat. "Like I told you a while ago, I'm not your type."

"I disagree."

"Haven't you heard about me?"

"Of course. I read about you in the *Wall Street Journal* all the time."

"Ah, that's business, though. Let me enlighten you about the personal side of things." He leaned down and whispered in her ear, "I never buy jewelry for women. Or cars or plane tickets or clothes or houses or hotel rooms. And I believe in splitting the check over dinner. Right down to the tip."

She hauled back as if he'd blasphemed.

He smiled. "I see you get my point. Trust me, you'll be much happier with someone else."

As he turned away from her and walked over to the bar, he had to laugh. The thing was, he hadn't said those things just to get rid of her. They were the God's honest truth: For him, Dutch was the rule with women.

The minute he'd made his first big chunk of cash, he'd become a target for that kind of predatory female and he'd gotten burned. Back over a decade ago, after having lived for years as the poor relation to his room-mates and friends at Harvard, he'd finally put together a deal with a percentage point or two in it for him.

The cash had been an avalanche. More than he could ever have imagined filling his account. And within a week of him throwing some of it around, a very sophis-ticated blonde, not unlike Candace, had shown up on his doorstep. She'd been everything he'd ever wanted, proof positive that he'd arrived. Elegant, cultured, an antiques dealer with style, he'd felt invincible with her on his arm.

He'd done his best to buy her anything she wanted and she'd been more than happy to trade her presence for the things he got her. At least until she'd found someone who could write even bigger checks. On her way out the door, she'd told him, in her Upper East Side, long-voweled way, that even though he was just a roughneck from South Boston, she could tell he was going places...so he should never hesitate to call her if he was ever in the market for oil paintings.

Lesson learned.

Now, it was easy to pick out women like that, although not because he was a genius at reading minds. Pretty much anyone he met in a dress was after money.

Just like anyone in a suit, too, come to think of it.

After he ordered a Tanqueray and tonic from the bartender, he noticed two young guys edging their way over to him. They were dressed well, real spit and polish, Ivy League shiny, and their faces were composed as if they were prepared to play it cool.

Except both of them were rubbing their right palms on their hips as if they were worried they'd offer him a wet handshake.

"'Evening, Mr. O'Banyon," the taller one said.

Sean got his T&T and pointed to the guy. "Fred Wilcox. And...Andrew Frick, right?"

The two nodded their heads, clearly astounded he knew their names. But you had to keep up with the FNUGs. Some percentage of them were going to make it and thus become useful, and besides, he liked the look of this pair. Smart eyes, but none of that showboat crap some of the other young hardies tried to pull. Plus, if he remembered correctly, they were both HBS like him.

"How you boys doing tonight?" he said.

They stammered over some social nonsense then fell completely silent as a cloud of perfume wafted in. Sean glanced behind his shoulder and then smiled honestly for the first time since walking into the gala.

"My lovely, Elena," he murmured, leaning down and kissing the smooth cheek of a stunning brunette. As she greeted him in Italian and he replied, he could positively feel the hero worship coming at him from the young guys. He glanced at them. "Will you excuse us?"

"Of course, Mr. O'Banyon."

"Absolutely, Mr. O'Banyon."

"Wait up," he said on impulse as they turned away. "You two want in on some fun?"

Frick blinked. "Ah, yes, sir."

"Call my assistant tomorrow morning. She'll put you in touch with the Condi-Food analysts and they'll find you a little slice of the deal to work on. Don't worry about your boss. I'll call Harry and tell him you're going to come play with me for a while."

As their eyes bugged as if they'd been goosed by a pair of pliers, Sean smiled. Man, he remembered what that felt like. To be young and green and desperate to be given a shot at the big time…and have a door opened.

The thank-yous from them started to roll fast as marbles on a bare floor. "No problem," Sean said, then narrowed his eyes. "Just stay tight and use your brains and everything will be fine."

He turned his attention to Elena. She looked very beautiful tonight, dressed in a red sheath with her hair up high on her head. Rubies glowed from her neck and her earlobes.

"Sean," she said with her lovely accent, "I have a favor to ask you."

"What, baby?" As she smiled, he had to imagine that no one ever called her *baby*. She was a descendent of the Medicis and as rich as her ancestors had been back in the Middle Ages. The thing was, though, in spite of her bloodline and her money, she was a very nice person. They'd met years ago and had shared an immediate, mutual respect.

"Excuse me," one of the photographers cut in. "May I take a picture?"

Sean flipped into social mode, gathering Elena against him and staring into the lens. There was a flash, a thank-you from the guy, and then he and Elena went back to their conversation.

"What kind of favor do you need?" Sean asked.

"An escort to the Hall Foundation Gala."

Oh, okay, he knew what this was all about. Her recent marital separation had been messy and public and had involved infidelity on her husband's side. To top it off, the guy was trying to suck tens of millions of dollars out of her in the divorce...despite the fact that he was still with the masseuse he'd gotten pregnant.

The details of the split had been written up in *Vanity Fair* and *New York Magazine,* but that wasn't the worst of it. Everyone on the A-list circuit was talking about what had happened and not with kindness. They were whispering that Elena had gone out and bought herself a younger man then hadn't been able to keep him. And that he'd wandered because she couldn't have children. And that Elena was a cold fish.

Sean didn't know about the kids part, but he was certain that she'd been passionately in love with her husband when they'd gotten married. Too bad everyone else seemed to have forgotten that.

God, Manhattan could be a very cold place even if you lived in a penthouse on Park Avenue with perfectly good heating and ventilation. All it took was for your private life to become the scandal du jour and you became fodder, not friend. And gossip was like chum to the social sharks, sure to attract a frenzy.

If Elena didn't show up at the Hall Foundation Gala? She'd look as if she were weak and that would only incite the harping more. But if she arrived at the event with him, she'd appear strong and desirable.

He reached out and took her hand. "I'm there for you. One hundred percent."

She positively sagged with relief. "Thank you. This has been a very difficult time."

He pulled her forward and tucked her into his body as a friend or a brother would, for comfort. "You don't worry about a thing."

When his phone started to ring in his breast pocket, he took it out. The 617 area code made him frown because he didn't recognize the rest of the caller's number.

"I'll let you take that," Elena said, kissing him on the cheek. "And seriously, Sean...thank you."

"Don't go, baby. This'll just take a sec." He accepted the call. "Yeah?"

The pause that followed was broken by the wail of an ambulance siren. Then a female voice said, "Sean O'Banyon?"

"Who is this and how did you get this number?"

"My name is Elizabeth Bond. I got it from your voice mail. I'm...I'm so very sorry to tell you this...but your father has passed."

All at once, the sounds of the party drained away. The patter of talk, the winding chords of the chamber orchestra, the trilling laughter of a woman nearby—all of it disappeared as if someone had thrown a thick blanket over everything. And then the sight of the 150 people before him fogged out until he was alone in the vast room.

In fact, the very fabric of reality disintegrated until it seemed as if the world had become an intangible dreamscape and him a formless vapor: he couldn't feel the floor under his feet or the phone in his palm or the weight of his body. Nor could he remember what he was doing in this room full of crystal chandeliers and too much perfume.

"When?" The heavy word came out of his mouth without benefit of conscious thought.

"Less than an hour ago. He suffered a second heart attack."

"When was the first?"

"Six days ago."

"Six days ago?" he asked in an utterly level tone.

There was a hesitation, as if the woman on the other end was unsure what his mental state was. Funny, that made two of them.

She cleared her throat. "Immediately following his first, he was taken by ambulance here to Mass General, and though he was revived, the damage to his heart muscle was extensive. Following an angiogram, it was revealed that he had multiple blockages, but he was not stable enough for surgery."

Dimly, Sean heard the sound of ice tinkling in a glass and he looked down. His hand was shaking so badly his Tanqueray and tonic might as well have been in a blender. He leaned to the side and put the drink down on a table.

"What happens to him now?" he asked, shoving his hand in his pocket.

"He will be held here at Mass General until the family makes arrangements." When he didn't respond, she said, "Mr. O'Banyon? Will you be making arrangements? Um…hello?"

"Yes, I will. I'll fly up tonight. What do I need to do once I'm at the hospital?" As she proceeded to tell him who to call and where to go at MGH, he wasn't tracking. The only thing that stuck was that he could phone the general information number if he needed help or had further questions.

"I'm very sorry," the woman said and she obviously meant it. There was true sorrow in her voice. "I—"

"Are you a nurse?"

"Yes, I am. But your father wasn't a patient of mine. He was—"

"Thank you for calling me. If you'll excuse me, I need to make some calls. Goodbye."

He hung up and stared at his phone. Obviously his father had listed him as next of kin, which explained how the woman had gotten the number.

"Sean? Is everything all right?"

He glanced at Elena. It took a moment or two for him to recognize her, but eventually her worried mahogany eyes got through to him. "My father is dead."

As she gasped and put her hand on his arm, a booming voice barreled through the crowd at them. "Sean O'Banyon, as I live and breathe!"

Sean turned to see the owner of a shipping conglomerate lumbering over like a bear through the woods. The man was as ungainly as the mega-ton freight haulers he put out on the oceans and he had the mouth of a longshoreman. In typical Manhattan fashion, he was welcome here tonight only because he'd given five million dollars to the cause.

"I'll handle him," Elena whispered. "You, go now."

Sean nodded and took off, heading for the back exit while trying to dodge all the people who wanted things from him. As he fought through the crowd, he felt as if he couldn't breathe and a curious panic set in.

When he finally burst outside through a fire door, he had to lean down and put his hands on his knees. Drawing the sultry summer air down his throat and into his lungs only made the suffocation worse and he wrenched at his tie.

Dead. His father was dead.

He and his brothers were finally free.

Sean forced himself to stand up like a man and pushed a hand through his hair to try and clear his brain. Yeah…freedom had come with that phone call.

Hadn't it?

Tilting his head back, he measured the lack of stars in the sky and thought about the inflection in the nurse's words, the sadness and the regret.

How appropriate that the person mourning his father was a stranger.

God knew, his sons would never be able to.

Chapter Two

Lizzie hung up her cell phone and stared at the thing. Through the din of what sounded like a party, Mr. O'Banyon's son had been totally detached, his voice giving away no emotion at all. Then again, she was a stranger and the news had not been good or expected. He was no doubt in shock.

She'd wanted to find out when and where the funeral would be held, but that hadn't seemed like an appropriate thing to bring up. Worst came to worst she could always call him later.

An ambulance went by her, its lights flashing red and white, its siren letting out a single squawk as it left the Mass General complex and headed out onto Cambridge Avenue. The sight of it got her moving and she started for the parking garage. Part of her wanted to stay here and wait for the son to arrive, but it would take him hours to get into town. Plus it appeared that he was the type who'd rather deal with things on his own.

Besides, it was time to go to her second job.

Lizzie jogged across the road and took two flights of concrete stairs up to the second story of the garage. When she found her old Toyota Camry in the lines of cars, she unlocked it with a key as the remote no longer worked, and put Mr. O'Banyon's things on the backseat. Getting behind the wheel, she figured she'd leave the bag by the upstairs apartment's door for the son along with a note that if there was anything she could do to help she was always available.

The drive from Beacon Hill to Chinatown took her on a straight shot up Charles Street, then a jog around the Commons, followed by a scoot past Emerson College. Down farther, opposite one of the Big Dig's gaping mouths, was Boston Medical Center. Affiliated with Boston University, BMC was a busy urban hospital and its emergency department saw a lot of action. Particularly, and tragically, of the gunshot and stabbing variety.

She'd been moonlighting in the ED three nights a week for the past year because, though she worked days at the health clinic in Roxbury, she needed the extra income. Her mother lived in an artist's world of color and texture and not much reality, so Lizzie helped her out a lot, covering her expenses, paying bills, making sure she had enough money. To Alma Bond, the world was a place of beauty and magic; practical matters rarely permeated her fog of inspiration.

The extra income was also for Lizzie, however. Earlier in the year, she'd applied and been accepted into a master's program for public health. Though she couldn't afford to start this fall, her plan was to save up over the next few months and matriculate in the winter session.

Except now she wondered whether she needed to find a new place to live. Would Mr. O'Banyon's son hold on to the duplex? If he sold it, would her new landlord ask for more in rent? How would she find something equally inexpensive?

After driving through BMC's parking garage, Lizzie squeezed the Toyota in between two mountain-size SUVs and took a last look at Mr. O'Banyon's things. Then she got out, locked the car and strode toward the bank of elevators.

As she waited for the metal doors to slide open, Sean O'Banyon's hard tone and emotionless words came back to her.

Maybe that hadn't been shock. Maybe that had been genuine disregard.

God, what could cause a father and son to lose touch to such a degree?

It was 3:16 in the morning when Sean stopped his rental car in front of the Southie row house where he and his brothers had grown up.

The duplex looked exactly the same: two stories of nothing special sided in an ugly pale blue. Front porch was a shallow lip of a thing, more a landing than a place to sit outside. Upstairs was all dark. Downstairs had what looked like a single lamp on in the living room.

He wondered who was staying in the bottom unit now. They'd always rented it out and clearly that was still the practice.

With a twist of his wrist, Sean turned the engine off, took the key out of the ignition then eased back in the seat.

On the flight from Teterboro to Logan, he'd made two phone calls, both of which had dumped into voice mail. The first had been to his younger brother, Billy, who was traveling around to preseason games with the rest of the New England Patriots football team. The second was to an international exchange that was the only way he had to get in touch with Mac. The oldest O'Banyon boy was a special forces soldier in the U.S. Army so God only knew where he was at any given time.

Sean had told them both to call him back as soon as they got the message.

He looked up to the second story of the house and felt his skin tighten around his bones and muscles. Man, Pavlov had been right about trained responses to stimuli. Even though Sean was a grown man, as he stared at the windows of his childhood apartment, he felt his ten-year-old self's terror.

Dropping his head, he rubbed his eyes. The damn things felt as if they had sawdust in them and his temples were pounding.

But then stress'll do that to you.

He *so* didn't want to go into that house. Probably should have stayed at the Four Seasons, which was what he usually did when he was in town. Except on some molecular level, he needed to see the old place even though he hated it. Needed to go inside.

It was like peeling back a Band-Aid and checking out a cut.

With a curse, he grabbed his leather duffel as well as the two bags of groceries he'd bought at a twenty-four-hour Star Market, then opened the car door and stood up.

Boston smelled different than New York. Always had. Tonight, the brine of the ocean was especially heavy in the air, buffered by the sweet sweat of summer's humidity. As his nose ate up the scent, his brain registered it as home.

He followed the short concrete walkway up to the house then long-legged the five steps to the shallow front porch. He didn't have a key, but as always, there was one tucked behind the flimsy metal mailbox that was tacked onto the aluminum siding.

The door opened with the exact same squeak he remembered, and, hearing the hinge complain, his blood turned into icy slush.

That squeak had always been the warning, the call to listen hard for what came next. If it was a door closing underneath them, he and his brothers would take a deep breath because it was just the tenants coming home. But if it was footsteps on the stairs? That meant pure panic and running for cover.

As he stepped inside the foyer, Sean's heart started to jackrabbit in his chest and sweat broke out on his forehead.

Except, damn it, he was thirty-six years old and the

man was dead. Nothing could hurt him here anymore. Nothing.

Uh-huh, right. Too bad his body didn't know this. As he went up the staircase, his knees were weak and his gut was a lead balloon. And God, the sound of the wood creaking under his soles was awful in his ears. The dirge of his approach was the same as when his father had come home, and hearing his own footsteps now, he remembered the fear he had felt as a boy as the thundering noise grew louder and louder.

At the top of the landing he put his hand on the doorknob and the key in the lock. Before he went in, he told himself this was only a door and he wasn't stepping back into his past. The space-time continuum just didn't work that way. Thank God.

But he was still in a cold sweat as he opened up and walked in.

When he turned on the lights, he was amazed. Everything was exactly the same: the tattered Barcalounger with the TV tray right next to it; the rumpled couch with its faded flower print; the 1970s lamps that were as big as oil drums and just as ugly; the crucifix on the wall, the yellowed, exhausted lace drapery.

The air was stuffy in spite of the air conditioner that was humming, so he cracked open a window. The place smelled of cigarette smoke, but it was the kind of thing left over after a four-pack-a-day addict stops. The stench lingered, embedded in the room's paint and flooring and fabrics, but wasn't in the air itself.

As the breeze came in, he walked over to the TV tray and picked up the *Boston Globe* crossword puzzle that was mostly done. The date in the upper right-hand corner was from the previous Sunday, the last time his father had sat in the chair with a pencil in hand filling in little boxes with wobbly, capitalized letters.

Going by the script, it seemed as if his father had had hand tremors. Odd, to picture him as anything other than brutally strong.

Sean put the paper down and forced himself to walk through every room. It was about halfway through the tour when he realized something was different.

Everything was clean.

The cramped kitchen was tidy, no dirty dishes in the sink, no trash collecting in the Rubbermaid bin in the corner, no food left out on the counters. The room he'd shared with Billy had both beds made and a vacuumed rug. Mac's bedroom was just as neat. Their father's private space was likewise in wilted but tidy condition.

Back when Sean had lived here, there had been cobwebs in the corners of the rooms and dirt tracked in the front door and beds with rumpled sheets and dust everywhere. There had also been a lot of empty bottles.

With a compulsion he couldn't fight, Sean went through all the closets and cupboards and dressers in the apartment. He looked under each bed and the couch. Checked behind the TV and then went into the kitchen and moved the refrigerator out from the wall.

Not one single booze bottle. Not one beer can.

No alcohol in the place.

As he threw his shoulder into the fridge and forced the thing back into place, he was flat-out amazed. He'd never have thought their father could kick the sauce. The drinking had been as much a part of him as his dark hair and the hard tone of his voice.

Sean stalled out, but then went into the living room and figured it was time to score some shut-eye. First thing tomorrow, he was going to make arrangements with Finnegan's Funeral Home for the cremation and the interment. After that, he'd have to pack up the apartment. No question they would sell the duplex. There was no reason to come back here ever again.

He glanced around. God, how long had it been since he'd stood in this room?

As he went through the years, he was surprised to realize it had been all the way back when he'd gone away to Harvard as a freshman. Made sense though. College had been his ticket out, and once he didn't have to sleep under this roof, he'd made damn sure he never showed up again. It had been the same for Billy when he'd gotten a football scholarship to Holy Cross. And for Mac, who'd joined the army the very month Billy went off to college. They'd all left and never returned.

Go figure.

Sean went over to his duffel, stripped down to his boxers and grabbed his toothbrush. After he hit the bathroom in the hall, he picked a pillow off his old bed and headed for the couch.

No way in hell he was sleeping in his room.

Lying flat on his back in the dark, he thought of the penthouse he lived in down in Manhattan. Park Avenue in the seventies, a perfect address. And everything in that showstopper of a place was sleek and expensive, from the furniture to the drapes to the kitchen appliances to that million-dollar view of Central Park.

It was about as far away from where he was now as was humanly possible.

Sean screwed his lids down, crossed his arms over his chest and concentrated on going to sleep.

Yeah, right.

He lasted not even ten minutes before he was on his bare feet and pacing up and down over the knobby area rug.

Lizzie parked the Toyota in front of the row house and got out with the bag of Mr. O'Banyon's things. Her feet were killing her and she had a headache from having had too many coffees, but at least she didn't have to be at the clinic until noon today because she was working the later shift.

As she stepped onto the duplex's concrete walkway, she stopped and looked up. No lights were on upstairs, but that wasn't because someone was sleeping. It was because no one lived there anymore.

Tears stung her eyes. It was hard to imagine her cranky old friend gone. Hard to internalize the fact that there would be no more blue glow from his TV at night, no more sound of him shuffling about, no more trips to buy him the chocolate ice cream he liked.

No more talking to him the way a daughter talked to a gruff father.

She tightened her grip on the bag's handles and hoped he hadn't struggled at the end, hadn't felt horrible pain and fear. She wished for him a peaceful slide as he passed, not a bumpy, frightening fall.

As she went up to the house, she felt as if there was a draft licking around her body, as if the night had turned frigid though it was in fact balmy.

It was just so hard to come home this morning. To her, there was only empty space above her now. The man whose life had animated the furniture and the objects in the other apartment was gone and the silence overhead was only going to remind her of what had been lost.

After Lizzie let herself into her place, she put her keys in a dish on her little painted table and shut the door. She was setting down the plastic bag when she froze.

Someone was walking around upstairs.

Her first thought was totally illogical: for a split second, she was sure that someone had made a mistake with Mr. O'Banyon and he'd been discharged because he was perfectly healthy.

Her second thought was that a burglar had broken in.

Except then she realized whoever it was was pacing. Back. Forth. Back. Forth.

The son had come into town.

She started for the door, but then stopped because going up to see him was ridiculous. Though she'd been close to the guy's father, she didn't know the son at all and it was just before dawn, for heaven's sake. Hardly the time for a sympathy call.

After she took a shower, she sat in her living room with a bowl of corn flakes in her lap. Instead of eating the cereal, she played with it until it turned to mush, and listened to the man above her wear out the floorboards.

Twenty minutes later, she put on a pair of jeans and went up the stairwell.

The moment she knocked, the pacing stopped. Just in case *he* thought she was a burglar, she said, "Hello? Mr.—ah, Sean O'Banyon?"

Nothing could have prepared her for who opened that door.

The man on the other side of the jamb stood about six inches taller than her and wore nothing but a pair of boxers and a whole lot of muscle. With a gold cross hanging from his neck, an old tattoo on his left pec and a scar on one of his shoulders, he looked a little dangerous…especially in the face. His hazel eyes were sharp as razors, his jaw set as if he was used to being in charge, his lips nothing but a tight, hard line.

She could totally imagine the cold tone she'd heard over her phone coming out of that mouth.

"Yeah?" His voice was very deep.

"I'm Lizzie—Elizabeth Bond. I talked to you today—yesterday. I live downstairs."

All at once his face eased up. "Ah, hell. I'm making too much noise, aren't I? Worse, I've been at it for a while." His South Boston accent flattened out his vowels and sharpened his consonants. Funny, she hadn't noticed the intonation over the phone, but it was clear as day now. And she'd seen him somewhere. Then again, it was probably because he looked like his father.

"Anyway," he said, "I'm sorry and I'll cut it out."

"Oh, that wasn't why I came up. And I just got home

from my shift so I missed most of the pacing." She took a deep breath and smelled...whoa, a very nice cologne. "I'm truly sorry about your loss and I—"

"Hey, you want some breakfast?"

"Excuse me?"

"Breakfast." As he pushed a hand through his thick dark hair, his bicep flexed up and the gleaming cross shifted between his pecs. "I'm not going to sleep anytime soon and I'm hungry."

"Oh...well...that's not necessary."

"Of course it isn't. But you just got home from work, didn't you?"

"Ah, yes."

"So you're probably hungry, too, right?"

Come to think of it she was.

"And I'll even put my pants on for you, Elizabeth."

Absurdly, a rush went through her. And she had the illicit, inappropriate thought that while he was making love to a woman, his voice would sound fantastic in the ear.

God, how could she even think like that?

"Lizzie," she said, walking in. "I go by Lizzie."

Sean tracked the woman as she went by him, very aware of her smooth, gliding stride. Tall and lean, she was wearing an old pair of blue jeans and a four-sizes-too-big Red Sox T-shirt he was willing to bet she'd be sleeping in later. Her shoulder-length blond hair was pulled back in a no-nonsense way and the ends were damp as if she'd just showered. She smelled of Ivory soap.

Which he liked.

"Lizzie it is, then," he said as he closed the door. "And you can call me Sean, of course."

As he spoke, he realized his Southie accent had resurfaced and it was strange to hear the speech pattern of his childhood back in his words again. During his years at Harvard, he'd assiduously tamed the telltale *r*s and learned a different, less regional way of talking.

Less regional. Ha. Try more upper-class.

Lizzie stopped in the middle of the room, her pale green stare going over everything as if she were inspecting the place. She had smart eyes, he thought.

"So you're a nurse?" he said.

"I am, but I wasn't treating your father. I was a friend of his."

Had he heard that right? "A friend."

"Yes. I've lived downstairs for the past two years so we got to know each other. He was lonely."

"Was he."

"Very." As she nodded, she ran her hand over the back of the Barcalounger. "We had dinner together a lot."

For some reason, the sight of her touching his father's chair creeped him out.

"Well, then, I guess you know the way to the kitchen." Sean reached into his duffel for some jeans. "You mind if I don't put on a shirt? Damn hot up here."

He was surprised when she blushed. "Oh…no. I mean, yes, that's fine."

As she headed out of the room, he pulled on his pants and thought of his father.

Lonely. Yeah, right. Not with this tenant around.

Eddie O'Banyon had been a loner by nature, but it was funny how a pretty young woman could get a man to feeling sociable.

And she'd obviously spent a lot of time up here. Not only did she know where the kitchen was, but along the way, she shifted the edge of a cheap picture that had tilted off center and straightened a pile of mail. He had the feeling she was the reason the place was so clean.

While Sean worked his way up his button fly, he was willing to bet she was also the reason his father had gotten off the booze, too. Nothing like love or some serious attraction to the opposite sex to turn a guy around. At least temporarily.

Except what had she seen in him?

Sean cursed under his breath. Like he had to even ask that? On impulse, he removed his gold watch and tucked it into his duffel. If she'd been attracted to what little cash his father had had, there was no reason for her to know he was swimming in the stuff.

As he went into the kitchen, he wondered if she knew who he was. He figured chances were fifty/fifty. His face had been in the newspapers often enough, but it was the kind of thing that, unless you were into the world of high finance, you'd probably overlook. Although maybe his father had mentioned something.

Not that Eddie had known much.

"So cop a seat and I'll cook for you," Sean said, nodding to the table in the center of the room. "All I got are eggs and bacon, but the good thing is that's hard to screw up."

"Sounds perfect."

He went to where the frying pan had always been kept and what do you know, the thing was still there. "Scrambled okay?"

"Fine."

As he got the bacon going and grabbed the eggs out of the fridge, he kept his tone casual. "So you knew my old man well, huh?"

"He was very kind to me."

I'll bet. "You lived here two years, you said?"

"Since I got out of nursing school. I wasn't around much as I work at a clinic in Roxbury and I moonlight at BMC a lot, but we spent some time together." A sad smile lifted her mouth. "Your father always said I worked too hard."

Did he? What a prince. "And you took care of this place, too, didn't you? I mean, it's pretty obvious. He never was into housekeeping when I knew him."

"Well, at first he wouldn't let me. But after a while, he needed help." She cleared her throat. "When was the last time you saw him? If you don't mind my asking."

"A while. He told you not to call me until it was over, right?"

As she stayed quiet, he cracked eggs into a bowl and started to beat them with a fork. The choppy, liquid sound cut through her silence.

He looked over his shoulder. "Didn't he?"

"Yes. It felt wrong not to, but I respected his wishes."

When her green eyes lifted to his, he stopped dead.

Check out that stare, he thought. So compassionate. So…kind.

As he looked at her face, something popped in his

chest, like a lid being released. And what came out of his inner soda can was a yearning that unsettled him. He literally wanted to dive right into those warm eyes of hers.

"I think the bacon is burning," she said.

He cursed and got back with the program. As he transferred the strips onto a paper towel–covered plate, he asked, "So where are you from?"

"The north shore. Essex. My mother is still up there." Lizzie laughed a little. "I was hoping to introduce your father to her. Maybe they could have been friends. But your father liked to keep to himself."

Or maybe keep *Lizzie* to himself? "You got a husband or a boyfriend there, Lizzie?"

As she blushed again, he became absorbed in the pink tint on her face. To the point that when she dipped her head, he found himself leaning to the side so he could keep measuring her cheeks.

Man, the women he knew in Manhattan did not blush and he realized he liked it. Or hell, maybe he just liked this particular woman turning red.

"Lizzie? Was my question too personal?"

"Not at all. I don't have a husband. Or boyfriend. Too busy."

Good, he thought. Then frowned.

Wait a minute. Not *good*. Doesn't matter. None of his business.

Besides, maybe she'd been saving herself for his *father*. God, what a cringer that was.

"What about you?" she asked. "Are you married?"

"Nope. Not my thing."

"Why not?"

Well, there were a whole bunch of why nots. The first of which was prenups could be broken and he had no intention of someone in stilettos walking off with his hard-earned cash. More than that, though, you had to trust your wife wouldn't play you. And he'd long ago lost the illusion that faith in lovers or business associates could be justified.

Hell, maybe he'd never had it. His two brothers were really the only people on the planet he believed in.

"No particular reason," he said, dumping the eggs into the pan. As a hiss rose up from the hot iron, he tacked on, "Other than I'm a loner."

She smiled. "Like your father."

He whipped his head around. "I am *nothing* like my father."

As she recoiled, he didn't apologize. Some things needed to be stated clearly and he was not like that abusive, drunken bastard on any level.

"You like a lot of pepper in your eggs?" he said to fill up the silence.

Chapter Three

Sean O'Banyon might be a little touchy about his father, but he made a very good breakfast, Lizzie thought, as she put her fork on her clean plate and eased back in the chair.

Wiping her mouth on a paper towel, she glanced across the table. Sean was still eating, but then again he had twice the food she'd taken to get through. And he was slow and meticulous with his meal, which surprised her. He seemed like the kind of tough guy who wouldn't bother with good table manners. But his were beautiful.

And...boy, yeah, the way he ate wasn't the only beautiful thing about him. That chest of his was sinfully good to look at. So were his thick eyelashes. And his mouth—

Lizzie cursed in her head. What was her problem? The man asks her in for breakfast right after his father dies and she's checking him out as if he were an eHarmony candidate?

Then again, it was probably biology talking. After all, when had she last been alone with a man? As she counted up the months, then hit the one-year, then two-year mark, she winced.

Two and a half years ago? How had that happened?

"What's wrong?" Sean asked, obviously catching her expression.

Yeah, like she was going to parade her Death Valley dating life in front of him? "Oh, nothing."

"So what was I about to ask you? Oh…your mother. You said she's still up in Essex?"

"Ah, yes, she is. She's an artist and she loves living by the sea. She keeps busy painting and sketching and trying out just about every kind of creative endeavor you can think of."

To keep her eyes off him, Lizzie folded her paper napkin into a precise square—and thought about her mother's origami period. That year, the Christmas tree had been covered with pointy-headed swans and razor-edged stars. Most of them had been off-kilter, mere approximations of what they were supposed to be, but her mother had adored them, and because of that, Lizzie had loved them, as well.

For no particular reason, she said, "My mother is what they used to call *fey*. Lovely and…"

"All in her head?"

"Precisely."

"So you take care of her, huh? She relies on you for the practical stuff."

As Lizzie flushed, she murmured, "Either you're very perceptive, or I'm quite transparent."

"Little bit of both, I think."

As he smiled, her heart tripped and fell into her gut. Oh…God, he was handsome.

"How long are you in town?" she blurted. And then couldn't believe she'd asked. It wasn't that the question was forward on the surface, but more because she was angling to see him again in a situation just like this. The two of them alone.

Can you say *desperate,* she thought.

"I'm going back to the city tomorrow—well, that's today, isn't it?" He wiped his mouth and took a drink from his glass of orange juice. "But I'll be back. I've got to clean out this place."

"Are you going to sell?"

"No reason to keep it. But I'll make sure you're in the loop."

"Thank you. I really liked living here."

"Hopefully you won't have to leave. I can't believe anyone would want to turn this into a one-family."

"I think I'm going to want to move, though."

"Why?"

She looked around. "It won't be the same without him."

Sean frowned and fell silent so she got up and took both their plates to the sink. As she washed them with a sponge she'd bought a week and a half ago, she tried not to think that Mr. O'Banyon had still been alive back then.

"So you and my father were real tight, huh?"

She held a plate under the rushing water. "We used to watch TV together. And we always ate dinner up here on Sundays. We also looked out for each other. It was nice to think someone wondered whether or not I made it back from my night shifts. Made me feel safer."

And cared for.

With her mother, Lizzie had always been the watcher, the worrier, the keeper...even when she'd been young. For the time she had known Mr. O'Banyon, it had been really nice to be something other than a ghost on the periphery of someone's artistic inspiration.

Feeling awkward, she asked, "So do you live right in Manhattan?"

"Yeah."

"I've always wanted to go there," she murmured as she put the plate in the drying rack. "It seems so exciting and glamorous."

"City's not far from here. Just drive down some time."

She shook her head, thinking of the time she would have to take off from work. "I couldn't really afford to. With two jobs, my hours are long and my mother needs the money more than I need a vacation. Besides, who am I kidding? I'm a homebody at heart."

"And you were happy being a homebody here. With my father."

She picked up a towel and began to dry what she'd washed. "Yes, I was."

"Were you lovers?"

"What?" She nearly dropped the skillet. "Why would you think that?"

His eyes were cold and cynical as he said, "Not unheard-of."

"Maybe to you. We were friends. Good Lord…"

She quickly put away the dishes, hung up the towel and headed for the exit. "Thank you for breakfast."

He rose from the table. "Elizabeth—"

"Lizzie." She stepped around him pointedly. "Just Lizzie."

He took her arm in a firm grip. "I'm sorry if I offended you."

She leveled her stare on his hard face. His apology seemed sincere enough; though his eyes remained remote, they didn't waver from hers and his tone was serious.

She reminded herself that he was under a lot of stress and it was four—well, almost five in the morning. She cleared her throat. "It's all right. This is a hard time for you right now."

"Hard time for you, too, right?"

"Yes," she said in a small voice. "Very. I'm going to miss him."

Sean reached out and touched her cheek, surprising her. "You know something?"

"What?"

"A woman like you should have someone waiting up for her, Lizzie."

In a flash, she became totally aware of him down to the details of his beard's dark shadow and the hazel of his eyes and…

And the fact that he was looking at her mouth.

From out of nowhere, an arc of heat supercharged

the air between their bodies and Lizzie had to part her lips to breathe.

Except just as she did, his face masked over and he dropped her arm. "I'll walk you to the door."

He turned away as if nothing had happened.

Okay…so had she just imagined all that?

Apparently.

Lizzie forced herself to walk out of the kitchen and found him standing next to the apartment's open door. As if she'd overstayed her welcome.

As Sean waited for Lizzie to come from the kitchen, he figured he either needed to put his long-tailed button-down shirt on or get her out of here. Because his body was stating its opinion of her loud and clear, and he didn't want to embarrass the poor woman.

He was totally, visibly aroused. And the quick rearrange he'd done as he'd walked through the living room had only helped so much.

Then things got worse. As she came over, he started to wonder exactly what was under that baggy shirt of hers—and his "problem" got harder.

"Are you going to have a funeral for him?" she asked.

Well, at least that question slapped him back to reality.

"No. He'll be cremated and interred next to my mother. Told me ten years ago he didn't want any kind of memorial service." Man, that had been an ugly phone call. His father had been drunk at the time, naturally, and had maintained he didn't want his three sons dancing on his coffin.

Sean had hung up at that point.

"That's a shame." Lizzie tucked a piece of blond hair behind her ear. "For both of you. People should be remembered. Fathers should be remembered."

As those green eyes met his, they were like looking into a still pond, gentle, calming, warm. Teamed with the heat that had sprung up in his blood, the impact of her compassionate stare was like getting sucker punched: a surprise that numbed him out.

Unease snaked through him. Stripped of defenses and vaguely needy was not what he wanted to be, not around anyone.

His voice grew harsh. "Oh, I'll remember him, all right. Good night, Lizzie."

She quickly looked away and scooted past him. As she hit the stairs at a fast clip, she spoke over her shoulder. "Goodbye, Sean."

Sean shut the door, crossed his arms over his chest and leaned back against the wall. As he thought about his arousal, he reminded himself that there was nothing mystical or unusual at work here. Lizzie was attractive. He was half-naked. They were alone. Do the math.

Except there was something else, wasn't there?

He thought back to the past. Though his memories of his mother were indistinct, he recalled her as warm and kind, the quintessential maternal anchor. From what he'd learned about her, she'd come from a very good family who'd disowned her when she'd married a blue-collar Irish Catholic. Her parents had even refused to come to her memorial service.

Back when she'd still been around, their father had

been relatively stable, but that had changed after she'd died when Sean was five. After they'd buried her, all hell had broken loose and hard drinking had moved into the apartment like a mean houseguest. Turned out Anne had been the glue that had held Eddie together. Without her, he'd spiraled fast, hit bottom hard and never resurfaced.

Sean stared at the Barcalounger.

Dimly, he heard the water come on downstairs and he imagined Lizzie brushing her teeth over a sink. When the whining rush was cut off, he saw her stripping off those jeans and sliding between clean white sheets.

She looked like the kind of woman who had sensible sheets.

She hadn't been his father's lover, he thought. The outrage on her face had been too spontaneous, the offense too quick. But that didn't mean she hadn't been stringing Eddie along for money.

God, one look into those green eyes and even Sean had been hypnotized.

Picturing her face, he was surprised that he wanted to believe she was a well of compassion and goodness. But the Mother Teresa routine was tough to buy. That talk about wanting to go to Manhattan, but needing to hold down two jobs to help out her fey, artistic mother? It was almost Dickensian.

He went back over to the couch and lay down. As he put his arm under his head, a small voice he didn't trust told him he was reading her wrong. He ignored the whisper, chalking it up to the fact that he was off-kilter because he was back in his father's place.

When his cell phone went off at 6:00 a.m., he was

still awake, having watched the sun rise behind the veil of the old lace drapes.

Sitting up, he grabbed his BlackBerry and checked the number. "Billy."

His brother's low voice came through loud and clear. "I was crashed when you called and just woke up for practice. Are you okay—"

"He's dead, Billy." He didn't need to use any better word than *he*. There was only one *him* among the three O'Banyon brothers.

As a long, slow exhale came over the phone, Sean wished he'd told Billy in person.

"When?" Billy asked.

"Last night. Heart attack."

"You call Mac?"

"Yeah. But God knows when he'll get the message."

"Where are you?"

"Home frickin' sweet home."

There was a sharp inhale. "You shouldn't be there. That's not a good place."

Sean looked around and couldn't agree more. "Trust me, I'm leaving as soon as I can."

"Is there anything I—"

"Nah. There's not much to do. Finnegan's will handle the cremation and he'll be interred next to Mom. I'll go back and forth until I've packed everything up here and put the house on the market. I mean, I don't want to keep this place."

"Neither do I. Mac'll agree."

In the long silence that followed, Sean knew he and

his brother were remembering exactly the same kinds of things.

"I'm glad he's gone," Billy finally said.

"Me, too."

After they hung up, Sean felt exhaustion settle on him like a suit of chain mail. Stretching out on the sofa, he closed his lids and gave up fighting the past, letting the memories fill the space behind his eyes. Though he was six foot four and worth about a billion dollars, in the dimness, on this couch, in the apartment that had been a hell for him and his brothers, he was as small as a child and just as powerless.

So he was not at all surprised when two hours later he woke up screaming and covered in sweat. The nightmare, the one he'd had for years, had come for another visit.

Jacking upright, he gasped and rubbed his face. The summer morning was bright and cheerful, the light barging into the living room through the windows like a four-year-old wanting to play.

Amid the lovely sunshine, he felt positively elderly.

In a desperate, misplaced bid to cleanse his mind, he took a shower. Didn't help. No matter how hard he worked his body with soap, he couldn't lose the head spins about the past. It felt as if he were trapped in a car on a closed track, going around and around without getting anywhere.

As he stepped out of the water and toweled off, he knew his best hope was that his mind would run out of gas. Soon.

Man, he couldn't wait to get back to Manhattan tonight.

Chapter Four

Two days later, Lizzie lost her job at the Roxbury Community Heath Initiative.

It was the end of a long Friday and she was in the medical-records room when her boss came to find her. "Lizzie? You have a minute?"

She glanced up from the patient charts she was pulling. Dr. Denisha Roberts, the clinic's director, was in the doorway looking exhausted. Which made sense. It was almost five in the afternoon and it had been a week full of challenges. As usual, finances were very tight and their waiting room busier than ever.

Lizzie frowned. "What's wrong?"

"Can you come down to my office?"

Lizzie hugged the chart in her hands against her

chest and followed Denisha to the back of the clinic. After they'd gone into the office and Lizzie was in a chair, the director took a deep breath, then shut the door.

"I don't know how to say this so I'm just going to come right out with it." Denisha sat on the edge of her desk, her dark eyes somber. "I've been informed that our funding from the state is going to be cut substantially for the upcoming year."

"Oh, no…don't tell me we're closing. The community needs us."

"We'll have enough to stay open and I'm going to put some grant applications out there, which hopefully will generate some funds. But…I need to make some staffing changes."

Lizzie closed her eyes. "Let me guess, first in, first out."

"I'm so sorry, Lizzie. You make a tremendous contribution here, you really do, and I'm going to give you my highest recommendation. It's just that with everyone else doing such a good job, seniority is the only thing I can base the choice on. And I have to make the cut now, before the funding shrinks, because we need that new X-ray machine."

Lizzie smoothed her hand over the patient file in her arms. She knew exactly the person it detailed. Sixty-eight-year-old Adella Thomas, a grandmother of nine, who had bad asthma and a gospel voice that could charm the birds to the trees. Whenever one of Adella's granddaughters brought her in for her checkups, she always sang for the staff as well as the patients in the waiting room.

"When's my last day?" Lizzie asked.

"The end of this month. Labor Day weekend. And we'll give you a month's severance." There was a hesitation. "We're in real trouble, Lizzie. Please understand…this is killing me."

She thought for a moment. "You know…I can line up moonlighting work easily enough. Why don't we say a week from today so you can get me off the books? I'll still have a month after that to find a day job."

"That would be…the best thing you could do for us." Denisha looked down at her hands then twisted her wedding band around and around. "I hate doing this. You can't know how much we'll miss you."

"Maybe I can still volunteer."

Denisha nodded her head sadly. "We'd love to have you. Any way we can."

When Lizzie left the office a little later, she thought she was likely losing the best boss she'd ever have. Dr. Roberts had that rare combination of compassion and practicality that worked so well in medicine. She was also an inspiration, giving so much back to the community she'd grown up in. The joke around the center was that she should run for governor someday.

Except the staff really meant it.

Lizzie walked down to the medical-records room and finished pulling charts so that the Saturday-morning staff would be ready for their first five patients of the day. Then she grabbed her lunch tote from the kitchen, waved goodbye to the other nurses and headed out into the oven that was your typical early August evening in Boston.

On her way home, she called Boston Medical Center and asked her supervisor to put her on the sub list so she could hopefully log more hours in the ED. She would need a financial cushion if she couldn't find another day job right away and she might as well prepare for the worst.

When she pulled up to the duplex, she told herself it was going to be fine. She had an excellent job history, and with the number of hospitals in and around Boston, she would secure another position in a week or two.

But God…wherever she ended up it wasn't going to be as special as the clinic. There was just something about that place, probably because it was run more like an old-fashioned doctor's office than a modern-day, insurance-driven, patient-churning business.

Lizzie's mood lifted long enough for her to get through her front door, but the revival didn't last as she hit the message button on her answering machine. Her mother's voice, that singsong, perpetually cheerful, girlie rush, was like the chatter of a goldfinch.

Funny how draining such a pretty sound could be.

"Hi-ho, Lizzie-fish, I just *had* to call you because I've been looking at kilns today for my pottery, which is *critical* for my new direction in my work, which as you know has recently been drifting *away* from painting and into things of a more three-dimensional nature, which is really *significant* for my growth as an artist, which is…"

Lizzie's mom used the word *which* as most people did a period.

As the message went on and on, Lizzie put her purse

and her keys down and leafed through the mail. Bill. Bill. Flyer. Bill.

"Anyway, Lizzie-fish, I bought one this morning and it's being delivered tomorrow. The credit card was broken so I wrote the check for two thousand dollars and I had to pay more for Saturday delivery…."

Lizzie froze. Then whipped her head around to stare at the machine. Two thousand dollars? *Two thousand dollars?* There wasn't that kind of cash in their joint account. And it was after five so Lizzie couldn't call the local bank to stop payment.

Her mother had just bounced that check good and hard.

Lizzie cut off the message and deleted it, then sat down in the quilt-covered armchair by the front bay windows.

The credit card was not "broken." Lizzie had put a five-hundred-dollar limit on the thing precisely so her mother couldn't charge things like kilns, for God's sake.

At least this situation was repairable, though. First thing tomorrow morning, she'd call the bank and cancel that check, then she'd get in touch with the one art-supply store in Essex and tell them the purchase was off. Hopefully, she'd catch them in time.

A thump drifting down from above jerked Lizzie to attention. She looked at the ceiling then out the window. Another rental car was parked at the curb, this time a silver one, but she'd been too caught up in the drama over her job to notice when she'd arrived.

Sean O'Banyon was back.

Sean stood in his old bedroom and wondered how many boxes he'd need to clean out the space. On his way into Southie from the airport, he'd hit U-Haul and bought two dozen of their cardboard specials, but he was probably going to need more.

He went over and opened up the closet door then tugged on a white string that had a little metal crown at the end. The light clicked on and the dusty remnants of his and Billy's high-school wardrobe were revealed. The two of them had shared clothes for years because Billy had always been so big for his age, and when Sean had left for college, they'd divvied up the best of the stuff. All that was left now was a wilted chamois shirt with a hole under one pit and a pair of khakis they'd both hated.

His cell phone rang and he answered it offhandedly, distracted by thoughts of his brother. It was the team of analysts from his office about the Condi-Foods merger, and he started to pace around as he answered their questions.

When he got off the phone with them, he looked back across the room at the closet and frowned. There was something shoved in the far corner of the upper shelf, something he'd missed on the booze hunt that first night he'd been here.

A backpack. His backpack.

He went over, stretched up and grabbed on to a pair of nylon straps. Whatever was in the damn thing weighed a ton, and as it swung loose from the shelf, he let it fall to the floor. As it landed, a little cloud of dust wafted up and dispersed.

Crouching down, he unzipped the top and his breath

caught. Books… His books. The ones from his senior year in high school.

He took out his old physics tome, first smoothing his palm over the cover then fingering the gouge he'd made on the spine. Cracking the thing open, he put his nose into the crease and breathed in deep, smelling the sweet scent of ink on bound pages. After tracing over notes he'd made in the margins, he put it aside.

Good Lord, his calculus book. His AP chemistry. His AP history.

As he spread them out flat on the floor and arranged them so the tops of their multicolored covers were aligned, he had a familiar feeling, one he used to get in school. Looking at them he felt rich. Positively rich. In a childhood full of hand-me-downs and birthdays with no parties and Christmases with no presents, learning had been his luxury. His happiness. His wealth.

After countless petty thefts as a juvenile delinquent, these textbooks had been the last things he'd stolen. When the end of his senior school year had come, he just hadn't been able to give them back and he hadn't had the money to pay for them. So he'd marked each one of the spines and turned them in as you were supposed to. Then he'd broken into the school and the gouges he'd made had been how he'd found the ones that were his. He'd gathered them from the various stacks, put them in this backpack and raced away into the night.

Of course he'd felt guilty as hell. Strange that palming booze from convenience stores had never bothered his conscience, but he'd felt that the taking of the books had been wrong. So as soon as he'd earned enough from his campus job at Harvard, he'd sent the high school three hundred seventy-five dollars in cash with an anonymous note explaining what it was for.

But he'd needed to have the books. He'd needed to know they were still with him as he went off to Harvard. On some irrational level, he'd feared if he didn't keep them, everything he'd learned from them would disappear, and he'd been terrified about going to Crimson and looking stupid.

Yeah, *terrified* was the right word. He could clearly recall the day he'd left to go to college...could remember every detail about getting on the T that late August afternoon and heading over the Charles River to Harvard. Unlike a lot of the other guys in his class, who'd come with trunks of clothes and fancy stereos and TVs and refrigerators—and BMWs for God's sake—he'd had nothing but a beat-up suitcase and a duffel bag with a broken strap.

He'd gone alone because he hadn't wanted his father to take him, not that Eddie had offered. And as he'd been forced to go on foot, he'd had to leave his books behind. There had been no question that he was coming back for them, though. He'd returned home that weekend to get the backpack...except his father had said he'd thrown it out.

That had been the last time Sean had been home. Until three nights ago.

A knock brought his head up. Getting to his feet, he walked down the hall to the living room, opened the door and—oh, man—looked into the very pair of green eyes that had been in the back of his mind over the past few days.

Lizzie Bond was dressed in a little white T-shirt and a pair of khaki shorts. Her hair was down on her shoulders, all naturally streaked with blond and brown, and there wasn't a lick of makeup on her pretty face.

She looked fantastic.

"Hi," he said with a slow smile.

In characteristic fashion she flushed. "Hi. I'm…ah, I'm sorry to bother you." She held out a clear plastic bag full of clothes. "I meant to give this to you before. They're your father's things."

He didn't want whatever was in there, but he took the thing anyway. "Thanks."

She glanced around his shoulder at the stack of collapsed U-Haul boxes. "So you're starting the packing."

"No reason to wait." He stepped back and motioned her in. "Listen, if you want any of the stuff around here, you know, the furniture or anything, it's yours."

"Won't you want to keep some?"

"My place is furnished." Sean shut the door to keep the air-conditioning from leaking down the stairwell. And also because he wanted her to stay for a little longer. "So is my brother's."

Her brows shot up. "You have a brother?"

"He didn't mention that?"

"No, he only told me to call you."

Well, hadn't he won the lottery. "There are three of us, actually. Billy, Mac and me. I'm in the middle. Billy's the youngest."

"Oh." She tucked some hair behind her ear, something he had a feeling she did when she felt awkward. "I had no idea. Where are the other two?"

"Here and there." Or in the case of Mac, God only knew where. Matter of fact, he still hadn't returned Sean's call. "Seriously, Lizzie, check out the furniture, tell me what you want and I'll help you move it down-stairs. Except for the couch, at least for the time being. I'm going to be sleeping on it until I'm through here."

She gave him an odd look, as if she was thinking there were plenty of beds in the place and was wonder-ing why he didn't use them. But she didn't make any comment, just walked around the living room then headed for the kitchen.

As she wandered around assessing furniture, he found himself wishing he could take the offer back. For some reason, he didn't want this stuff in her home…as if what had taken place here could contaminate where she lived. Which was ridiculous. Domestic abuse wasn't a virus. And sure as hell if it was, you couldn't pick it up from a ratty Barcalounger.

When she went into his and Billy's bedroom, Sean followed, his eyes locking on the sway of her hips as she walked. He let his gaze wander up her spine to her shoulders and her neck. With a flash of inspiration, he wanted to pull her up against him, draw his fingers in deep through her hair, tilt her head back—

"Look at the books!" She crouched down. "These are from high school, right? Were they yours?"

Sean quickly knelt and started stuffing the things into the pack. "They're nothing. Nothing special."

She sat back and he knew she was watching his

frantic hands, but he couldn't stop himself. He'd always had to protect his books and evidently the compulsion hadn't lessened with age. When they were all safely zipped in the bag, he hefted them back onto the shelf in the closet and shut the door.

"So the furniture?" he prompted with an edge. "You want any?"

She got up slowly. "I think not. Thank you."

As she turned away, he knew she was hightailing it for the exit and he didn't blame her. Goddamn it, he'd all but bitten her head off.

"Lizzie?"

She paused in the bedroom doorway, but didn't look at him. "Yes?"

"If I promise to be more polite, would you like to go out for some dinner?"

When her head swiveled around, her eyes were grave. "You don't like it here, do you?"

For some stupid reason, he found himself shaking his head. "I'd rather be just about anywhere else in the world."

"Why?"

"No reason."

The lie was no doubt painfully apparent, yet he was sticking with it. Some things you never shared. Not because you were weak, but because you were strong.

Lizzie stared at Sean and idly thought he looked better than any man should. The black T-shirt and low-hanging jeans were just too attractive. And the fact that he was barefoot was really sexy. Even his feet were nice.

In the silence between them, she was reminded keenly of his father. No matter what Sean said, he and Mr. O'Banyon were a lot alike. Very private. Very closed.

Though she had known Mr. O'Banyon for quite a while, there had been so many things the man had hidden, just as Sean was doing now. And the two of them did it the same way. Their faces just walled up tight, their eyes going blank, their mouths drawing into a line.

"So what do you think?" Sean prompted. "Dinner?"

The thing was, the shutdown happened fast. Literally in a moment, they were gone and you were talking to a two-dimensional likeness of who they really were.

It made her want to dig to find out what had happened in this apartment, what had caused a father and son to split so irrevocably.

Son? *Sons,* she corrected herself. She couldn't believe Mr. O'Banyon hadn't mentioned he had multiple children.

"I'll get my purse," she said, heading for the living room.

"How about Little Italy?" Sean said as he followed.

"Sounds like heaven."

She waited as he shoved his feet into a pair of Nikes, grabbed keys from the table next to the couch and slipped a black wallet into his back pocket.

After a quick stop by her place, they got into his rental. As they pulled away from the curb, she noticed that the tension in his face had eased up considerably and she had a feeling it was because they were leaving.

"Sean?"

"Yeah?"

"About the furniture upstairs? Come to think of it, I could really use that kitchen table and those chairs."

"No problem. When we get back, I'll hump them down to your place."

"That would be great."

She and Mr. O'Banyon had never sat in the kitchen during their Sunday dinners so she didn't have any deep associations with the little dining set. And she needed one. She was tired of eating either standing up in the kitchen with her butt against the counter or off her lap on her couch.

And maybe there was a little part of her that wanted to keep something of Mr. O'Banyon's. As she'd looked at all those boxes Sean was going to use, she'd felt an odd fear...as if her friend were truly disappearing even though he was already gone.

A half hour later she and Sean were standing in line outside Bastianelli's. The restaurant was a Little Italy favorite, barely bigger than a closet with the best Italian food in town. Part of the tradition of eating there was the long line and she always enjoyed the forced slowdown. With nothing to do but inch forward toward the glossy black and brass door, Lizzie found herself calming out and forgetting about the fact that a dear friend had died and she'd lost one of her jobs and her mother was the Imelda Marcos of art supplies.

As the sun set, the heat rolling over the city eased up and a gentle breeze suffused with the scents of oregano and garlic wafted by. The patter of talk from other people in line was like soft, indistinct music, more rhythm than words.

Lizzie lifted her face to the gloaming sky and took a deep breath. When she felt something touch her neck, she jumped.

Sean's hand hesitated then brushed behind her ear. "Loose strand of hair."

In slow motion, his fingers drifted over to the other side of her face and did the same thing. "And another one."

Abruptly, she couldn't breathe at all. Which was fine. Looking up into his hazel eyes, she didn't need air to live.

His thumb passed over her cheek and his voice dropped an octave, becoming nothing more than a deep rumble in that muscled chest of his. "You've got bruises under your eyes from lack of sleep. What's got you so tired there, Lizzie?"

She blinked. Then wanted to wince because obviously he thought she looked like hell. "Just have a lot on my mind."

"Like what?" he said in a lazy drawl.

Oh, God…where to go with that one? Because the truth was that she'd stayed awake thinking of him. "I'm out of work," she blurted.

All at once, his voice shifted back to its normal bass and he dropped his hand. "What happened?"

Way to ruin a moment, Lizzie.

She cleared her throat. "Well, the health clinic in Roxbury where I work is losing state funding so they have to reduce staff. We're just a small community center and we don't—*they*…don't have enough resources to afford my position anymore."

His brows came together. "This because of the new budget?"

"Yes. Tax dollars are tight and I can understand that. But the state has to support facilities like ours. I mean...theirs." She exhaled in a rush. "It's a social imperative."

As they moved forward again, she realized there was one more couple and then they'd be in the door and at a table.

She looked through the restaurant's window at the people who were eating inside and murmured, "I'm going to miss working at the clinic so much. The patients are wonderful and I've really gotten to know the community. But I'm going to volunteer there or at least try to."

"How long do you have until you're out?"

"Next Friday. But I'm sure I'll find more work. Nurses are always needed in Boston. Besides, I still have my moonlighting. I'll be fine." When there was a silence, she glanced over at him. "Why are you looking at me like that?"

"Like what?"

"As if you're measuring me."

Sean's lids dropped and a slow, very masculine smile appeared on his face. "Well, you're kind of measurable, Lizzie Bond."

Whoa.

Flustered, she said, "It's hot out here."

"Yeah, it is."

And didn't that drawl of his just make it hotter?

Abruptly, he laughed. "You are a blusher."

"Not usually."

"Well, then I appreciate your making the effort on my behalf. It suits you."

Oh…hell. She had to smile at him. Just couldn't resist looking up into those deep-set hazel eyes and grinning like a fool.

The door to Bastianelli's opened and a little man with a mustache and a big belly motioned them in with a broad smile. As they stepped into the restaurant, Sean put his hand on the small of her back and she found herself inching closer to his body.

And not because the place was crowded.

As they made their way to the table, Sean leaned down to her ear, the spicy scent of his cologne enveloping her like a caress. "You've surprised me."

"I have?" God, even though they were in a public place, she suddenly felt as though they were all alone. And she liked it.

His chest brushed up against her shoulder blades. "I didn't know I liked women who blushed. Also didn't know I liked Ivory soap so much."

"How did you know I used…"

Her words dried up as his fingertip ran down the nape of her neck. "I can smell it on you."

Okay, so now *hot* didn't cover it. She was inside of a volcano.

The maître d' stopped by a little table in the corner that had a red candle burning and two place settings on it. "For you! *Mange bene!*"

As she and Sean sat down, she fumbled with her napkin, aware that she was blushing a little. And that he was looking.

"So how do you feel about red?" he asked, flipping open the wine list.

"Perfect." She was getting to know the color ever so much better with him around.

"Do you want to pick?"

"No, thanks." She took a look at her menu and didn't see a thing. Surely she wasn't reading into things with him. He'd caressed her neck, for heaven's sake. "I'll trust your choice."

"Lizzie?" When she glanced up, he smiled and said softly, "Just wanted to see the blush. That's all."

As her cheeks flamed even further, the waiter came over with some fantastic fresh bread and a plate of olive oil. After the specials were recited, Sean ordered a bottle of wine and they made their selections.

When they were alone, he offered the basket of bread to her. "You know…really, this candlelight suits you."

It was right then that Lizzie knew for sure…she was on a date.

Chapter Five

An hour and a half later, Sean smiled to himself as he put his espresso back down on its little saucer. He couldn't remember when he'd had a more enjoyable dinner with a woman. He and Lizzie had talked about books and movies and food and music.

And they didn't agree on anything. Which was the fun part.

"I can't believe you don't like any of the Impressionists," Lizzie said, shaking her head over her cannoli.

"Oh, please." He smiled more widely. "Rorschach tests and finger painting do more for me."

"So what kind of art do you like?"

He forked up a little more of his crème caramel. "Medieval. Definitely medieval."

"Really?"

He laughed. "Why so surprised?"

"It's not what I expected."

"And what exactly would you expect? Edward Hopper? No, wait, LeRoy Neiman?"

She sipped some of her cappuccino. "Well, I, ah…I'm just surprised you care about art at all. Or know so much about it." She rushed to qualify. "Not that I think you're uncultured or anything. It's just…"

He leaned back in his chair, feeling a little awkward for the first time. "Just that considering where I come from, men aren't usually into that stuff?"

She winced. "That sounds bad doesn't it? I don't mean to offend you or generalize."

"Nah, it's okay. Beautiful things should be valued, so I like art. No big deal."

The awkward feeling persisted. Thing was, he liked that she thought he was just another Joe from Southie, that she seemed to have no clue who he was. He'd been Sean O'Banyon, Big Shot Wall Street Money Man, for so long, it felt liberating to leave that identity behind.

And just be himself.

Except he was leaving a hell of a lot out and that didn't sit well.

She took another bite of the cannoli and wiped her mouth. "You know a lot more about literature than I would have thought, too."

"Always been a big reader."

She smiled and he loved the curve of her cheeks in the candlelight. "So tell me, what do you do? I've been meaning to ask you."

The waiter showed up at Sean's elbow. "Another espresso? More cappuccino?"

"Not for me, thanks. Lizzie? No? Okay, the check would be great."

The waiter left and Sean folded his napkin and put it on the table. God, how to answer her. This had been the best date he'd been on in…forever. All it had been was two people getting to know each other and he didn't want to ruin it.

Especially because he didn't know for a fact that she hadn't been using his father for money.

Except, damn it, Lizzie just did not seem like that kind of woman.

Sean cursed in his head. Yeah, well, neither had the one who had taken him for such a ride way back when.

"My work?" He shrugged…and recalled the conversation he'd had with his team before he and Lizzie had gone out. Nothing but interest-rate analysis and speculation on whether the Fed was going to raise the rates in the next quarter. Dry. Very dry. "You know what, it's not that interesting, I'm afraid."

"Are you in construction?"

His brows shot up. "What makes.you think that?"

As Lizzie turned bright pink again, he wanted to lean across their empty cups and kiss her. So much so, he planted his palms on the table and started to rise.

But come on. Trying to do that for the first time in public? Not smooth.

As he forced himself back into the chair, he knew he was going to end up putting a move on her at the end of the night. He *knew* it. It was probably a bad idea but she was so different…so natural…so real. A woman, not a social shark in a skirt.

Or at least she appeared that way.

"Why do you think I'm in construction, Lizzie?"

"Your chest is really…ah…developed. So I thought maybe what you did had a physical component to it." Then she frowned and looked down. "Except your hands aren't callused. Are you a trainer at a gym?"

"I do train folks, yeah." And this was not a lie. He worked a lot with the membership of his triathlon club, getting folks ready for events. "I'm into sports."

"What kinds?"

"Every year I do the Ironman Triathlon. I hit a number of others, but that's my big one. I like to compete. And I like to win."

"You like to push yourself, then."

"Yeah, I do. So do my brothers. We're like that."

"Why?"

The question made warning bells go off in his head. He and Billy and Mac were all driven to the point of obsession and the root cause, he suspected, was in the ugly past: every day, they ran without running.

Time to switch the subject.

Sean shrugged. "We're just like that. So tell me more about your mom. What kind of art is she into?"

God, he was a liar, wasn't he?

And she knew it. Her smart, level eyes told him that.

Lizzie smiled at him, and it was the smile of a Madonna, all-knowing, very kind. "It's okay, Sean. I'm not going to push."

Crap. Now he was the one flushing. Imagine that. "I'm not into talking about myself much."

"That's all right. You're really good company anyway."

Sean's heart stopped. He couldn't think of the last time a woman had told him he was really good company. Hell, maybe one never had. And he was so used to being seen as a "catch" that the idea someone just liked his words and his opinions was…disarming.

"You're some good company there, too, Lizzie." His voice was a little husky and he hoped she didn't notice it. He cleared his throat. "I am curious about your mom, though. What's she like?"

Lizzie took a deep breath, as if she were about to lift something heavy off the floor. "My mother calls herself a free-range art-ellectual. I'm not too clear on what exactly that is, but I can tell you that she's into pottery now. I don't think it's going to stick. Over the past two decades, she's been through almost everything. Painting in watercolor and oil. Sculpting in clay, marble and brass. Pastels. Photography. Macramé. Toothpicks. Recycle art—that's garbage by the way. She follows her whims where they take her."

"She sell any of her work in galleries?"

"She's more into the creation end of things rather than the retail." Lizzie sipped at her cappuccino. "And well…honestly? She's not that good at it."

"Sounds like an expensive hobby then."

Lizzie's voice grew wry. "Yeah. But the thing is, it makes her happy. So I support it."

"Where's your father?"

"He left about five years ago for the third time and

it finally stuck. My mother is enchanting, but she can be difficult to handle. She's a child in many ways, and like a child, she's both irresponsible and beguiling. So I can't say I blame him."

"Do you see him?"

She shook her head. "When he left, he left us both. Said a clean cut was best. It was no big change, though. She was always what held his interest, not me."

Good Lord, he thought. "That's harsh."

"Oh, I don't mean to come across that way."

"Not you, Lizzie. Him. To leave his daughter like that?"

There was a quiet moment. Then she murmured, "I think it's hard for him to see me. I look a lot like her and our voices sound the same. To him, I am the younger version of her."

"So what? He should man up and get over that."

Her eyes flipped to his, and as he saw the sadness in them, he wanted to hunt down her father and yell at the guy for dumping his daughter.

The urge got even stronger when she said with dignity, "It is what it is. I used to hope he'd be different, but he is who he is and it's better for me…healthier…to accept him and move on. Waiting for change is hard and not all that realistic."

Yeah, well, Sean respected the fact that she wasn't looking for sympathy and he could see her point, but it still sucked. "You don't have any brothers or sisters do you?"

"No."

"Which means you deal with your mom all by yourself."

"Yes, but it's not that bad. The house is paid for and her expenses aren't that high. Usually."

He kept his curse to himself. "No offense, but it strikes me that the parent-child thing is ass-backward."

"But I love my mother. And without me…"

"She'd be forced to grow up?" In the silence that followed, Sean cursed out loud. "I'm sorry. I don't mean to get in your face about this."

There was another long pause. Then she said, "I don't tell people this usually, not because I'm ashamed or embarrassed, but because I'm not interested in pity…. My mom's mentally challenged. She can function independently to a point, but she's always going to need help. First my father was that for her. Now I am."

Sean's eyes widened. "Oh, God…Lizzie, I'm sorry."

"Don't be." She smiled. "There is no tragedy here and no shame, either. You know, it's interesting. My father is much older than my mom and I assume in the beginning he thought that she was just young and eccentric. Like she'd grow out of her ways or something. It wasn't until I was in my early teens that he took her to doctors and we learned that it was not an issue of maturity. But again, there is no catastrophe here. My mother's happy and healthy and she's full of joy. So it's okay. But can you understand why things between her and I aren't just a case of a parent dropping the ball?"

"Yeah. Totally."

The waiter showed up with the check, and without even thinking, Sean took out his wallet.

"How much do I owe?" Lizzie asked.

Sean froze. He'd been about to pay the whole thing and to hell with his Dutch rule.

Get back with the program, he told himself. Stay tight.

Doing some quick division in his head, he said, "Sixty-seven dollars."

Her eyes flared, but she reached for her purse.

"Let me pay for the wine, though," he cut in. "I picked it."

"No, that's okay. I drank my share."

As she put three twenties, one five and two ones on the table, he noticed that the edges of her purse were worn through. In a rush, his net worth funneled into his brain, that cool billion dollars or so in stocks and cash and annuities and T-bills and gold.

He reached out to push her money back to her.

"Wow, that's a beautiful wallet you have."

He stopped, jarred as his normal mind-set about women returned.

Man, that stuff about Lizzie losing her job had seemed true enough and so had all those blushes and the revelation about her mother. But he got tangled whenever he thought about her relationship with his father. Surely she couldn't have enjoyed that miserable bastard's company. So that left Good Samaritan-itis. Or her being after something.

Sean looked into her eyes and mined for the answer to his unspoken question: Was Lizzie Bond different than the women he knew or exactly the same?

After a moment, he found himself slowly moving her money back toward her. "My treat."

"Are you sure?"

"Yeah." Keeping his titanium American Express card out of sight, he put a crisp hundred-dollar bill and three twenties on top of the table. "Let's go."

"Wow, that's a big tip."

"They deserve it."

She smiled at him. Then stood up...only to put her hand on the wall to steady herself. "Oh, this is bad."

"What?"

"That wine was awfully good and I have no tolerance whatsoever."

"Lean on me, then."

As he came around and drew her against him, their bodies fit together so perfectly it momentarily stopped him in his tracks.

"Sean? You ready to go?"

He tightened his hold on her waist. "Yeah."

He led her through the crowded restaurant, and as he urged her out the door first, he wanted to keep his arm around her. Like for the rest of the night.

When they were outside, she took a couple of deep inhales and said, "Maybe it was just hot in there."

"It was stuffy. You feel better?"

"Much." She glanced to the sky. "I heard we're supposed to get storms tonight."

"Hot enough for it."

"Yes."

He had no idea what they were talking about. Maybe the weather? Whatever. He was caught up in her profile, most specifically her lips. Oh, man...he wanted to grab her around the waist, get her against him from shoulder to knee and kiss the ever-living breath out of her.

"The car's this way," he said roughly.

On the way back to Southie, they went without air-conditioning and both put their windows down. The summer night was gentle and warm as it flooded into the rental car and he stole glances across the seat at her as if he were sixteen.

When they pulled up to the row house, he stopped the sedan and turned off the engine, but he made no move to open his door.

"Thank you," she said with a smile that melted him. "This was lovely."

"You're welcome."

In the silence, he thought of the last time he'd taken a woman out in Manhattan. The two of them had gone to Jean Georges in his limo. She'd been wearing diamond studs the size of marbles and a dress by Chanel; he'd been in one of his Savile Row suits. They'd worked the crowd on the way to their A-lister table then flirted as sophisticates did, one-upping each other. Afterward, they'd gone back to his penthouse, but she hadn't spent the whole night—yet another of his rules with women.

It had all been very glamorous…and utterly forget-table.

Tonight with Lizzie was not. Here in this Ford Taurus, with the summer air on his face and the sound of crickets in his ears and the dark night wrapped around them, this moment was totally vivid to him. He was not on social autopilot. With Lizzie…he was alive.

And he wanted more. He wanted the privacy of her

apartment. He wanted to be in between her sheets. Tonight, he craved the sweetness in her, needed to be naked against her kindness. And though he was very aware that he couldn't give anything back to her other than pleasure, he vowed to make sure that was enough for her if she let him in.

He pushed his door open. "Let's move that kitchen table down."

"Are you sure?" She smiled as they went up onto the porch. "It's late. We could do it tomorrow as I'm off."

"Won't take long. Besides, it'll give me some room for the boxes."

"Oh, in that case, let's do it."

They went upstairs, and as she headed into the kitchen, he walked over to his duffel bag of clothes and took out his shaving kit. As he slipped a condom in his back pocket, he didn't like the ache in his chest, but he didn't stop himself. After all, if she told him no, he would absolutely back off.

"Sean? You coming?" she called out.

"Yeah." He rubbed his sternum and went into the kitchen.

"This is going to be a tight squeeze." She bent to the side and eyed the table's girth. "The stairs aren't that wide."

"Don't worry, we'll take it slow."

Getting the thing down the stairwell took some maneuvering, but they managed not to mash anyone's fingers on the railing or the doorjamb into her apartment.

As they took a breather in her living room, his chest burned even more as he looked around. Everything was tidy and very clean, but thrift-shop worn: the couch had a pretty flowered blanket tucked into what undoubtedly were frayed cushions. The chair by the window had threadbare patches on the arms and was covered by a quilt. There was no TV and just one lamp. Nothing on the walls.

He thought of her purse with its worn corners.

"Sean?"

"I'm sorry, what?"

"Only a little farther." She nodded over her shoulder. "To my kitchen?"

"Right." He picked up his end of the table.

The kitchen was likewise sparkling from regular cleaning—hell, you could have eaten off the floor or the counters. But there was nothing around, no decorations, no extra appliances. Just the basics.

He thought of his own kitchen back in Manhattan with its Viking stove and its granite countertops and its wine fridge and its matching toaster and mixer and espresso machines. None of which he'd ever used.

"Would you like to wait to do the chairs?" she prompted, making him realize he'd been standing stock-still and saying nothing.

"Nah, let's do them now."

Two joint trips up and down and everything was set up in the middle of her kitchen. As Lizzie eased one of the chairs into the table, her hands lingered on its back. The furniture was well used, but she treated it as if it were precious.

"Thank you," she said. "I've always eaten on the couch. Now I have a real table."

Sean rubbed his chest again. How she shamed him with her pleasure at this gift that meant nothing to him.

"You're welcome," he replied, aware he'd made up his mind. "Good night, Lizzie. Sleep well."

As he headed out of the kitchen, he glanced down the hall and saw into one of the bedrooms. It was empty, just four walls and a bare floor. He was willing to bet she only had a bed for herself.

He walked even faster toward the exit.

"Sean?"

He paused with his hand on the door and didn't look back. "Yeah?"

As she hesitated, he guessed she was surprised he wasn't putting a move on her.

"Ah…thank you again for dinner. That was very generous."

Generous? The night before, he'd spent seventeen hundred dollars hosting two people at the Congress Club in Manhattan. But sure as hell, he'd enjoyed the dinner with her in Little Italy so much more.

She cleared her throat. "Maybe I can pay you back sometime."

Now he glanced over his shoulder at her. Standing across the room from him, she was lovely in the way of a summer afternoon. Warm. Inviting. Something you missed during winter.

"Don't worry about it," he said and turned away.

As he closed the door behind himself, he knew if she'd been any other woman he would have stayed. But Lizzie Bond deserved better than a quick roll. And that was all he had in him.

Chapter Six

Lizzie watched Sean walk out her door and wondered yet again if she hadn't read him wrong. She'd been convinced he was going to kiss her, especially after he'd put his arm around her while they'd left the restaurant. She'd even figured that moving the table was just an excuse for him to come into her apartment.

But maybe she'd let her own attraction to him color her interpretation of his actions.

She sucked at dating. Or whatever tonight was.

As she locked her door, she listened to his heavy footsteps going up the stairs and then moving around above her. All things considered, it was probably better for the night to end like this. She could see herself getting attached to him and getting hurt.

It still was a letdown though.

Unsettled and vaguely depressed, she took a quick shower, turned the temperature to low on the AC unit and got into bed.

The lightning came hours later, flashing on the other side of the Venetian blinds, startling her out of sleep. As her heart rate slowed, she listened for the thunder, and after a long pause, a crack dissolved into a bass rumble.

She reached for the remote to the AC and shut the thing off so she could hear better. She'd always loved storms, especially the—

What was that?

She frowned and looked at the ceiling. An odd noise was coming from upstairs, some kind of... Well, she didn't know what that was. She sat up, as if that would help her ears do their job, and held her breath.

There it was again. A low, uneven sound.

Slipping from bed, she walked out into her living room and got really quiet as she absorbed the sounds in the duplex.

Whatever it had been seemed to have stopped.

Except then the next burst of lightning came, and in the dead space before the thunder, she heard what had to be a moan. She opened her door, stepped into the foyer, and put her hand on the staircase's railing. When the low, aching groan came once more, she jogged up and knocked.

"Sean?"

Thunder rolled through the house like a wrecking ball, making the walls vibrate and the darkness of the stairwell seem horror-movie oppressive. Then a hoarse yell came through the door.

She tossed out all propriety and tried the knob. As it was unlocked, she shoved hard and burst into the apartment.

Sean was on the couch, his big body contorted, his boxers twisted around his hips, one arm rigid and gripping a cushion. His head was thrown back, his neck straining, his mouth open as he breathed in ragged pulls. Next to him on the floor was the backpack full of books.

She rushed over and put her hand on his shoulder. "Sean…wake up."

He shot out of the nightmare like a bullet from a gun, sitting up in a rush, shouting loudly. As he swiveled his head toward her, his eyes were stark wild and the moment he saw her, he cowered back, lifting both arms to cover his head as if she were going to strike him.

"No…" His voice didn't sound at all like the one she knew. "No, *please*."

"Sean?" She touched his thick bicep only to have him flinch away and tremble as lightning flickered through the room.

Another crack of thunder broke out, so loud it was as if the house next door had been struck. Both of them jumped. Then Sean dropped his arms and looked around as if he wasn't sure what had happened.

"You had a nightmare."

His eyes went to her face and locked on her as if he were using the sight of her to pull himself out of where he'd been. As he stared up at her, he was breathing hard, the sheen of sweat on his bare chest catching the reflection of yet more bolts of lightning.

He moved so fast, she couldn't have pulled back if she'd wanted to. His hands clamped on either side of her face and he brought her down hard to his mouth.

He kissed her with erotic aggression, the pent-up energy in his body tunneling into her and lighting her on fire through the shifting contact of their mouths. As she gasped, his tongue shot into her mouth and he pulled her on top of him until she felt him from her collarbones to her ankles. Moving fast and hot, he devoured her, holding her with heavy hands, thrusting his hips up into her so she felt his erection.

When he pulled back, they were both panting.

"Leave now," he said roughly. "If you're going to."

She should go, she really should. She'd never been with someone outside of a relationship, and she and Sean definitely didn't have one of those.

Except this moment, this raw, incendiary moment, was too enticing to walk away from.

Sean lowered his hands and held out his arms as if wanting to make sure he wasn't forcing her in any way. "Lizzie, make up your mind. And do it now."

She shook her head. "I don't want to go. I'm not going to stop this—"

He was all over her in the next heartbeat, kissing her like a man possessed, like a man who was starving. His mouth and tongue devastated her, and in the back of her mind, she had some dim thought that he was very good at this, had no doubt had a lot of practice.

Her heart ached at the passing realization, but the

sting didn't linger. She refused to let it. She had him here and now and he was…on fire.

His thigh pushed between hers and his need rubbed on her lower belly, a stunning length that left her shivering. As the storm swept in and the rain came down, he stripped off her shirt and pulled her up his body so he could take one of her breasts into his mouth.

She cried out and arched her back, feeling his hands grab on to the backs of her thighs and squeeze. It was impossible to keep up with him and unthinkable to slow him down and unbearable to imagine him ever stopping. Somehow her panties disappeared, probably because he ripped the side apart.

And then he was touching her.

As she cried out, his hips surged up and he cursed in a low, desperate sound, as if the feel of her was almost too much for him. It certainly was too much for her. She shattered apart, going rigid on top of his bare chest, her body torquing wildly as she climaxed. His mouth latched onto her throat and he sucked hard as he helped her ride out the sensations, his hand between her legs keeping her going.

When it was done, she collapsed against him, her face falling into his neck. She was limp as he rolled her over and she should have been embarrassed as she lay sprawled on the couch, but she just closed her eyes in bliss.

She felt the sofa wiggle as he stood up. Heard the shift of cloth as he took off his boxers. Then there was a soft tearing sound.

He stretched out on top of her, splitting her thighs

with his knees. His skin was griddle hot, his body flexed and straining with his need to finish.

At the first blunt brush of his arousal, her eyes popped wide.

"You're protected," he said. "I took care of it."

Her lids settled and she ran her hands up his thick shoulders. As his hips began rocking against her, he stared over her head, his face dark with concentration and barely leashed energy.

He went slowly, but even still she had to wince. In spite of how careful he was, and even though her body wanted him, the discomfort made her stiffen beneath him.

He stopped. Retreated a little. "Lizzie?"

Before he could say anything else, she blurted, "It's been a while for me."

As he looked down at her, his eyes became remote. "How long?"

"A while." When he just stared at her, she whispered, "A year or two."

Now he was the one wincing.

With an abrupt shift, he lifted off her body, pulled a throw blanket over her and sat down at the far end of the couch. Putting his elbows on his knees, he rubbed his face then reached between his legs. There was a snapping sound as he pulled off the protection.

In the silence that followed, Lizzie tucked the blanket in tight to her neck and stared at him. She was pretty sure why he'd stopped. The question was whether he'd be honest.

"I'm sorry." He rubbed his face some more. "I don't want to use you for sex, just to get rid of that dream."

As if that was the only reason he'd wanted to be with her. *Ouch*.

And damn, she hated being right. Good thing they'd stopped when they had.

She sat up, holding the blanket to her breasts and thinking she had to get out of this apartment fast. Thank heavens her T-shirt was right on the floor next to the couch. She picked it up and managed to get it on even though her hands were shaking. Where were her panties—oh. They were unwearable.

She got to her feet and wrapped the blanket around her hips, prepared to leave without another word.

Except then he said, "Can I come with you?"

She looked over at him. "What do you mean?"

"Can I, ah… Can I sleep with you? As in sleep, sleep with you?" He glanced up at her. "God, that sounds lame."

Her first and only thought was…she would love to have him in her bed like that.

He cursed and muttered, "Forget—"

"Yes." She held out her hand. "Yes, you can."

As Sean settled into Lizzie's bed, he let out a deep sigh. Man, this was good. The sheets smelled like her and so did the pillow his head was on. From over on the left, the rain softly hitting the window made him think of cats padding over hardwood floors. Lightning still flashed and thunder still rolled, but the storm was winding down.

This was better than good.

Lizzie came in with two glasses of water. She put

one on the bedside table next to him and took the other around to her side. She was awkward and lovely as she dropped the throw blanket and scooted under the covers with him. Then the lights went off and they were together in the dark.

He turned toward her, feeling needy and hating himself. "Can I hold you?"

She rolled right into him and he fit her warmth to his body, tucking her head under his chin, intertwining his legs with hers.

"What sort of nightmare was it?" she asked.

"The old kind." Yeah, the really old kind. The one where his father came into his room after he'd finished off with Mac. Mac had always been able to take a lot, but sometimes he broke and then it was Sean's turn, if their father was still angry. As the third in line, Billy had almost never been worked over. He'd just had to listen to the sounds and wonder if he was going to be next.

Which had been a head screw nonetheless.

Man, the not knowing had been the worst. You never knew whether it was going to be this night or another.... Whether the monster was going to come after you because your brother couldn't handle it... If it was going to hurt less or more than before—

"Are you cold?" Lizzie asked, inching even closer to him. "You're shivering."

Sean squeezed his eyes shut and wondered what all those people on Wall Street would think if they could see him now, curled up for comfort against a woman he barely knew because she was all he had to turn to.

He kissed Lizzie's hair then rubbed his face against it, dragging himself back from where he'd been.

Unfortunately, what he tuned into was her body.

Upstairs, his response to her had been all about pent-up fear and anger, an unleashing. But now in this quiet room, with the storm outside receding and the soft dripping of rain all that was left of the weather's fury, he found himself wanting to make love to her, not just have sex with her.

His body began to hurt with need denied and now renewed.

Except he knew it was wrong. Over the next couple of weeks, he was going to pack up the apartment upstairs, sell the house and never look back. Meanwhile, she was a woman who wasn't into short-term lovers—her history said it all.

"Sean?" she whispered into his neck.

The brush of her breath against his skin made him jerk. And his reply was nothing more than a growl.

Her palm slid over his waist and down to his hips and… He hissed sharply as she found the ache behind the boxers he'd thrown on.

Unconsciously, his hips moved, pressing his flesh into her grip. But then he reached down and brought her hand to his lips. Looking into her eyes, falling into them, he wanted her in ways he couldn't name. Refused to name.

God…maybe he was protecting himself, as well, by not being with her.

"Lizzie—"

"At least let me…take care of you. Your body isn't going to let you sleep."

He went still, lungs ceasing to draw. Oh, man, he wanted her to make him finish and not just because she was right about the not sleeping. He wanted her to be in charge of him.

Slowly, he put her hand back where it had been.

Lizzie urged him over onto his back, and as he complied, she pulled the sheets free of his body. Going up on her knees, blond hair falling forward, shirt hanging loose, she reached down and dragged his boxers off his legs. His arousal landed flat on his belly, swollen and straining.

She came up to his mouth and kissed him with the sweet, hesitant style of a woman more passionate than experienced.

And it was just about the most erotic thing he'd ever had done to him. Many women had touched his body over the years; ever since he was sixteen and had embarked on his sexual life, he'd had no shortage of lovers. And yet he couldn't remember feeling so delighted by one. Or so turned-on.

"How do you like to be…" She couldn't finish the sentence.

He put his hands up to her face, feeling the burn in her cheeks. "Do what you like to me. I'll love it, whatever it is."

Sean gasped as she took him in hand then moved down his body. With a rush of breath, he let his head fall back onto the pillow and balled the sheets in his fists. He gave himself to her with no barriers, nothing contrived, no calculated sensual tricks.

In return, she gave him…everything.

At the last moment, just before he went over the edge, he pulled her up to his mouth. As he spilled himself into her hands, he kissed the lips that had pleasured him.

For some completely ridiculous reason, he found himself wanting to weep.

When morning came, Lizzie woke up in a furnace.

Okay, not a furnace. She was under a thin sheet and on her bed…. She just *felt* as if she were in an industrial boiler.

But she was very okay with the heat.

Sean had chased her over to the far edge of the mattress, snuggling up so close he might as well have been under her own skin. His chest was against her back, his head tucked into her nape, his legs twisted around hers.

She chuckled, thinking she now knew what pretzels felt like.

"I'm crowding you, aren't I?" he said in a lazy, gravelly voice.

"I don't mind at all."

"Good." His hand smoothed down her arm, found her palm and gave it a squeeze. Then he somehow managed to get even closer.

Which gave her a clear impression that however sleepy he was, there was one part of him that was wide-awake. With a soft growl, he rubbed that part in a slow circle against her bottom. When she gasped and arched into him, he made a purring sound.

"You're hell on my good intentions there, Lizzie."

His voice vibrated in his chest as he nuzzled the back of her neck. "Pure hell."

"Am I?" She deliberately moved with him and smiled at the rumbling curse she got in response.

"You know you are." His lips traveled to her shoulder and he sank his teeth into her, tugging a little then sucking the spot through her T-shirt. "You treated me fine in this bed last night."

God, she loved that South Boston accent of his, that rough tone, that need. "Just returning the favor," she murmured.

"So I guess it's my turn again, Lizzie." His hand slipped under her shirt and found her breast. "I'm wicked tired, though. Guess I'll have to go real slow."

He shifted down her body, tunneling under the sheets, rolling her onto her stomach. His mouth found her spine and followed it all the way to her—

The phone rang with an ear-splitting peal.

Sean paused, but didn't stop.

Unfortunately, neither did the phone. And what if it was her mother having burned the house down or given the car away or done any one of a thousand things that spelled disaster?

As Lizzie stretched up to the bedside table and popped the phone off the cradle, Sean's response was to start in on the backs of her thighs.

Man, if this was a telemarketer, she was going rip his or her head off. "Hello?"

"Lizzie, it's perfect!"

"Mom?" Thankfully, Sean eased up and she caught her breath. "Mom…now's not a good t—"

"The kiln is working beautifully!"

"It's working...*what?*" Lizzie looked at the alarm clock with panic. Eleven. Eleven o'clock...oh God, she and Sean had overslept and the kiln had been delivered and her mother was now using the thing so the chances of getting the art store to take it back were next to nil. "Mom—"

"I'm positively inspired.... The wings of creation are fanning me...." As her mother started in on one of her soliloquies about artistic vision, Lizzie just let her go on.

All she could think about right now was that two thousand dollars they'd lost.

The call didn't so much end as flame out, with her mother getting more and more caught up in her own excitement until she had to go express herself.

As Lizzie hung up, Sean appeared from under the sheets, his dark hair tousled. "Trouble with mom?"

"Nothing unusual. Unfortunately."

He eased onto his side and propped his head up with his hand, the gold cross around his neck lying flat on the mattress.

He ran his finger down her cheek. "You know something, Lizzie, I have an idea."

"What?"

"Let's play hooky today."

"Hooky?"

"Yeah, let's grab some eats and a blanket and drive over to Esplanade. We can sit by the river and just forget about everything." When she hesitated, he murmured, "Unless you have other plans?"

While she thought about the day, he idly lifted her hand to his mouth and sucked her forefinger between his lips. As he swirled his tongue around, the circling movement was liquid and warm and oh so smooth. His eyes flipped to her face and he stared at her from under heavy lids.

Other plans? As if her job search couldn't wait until tomorrow?

"No…" she said. "I don't have anything I have to do."

He released her finger and slowly rolled on top of her, his body flowing over hers, a heavy weight full of strength. As his thigh fell between her knees, she yielded to him.

He suspended his torso on muscular arms and looked down into her face, hovering above her like some great bird of prey, all latent power. With the way he looked at her now, he made her feel marked and she knew then without a doubt they were going to be together.

Even though he would leave and never look back and she would miss him for a long, long time, she was going to have him.

He dropped down and kissed her lightly. "I'll see you in twenty minutes."

When she nodded, he leaped out of bed and disappeared through the door.

Before she got up, she made two quick phone calls. One was to the art store's manager, who confirmed there was no returning the kiln now that her mother had used it. The other was to the bank, which informed her that her only option to keep the check from bouncing was to do a credit-card transfer.

Two thousand dollars at nineteen-percent interest. Terrific.

She hung up the phone and told herself that at least the kiln could be sold when her mother moved on to her next big inspiration.

So everything was going to be okay. Eventually.

Chapter Seven

Lounging beneath a blue sky dotted with cotton-ball clouds, Sean stretched his legs straight out in front of him and crossed his ankles. Lizzie was next to him on the plaid blanket, curled on her side, eyes closed, a little smile on her mouth.

Life was just about perfect right now, he thought.

After they'd staked out a stretch of grass on the Esplanade, they'd had turkey subs for lunch and backed up the foot-longs with oatmeal cookies the size of hubcaps. Now, in spite of the shouts from some guys playing Frisbee and the barking of dogs and the occasional horn on Storrow Drive, Lizzie was fading like a sunset.

And just as lovely.

Abruptly, he thought about all the hours she pulled

between being at the clinic and moonlighting downtown. He frowned. Although he respected people who worked as hard and as long as he did, for some reason, Lizzie's going around the clock bothered him.

Probably because she seemed so delicate right now, the fine bones of her face showing too prominently under her pale skin.

She covered her mouth with the back of her hand and yawned. "I'd better sit up soon."

"The hell you should. Don't you know how to play hooky?"

She laughed and opened a pair of very sleepy green eyes. "I'm afraid I always followed the rules in school. So I'm not all that familiar with the hooky routine."

"Well, learn from the master. Hooky means you do whatever you want. And I'm no mind reader, but you look like you're really jonesing for a nap."

"I am." She yawned again and smiled up at him. "Were you a rebel in high school?"

"Yup." A rebel who had pulled As, but trouble nonetheless.

"And you still are, aren't you?"

He grinned at her. "My tattoo is an old one, I'll have you know."

"Except it's not the ink in your skin, it's your nature. I could tell by the way you looked at me that first night. You weren't all that interested in social pleasantries. But you weren't mean, though. Your father was the same way."

Sean's eyes shifted out to the Charles River. His father not mean? Yeah, right.

He felt his hand get gripped. "What happened with

your dad, Sean? I know you don't like to talk about it, but…"

As her words drifted, he absently rubbed her palm with his thumb and watched a crew boat stroke under one of the bridges that stretched over the water. Eventually, he said, "Nothing happened that matters now. It's all over and done."

"Do your brothers feel the same way?"

"Yeah." Although actually, he didn't know that for sure. None of them had ever talked about it. Especially Mac, who'd taken the lion's share of the abuse.

"Do you see your brothers often?"

Sean smiled a little. "Billy and I are tight. He comes down to the city a lot on the off season and we have a great time."

"Off season?"

"He's a football player. Linebacker for the Patriots."

"Boy, what a life that must be."

"Yeah, he gets around. And I'm not just talking about all the traveling he does. My brother's a real ladies' man, but he's also a spectacular athlete. Think the world of the guy, I really do."

"And your other brother?"

Sean shrugged. "I love him just as much, but no one knows Mac well, not even us."

"What does he do?"

"He's in the army. Special forces." At least that was the story. Mac had been very quiet about his job so both his brothers suspected he was involved in some very high-level covert ops.

Yeah…there was some possibility Mac was an

assassin. Although that was based on one dropped comment made years ago.

"Where does Mac live?"

"He has a place just outside of D.C., but he's not there all that often." Not there at all, frankly.

"What was your mother like?"

"She died when I was very young."

Lizzie lifted her head. "I'm so sorry. Do you remember anything about her?"

Sean broke the contact of their hands. The idea that secrets were escaping him, that revelations were being made that he couldn't retract, that she was getting into his head, made him twitchy. In the home he'd grown up in, and in the profession he excelled at, vulnerabilities were used against you.

Silence was safety.

He brushed his finger down her straight, slightly freckled nose. "So how about that nap for you?"

She smiled and closed her eyes. "I'll stop prying."

In the silence that followed, Sean frowned, thinking there had been no censure in her tone. Just acceptance. The fact that she didn't get on him made him feel grateful...and even closer to her.

"You don't mind?" he said softly. "That I'm not a big talker?"

"Not at all, Sean. Just being out in the sun with you is enough for me."

He stared down at her for the longest time, thinking how perverse it was that now that he knew she didn't care whether he said another thing, he found himself wanting to talk.

He looked back out to the river and watched the sun glimmer across the Charles with poetic glory, all golden sparkles over gentle waves. On the far side of the water was Harvard, that mountain of red brick and wrought-iron fencing. His eyes shifted up to the bright-blue dome that marked the horizon.

"I liked school and I was good at it," he said for no particular reason. "I liked reading and studying. Liked to see my report cards. Liked to be at the top of my class. In high school, I would have graduated valedictorian, but I got arrested for stealing a car my junior year and that took me out of the running no matter how high my GPA was. Yeah...school was all I had really, growing up. The only constant."

When there was no response, he glanced down. Lizzie was sleeping soundly, her eyelids flickering a little as if she were dreaming.

He told himself it was just as well. Didn't quite believe it.

Taking a page from Lizzie's book, he lay all the way down and rested his head on the back of his forearm. As a sailboat bobbed by right in front of them, he had some dim thought that he hadn't had a vacation in...ever? How was that possible?

Surely he'd taken a week. A long weekend. Something.

Good God, no, he hadn't. He'd worked through his college vacations as a member of the grounds crew to make extra money. Then in the years that had followed, he'd been too busy getting an MBA and making a name for himself. Now, any traveling he did was for business:

captive insurance meetings in the Bahamas or the Caymans, trips to Tokyo and London and Hamburg and South America, financial summits in Switzerland. And as for the triathalons he entered? That was still all about competing and winning, not recreation.

Hell, he couldn't remember the last time he'd done something like this.... Just sat on the grass and let his thoughts drift with the breeze.

"Heads up!" someone hollered.

Sean glanced to the right and saw a Frisbee flying through the air, heading straight for Lizzie.

Lizzie heard a curse and then felt herself get covered by the weight of Sean's body. As her eyes flipped open, she saw him deftly catch a Frisbee...that would have hit her right in the face.

"Sorry, man!" a guy said as he ran over. "Everyone okay?"

Sean balanced his upper body on one arm as he reached up to give the thing back. "Yeah. Watch it though."

"We will," the guy promised. "Hey, great save, by the way. Wanna play?"

The light that came into Sean's eyes made Lizzie smile. "Go ahead," she said. "I'm sure you're terrific at it."

The guy with the Frisbee looked at her. "And you're welcome, too."

"Thanks, but I'd rather be on blanket patrol."

"You don't mind?" Sean asked her with a frown.

"Not at all."

"Okay. I won't be long, though." He kissed her quick

and leaped to his feet. In a smooth move, he took off his shirt and let it fall to the blanket. "Don't want to get this sweated out in case we head off to dinner."

Sean jogged over with the guy and shook hands with the other players. On the bright green grass, he fit in perfectly with them, one more strong set of shoulders, one more defined chest. The bunch of them went at it hard, until there were three disks going at once between five guys. Sean was amazing, all lithe power and razor instincts, his big body moving with elegant speed, his loose jeans hanging low on his hips, his gold cross bouncing against his chest as he ran around.

Those red and yellow Frisbees went faster and faster and the guys got more outrageous. Eventually, Sean went for a flying catch, springing up into the air and going horizontal to the ground—right as another guy came from the opposite direction. The two collided and fell hard.

Lizzie started to scramble to her feet…but they were fine as they rolled onto their backs and laughed. As she took a deep breath, Sean flashed her a thumbs-up then stood and went back into the fray.

While the horsing around went on, she felt as if she were playing with him even though she was on the blanket. Every few minutes or so, he would look over at her and wave. Or wink. Or he'd deliberately run by and do some wild catch around his back or pull off a crazy, convoluted toss.

He was showing off. For her.

Which was pretty darned charming.

By the time he came back to the blanket forty-five

minutes later, he was breathing hard and a sheen of sweat covered his smooth skin.

"That was great," he said. "Thanks." He sat down, putting his forearms on his knees to air himself out as he regained his breath.

God, she wanted him. "You looked like you were having a wonderful time."

"It's been a while since I've just run around for no good reason." He reached into the Deluca's paper bag and took out a Poland Spring bottle. As he cracked the top, he shot her a quick smile then tilted his head back and poured the water down his throat, his Adam's apple working in a rhythm.

When he brought his head back to level, he pointed at her, bottle in hand. "So what can we do for you? I mean, I've had my fun. We should do something you want to now."

As she considered the offer, she prayed he couldn't read minds. Because all she could think of was him moving down her body this morning…and how much she wanted him to do that again. Without interruption.

Sean frowned. "Hey, do you have enough sunscreen on? You look a little red."

Uh-huh. Go figure. "Ice cream."

"I'm sorry?"

"I would love some ice cream." She put her hand on her stomach. "Even though I shouldn't—"

"Ice cream it is." He finished the water and sprang to his feet as if he hadn't just run miles chasing a Frisbee. "You have a favorite place?"

"I'm easy." Lizzie got up as he tucked his shirt into

the back pocket of his jeans and together they folded the blanket. "As long as it's cold and sweet, I'm happy."

Just as they were about to leave, she frowned. "Wait a minute."

"What?"

She looked around. She had her purse and he had the blanket and the bag of food and they'd left no trash. But something was off.

When she ran her eyes up and down his chest, she realized what it was. "Your cross. It's missing."

Sean's hand snapped to his heart, and though he tried to fight it, she could see panic in his eyes.

"Don't worry, we'll find it," she told him.

They walked the area he'd played in, but it seemed hopeless as he'd covered a lot of distance during the game. Then she remembered. Where had he fallen with the other guy? She headed over to where she thought he'd hit the ground and began crisscrossing the vicinity.

She was about to give up when she saw a flash of gold in the cropped blades of grass. "I've got it!"

Sean came running over and as she held out her hand he sagged in relief. He took the necklace and inspected the clasp, then put it back on.

"Don't know how it fell off," he said. "Everything seems okay."

"You should get it checked."

"I will." His hazel eyes lifted and met hers, then he bent down and kissed her. "Thank you," he whispered against her mouth. "Just…yeah, thank you."

"You're welcome." As he pulled back, he was

gripping the cross so hard his knuckles were white. "It obviously means a great deal to you."

He glanced down. "Mac gave one to me and to Billy and kept a third for himself. I wear it because…hell, I don't know."

Abruptly, his lids dropped over eyes that had gone deliberately blank.

She squeezed his hand. "Let's go."

Sean kept it together as they walked away from where the necklace had been lost, but he cracked a couple minutes later.

The two of them were on the Arthur Fiedler pedestrian bridge that arched over Storrow Drive when he put his arm around Lizzie's shoulders and drew her tight to his side. A few feet farther and he stopped altogether, gathered her in his arms and put his mouth to her ear.

"Lizzie?"

"Yes?"

"If I had lost that necklace…it would have killed me."

"I'm so glad we found it." As she hugged him, he absorbed her kindness, fed off it.

"Mac got the crosses for us right after he went through basic training and before he shipped out for the first time." Sean kept speaking right into her ear, the only way he could continue. "I haven't seen him in a decade and I talk to him once a year if I'm lucky…when he calls me on my birthday. So the necklace is all I have of him. Lose it, lose him." Sean cursed as he heard what he was saying and pulled back. "Sorry, don't mean to get melodramatic."

Her arms tightened around his waist. "You're not."

Looking into her eyes, he felt as though the essential loneliness of his life was exposed, laid bare to the summer day and to her. For all the people he dealt with every hour of the week, for all the women he'd been with and the men he competed against, he was nonetheless alone.

Except he didn't feel alone now.

He kissed Lizzie at first just in thanks for her understanding and acceptance. Then he kissed her some more because he didn't want to stop.

As the sun fell on his bare shoulders and people walked by and cars zoomed underneath them, he dropped the bag and the blanket he was carrying, dug his hands into her hair and tilted her head back so he could go deeper into her. In response, she settled against him like warm water, flowing over his hard edges, both soothing him and exciting him.

He closed his eyes and let himself get good and lost in her. Oh, man, did he have plans for them. Tonight, he was going to go back to her apartment and make love to her. Slowly. Thoroughly. He was after the closeness, not just the orgasms, and he was going to hold her afterward until he was ready to do it again. Then he was going to sleep next to her and wake up looking into her face.

When he finally pulled back from her mouth, he brushed her lower lip with his thumb. "I can't feel my legs. How about you?"

She laughed a little breathlessly. "I'm on fire."

"Then we'd better cool you down." He kissed her quick. "How's Ben & Jerry's sound?"

"Perfect. I'd love some of their Mint Oreo in a waffle cone."

"Ask and ye shall receive."

They meandered off the bridge and hooked up with Newbury Street, joining the crowd that strolled down the sidewalk. There was a line in front of Ben & Jerry's, but the breeze was nice and soon enough their cones were being handed to them. As he pulled a twenty out of his wallet, Lizzie went for her purse.

"No, wait. Let me—"

"My treat," he said. After he gave the bill to the kid behind the register, he nodded to the door. "Shall we?"

The kid called out, "Don't you want your change?"

"Yeah. In the tips jar."

"Hey, thanks, man!"

Sean smiled and followed Lizzie out into the sun.

"I really like that about you," she said as she stuck a white spoon into her waffle cone and brought some of the chunky ice cream to her mouth.

"Like what?"

"That you tip generously. Mmm, this is so good."

Sean watched her lick her spoon clean and had to put the blanket in front of his hips. God, men were letches, weren't they? But man...he wanted her.

He cleared his throat. What had they been talking about? Oh, yeah... "Well, I know what it's like to live off tips. I've waited a lot of tables in my day—"

"Sean? Sean O'Banyon?"

Sean frowned at the male voice and looked over his shoulder. When he saw who it was, he felt an absurd impulse to shield Lizzie, to protect their day together.

Except it was too late. As a well-dressed man headed right for them, he knew that the bubble he'd been in all afternoon was about to burst.

Chapter Eight

Lizzie smiled at the gentleman who was hustling up to them. He looked very *Great Gatsby* in his white linen slacks, crisp blue button-down and navy-blue blazer with a kerchief in the pocket. His loafers were shiny and tasseled and his round glasses were made of tortoiseshell.

He looked very pleased to see Sean. "Sean! How do? I haven't seen you since—"

"Rolly, it's good to see you." Sean stuck his hand out. "How are you?"

"Fine, fine. And you? I've heard you're doing great things with—"

"So how is it possible you're in town on a sunny Saturday? Is the whole family here with you, too?"

"No, no. Sarah and the kids are at the house on the

Vineyard, lucky devils. I had to come in for business. I'm sure you know how that—"

"I'd like you to meet my friend, Lizzie. Lizzie, this is Rolly."

The man smiled, revealing perfect teeth. "Good Lord, where are my manners? It's a pleasure."

Lizzie shoved her spoon into her cone and offered her hand. "Nice to meet you."

"Enjoying the day with Sean, are you?" he said as they shook.

"Very much."

"You know, I didn't think the great SOB ever wandered around—"

"You need to give my regards to Sarah," Sean cut in.

"Of course, and I hope you'll come out and visit us sometime on the Vineyard?" Rolly smiled at Lizzie. "Friends are always welcome, too. We have a big house and the more the merrier. Well, I must off to the club. I'm late, which I despise."

As the man waved and dissolved into the pedestrian stream, Lizzie glanced at Sean. His brows were down low and his mouth set tight.

She was not surprised when he said, "How about we head home? I could use a shower."

"Sounds good," she said. Even though it didn't. She wasn't in a hurry for the day to end, but she sensed that even if they kept walking around now, it would be over anyway. Sean had gone somewhere in his head and his mood had changed. Which was odd. Rolly Whoever-he-was had seemed perfectly nice, yet Sean had been in a hurry to get rid of him.

They were quiet as they walked down Newbury then went through the Commons and down into the parking garage. Sean didn't say much on the way home, and when they pulled up to the row house, she had a feeling he was going to make an excuse to go upstairs.

She told herself it was better this way as she could start getting her résumés out.

Yeah…right.

As they got out of the car and went up to the shallow front porch, she said, "Well, thank you for the day. I had a wonderful time."

Sean stopped. Looked her in the eye. Took her hand in his. "I'm sorry, Lizzie. About being a buzz kill."

"Why did running into that man bother you so much?"

Sean glanced across the street, but she was sure he wasn't seeing the other row houses. "He and I went to college together." In a dry voice, he added, "I was on scholarship, Rolly wasn't."

Oh, that explained it. It must be hard to see people who were so much more successful, who had so much more.

"Money isn't everything, Sean."

He smiled his disagreement. "Sometimes it feels that way. Sometimes I think my whole life is about chasing the stuff."

"I totally get that," she said as she thought about her mom. "But come on, how much did today cost us? The two sandwiches were eight bucks. The cookies were what…four dollars? A six-pack of water was a dollar ninety…on sale, I might remind you. And the cones were nine dollars with an eleven-dollar tip. For thirty-three dollars and ninety cents, which could have been even less if you hadn't left so much at Ben & Jerry's, we had a perfectly lovely afternoon. After all, the sun and the Frisbee game were—"

He swooped in and kissed her, his mouth lingering on hers before he pulled back.

"—free," she finished.

Sean ran his fingertip down her cheek then took a deep breath, as if he were bracing himself for something. "So you wouldn't think of me differently, rich or poor?"

"I enjoyed today because of you. The fact that you're not wealthy never even occurred to me."

His eyes grew shrewd as if he were assessing her down to her DNA. Then he nodded once, took out his keys and put one in the lock. When he paused, his stare shifted over to hers and the hazel in it burned.

"Do you want to get together tonight?" he asked in a very low voice.

Lizzie swallowed hard, knowing very well what it meant to say yes to the question. She took a deep breath. "Yes."

"I'll come down right after I shower."

He pushed the door wide and held it open for her. As she walked by him, a horrible realization hit her and she wanted to curse.

Oh God…in the space of two days, she'd somehow become attached to this man.

And she feared there was no going back.

* * *

In the shower upstairs, Sean soaped his body up and rinsed off as if he were an Indy 500 pit crew. He shaved just as fast and managed to nick himself under the chin, which necessitated tearing off a piece of Kleenex and sticking it to where he bled. After brushing his wet hair back, he did the cologne thing and inspected the razor cut.

With relief, he ditched the little white square. Man, there was no looking good with that kind of thing on your puss.

Boxers went on without incident as did a fresh black polo. Pants were an issue because his jeans were grass-stained, so in the end, he pulled on his suit slacks. Thank God they didn't have any pinstripes, so he didn't look ridiculous.

On his way out the door, he slipped a couple of condoms in his back pocket out of necessity and picked his BlackBerry up out of habit.

Oh…crap, he thought as he stared at the phone.

He couldn't believe he'd left the thing behind today. How had that happened?

Then again, the oversight had been a blessing. Part of the reason the afternoon had been so relaxing was that the ringer hadn't gone off constantly.

He flipped through the screens. He had an in-box full of e-mails and seven voice messages waiting for him. He almost started checking it all, but at the last moment, he stopped. He didn't want to know what was falling apart. All he wanted was just a little more time with Lizzie. Then he'd get back to real life.

Shoving it into his pocket, he left the apartment and

was at her door in three heartbeats. After he knocked once, he heard her call out and he went inside.

She ducked into the living room wrapped in nothing but a towel, her hair in damp ringlets. "Hi, I'll just get dress—"

She didn't have a chance to finish the sentence.

Sean went to her in two long strides, clamped his hands on either side of her face and dropped down, fusing his mouth to hers. As he pushed her back against the wall, he was hard, hot, hungry, his hands finding the edge of the towel and stripping it away.

With a quick move, he picked her up and carried her to her bed, laying her out flat on the comforter. He tore his shirt over his head, kicked off his shoes and covered her body with his own, all but out of control as he kissed her deep and long. He kept at it until they were both breathless, then went to work on her neck.

"I need to…" His voice cracked as he palmed her hip and squeezed. "I need to be inside you."

She nodded with a jerky head bob then dug her hands into his hair and pulled him up to her mouth again. It was the perfect move because he couldn't get enough of her lips, her scent, her crazy moaning…. The way her legs were scissoring underneath his was driving him insane.

Somehow, his pants disappeared along with his boxers. He wasn't sure how and didn't care; maybe the damn things walked off his legs by their own volition. What mattered was that he and Lizzie were both wild and naked and he was pressing into the soft space between her thighs with razor-edged desperation.

He needed this so badly. He needed *her* so badly.

* * *

Sean was all carnal demand and Lizzie loved it. Especially when his fully naked body came down on hers and his thighs split her open to him. His skin burned as if he had a fever and his hands were rough and his mouth was hungry and he was going to take her hard just the way she wanted him to. It was the kind of full-tilt sex she'd only heard about and had assumed was wildly exaggerated.

And yet as she cried out, he went still. "Lizzie…I'm sorry. I'm so sorry. I'm going too f—"

She locked her legs around his hips and went for his mouth, frantic for more of him. As her tongue pierced his lips, he groaned wildly and his arms shot around her, his hips falling into a grinding rhythm that blinded her. Everything was fast, fast and edgy and just a little reckless, nothing she was used to and everything she wanted.

"Lizzie…can I—"

"Yes."

He reared back and rose off her, his arousal jutting out from his hips, proud and ready. He ripped a condom wrapper open with his sharp white teeth, spit out the corner, then he sheathed himself with quick, sure hands. His heavy weight came back down on her and she trembled, ready, but bracing herself for a powerful thrust.

Instead, he eased into her. As they slowly came together, his head dropped down beside hers so they were ear to ear.

"Are you okay?" he asked hoarsely. "This okay?"

His ragged breath and the sweat on his skin gave her an idea how much his self-control was costing him.

She dug her nails into the small of his back and arched. "More."

With one smooth push, he locked his hips against hers and they both moaned as their pelvises merged. Their bodies took over, meeting and retreating, his advancing, hers receiving. As he moved inside of her, his muscles bunched and relaxed in his shoulders and his legs, and his slick skin slid over hers. The rhythm of it all intensified until she was nothing but sensation and instinct.

"Lizzie…Lizzie, I'm about to—"

A phone started ringing right by the bed, but it wasn't one of hers.

As it went off again, Sean froze then cursed and squeezed his eyes shut.

She cleared her throat. "Ah…do you want to get that?"

His answer was a straight, to the point expletive followed by the word *no*.

As the ringer kept going off, he resumed pumping, falling into a driving, primal pace that took her right over the edge. As she soared beneath him, he fell over the brink himself, his head tilting back, his neck straining. He roared, more beast than man in the beautiful moment that he gave himself to her.

When he stopped bucking against her, he collapsed, his heart pounding so hard she could feel every beat in her own chest.

With the phone now silent, the only sound in the room was their breathing.

As passion's heat faded from their bodies, her chest ached although she wasn't sure why.

* * *

Sean was utterly sated as he rolled to the side and took Lizzie with him. Looking into her face, her eyes were so clear and guileless he wondered how he could have ever thought she was calculating, and he loved that she was so transparent.

What he didn't like was the fact that she seemed a little rattled.

"Lizzie…" He kissed her softly. "You okay there?"

She ran her hand up the back of his arm and nodded.

"Lizzie? Did I hurt you?"

"Oh…no…it's not that."

"Talk to me."

"I…ah, I didn't know…" Her eyes dropped. "I didn't know it could be like that."

Sean went utterly still; he didn't even breathe. Time became a meaningless measure of nothing important. "Lizzie—"

His cell phone went off again, the soft tone landing like a bomb.

With a curse, he shot out of bed and grabbed his boxers, holding them in front of his hips as he headed for his pants.

"What?" he snapped as he answered the damn thing.

"Where the *hell* have you been?" Ah yes, Mick Rhodes. Lawyer. Friend. And when in that tone of voice, bearer of bad news.

"Just spit it," Sean muttered. "What's on fire?"

"Condi-Foods. Name ring a bell? Damn it, I called you five times this afternoon. Where have you been? You know the deal is shaky—"

"Skip the lecture and give me details."

Mick swore a couple of times then launched into a news flash that set Sean's teeth on edge. "The revised tender offer from the acquirer is coming in two hours from now. Condi-Foods' board chair wants you and only you to render the opinion and he wants to hear it in person. So you need to drop whatever you're doing and get your ass into Manhattan *now*."

Sean cursed and reached back down for his trousers. Then realized he wasn't getting dressed unless he made a quick trip to the bathroom. "I'm on my way."

"Hey, there's an idea—"

"I'll call you from the plane." Sean hung up. Dropped his arm. Looked over his shoulder. "I have to go."

"Was that your boss?"

"Basically." Actually, he was Mick's boss, as he'd hired the guy to work on the legal aspects of these deals. But his pal was right to goose him. He'd left a two-billion-dollar negotiation hanging in the breeze today. So he could play Frisbee for God's sake.

Not a smart career move. Or a responsible one.

Sean went into the bathroom, snapped off the condom and washed up. Without looking at himself in the mirror, he put on his boxers and his pants and headed back to the bedroom.

"I'm really sorry about this," he said, picking up his shirt from the floor. He pulled it over his head and shoved his feet into his running shoes. "I'll call you."

Lizzie's eyes grew remote. "Have a safe trip."

"Lizzie, I'll call you. I promise."

She smiled slowly. "Okay…I'd like that. I'd really like that."

Chapter Nine

Four nights later, in a conference room high above Wall Street, Sean lost it. Just *lost* it. And not in a calculated way intended to impact difficult negotiations.

He simply hit the wall. Then plowed right through it.

"To hell with this." He planted his big hands on the glossy mahogany table and rose from his seat. Leaning into his arms, he glared good and hard at the idiots who were wasting his and Condi-Foods' time. "Get out."

The head of the acquirer's investment team blinked like a bad lightbulb in his Brooks Brothers suit. "Excuse me?"

"Get. Out." This meeting had been a bad idea to begin with, but as the deal was at a standstill, Sean had agreed to the request for some face-to-face. He was not surprised they remained deadlocked, but it sure as hell didn't put him in a good mood.

Then again, since he'd left Lizzie's Saturday night, nothing had given him a jolly.

"Our share price is fair!" the man across the table hollered.

"No, it isn't, and it's backed up by air. You find yourself some better financing and come up on your number, then we'll talk."

"Damn it, O'Banyon! We've been working on this for the last four days—"

"And time has not improved your offer. Get. Out."

There was a long pause and then they just started yammering on again about their low-ball valuation of Condi-Foods' assets. One of them even had the nerve to push a spreadsheet at him.

Sean balled the thing up and tossed it into a waste-paper basket across the room.

Which effectively ended the meeting.

All six guys across the table stood up and, amid much huffing and offense, funneled out of the room as if the door were a drain. Before he left, the team leader glanced back at Sean. The man's eyes were shrewd and that was when Sean knew. What had just transpired was a test of his resolve by the opposing side, not any kind of genuine stalemate.

They were going to meet his demands. He could feel it. And as Mick Rhodes chuckled a little in the seat next to him, it was clear his buddy knew it, too.

In the aftermath of the drama bomb, Sean eased down into his chair.

As silence reigned, the two young guys he'd picked up from that gala, Freddie Wilcox and Andrew Frick, were frozen-statue speechless.

"Do we leave now?" Freddie asked.

"Nope," Mick replied. The lawyer's sardonic grin, which was as sharp as his Brioni suit, made a quick appearance. "Twenty-seven, SOB. Don't you think?"

Sean rubbed his face and played along out of habit, not because he was interested in the game. "Thirty-nine. Because I balled their—what did I throw?"

Andrew spoke up. "I believe it was their financial projections for the coming fiscal year."

"Ah, then I put them in the right place." Sean leaned back in his chair and rolled his Montblanc between his thumb and forefinger. The fountain pen was one of his signature props, a big black cigar of a writing instrument known on Wall Street as the Club for all the damage he'd done with it.

Usually at this point, when he knew in his gut he was going to get what he wanted, he'd feel a simmering triumph. After all, making the other side break and submit was the goal, and sure as hell, those highfliers who'd just fluffed out of here were going to call back within the hour with a reasonable offer that he could recommend to the Condi-Foods board.

He'd been through this countless times. It was the cycle of challenge that had kept him juiced for years.

But the problem was, on this particular walk through the minefield, he really had lost his temper. Unlike the other side, his anger hadn't been for show. His frustration level had been on hard-boil since he'd come back to the city and now he was stretched as thin as a hair. The three-ring circus of these negotiations, coupled with that grossly inadequate offer, had just pushed him over the edge.

And there was nothing more dangerous in a multi-billion-dollar negotiation than one of the principals getting truly emotional.

He told himself he was just strung out. Hell, he'd been working until three in the morning every night since he'd come back, and although that wasn't un-precedented, it certainly didn't put him in his happy place. Plus the fact that these negotiations had been going so slowly made it all worse—

Oh, who was he kidding. It wasn't business that was razoring him up.

His conscience was wearing on him. Badly.

Lizzie Bond was wearing on him.

He got to his feet and started to pack up his brief-case.

"You're leaving?" Mick said.

"I already know what they're going to do." Sean slipped the Club into his breast pocket then text messaged his limo driver. "They're going to come up twenty-five cents a share and get real on the interest payments before the balloon five years out of closing. And I will accept that. Call me when the new offer comes through."

Andrew cleared his throat. "But how do you know that's what they're going to counter with?"

Sean picked up his leather document holder. "Because it's the only move they have. If they back out after getting this close, everyone on the Street will think it's because they don't have the corporate will to be a player and that lack of confidence would be bad news for their stock. As usual it all comes down to pride and math."

The hero worship that flared in the kid's eyes was hard to bear so Sean looked around the room. "Ladies and gentlemen, it's been real. Mick, I'll be hearing from you shortly."

On his way out, he checked in with his assistants and picked up a stack of phone messages as well as the schedule for the next week and the so-called social file. When he told his staff he was going home, they looked relieved, as if they needed a break from him.

He didn't blame them in the slightest.

He hit the elevators and exited the building. His limousine was waiting out front in the sweltering heat and he slid into the air-conditioned backseat with relief. As the Lincoln eased into traffic, he opened the social file with no enthusiasm. The thing was stuffed with invitations to galas and messages from women and favors he was being asked. Typically he would run through the morass in about ten minutes, turf the RSVPs to his assistants and call back a couple of the ladies.

Instead, he closed the cover and took out his Black-Berry.

Lizzie's face came to him, as it had on a regular basis, and he rubbed the center of his chest.

He'd wanted to talk to her since landing in Manhattan, but he'd been dealing with one problem after another in the Condi-Foods negotiations. The way things had been going, the only time he had to himself was either well after midnight or just around noontime. Neither of which were good times to reach her.

He'd tried to leave messages, but had just ended up deleting them halfway through. Even though he'd spoken thousands of sentences since getting back to the city, he somehow couldn't find the words to let her know how much he was thinking about her. And the longer he went, the worse he choked.

He checked his watch. Nine o'clock at night.

Damn it, he had to call. Considering all the crap that was going down with Condi-Foods, he wasn't going to get back to Boston for another week. And that was assuming the acquirer's offer finally did make sense.

As his limo slowly progressed down Wall Street, he dialed his BlackBerry, put the thing up to his ear and loosened his tie.

After the second ring, Lizzie's voice came through loud and clear. "Hello?"

God, she was home. "Lizzie…"

"Oh…hi." There was a shuffling sound as if she were switching her receiver to her other hand. "How are you?"

He thought about all the ways to answer the question. The replies disturbed him because they were all about missing her. "Good. Busy."

"I'm sure you have been." Her voice was level. Calm.

"Work's been hectic." The limo came to a stop at a traffic light, a thoroughbred among the herd of taxi ponies. As it occurred to him that she'd be surprised he was sitting in something like the stretch Lincoln, he felt like a liar.

Maybe everything he was holding back from her, rather than his schedule, had been what had prevented him from calling.

Screw the *maybe*. "Lizzie, I need to tell you—"

"You don't have to explain. We had a lovely evening, not a relationship." Oh, man, her tone wasn't just level. It was impersonal.

"Are you near a computer?" he said.

"I—ah, yes."

"Do a search under the name Sean O'Banyon."

"Why?"

"I want you to know who I am."

"I already do."

"No, you don't." And he wasn't sure how to tell her without sounding like a pompous ass. "Sean O'Banyon. Do it."

He heard the sound of keys typing. Then silence.

He knew what the search engine would pull up: References to articles on him in the *Wall Street Journal*. *The New York Times*. *Forbes*. *Fortune*. *Time*. Interviews logged on MSNBC and CNN and the FOX News network. Books on finance that had his name in them.

"What is all this?" she murmured.

"Me."

More silence. "Guess you're really not a construction worker."

"No, I'm not."

"Clearly."

"Lizzie—"

"Hey, you met with the president, huh."

"I didn't tell you because—"

Her voice sharpened. "Because you didn't trust me. Or you thought I was beneath you. Which one was it?"

"I didn't know you."

"And I guess a week away has made me more knowable?"

"I just don't want to lie by omission anymore. It's not right."

He heard her exhale. Heard a mouse clicking. "God, you must have really hated your father."

"Excuse me?"

"Do you know how hard he struggled to pay for his medications and his doctor visits? I mean, I doubt it would even make a dent in—oh, look, here's your net worth. Yeah, whoa…wouldn't even be couch change to you."

"This has nothing to do with him."

"Yeah…and you know what? I don't think it has anything to do with me, either."

God, he wished he'd left a couple of messages on her phone. Maybe this would have been easier. "It does, though. Damn it, Lizzie—"

"Do you think I was after your father for money? You did, didn't you? And you figured if I knew you were loaded I'd glom on to you, too."

"Look, like I said, I didn't know you. And why wouldn't I be suspicious? You mean you've never heard of that kind of thing?"

"Hey, check this out. You gave away a million dollars last month to the Hall Foundation. How generous." Her voice grew heated. "Good Lord, Sean, do you have any idea how tough these last few years have been on your father? You could have helped him. You *should* have helped him."

Okay, that was not a good topic to get on, Sean thought. Because he couldn't be civil about the fact that his father had obviously *poor-little-old-me*'d her.

"I'm not going to discuss him."

"Oh, that's right. Closed-door policy on that."

"Lizzie, no offense, but you don't know a thing about my father."

"Funny, the same could be said of you. I don't think you knew him very well, either."

Sean's hand curled around his BlackBerry. As he fought to rein in his temper, he reminded himself that she had no way of knowing about the past and that people, even his father, could present many different faces to the world.

"Let's keep this just to us, Lizzie. We'll get further."

She exhaled sharply, which he didn't take as a good sign. "You know what? Let's forget about us going anywhere, okay? Let me know about the house sale when you can. Goodbye."

She hung up on him.

Sean let his head fall back against the plush leather seat. Closing his eyes, he tried to tell himself it was for the best. She stirred up too much in him. Went in too deep. Made him feel too much.

It was better to be alone than in chaos.

Taking a deep breath, he put his palm under his tie and rubbed his sternum.

Damn, his chest hurt.

When his BlackBerry went off, he answered it without looking at the caller ID.

Mick Rhodes was in midlaugh. "Twenty-two minutes. I win."

"What did they come back with?"

"Up twenty-five cents a share and much better financing, at least to my eye. You're a genius, SOB."

"Tell them to get the papers to me."

"Will do."

Genius? Sean thought as they hung up. What a crock of crap that was. He felt like anything but.

After she ended the call, Lizzie just stared at the photograph on her laptop's screen. It was a picture of Sean looking like a total power player: Black suit. White shirt. Red tie. A hard smile and harder eyes.

A stranger.

Oh, but then he'd been that before, hadn't he?

She glanced at the date. The photo had been taken at a gala on the night Mr. O'Banyon had died and she thought back to when she'd called Sean with the news. Evidently this fancy party had been the noise she'd heard in the background.

She shut off the computer to get away from the image and let herself sink back into the sofa.

All around her, everything seemed too quiet. The drone of the AC unit. The dulled murmur of a passing car. The soft wind catching a piece of siding and making it whistle.

She wished she had to go to work or had someplace

to go. The only thing she had here at home was a whole lot of smothering introspection that she could do without. Trouble was, she wasn't moonlighting until tomorrow night and she was not the bar-hopping type.

Exhausted and cranky, she headed for bed for lack of a better alternative, but she was pretty sure she wasn't going to sleep. Sure enough, as she turned off the light and lay back, the mattress beneath her felt as if it were stuffed with gravel and her sheets were like sandpaper against her skin.

Man…this thing with Sean was such a mess.

She'd spent the last four days waiting for the phone to ring, if she was home, or checking her message light first thing as she came in the door. Naturally, when she'd decided he was never going to call, he did…only to drop this news flash that he was a big shot.

A big shot who evidently hadn't had enough cash to spare for his father in spite of being on the Fortune 500 list. Which was just wrong. Granted, Mr. O'Banyon hadn't starved, but things could have been a lot easier on him if he'd had a visiting nurse and if his medical bills had been covered.

Lizzie pictured the photograph of Sean she'd just seen. How he must have laughed at her. Thinking that he was a construction worker—

The phone started to ring in the living room, the cheerful chirping sound coming down the hall as if the noise were skipping.

The first ring she ignored. The second ring she ignored. On the third, she almost got up, but then she let the call dump into voice mail.

She didn't care what he had to say.

Crossing her arms over her chest, she closed her eyes.

Three minutes of pulling the mummy routine and she was out in the living room, finding the phone. There was a message so she dialed into the system and held her breath.

Her mother's voice was excited: "I have had a break-through with the clay! My fingers are singing! This is such a revelation, which…"

Lizzie closed her eyes and let the message roll on. After she deleted it and hung up, she stared at the phone and knew going back to bed was not an option.

She went to the couch, fired up her laptop again and logged into the *Boston Globe*'s online classifieds site. Since she was not going to get some shut-eye anytime soon, she might as well focus on something that would help her.

Which stewing about Sean O'Banyon would definitely not.

Plus it was about time she got into her job search. She'd moonlighted every day this week so she would earn some extra cash, but as a result, she hadn't been able to find time to apply for a new position.

Two hours later, she had her résumé updated and had made online submissions to four jobs: one down on the South Shore at Quincy Hospital's ED and one each to Boston Medical Center, New England Medical Center and Brigham & Women's.

Next she hit the apartment ads. Even if Sean wasn't going to sell the house right away, she had to get out of here. There were just too many memories. And now too many complications.

She braced herself for what she'd find. She knew that the Boston real-estate market for rentals was tight right now because of all the college students returning for school in August. And it would probably make more sense to wait until she knew where she would be working, but she figured it couldn't hurt to start looking this Sunday when there'd be some open houses scheduled.

Oh…*man*. Everything was so expensive compared to what she was paying now. Part of it was that Eddie had refused to raise her rent over the two years she'd been here. The other half was simply supply and demand coupled with inflation.

She put the laptop aside and stared out the bay window. With her job at the clinic ending tomorrow, she was relieved to have plenty of moonlighting work lined up. But that was not the way she wanted to live. Pulling night shifts on a regular basis really screwed up your life.

Besides, she had her sights set on bigger things than being a floor nurse. What she wanted to be, eventually, was her boss, Denisha Roberts. She wanted to run a clinic like the one in Roxbury, and to do that, she needed more education and some experience on the administration side of patient care.

Unfortunately, she had a feeling school was going to be delayed for a while.

She turned off the computer and the lights, then went over to the armchair in front of the big window. Sitting down, she curled her legs up under herself and let her head fall to the side. Through the slits in the blinds she saw the dark path of the road and the sidewalk's ghostly glow and the bulky outlines of the houses across the street. As the night went on, occasionally a car would float by like a boat on a still river, its headlights flaring white then its brake lights glowing red.

Funny how losing a job made you look over your life and reassess things.

And the ending of a relationship did that, too, didn't it?

Except, had she even had a relationship with Sean? Not really. Just a couple of days… Still, the effect was the same. In the quiet darkness, she found herself thinking back to her two earlier boyfriends. Neither one had come close to Sean for intensity. But then she couldn't imagine many men did.

Just her luck.

Lizzie was still sitting in the chair a couple of hours later when a car pulled up in front of the house. The headlights went off, one of its doors slammed and a huge shadow of a man came up the walkway.

She got to her feet in disbelief and went to the blinds. Sean couldn't possibly have come all the way up from New York. In the middle of the night. Could he?

Good…Lord, he had.

In the glow of the porch light, he looked totally out of place, more like he should be walking up to the door of a Park Avenue penthouse rather than a well-worn duplex in South Boston. He was wearing a beautifully tailored dark suit with a fancy black-and-peach–colored tie, and as he reached forward to put his key in the lock, a big fat gold watch gleamed on his wrist.

Lizzie stepped back from the window. Maybe he hadn't come to see—

The knock on her door was a single, sharp rap.

His voice came through the panels. "Lizzie, I saw you at the blinds. I know you're up. Can we talk?"

Holy hell, she wasn't sure she was ready to see him. And even if she was, she felt as if she should throw on a dress and some heels before she opened her door. "It's late."

"I know."

"I should go to bed. Maybe tomorrow."

There was a brief silence. "I have to go back tomorrow morning."

She frowned and glanced at the clock on her wall. "But it is tomorrow morning."

"I realize that. I have to go back in three hours."

"You came all the way up here for three hours?"

"Some things need to be said in person."

Stunned, she walked over and opened the door. Wow…he seemed so much taller in the suit, even though the top of his head was no higher off the ground than before.

"You don't look the same to me," she murmured. And it wasn't just because of his clothes.

"Can I come in?"

She stepped aside, and as he walked by, she looked him over. Even after having traveled five hundred miles, and in spite of the fact that it was now almost three in morning, he was as polished as the hood of a Ferrari.

But then maybe that was what expensive clothes got you. Perma-gleam.

As she closed the door, she resisted the urge to tug at her sweatshirt. Rearranging it wasn't going to change the fact that she'd paid nineteen dollars for it at Target. And anyway, she liked the darned thing. It was soft and comfortable…which was evidently more than could be said for what Sean had on. While he paced around, he yanked his tie loose as if he were dying to take it off.

He stopped and faced her. They both spoke at once.

"Sean—"

"Lizzie—"

She shook her head. "You first."

"No, what were you going to say?"

"Would you like something to drink?"

"I was wrong to think you were bilking my father. And I'm very sorry."

Lizzie's brows shot up. So much for social pleasantries and just as well. "I didn't use him, Sean."

"I know." He went over to the Venetian blinds, fingered them apart and peered outside. "I just couldn't figure out why you would be so close with him. Other than that."

"He was kind to me and he needed help." Censure creeped into her voice. "He had no one."

"Indeed." He dropped his hand and turned back to her. "Anyway, I'm honestly sorry."

"Apology accepted." Boy, he looked tired. "You know, you really could have said this over the phone."

"Assuming you'd have answered my call. And I wouldn't have blamed you if you didn't." He ran his hand down the length of his beautiful tie. "I should have told you about me earlier, but I liked the anonymity. I wanted to just be me with you."

"So you really thought I was a gold digger, huh?"

"Maybe."

"Definitely."

He shrugged. "Most of the women I've been with are fiscally minded. And not because they're in banking."

"Your poor choices, not my fault. Dear God, I don't want your money. Sure, I've got some problems with my job situation and my mother, but I wouldn't solve them by using you. I liked being with you."

He frowned. "Liked…past tense."

"Come on, Sean. You left and didn't look back this week. And besides, what do we have in common?"

His eyes traced over her face. "I thought of you the whole time. I wanted to call you, but the deal I'm working on is complex and at a critical—"

"People make time for what they want to do. They make the time." She shook her head and wrapped her arms around her waist. "It's okay, though. I mean—"

"I also didn't know what to say. I just didn't know how to tell you I missed you. I haven't missed anyone in a long time. I'm not used to it."

Lizzie's body stilled until her heart barely beat. The apology she expected. The revelation was a surprise.

"You mind if I sit down?" he said as he wrenched his tie off altogether and stuffed it in his jacket pocket.

"Ah, no…please do."

His big body sank into her sofa and he crossed his legs, ankle on knee. Stretching one of his arms out over the top of the cushions, he looked not just tired but depleted.

In the silence, she tried to see past the fancy suit and

the big-shot job and the net worth to the man she had been with before.

Because she'd really liked the person she'd watched playing Frisbee.

She truly had.

Chapter Ten

As Sean sat on the sofa, he had to hold on to the back of the damn thing to keep himself in place. He'd been fighting the urge to hug Lizzie since the moment she'd peaked out from between the blinds, and now that it looked as if she'd partially forgiven him, he wanted her against him so badly.

Plus she looked adorable in her baggy blue sweatshirt and those loose men's boxer shorts.

A surreptitious glance at her smooth legs had him tightening his grip on the couch. Oh, man, he really didn't trust himself to stay away from her. He was feeling the effects of a week of not sleeping on top of his manic rush to the airport, the hour-long flight and the drive into Southie.

So he was weak right now. Or rather, his hold on himself was weak.

What he wanted was to reconnect with her skin to skin and to hell with the talking. But he respected her too much to try and seduce her, and besides, it was clear she was wary of him, as well she might be. Hell, he was wary of himself. Nothing about this thing with her was making any sense to him, and when he felt off-kilter, he tended to get more aggressive, not less.

Letting his head go lax, he eased back into the cushions and eyed her from beneath his lids. She was pretty, her hair all disheveled, her face clean and a little shiny. She reminded him of things that were real, not pretension.

"You look exhausted," she said.

"I am."

"When does your plane leave?"

"Whenever I tell it to."

Her eyes dropped away. "Oh…yes, of course."

He waited for her to say something else. When she didn't, he realized he hadn't reached her far enough. His apology had been accepted, yes. But there was no going back.

So he should head out.

Sean sat up and put his hands on his knees, feeling as if there were an anvil on his chest. "Well, I—"

"Have you eaten?"

"Ah…no."

"Would you like to? Because I owe you one. You made me breakfast."

Okay…maybe there was a little light at the end of the tunnel. "I would love something. Thank you."

She nodded once and turned away.

"Lizzie?"

Her eyes bounced around the living room, avoiding his. "Yes?"

He wanted to keep pressing the apology stuff until she not only believed him but forgave him for having had so little faith in her.

"I don't care what it is. The breakfast, I mean. I'll love whatever you give me."

She nodded and turned away. As he watched her go, he let his head fall back again and he closed his eyes. Just for a moment.

He wasn't sure what woke him up or how long he'd been asleep, but it was still dark out when he came to. As he shifted and looked around, his neck was stiff and his jacket was wrinkled. There was a quilt around his legs as well as a plate with a sandwich on it and a glass of water on the table next to him.

He downed the water, ate the sandwich and went to find Lizzie.

The door to her bedroom was ajar and he pushed it open a little farther. Oh, man, just where he wanted her to be: curled on her side, her hair on her pillow, the room dim and cool.

He was such a bastard, he thought. Because he was going to get into that bed with her.

He quietly kicked off his wingtips and got out of his jacket then went over to the side he'd slept on before. As he lifted the covers, he eased his body in, but there was no way his two-hundred-and-ten-pound self wasn't making a dent in the mattress. As he got horizontal,

Lizzie was sucked into the hole he made, coming flush against him.

She was warm with sleep, a little ball of sumptuous ember, and he pulled her against his chest. As his head went down on the pillow, it found the crook of her fragrant neck.

He didn't mean to kiss her there. It just happened when she made a noise deep in her throat and undulated against him. As she arched, her skin met his lips.

It was a match to gasoline situation for them both.

They went body-to-body in a single surge, melding together through his clothes and hers. As he found her mouth, he kissed her deeply, taking what she offered even though he had no idea where they stood. The only thing he knew as they devoured each other was that his curious desperation for her was his undoing.

He broke away from her only long enough to split his shirt down the middle, and as the buttons flew, she took her own top off and shrugged out of her boxers.

He stopped with his hands on his belt and cursed. "I didn't bring any..."

"I got some in case you ever...um...we ever..."

His relief came out as a hoarse groan and he quickly ditched his trousers, tossing them to the floor as if they were trash.

"Where?" he groaned as he landed on top of her and pushed her legs apart with his own.

As she stretched out an arm to open a drawer on the bedside table, he latched onto her breast. There was a clatter as something hit the floor and then she was pressing a foil packet into his hand.

"I have no patience tonight," he warned against her nipple. Then he lifted his hips from hers and ripped the wrapper open with his teeth.

Her eyes were heated as they locked on to his body. "I don't want your patience."

"Good." He spit a piece of foil out, covered himself and then took her in a rush.

They both shouted and her nails scored his back as a climax rolled over her, through her. He absorbed the sensations of her grabbing on to him and then he let loose until he was heaving on top of her, riding her hard, driving them both into a frenzy.

Lizzie was mindless underneath Sean's rhythm, nothing but the sensations in her body. Just as he growled low in his throat and his body tensed from shoulder to thigh, she seized up again and arched into him. They shuddered together, his arms shooting around her and squeezing tight.

It was a while before either one of them could catch their breath and he rolled off her slowly as if he didn't want to leave. "You okay?"

She smiled at the hoarse sound of his voice. "Are you always going to ask that?"

"If things keep up like this, yes."

"I'm fine."

"Be right back."

As Sean disappeared into the bathroom, she lost her grin and the bed got cold fast.

What was she doing? This…whatever it was…with him was so awkward. Even though they were great together in bed, she didn't know whether there could be anything else between them.

She sat up and looked around for her T-shirt. She found it just as he came in.

"Can I stay?" he asked as she pulled the thing over her head.

Yanking her hair free of the collar, she said, "Sean...I don't know. What just happened was probably a mistake."

As he put his hands on his hips, she had to fight to ignore how astoundingly beautiful he was naked.

She cleared her throat. "I think you should go."

Because given that she was conflicted, if he stuck around, she was liable to be swayed by his proximity.

Good Lord, who wouldn't be swayed by a man like this?

For a moment, she thought he was going to argue, but then he nodded and bent down to the floor. He pulled his trousers on commando, picked up his boxers and his shirt and jacket and went to the door.

"Mind if I call you?"

"Don't ask me that, Sean. Do it or don't."

His brows dropped down low. "Fair enough."

He turned away and didn't look back.

As his footsteps went down the hall, her heart felt like a lead ball in her chest.

Just as she heard the front door open, something made her spring out of bed and run for the living room. She stopped herself in the hall, though.

Desperation was not good in situations like this.

Keeping herself in check, she watched him shut her

door then listened to him go up the stairs and settle directly above her.

He was sleeping on the couch again.

As she went back to her bed, she wondered why he did that. And was reminded of why a relationship would be so difficult with him.

It was hard to fall in love with someone who couldn't share himself with you.

In Sean's dream, the one that really got to him, the one that was the worst of the bunch, he was ten years old and coming home from dinner at a friend's house. It was winter and the snow was falling. His too-small boots were squeezing his toes until they were numb. His mittens had holes at the tips of the fingers and the pads of the thumbs. His jacket was thin and dirty.

But his stomach was full and that made all the difference. His school buddy, Butch O'Neal, had a mother who was a cook and a half. And as the O'Neals had five kids, one more mouth was no big deal.

Sean went over to their house a lot.

As he walked along in the dark, the snowbanks came up to his shoulders and he imagined himself on the ice planet Hoth from the *Star Wars* movies. He was Han Solo back from rescuing Luke…and Princess Leia was waiting at home for him.

He smiled, picturing himself as a hero.

Except then he came up to his house. All the lights were off on the top floor and the TV was flickering blue and green in the front window.

Lights off was a bad sign.

He looked at the downstairs unit. It was dark, as well, because the tenants had moved out a week ago. That always made things worse.

It happened a lot. Those first-floor people never stayed long. He had a feeling they didn't like the noises that came from upstairs and he could understand why. He didn't like the noises, either. He would have moved out if he could have.

Though his teeth were chattering, he hung around outside, packing snowballs and watching the TV do its thing in the living room. He wondered where his brothers were. He figured Mac would be at work still and Billy would be in their room in bed. Billy was always asleep if he was home. Didn't matter what time of the day it was, if he was there, you'd find him with his head under his pillow and the blankets up to his chin.

When Sean couldn't stand the cold any longer, he walked up the front steps and went to the door. He had to turn the knob a couple of times because his mittens were slippery from the snow and his hands were stiff.

And maybe because he would have given anything to have somewhere else to go.

He stepped into the foyer and was careful to be very quiet as he went up to his apartment. The higher he got on the stairs, the drier his mouth became until he was swallowing nothing at all and his tongue was like sandpaper.

He took off his right mitten and went for the doorknob. It was locked.

He closed his eyes and shivered. He knew why his father did this and it wasn't to keep out thieves. It was so Eddie O'Banyon would have to be inconvenienced when his sons came home. So he would have to get out of his chair and weave across the room. So he would be justified in what came next.

Sean lifted his little hand and formed a loose, insubstantial fist. He knocked as quietly as he could, as if maybe it would bother his father less.

Didn't work.

A monster opened the door. And a monster dragged him inside. And a monster ripped his dirty snow jacket.

But before things got really bad, Mac came bursting into the apartment, home just in time. Sean had some impression of getting thrown in his room, not by his father, but by his brother. And then his door clapped shut.

As he landed in a heap, his face was throbbing to the beat of his heart and his knees were weak and the food that Mrs. O'Neal had made was a lead weight in his gut.

He started in with the dry heaves.

"W-w-wait! D-d-don't throw up on the r-r-rug!" Billy stammered.

There was a scramble over by the desk and then a wastepaper basket was shoved under Sean's face. Billy held him off the floor as he threw up Mrs. O'Neal's dinner and the only good thing about the retching was that it drowned out the noises from the living room.

Except then the nausea passed and they heard everything.

"Oh God…" Sean whispered as a loud thump hit the wall just outside their bedroom.

Billy started to cry.

The two of them ended up in Sean's bed with the

sheets pulled up over their heads. They trembled together as they listened. Eventually, it all went silent.

Sean waited for exactly one hour. He timed it, watching the alarm clock on the bureau, the one that got them up for school.

Then he shifted off the bed.

"Where are you g-g-going?" Billy whispered.

Sean didn't want his little brother to come. Didn't want Billy to see. "Go back to sleep."

"B-b-be careful."

"Shh."

Sean cracked open the door and winced as the thing creaked. Going utterly still, he waited while his heart pounded, and when nothing came at him, he slipped out into the hall. The TV was still on, still flickering, the glow throwing shadows as if things were coming at him.

There was something wet on the floor.

Sean was shaking as he went into his older brother's bedroom and he was careful as he shut the door behind him. Quiet. Had to stay quiet. He didn't want to wake the demon, although their father was likely passed out cold.

"Mac?" The room was dark and he couldn't see much, just the outline of the furniture. "Mac?"

There was a shuffling noise, as if someone had moved a leg or an arm.

With his eyes still adjusting, he went over to his brother's bed out of memory. But there was no one in it.

"Where are you?"

Another shuffle.

Sean tracked the sound over to the corner.

And that was where he found his fifteen-year-old brother, on the floor in a ball, hidden on the far side of his bureau.

"Mac, are you okay?" He went over and when he reached out, he felt something wet. He knew it wasn't tears. Mac never cried, no matter how bad it got. "Mac?"

"Go to bed." The voice was nothing but an exhausted whisper, more hoarse breath than words.

Sean patted his brother because it seemed like something their mom might have done. But Mac jerked away as if it hurt then groaned as if any kind of movement was a problem.

"Mac…I'm scared. What do I do?"

"What I told you. Go to bed."

"You're hurt."

"Go to bed."

Sean started to cry, and though he did his best to stop, the sniffles won. As his brother's hand landed on his shoulder, he was ashamed.

"Billy's wicked scared, right?" Mac said roughly.

"Yeah."

"So go take care of him. Go on."

"But you're—"

"If Dad finds you in here, we're all in trouble. *Go.*"

That got Sean moving like nothing else could. He scooted back to his room, back to Billy. Who was indeed wicked scared.

"I d-d-don't want to l-l-live here anymore," Billy said.

"I'll take you away. I'll take you and Mac away."
Sean lay back down, closed his eyes and thought of Han
Solo the hero. Fearless and strong. Protector of the
weak. Champion. "I promise, Billy."

Sean sat up in a rush and nearly flipped himself off
the couch. He blinked hard and raised his arm to shield
his eyes. Light was spilling into the living room, all
bright and cheerful, but it registered as glare.

As he thought about the dream, his stomach rolled.
In the end, he hadn't been able to keep that promise to
Billy; he hadn't managed to get his brothers out. Time
had been their slow, disinterested savior, their age of
majority all that had rescued them. Mac, who'd taken
the brunt of the beatings, had been the last to leave,
staying until Billy was out then disappearing into the
army.

Never to be seen again, really.

Sean couldn't blame the guy for that. After years of
running interference, no wonder Mac had had it with
his younger brothers. He'd more than paid his dues.
Besides, Sean often wondered whether his brother
thought less of him and Billy. Mac had rarely cracked,
but Sean and Billy had. Often.

With his older brother on his mind, Sean checked his
watch and calculated what time it was on the other side
of the globe. Not that it would matter. Mac wouldn't
answer the number he'd left for calling. Never did.

Sean grabbed his BlackBerry, dialed what he'd been
given and laid down another message, all no pressure,
just-give-me-a-buzz-when-you-can. He figured he'd let

one more week go by and then he'd just tell the recording that their father had died.

After he hung up, he showered and made some phone calls to New York to keep his mind off Lizzie. He wanted nothing more than to go down to her place, and not just because he was rattled from his dream. He was worried that they'd had their last night together and the concern wasn't sitting well.

His instinct was to press her, but that wasn't fair. Best thing was to give her a little space and pray that she came around. Hell, he wasn't sure exactly what he wanted out of a relationship with her. It wasn't as if he had the capacity to fall in love with anyone. But he knew that he wanted to see her again.

Maybe even *had* to see her again.

Man…he didn't enjoy feeling like this. Especially as he couldn't seem to pull himself out of the emotions.

But at least work wasn't a problem this morning. There was good news on the Condi-Foods deal. The memorandum of understanding from the acquirers had hit his offices at 4:00 a.m. for his review, and the share price and interest payments had been adjusted to what they'd agreed on. Which meant they had the bastards in writing.

As soon as he got back to Manhattan this morning, he was going to double check the documents then meet with the board chair to give his go-ahead. It was going to be big news on the Street, though the leaks were already out there. The news outlets had started calling his office.

Sean got dressed, throwing a polo shirt on under his

suit for the trip back because he'd shredded his button-down. He was just about to lock up when he heard the sound of a car engine turning over and wheezing out. There was a pause. Then the starter's whirring noise went off again only to fade after nothing caught.

He went over to the bay window and looked through the old lace curtains.

In the street down below, Lizzie got out of her Toyota and marched back into the duplex.

Sean descended the stairs at a clip and leaned into the open doorway of her apartment. "You need help?"

Lizzie was holding the phone to her ear and tapping her foot in frustration. Dressed in the loose scrubs of a nurse, her face was clean and shiny, her hair softly curling up as if it were only partially dry from a shower. She was frazzled, her mouth set with frustration, that foot going like the third hand on a watch, but she looked fantastic to him.

She lowered the receiver from her mouth. "My car does this sometimes. Just refuses to wake up."

"And you're late?"

"I wanted to get in early for my last day today. Boy, that starter motor has always had perfect timing. Perfectly *bad* timing."

"Can I drive you somewhere?"

"No, thanks. I'm on with the cab—" She cleared her throat and spoke into the phone. "Hi, I'd like a pickup at…"

As she talked with the taxi company, Sean stared at her, thinking he was the one who should drive her to work.

"I'm sorry, how long?" she said. "*Forty*-five minutes?"

"Let me take you," he cut in.

"I...ah—"

"Lizzie, I'll take you wherever you need to go. Let me do it."

Her eyes shifted to him. There was a pause. Then she said into the receiver, "Sorry, yes, I'm still here. But...ah, I don't need the cab. Thank you." She hung up. "You look like you're about to leave, though."

"I am. Right after I take you to work."

"I'm going to Roxbury."

"Then so am I."

"Okay...thank you. I just need to call the garage." She was quick and to the point with the mechanics, and after she hung up, she grabbed her purse and keys. "They're going to send a tow for it. They're used to me."

Damn it, he hated that her ride was unreliable. But as he followed her outside, he kept his yap shut. It wasn't as if she needed to hear that right now because she was no doubt thinking the same thing.

Without saying a word, they both paused on the shallow porch. The sun was a golden yellow, the sky a brilliant robin's-egg-blue, the trees as green as emeralds. It was as if the world had been colored by children's crayons.

"Beautiful day," he said.

"Yes." She looked around. "Like a cartoon almost. Reminds you of when you were young, doesn't it? So simple and clear and beautiful." She made an awkward sound. "Guess that's silly."

"Actually, it was just what I was thinking."

Her eyes shifted over, and for a split second, the

connection was there between them again, as invisible as the air that separated them, but as warm and real as the sunshine on their faces.

"Lizzie," he breathed.

"We…better go." Except she didn't look away. And neither did he.

Sean leaned down and put his lips on hers. There was so much he wanted to say, but he kept it simple and clear as the day. "I'm glad I'm taking you to work."

He took her hand and they walked to the rental in silence. After he opened her door for her, he waited until she was settled, then went around to the driver's side.

As they headed off for Roxbury, she said, "I wanted to let you to know I'm moving out."

Sean's hands cranked down hard on the wheel and he had to force them to relax. "You don't have to."

"I want to leave."

"Why?" Even though he knew.

"Too many memories." Then she quickly added, "Besides, if I end up working downtown during the day, it would be better if I lived closer to a T-stop."

He frowned. "How is the job search going?"

"It's going. Just started, really."

He glanced across the seat. Her eyes were trained out the side window, but they were unfocused, as if she were reviewing her situation in her head.

Sean thought about her mother. Her broken-down car. The fact that she was working nights in a rough part of town.

"Listen, you can forget about the rent," he said. "I mean, until I sell the place."

She looked at him in surprise then shook her head. "Oh, no. That's okay. I'll be fine, but thanks."

Man... First time he could remember a woman turning him down for money. But then Lizzie wasn't fitting the pattern in any manner, was she?

"Well, the offer stands," he said. God, he was a bastard to have ever doubted her for a moment. No way she'd been after his father for cash. No. Way.

After hitting all the red lights in Boston and getting slowed up by some sewer work, they eventually made it to Roxbury.

"It's on the next block." Lizzie pointed out the windshield. "Right here."

The community health center was set up in a two-story building constructed of concrete bricks and marked with windows that had chicken wire in the glass. But it wasn't dour. There were flowers in pots in front of the door and a lovely maple on the front lawn. And everything was neat as a pin: the grass between the sidewalk and the foundation was trimmed, and the juniper bushes were clipped nice and tight and the entryway was swept clean. Sun glinted off the front doors and made the brass sign that read Roxbury Community Health Initiative glow.

There were some people milling around, two of whom were in white coats and obviously doctors or nurses. The others seemed like a family: the woman with a baby in her arms and a toddler latched onto one leg, the man with a five-year-old up on his shoulders.

"Nice-looking place," Sean said.

"It is. The people who work here are so committed.

And the patients we treat are very special. I've been lucky to be a part of it."

"Even with the cuts in funding, it'll still stay open, right?"

"The question is for how long. We're—*they're* close to the bone already, working with equipment that needs to be upgraded in a facility that's really too small. The thing that scares me is, I don't know what this community would do without these services. So many folks aren't able to get downtown to the big medical centers, either because they don't have the money to travel that far or there are child-care issues or they can't take off the time from work to spend all afternoon in a doctor's office that's miles away." She shook her head and put her hand on the door. "Anyway…thanks for the ride."

"Wait, how long have you worked here?"

"Two years." Her eyes shifted back to the center. "Two years and two months. Like I said, I was right out of nursing school when I came onboard. Hard to believe it's my last day. I'm going to miss this place."

As Lizzie got out, the folks around the front door called her by name and she greeted them as one would friends, not patients or colleagues.

She leaned down into the rental car. "Thanks again, Sean."

"Lizzie?"

"Yes?"

"When do you get off?"

"Late today because they're throwing me a goodbye party. So not until sevenish. Why?"

"Just wondering. Take care."

Chapter Eleven

"So who *was* he, Lizzie?"

As the little conference room went silent, Lizzie looked up from her slice of We'll Miss You cake. The question had been popped by one of the other nurses, and with all the attention on her, Lizzie figured she had few options for response: Just a friend. No one special. Son of her landlord.

Or she could go with the truth: Wall Street tycoon with whom she'd had a very short-lived affair. Who was kind of still hanging around.

Ugh.

"Who are we talking about?" someone else asked.

"The guy who dropped off Lizzie today. The very handsome guy."

Keep it simple, stupid, Lizzie thought. "He's just a friend. My car died again."

"Well, from what I saw," a third person cut in, "a friend like him would be good to have."

Everyone smiled at her and piled on with good-natured ribbing. Which naturally caused Lizzie to turn as red as a stop sign.

Thank heavens the conversation was cut off by Denisha. The hollow sound of a plastic fork tapping on a plastic cup shifted the focus to the director. "I just want to take a minute to thank Lizzie for everything she's done."

"Hear! Hear!" came the chorus.

As people said a lot of really nice things, Lizzie looked down and pushed a wedge of frosting around her plate. She couldn't meet the eyes of her colleagues. Not with the tears that were threatening to spill at any minute.

"Lizzie?" Denisha said. "We have something for you."

Lizzie glanced up. "Really, that's not—"

The director held out an envelope. "This is for you."

Lizzie put her little plate down and took it. After working the flap free, she pulled out a homemade card with…oh, God…hundreds of signatures on it: patients and colleagues and the cleaning staff and the lawn men she'd helped with the flowers and the UPS guy and the medical reps who visited regularly.

She blinked fast so that only one tear escaped and hit the card. "You have no idea…what this means to me." She put her present up to her chest as if she could embrace at once all the people who had cared enough to sign it. "I will miss you so much."

A group hug bloomed all around her, people sniffling and smiling and holding on.

It was a sweet, sweet moment, proving that one person could make a difference to others. And it reminded her of why she'd become a nurse. There was great satisfaction in being a part of something like this, part of a place that cared about a community and healed the ill and infirm. She only hoped she could find something half as fulfilling somewhere else.

When the party broke up, she tidied the conference room with the others, grabbed her purse and her card of signatures and went out to the front desk to call a cab.

She was dialing when one of the nurses said, "He's back."

Lizzie didn't pay much attention as her call was answered by the taxi company. "Hi, I'd like a cab—"

"You don't need one, Lizzie. Your friend's back. And…wow is all I can say."

Lizzie frowned then leaned over the desk and looked out the double doors. A rental car was parked in front and Sean was lounging against the side of it, facing the community center. Wearing jeans and a New England Patriots T-shirt, he looked sexy as hell with his thick arms crossed over his chest and his sunglasses on.

Lizzie mumbled something to the cab folks, put the phone down and walked over to the door. "He isn't supposed to be here."

"Honey, man like that shows up for you, I'd say he's supposed to be here. And that you won the lottery."

As Sean lifted his hand and waved to her, she realized she was just staring at him like an idiot.

Shaking herself into focus, she gave a quick hug to her colleague then gathered her things and pushed open the door. The evening was a balmy benediction as she stepped outside.

"Um…I thought you were going back to New York."

"I did. Flew in for the meeting I had and came back. I figured I'd stop by here on the way home from Logan. How's your car?"

"Still getting worked on. I…I can't believe you came back."

"I have an ulterior motive."

She swallowed. "You do?"

"Yeah, can you give me a tour?" He nodded at the center. "Or is it too late at night?"

He wanted to see the center? "Ah…of course. The director is still here. I can introduce you to her and she can—"

"No, I want you to take me around. I want to see it through your eyes."

"Okay. But…Sean, why?"

"I'm always interested in businesses, but in this case, I might be able to help. The governor of this fine state happens to have been my college roommate and I'm not above hard-core lobbying for the right cause."

As Sean smiled, she found herself returning the expression. And tried not to let her heart soar. "Anything you could do would be appreciated, but I don't think it's the governor, actually. The legislature has been blocking his bid to get more funding to us. That's where the bottleneck is."

"Well, I'm glad to know your fine governor is

already onboard. It will make things so much easier on him when I start hammering him about your state-house." Sean stepped out of the car. "Shall we?"

Lizzie took him inside and led the way to Denisha's office so they could make sure the tour was okay. When Denisha gave her approval, Lizzie showed Sean around the exam rooms and talked to him about some of the patients they treated.

On the way to the lab facilities, she stopped in the doorway of the radiology room. "We really need better equipment. We have to send some patients out to other facilities to get certain films done and that is a hassle for them—more expensive, too. The advantage to us being in the community is that folks don't have to travel when they're sick. We're right here. And because we're user-friendly, important health screens for breast cancer and diabetes and high blood pressure are more likely to be conducted because patients adhere to their yearly checkups more often. If this center closes, or has to outsource too much, I really worry about the people we serve."

Sean frowned. "How tight is your budget?"

"Reimbursements from Medicaid and Medicare are not what they once were and our expenses are always higher so it's a thousand small cuts. If this continues, we're not going to be able to meet the standard of patient care because we'll be too understaffed and technologically compromised. And we aren't the only clinic in this situation. There are a number of facilities just like this, serving at-risk populations as we do. I mean…they."

Sean shook his head as the two of them came back

to the front desk. "Does this place have an endowment? I mean, what kind of philanthropic support do you get?"

"Some. Not enough. And no, we don't have an endowment."

Denisha came out of her office. "Did you enjoy your tour?"

Sean offered his hand and they shook. "You're doing really wonderful work here."

"Thanks." Denisha glanced over. "And Lizzie is one of our best. We're really going to miss her."

Lizzie looked away, not wanting to get emotional in front of Sean. "But I'm going to volunteer. So I'll be back."

"Good."

A few more things were said, but Lizzie wasn't really following. She was too busy looking at the crayon drawings that some of the kids had done while in the waiting room. The white papers with rainbow marks were taped up on the hallway's wall, a quilt of exuberance and life drawn by the community's future leaders.

"Lizzie? You ready?" Sean said.

"Yes." Though she wasn't.

She hugged Denisha tightly, but didn't lose it, and was proud of herself for getting to the car without a lot of drama.

Sean opened the passenger-side door for her. "You got any plans tonight?"

"I'm moonlighting."

"Okay, I'll be your taxi."

"Really, Sean, you've already done too much.

Besides, I have the home trip covered. I'm catching a ride back with a friend of mine who's pulling a double shift tonight."

"Then at least let me take you there, okay?"

As he shut the door and walked around the hood of the car, she watched him move. All that lithe male grace was something to see and she couldn't believe she'd been with him. Naked. In her bed.

She was so in trouble with this man.

"Why are you doing this?" she blurted as he got behind the wheel. "I mean…going to all this effort?"

He turned the key in the ignition and glanced at her as the engine flared to life. His deep-set hazel eyes were so serious that she was taken aback.

"You said it best. People make time for what they want. And I want you." Sean hit the gas and pulled away from the curb, resuming a more normal expression. "So when do you go to work? You want dinner?"

"Are you seeing anyone else?" she blurted. "I mean, down in the city?"

He shook his head. "It's just you. Only you, Lizzie."

Oh crap. That was so the right answer.

She rubbed her temples, thinking that this felt a lot like a relationship. It really did. Part of her wanted to fight falling into it. Part of her couldn't stop herself.

"I—ah, I usually eat something at the hospital around midnight. But there isn't time. I'm due in at eight."

"Okay, so are you free tomorrow night? My brother's in town for a preseason game. You want to come with me? We usually go out for a bite after he plays."

She loved football. "I don't know."

As Sean looked back over at her, his eyes were serious again. "Yeah, you do. But you don't trust me. Look, I'm hoping that we can spend some time together so that maybe…yeah, maybe you'll get to trusting me again."

"Sean, I'm not interested in getting my heart broken."

"Then we have something in common. I'm not interested in breaking your heart. I made a mistake. I'm sorry. And I want to keep seeing you."

She was about to ask him why when she realized that sounded pathetic. She was a good person. A smart person. She might not have millions in the bank or a flashy lifestyle, but that didn't mean she wasn't worthy of him.

"So what do you say, Lizzie? Little football in the afternoon. Little bite afterward. You know, real regular date stuff."

She took a deep breath. "Okay. It sounds…great."

He reached across the seat and took her hand. Then melted her by bringing it to his lips and whispering, "Thank you for the second chance."

When they got back to the duplex, Sean opened her door for her then hung back against one of the jambs as she went inside.

Man, he was tired.

He'd killed himself to get back to Boston tonight in time to pick her up and that was on top of a long day. After he'd raced down to Manhattan this morning, he'd had the meeting with the Condi-Foods board chair, a video conference conducted with investors in Tokyo and a drawn-out argument with one of his partners. Then he'd hightailed it back here.

The whole time he'd been en route, whether in limos or on the plane, he'd been working on his laptop, processing the hundreds of details and decisions that went along with a complex acquisition like Condi-Foods. When he'd waited for Lizzie at the health center, he'd made an effort to appear casual so she didn't feel pressured or stalked, but it had cost him a lot to haul ass up and down the coast.

Why had he made the effort? He'd had to come back to her. He'd made the time.

"I won't be long," Lizzie said as she went over to her computer and checked her e-mail.

"Don't rush on my account." When she made a frustrated sound, he asked, "What's the matter?"

"Oh, nothing." She blew out her breath. "Well, actually, I applied for four jobs last night. Two have already been filled, one was mis-listed and another I've been told I'm overqualified for. Usually there are a lot of nursing jobs available, but the class that graduated over this summer has taken some of the opportunities I could have used. But, whatever. At least I have the night work at the emergency department. And I put in some other applications on my lunch break today. Maybe one of them will come through...." She let the sentence drift, then headed off down the hall. "I'll be right back."

As Sean heard the shower come on, he imagined what she looked like, taking off her scrubs, stepping under the warm water, soaping up her body. He leaned his head back against the jamb and stared at the ceiling.

Wanting a specific woman was a new experience, but it was very clear that he had a case of the desperates for Lizzie. His blood was running red-hot again and the only thing that was going to put out the fire was her.

His BlackBerry went off, which was a relief. With any luck, he'd get sufficiently distracted so that what was doing behind his fly wouldn't show by the time Lizzie came back out.

After checking caller ID, he put his phone to his ear. "Mick, what's the news?"

"Congratulations, buddy, you did it. The Condi-Foods board signed off on the deal. You're going to get the formal call in about ten minutes. Holy hell, biggest transaction on the books this year and it's all you."

Sean heard the shower turn off. "That's great news, my man."

Mick laughed. "You're always so tight about these things. Most guys I know would be hopping around the room and breaking out the Cohibas."

"Lot of work to get to the finish line even with the board's approval." As doors were open and shut down the hall, he imagined Lizzie walking around in a towel. "It's not over yet."

"We need to celebrate anyway. How long are you going to be up there in Beantown?"

"I'll come back on Sunday night."

"Your father's place almost boxed up?"

"Haven't started yet."

There was a pause. "So what's been going on in Boston?"

"Nothing."

"You're spending a lot of time there for someone who still has packing to do."

Lizzie's voice carried down the hall. "Almost ready, Sean."

"Who's that?" Mick demanded.

"I've got to go, buddy."

"The hell you do. You seeing someone up there?"

"Ah…kind of." Assuming she'd have him.

The laugh that came across the line was a low, very masculine *gotcha*. And it took Sean back to a similar conversation he once had with a friend. Yeah, except back then with Gray Bennett, his buddy had been the one falling for a woman. And Sean had been the guy laughing.

Guess this was payback.

"So who is she, SOB?"

"You don't know her."

"Then you need to bring her to New York. I want to meet the woman who's gotten you to travel *to* her."

Lizzie walked in, dressed in a fresh pair of scrubs. "I'm ready—oh, sorry."

As she made like she was going to duck out of the room, he shook his head to stop her. "Look, I've got to go, Mick. I'll call you later." As he hung up without waiting for a response, an odd sinking sensation washed over him. Would she ever come to New York? he wondered. "So where we headed?"

"Boston Medical Center." She frowned and tilted her head to one side. "Hey, your right eye is twitching. Are you okay?"

He rubbed at the thing, annoyed by the way it was making his vision flicker. "Yeah, just fine. Actually, I got some great news from work."

"Good." Her stare surveyed him in what suddenly seemed like a professional manner.

He brought his hand up again and tried to get his eyelid to quit the disco routine.

"Sean, when was the last time you slept for more than a few hours?"

He had to smile. "Probably back when I was in college. That was basically the only time I slept well. But it's no big—"

Sean stopped breathing and blinked hard. Then scrubbed both his eyes. As he looked at Lizzie, half of her was gone, dissolved in a shimmering halo.

"Crap."

"Sean?"

"I'm having a migraine."

"Have you gotten them before?"

"Once or twice."

"Do you have medication?"

"No, because they don't come frequently enough. I think you'd better call a taxi because I can't drive right now. Oh, man... This is going to be a big one."

When Lizzie got home at 4:00 a.m., she opened the door to her apartment quietly and snuck in. The place was dead dark and dead silent.

Carefully putting her keys and purse on a table, she kicked off her shoes and padded down the hall. She put her head through her bedroom door and was disappointed when she saw through the dimness that her bed was empty.

Before she'd left for work, she'd pushed Sean between her sheets and closed the blinds and the curtains and told him to stay put. Clearly, though, he'd gone upstairs at some point.

Which meant she was going to go check on him. She wanted to see how he was doing and give him some of the over-the-counter medicine she'd picked up at the hospital.

Before she went up, she headed for the bathroom and flipped on the overhead—

Lizzie froze.

Sean was on the tile, curled up next to her toilet, having obviously spent some time throwing up. Had he passed out? she thought with panic.

A moan came up from the floor. "Lights off. Please."

She quickly hit the switch, and as blackness returned, he let out a ragged breath.

Kneeling by him, she whispered, "I have something for you to take if you'd like. Excedrin Migraine. It works very well or so I've heard."

His voice was reedy, nothing like the deep bass she was used to. "Don't think I could hold anything down."

"You want to go back to the bed?"

"Not yet."

"Do you need to go to the ER?"

"No."

She left and came back with a pillow and a blanket. Then she did the kindest thing she could for him: she left him alone.

After using the hall bath, she got into bed and stared

at the ceiling. Stress was a classic trigger for migraines and she was willing to bet his father's death coupled with whatever news had come from New York, even though it had been positive, had been what did it. All that travel couldn't have helped, either.

She thought of him lying in a ball on the floor. It was difficult to imagine someone as powerful as him being so fragile, but that was illness for you. As a nurse, she'd seen it so many times. Pain was the great equalizer, capable of stripping the crowns from kings.

She hated that Sean was hurting. And wished there was more she could do for him. Poor man…

She must have fallen asleep because sometime later the mattress wiggled. "Sean? How are you feeling?"

"Bad. Stomach has settled down though."

"Can I give you the meds?"

"Yeah."

She got the bottle, gave him two white pills with some water, and then lay back down beside him. As she turned to him, his hand came fishing through the sheets and the blankets and found hers. When he squeezed, she squeezed back.

"I'm right here if you need me," she said softly.

"Thanks." There was a stretch of silence. "I think I need you."

"You want something to eat? Drink?"

"No. I just…think I need you." He exhaled and fell silent.

She looked at the ceiling…and against her better judgment, beamed in the dark.

Chapter Twelve

"Could you please call my brother?"

It was late the next morning and Lizzie was standing over her bed, hands on her hips, clinical eye on Sean.

She ignored his request. "Have you ever had one that's lasted this long?"

"Yeah. It's been a decade, but yeah."

Boy, Sean was the color of kindergarten paste…except for the smudges of black under his eyes. His brows were cranked together, his breathing shallow. His big body was so still, it was obvious the slightest movement caused the headache to get worse. Still, he didn't seem to be in any medical danger. He was just miserable.

"So can you call Billy for me?" he asked. "I'm going

nowhere this afternoon. He'll also know how to get hold of Mick."

"How do I get in touch with your brother?"

"I'll give you his number."

She memorized the digits as he recited them. "You want anything?"

He managed to say the word *no* without moving his lips at all. Then tacked on, "Wait, my duffel bag from the car would be great. Has my toothbrush in it."

"Be right back."

After she got the bag and put it just inside her room, she shut the door and headed for the phone in the living room. While dialing his brother's number, she held her breath. She'd never spoken to a pro football player before.

The voice that answered was a low drawl. "Yeah?"

"Is this Billy O'Banyon?"

"Depends. Who are you and how did you get this number?"

Whoa. Evidently, linebackers had nice voices. "Assuming you are him, your brother Sean gave it to me."

There was a pause. Then the voice got sharp. "Is he okay?"

"He has a migraine. Bad one. He asked me to tell you that he won't be able to come to the game today."

"Oh, hell. Considering all that's been going on, I should have known one was coming. Where is he?"

"At your house."

"My house? Which one?" As if he had so many he couldn't keep track.

"Um…your father's house, I guess. In South Boston."

The man's tone turned incredulous. "He's still staying *there?*"

"Yes."

"Okay. Wow." There was another pause. "Tell him I'll stop over after the game."

"I'll pass on the message. Oh, and he wanted you to call Mick and let him know what's going on."

"Yeah, okay. Wait, who are you?"

"I live in the apartment below. I'm kind of taking care of him. My name's Lizzie Bond."

"Well, I appreciate your making the effort, especially because I'll bet you've got to tie him down to keep him still. That brother of mine never slows up."

"Well, he's slowed up now. Has been since last night."

"Poor bastard. How bad is he?"

"You can see for yourself. When you come by, just knock on the downstairs door. I'll be here, and considering how he's faring, so will he."

"I'll do that. And thanks again for watching over him."

As she hung up, she heard a noise from the bedroom and went down the hall. Sean was writhing on the bed, his big body twisting in the sheets, his brows drawn tight. He made a noise deep in his throat, a kind of strangled protest, then shook his head back and forth on the pillow.

She went over and touched his shoulder. "Sean?"

He woke up on a full recoil, his hands shielding his face as if he were about to be struck. In a voice that didn't sound like his at all, he said, "Please…no."

They'd done this before. The night of the storm.

"Sean?" she said gently, though she was thoroughly creeped out and worried about him. "Wake up. You're just dreaming."

"Mac?"

She frowned. "No, it's me. Lizzie."

He blinked a number of times, then sank back down into the pillows and closed his eyes. "Lizzie? Oh…yeah…yeah, I know. Sorry."

She stayed over the bed, the sound of his voice ringing in her mind. Mac was his other brother, right? And what had he been so afraid of? She had a feeling the dream was a repeater.

"Sean?" When he made an affirming noise, she said, "I'm going to go out for a little while, if you're okay?"

"I should probably leave, too. Not fair. Take up all your space." He started to push himself up, moving slowly as if he had an unbalanced load on his neck. Or maybe a ticking bomb.

"No, Sean. I want you to stay." The way he collapsed back down told her just how weak he was. "Listen, I have my cell with me and I've left the number by the phone, okay?"

"Don't want you to have to nurse me. 'Nough of that on your day job."

"I don't mind at all." She truly didn't. Although she was sorry he felt bad, she was glad he was in her bed, his hair dark against her pillows, his heavy shoulders filling out her blankets and covers. In her room, between her sheets, he was safe and she could care for him and he would be far more comfortable than upstairs on that couch he insisted on using.

"Thank you," he said in a garbled voice. "Once again."

Before she left, she had a consuming urge to kiss him on the forehead, but she resisted. "I'll be back."

She went out the front door a couple of minutes later and walked the long distance to the nearest T-stop. In the back pocket of her jeans was a list of open houses for apartments in Southie, Charlestown and Cambridge. She figured it was going to take a while to see them all.

She was right. And the prospects were bleak.

After three hours of hoofing it up and down stairs and taking the T around, she had a sense of what she could afford and it was not a lot. Prices had skyrocketed in the two years since she'd last been looking, and for what she was paying now, her only options were cramped studios in buildings that were kind of run down. Her only other choice was to look even farther out of Boston proper, to Watertown, for instance, but then getting to work would be more of a hassle.

On her way back home on the T, she called the service station and had to curse to herself. Her car was going to need a thousand dollars' worth of work. Evidently, it wasn't just the starter this time.

As the T trundled along and sank underground, she looked out and saw nothing but a rhythmic pattern of tunnel lights, some of which had burned out.

She really needed one of those job applications to come through. Fast.

For Sean, the migraine's pain started to recede about 250 years after it had started. Or maybe it was twenty-five minutes. Hard to tell. Time had warped, becoming like cloth that was bunched up and wrinkled. Maybe if he made an effort he could smooth it out and count the hours. But he really didn't care that much.

He rolled over onto his side and cracked an eyelid.

He was still in Lizzie's bed. Hell, he'd taken it over, lying in the middle as if he owned the damn thing. Man, bad enough to have been sick in front of her, but to have all but kicked her out of her own room? That was just awful.

He gingerly pushed himself onto his elbows and gave his head a moment to adjust to the altitude. Then he looked at the clock. It said nine and he was pretty sure that was nine at night. Yeah…no slits of sunlight through the drapes. Definitely nighttime.

He moved himself to the side of the bed slowly, feeling as if there were an anvil on the left side of his head. Still, the dull pain was a big improvement over the ax blade that had been there before.

As his feet hit the floor, he thought, okay, he could handle upright. And it was time to plug back into the real world. He needed to call Mick and get a status report on Condi-Foods. Had to check in with his office—

Whoa. The mere thought of doing either of those things brought the ax back. As his head started to pound again, he thought maybe he and his BlackBerry would stay estranged for a little longer.

Throwing the thoughts of work out the window, he concentrated on getting to the bedroom door in one piece. When that mission was accomplished, he opened the thing and followed the muted tapping of computer keys out to the living room.

"Hi."

Lizzie twisted around in the armchair by the window. "Hello!"

"I think I'm back in the land of the living."

"So you are. How's the head?"

"Still attached. Not real clear on whether that's a good thing, but at least I'm vertical."

"Good. Would you like something to eat?"

"I was thinking I'd get out of your hair, actually."

"Oh. Well, you weren't really in it. You've been a very quiet patient."

He pointed over his shoulder with his thumb. "I'm going to strip the bed. You got fresh sheets?"

"Don't worry about that. Besides, you look like you're about to fall over."

"I'm okay. Can't wait to have a shower though."

"Take one here if you want."

"No, thanks. I've intruded enough." With his energy already flagging, he glanced at the front door and wondered how he was going to make it to the second floor. But that wasn't what was really on his mind. "Ah hell, Lizzie, I've ruined your weekend."

"Are you kidding me? I wouldn't have done anything differently." She nodded at the computer. "Right now I'm all about the job search."

"Find anything?"

She shrugged. "A few. By the way, your brother said he was coming by, but I don't know how late."

Sean stopped breathing. "Here? He's coming *here?*"

"Yes." Lizzie frowned. "Is that bad? He's worried about you."

"No. It's just—" Sean cut himself off, thinking that if Billy was coming over, he didn't want his brother going upstairs. "You know what? I think I will shower down here, if you don't mind. And if he comes, would you feel comfortable just letting him in? He's a good guy. He only looks like a thug."

"Of course. Wait, what exactly does he look like? I don't watch football on TV."

"He's six-five, about 260 pounds. His hair's blond like my mother's was and he's got a jaw like a slab of rock."

"Sounds handsome."

In a flash, a good old-fashioned shot of jealous-for-no-damned-good-reason went through Sean's chest. *Handsome?*

"Ah, yeah, I guess he is," Sean muttered. Actually, his brother was a total looker and women always loved the guy. The bastard.

"Well, I'll watch out for him."

Sean nodded and headed for the bathroom, hoping to get in and out of it fast. And not just because he didn't want to keep his little brother waiting.

There was no reason to have Billy working out his charm on Lizzie.

Within moments of the shower starting, Lizzie heard the house's front doorbell ring.

She got up and went to the blinds. *Whoa...* There was a Greek god out on the porch: Billy O'Banyon just about defined jock handsome in his blue jeans and his white muscle shirt and his blond hair.

Yeah…wow. Check out those tattooed biceps.

Although it was funny. In spite of his obvious attributes, he couldn't hold a candle to Sean in her eyes.

She went out into the hall and opened the duplex's front door. "Hi, you must be Billy?"

The Adonis smiled, showing a row of white, even teeth. "I am. And you're Lizzie?" As she nodded, he stuck out his hand. "Nice to meet you. How's the patient?"

"Up and around. In the shower, actually." She stepped back and swept her arm toward her apartment. "He'll be right out."

When Billy stepped into the hallway, his demeanor changed completely. As his eyes drifted up the stairs, his face and his body stiffened, his charisma draining out of him.

He didn't move. Just stood there fixated.

"Um…he's in my shower," she prompted quietly.

"W-w-w-w." Billy shook his head. "I mean, what?"

"Sean… He's in my place."

"Oh. Yeah." Billy's eyes didn't leave the stairs. "H-how." More with the head shaking, as if he was trying to unstick his mouth. "H-h-how… *Damn* it, how is he?"

"Better. Much better."

"Good." Billy's massive chest expanded and then he looked at her. All at once, his face settled into a flashing smile that had about as much depth as water spilled on a counter. "I'm glad to hear it. He give you much trouble?"

"No." As Billy went into her apartment, she asked, "Would you like something to drink?"

"No, I hydrated before I came, but thanks." He looked around. "Nice place. Been here long?"

"Two years."

"Nice."

Standard social conversation, she thought, and she appreciated him making the effort, but she wished she could ask his what was wrong. The man who was standing in her living room was not the guy she'd opened the door to.

Down the hall, the shower shut off and there was the sound of a towel flapping around.

"Yo, Sean," Billy called out. "How you be?"

The door to the bathroom opened and Sean stuck his head out. His hair was sticking straight up like un-mowed grass and there was water dripping off his nose.

He looked fantastic. Until she got a gander at his eyes. They were locked on his brother and clearly worried.

"You okay?" Sean asked. Even though he'd been the one down for the count with that headache.

Billy nodded. "Y-y-yeah."

"Stay down here. You don't go up the stairs, okay?"

Billy nodded again as if he preferred not to trust his voice.

As Sean shut the door, there was an awkward silence.

Then Billy looked up to the ceiling. "You know my father at all?"

"Yes. We were friends."

His eyes shot to hers. As if he'd never expected to hear that word associated with the man. "Really. Huh. What was he like? As a friend?"

"He was good to me. I was grateful I knew him."

"Really. Huh." Same words, same inflection. As if his brain was multiprocessing and that was just what happened to spit out to fill conversational space. "He treat you good?"

"Yes."

"Really."

She waited for the *huh,* but it didn't come. "He looked after me in a way."

"Funny, I always thought he didn't care about people. Well, except for my mother. He loved her. But then she died and he changed. Everything changed. Forever."

The haunted quality of this big, beautiful man's voice made chills go up her spine. And the eerie feeling made her think of something Mr. O'Banyon had said once. It had been New Year's Eve and she'd been talking to him about regrets. He'd said he had none. What he had were things he could never atone for. Regrets... Regrets didn't go far enough.

She'd thought it was an odd way to put things, but he'd changed the subject and it had never come up again. Now, she looked back on that conversation and felt uneasy.

Billy brought his hand up to his chin. "Sometimes... Sometimes change isn't good, you know?"

She let the comment stand, because she was well aware he wasn't actually addressing her.

When a growling sound broke the silence, she frowned. Then realized it was Billy's stomach.

"Are you hungry?" she asked.

He looked down at his body as if surprised. "Yeah…I am."

"Come on, I was just about to make myself something to eat."

Chapter Thirteen

As Sean sat at his family's old table in Lizzie's kitchen, he had to give his brother credit. Billy was keeping it together, appearing to be what he was most of the time: a charmer of a guy with great people skills and a lot of bawdy stories.

But Sean knew the truth, knew how much it was costing his brother to be here. Billy had said he'd never come back to the duplex and it was clear the specter of what had happened upstairs was prowling around in the guy's head. Billy's eyes kept lifting to the ceiling as if he could see through the plaster and the Sheetrock and the framing boards into the past.

He was making an effort to keep tight, though, and Lizzie seemed to be having a great time as the two of them cooked then put dinner on the table. Man, it was a perfect summer meal. The hamburgers were stacked with juicy beef-steak tomatoes that spilled out of the bun as you bit down. The corn was sweet and tender. The lemonade was perfect and very chilly.

Except he didn't enjoy it as much as he could have. While they ate, he tried to get lost in the talk and the food, but it was tough. Even though he was in that post-migraine float zone where everything had soft edges, he kept thinking about Billy.

By the time a bag of oatmeal cookies was passed around, he was feeling the strain in his head.

After Billy told a real barn-burner of a story and Lizzie laughed so hard she was gasping for air, Sean's brother checked his sports watch. "I've got an early PT session tomorrow so unfortunately I have to take off soon." He got to his feet and picked up his plate as well as Lizzie's. "This has been great. Would love to do it again soon."

Lizzie grinned at him. "Yeah, well, I'd love to hear more stories from the locker room."

"I *knew* you were my kind of girl." The faux-leer Billy shot over his shoulder somehow managed to be both outrageous and respectful at the same time.

Which meant Sean didn't have to snap his brother's chain. Too hard. "Forget it, Billy, she's out of your league."

"I know. Too smart." Billy smiled at Lizzie. "You'd have to be smart to get through nursing school, right?"

"It helps," she said, winking at him.

Sean stood up. "I'll walk you to your car."

"Great." As Lizzie rose from the table, as well, Billy

stuck his hand out at her. "I'd hug you but I think my brother would hurt me."

"No, he wouldn't," she said.

Lizzie stretched up onto her toes and threw her arms around Billy. He was so big, she looked as if she were embracing the hood of a car, her reach not long enough by half. In response, Billy handled her gently, the way he did with all women. As a man who knew his strength, he was always careful around those more fragile than him.

Which was pretty much everyone on the planet.

"Okay, you can stop that," Sean said, putting his hand on Billy's shoulder and pulling back with a little tug.

Billy let go and wagged his eyebrows at Lizzie. "See. Told you."

She batted his tattooed bicep. "You know Sean's just kidding."

Yeah, the hell he was. "Come on, big man. Out."

As Billy laughed, Sean frog-marched him to the apartment's door, but they both got serious as he opened the thing. Stepping out into the foyer, he deliberately stood in the way of the staircase, trying to block as much of it as he could with his body.

Billy's eyes went up to the top landing and his mouth got grim.

Sean shook his head. "Come on, Billy. Let's go."

They went out of the house in silence and stayed that way while walking over to Billy's custom-rigged Denali.

"I didn't want you to come here," Sean said.

"Couldn't stay away forever."

"Yeah, you could have. And I'd have preferred that."

Billy's face tilted upward as he looked to the second-floor apartment. "What's it like in there?"

"Same. Exactly the same."

"Freak you out?"

"Yeah."

"You need help packing?"

"No." Not from his little brother, at any rate.

Billy rubbed his square jaw. "Did you see him dead?"

"Yeah."

"What did he look like?"

"Older. But like that damned apartment, the same."

There was a long period of quiet.

Down at the end of the street, a car turned onto the road. Its engine was a muted drone that got louder as it approached, then faded after it went by.

"You heard from Mac yet?" Billy asked.

"I left him another message a couple of days ago. Next time I'm just going to tell the voice mail."

"Wish he'd call."

"Me, too."

Billy leaned back against the SUV and cleared his throat. As he crossed his arms, his thick chest flexed. "So Lizzie's nice."

"She is."

"Not your usual type."

"And not yours, either." Which was a ridiculous thing to say but he couldn't help it.

Billy laughed. "Oh, relax yourself. I know she's off-limits. How long have you been together?"

"We're not."

"Bull."

"Fine. Let's just say…there are complications."

"Only if you want to have them."

"Please, no Dr. Phil, okay?"

Billy shrugged. "Just haven't seen you look at a woman like that before."

Don't ask. Don't ask. Don't be an idiot and— "How do I look at her?"

Idiot.

"Like you're actually seeing her."

"Whatever."

"Hey, I'm glad." Billy shoved a hand into his jeans pocket and took out a set of keys. "At least one of us might have a shot at getting married."

"I never said anything—"

"Touchy, touchy, touchy." Billy grinned and hit the car remote. As the Denali's lights flashed, the lock on the driver's side door made a little punching sound. "So you really do like her, huh?"

"Look, Billy, there's no—"

"You don't have to get defensive about it."

"I'm not being defensive!" As Billy laughed again, Sean cleared his throat. "I'm not."

"Oh. Really. Well, lemme remind you that as a line-backer, defense is my profession. So I'm good at spotting it."

"On the field, maybe."

Billy pointed to the ground. "And you're standing on grass as we speak."

While Billy got into the car and put the window down,

Sean cursed and stepped onto the sidewalk. "You going to be in town over the next couple of weeks?" he asked.

"I've got some away games, but other than that I'm here. You know, I'm sorry you missed today's match-up. But maybe you could come and watch me play some other time?"

"Yeah, absolutely."

"Bring Lizzie."

"We'll see." It would have to depend on whether she was around. God...he hoped she'd be around.

Billy stretched his arm out the window and the two gripped palms. There was a long moment as their eyes met.

"No looking back," Sean said. "We don't look back, remember?"

It was the credo they'd hung on to as scared children...then had reaffirmed as reckless college guys...and now lived out as best they could as adult men.

Billy nodded. "No looking back."

He put the car in gear and drove away.

As Sean watched the brake lights fade, he got pissed off that their father had been such a bastard. Billy might not have been hit as much, but he'd been ridden hard for being "stupid" because he was dyslexic and couldn't read very well.

Which was why he'd only been partially joking when he'd said Lizzie was out of his league because she was so smart.

"Your brother is very nice."

Sean turned around toward the house. Lizzie stood

in the front doorway, her body blocking the view inside, blocking the view to the stairs that went up.

Looking at her now, Sean didn't want her to know what had happened with his father. Ever. Nothing made him feel weaker or more ashamed than the past, and he wanted to be strong for her. He wanted to be a man for her.

Not a frightened little boy.

Besides, there was the relationship she'd had with his father. Though Sean couldn't understand it, it was clear she'd been close to the man and there was no reason to spoil her memories of him with stuff that didn't affect her.

Sean walked up onto the porch and wrapped his arms around her. As she embraced him back, he closed his eyes so he couldn't see the stairs.

"Did I tell you how beautiful you look tonight?" he said into her hair.

She chuckled a little. "This jeans and T-shirt combo isn't exactly Miss America–worthy."

He held on even harder. "The hell they aren't. To me, whatever you have on is a ball gown."

She stiffened, but then eased back into him. "You scare me when you say things like that."

"Why?"

"I'm afraid I'll start believing them."

He pulled back and looked her in the eye. "Believe them, Lizzie. Trust me and believe them."

Chapter Fourteen

The following Thursday, Lizzie raced for the phone in the living room, leaving a pot of water with a fistful of linguine in it boiling on the stove.

"Hello?"

"Hi." Sean's voice was warm over the line.

She smiled so wide her cheeks stretched. "Hi."

"How was your day?"

"Better now."

He laughed. "Funny, I feel the same way."

Over the past week, he'd surprised the hell out of her. He called her every day at least once, sometimes more often. And when she was moonlighting, no matter what time it was when she got home, the phone would ring as if he'd set his alarm to her schedule just so he could check she was safe and sound.

"Are you in a car?" she asked. "I hear a whirring noise in the background."

"Yeah, I'm on the road again."

"I don't know how you do everything you do." Boy, from what she'd learned, he earned every penny of the money he got for putting those billion-dollar deals together. He worked around the clock and there were very few times when there were no arguing voices in the background as they talked.

Yet, even though he was busy, somehow she was always his sole focus when he called. There had been numerous occasions when people had tried to interrupt and he'd put them off curtly. He even lingered over goodbyes as if he didn't want her to go. Every time.

"You sound tired," he said.

She headed back for the stove. "Just not as many daytime jobs in downtown as I'd hoped."

"Your car come back today?"

"Yes, thank heavens." She stirred the pasta with a fork. She was glad to have a set of wheels again, but cutting the check for all that work had pained her…and so was what she was about to ask him. The thing was, however, it was the end of the month and although money wasn't quite a problem, it was going to be in a little while. "Ah…Sean?"

"Mmm?"

"I hate to bring this up, but remember when you said I could live here rent free until you sold the—"

"Absolutely. Don't you dare write that check."

"Thank you…really, thank you. I hate to impose, but things are going to get tight for me."

"I'd offer you a loan, but I have a feeling you'd turn me down."

"Of course I would! But I do appreciate the break on the rent, even though I wish I didn't need it." She cradled the phone between her ear and her shoulder, picked up the pot and headed for the strainer in the sink. As she poured, a waft of steam shot up and she leaned back. "Whoa, hot."

"What is?"

"Spaghetti water." She put the pot back on the stove and jogged the strainer, making the linguine bounce. "So do you have another busy night planned?"

His voice deepened. "Oh, yeah. Very busy."

"I think you work too hard."

"Some kinds of work are a real pleasure."

"You love what you do, don't you?"

"I love what I'm going to be doing tonight." The whirring noise in the background got cut off. Then there were some dinging sounds followed by a dull *thunch*.

She poured the pasta back into the pot. "Mergers and acquisitions must really interest you."

"Mergers especially."

"What are you working on now or is it a secret—" The sound of a knock on her door brought her head around and her heart to her throat. "Sean?"

"Yes?"

She started to laugh and ran out to the living room. As she threw open the door, they both hung up their phones.

"What are you doing h—" She didn't get a chance to finish the sentence.

Sean dropped a duffel bag and dragged her against him, picking her up as he kicked the door shut. His mouth came down on hers and his hands gripped her hips as he carried her across the room.

She held on to his shoulders, so lost in the kiss she barely noticed that he was laying her on the couch and undoing the buttons down the front of her shirt…and working on the waistband of her jeans.

"I've missed my Lizzie," he growled as he peeled back one side of her bra. "Mmm…"

He closed his mouth on her nipple while he stripped off her Levi's and her underwear. Then he moved down her body, his lips going to the inside of her thigh and working their way to the very core of her.

He gave her shimmering pleasure, and when she came back into herself, she opened her eyes slowly. Sean was standing above her sprawled, satiated body, ripping off his tie and doing away with his button-down shirt. His eyes burned as he took hold of his fine leather belt and worked the buckle—then his deft fingers went to his fly and there was the sound of a zipper being dragged down.

His trousers hit the floor and she saw his arousal pushing at the thin cotton of his boxers. But then they were gone, too, his naked power revealed. She sat up, drawn by the sight of him, and encircled him with her hand.

"*Lizzie,*" he moaned, his head falling back.

She worshipped him until he made her stop by pulling her head back with a shudder. As he went for the pocket of his suit, his breathing was harsh and sweat gleamed on his muscular chest. He covered himself and got on top of her.

"I need to apologize in advance," he said with a rasp as he slipped inside.

After they both groaned, she mumbled, "For what?"

"I'm not going to last long."

And he didn't. But neither did she.

The next morning, Sean got up early and made Lizzie breakfast. He figured it was the least he could do considering the double shift she was going to pull today at the BMC emergency department.

As he fired up her coffee and got out a bowl and a spoon for her cereal, he listened to her moving around her bedroom…and realized this was probably why people got married.

Man, he loved this quiet morning peacefulness. Loved the idea he was helping her start her day. Loved the fact that when her work was done, she was going to come back and walk through the door and tell him how she'd spent the hours they'd been apart.

Domestic bliss indeed.

He put the milk carton next to the bowl and brought the box of corn flakes over from the cupboard. Not exactly eggs Benedict with hollandaise, but considering the time constraint and the fact that he only knew how to do hash-slinger stuff, she was more likely to enjoy the cereal.

"Chow's on," he called out.

She came right away and he poured the milk for her until she said when. Then he watched her eat. She was dressed in scrubs and not wearing makeup and her hair was all soft and blond and a little flyaway from the dryer.

To him she was the last word in female.

"So you're starting to pack today?" she said as she sipped her coffee.

"Yup." He leaned back with his own mug and studied the way the sunlight slanting through the kitchen window hit her cheeks and lips. He wished he had a photograph of her just as she was now, but he was going to have to rely on his memory.

"I'll help you tomorrow," she said.

"Thanks, but if you're home, I'd rather be doing other things with you." As she blushed, he tilted his head down and looked at her from under his brows. They hadn't slept much during the night because he'd been all over her. After having spent a mere five days away, he'd been insatiable. "Have I mentioned that I can't wait for you to get back tonight?" He reached out and brushed her cheek with his fingertips. "I want a repeat of how we spent last evening."

She turned even redder and kissed his palm. "Sean…"

He smiled. "I love it when you blush."

Her expression grew wry. "I do it often enough around you."

"I know."

As a soft chiming sound came from a clock, she pulled back. "Oh, darn…the time. I'm late."

When she took hold of her bowl, he said, "Don't bother cleaning up, I'll take care of it."

"You're so good to me."

"I want to be even better."

They headed for the living room together and he loved the soft, secret smile on her face—because he knew he was the cause of it.

The expression was lost as she went over to her purse and took out her wallet. Thumbing through the thing, she cursed softly.

"Not enough cash?" he said.

"I'll be okay—"

"Here." He picked up his suit jacket, pulled out his money clip and peeled off a hundred-dollar bill. "Take this."

She glanced over, eyes widening. "Oh, no…that's okay—"

"You're late, right? So it would be hard to stop at a cash machine."

"Well, yes, but at work they have—"

He pressed the crisp Benjamin Franklin into her hand and wrapped her fingers around it, finding an unfamiliar but vivid satisfaction in giving money to a woman. He just loved the idea he was helping her, providing for her. "Take it."

"Thanks, I'll pay you—"

He silenced her with a kiss. Then couldn't resist slipping his tongue between her lips. When he pulled back, he murmured, "Have I mentioned how I can't wait until you come home?"

"Yes. And I'll second that."

He walked her out into the foyer and ushered her to the front door, but hung back from the great outdoors because he only had boxers on. As she got into the old Toyota, he hated the thing she was driving. He wanted to buy her a new ride with state-of-the-art air bags and a steel crash cage and every amenity available to make her comfortable and safe.

With a wave, she pulled away from the curb and headed off. In her wake, he had to laugh at himself. Before meeting her, he'd refused to give women a dime. Now? He wanted to shower his money all over Lizzie Bond.

Not that she'd let him.

Fine. He was just going to drag his feet on the sale of the house, then. The longer he put it off, the more time Lizzie could be rent free and the less stressed she'd be as she looked for a job.

And maybe he could start working on her about the car thing.

Sean whistled as he went back in her apartment, cleaned up breakfast and started a fresh pot of coffee. He took a steaming mug upstairs with him, and as he opened the door to his father's place, he braced himself for the usual gut crank.

He was glad he hadn't eaten breakfast when it hit.

After casing the joint, he decided to start in the kitchen. It was the room with the fewest memories.

It didn't take long to develop a core competency getting those U-Haul boxes taped into shape. He filled them with dishes and glasses and cheap silverware, all of which would go to the church. He also started a trash pile. A lot of the cooking utensils were rusted from lack of use and he realized, as he threw out wire whisks and paring knives and measuring spoons, that what he was pitching had most likely last been touched by his mother.

Yeah, Eddie never had been much of a cook. Sean and his brothers had pretty much lived on peanut-butter-and-jelly sandwiches. Well, those and Mrs. O'Neal's handouts.

Sean had been in full clean-out mode for about an hour when he found a half-empty, dust-covered bottle of booze way in the back of a cupboard.

Ah, yes. The demon.

As he poured the cheap vodka out and watched the stuff funnel down the scratched porcelain sink, he wondered what quitting had been like for his father. As well as the why and the when of it.

It would have been hard, that was for sure. Alcohol and his father had been inseparable, the one relationship Eddie had valued, the one thing the man had connected with. Sean could even remember being jealous of the Popov. When Eddie wasn't loaded, he might actually talk to you.

At the very least, he didn't come after you.

A little later, Sean found another bottle in the broom closet. Again, dust-covered. This time when he emptied the booze, he didn't think of anything at all.

It took him the better part of the morning to finish up the kitchen and then he started in on the living room. As he worked, the number of stacked, marked boxes grew and he went through miles of packing tape.

He broke for eats around noon and then forced himself to hit the bedrooms. As he couldn't bear to go into his father's or Mac's, he whipped through his and Billy's then took care of the bathrooms. When he was through with them, it was only seven o'clock. Lizzie wasn't going to be home for another five hours and there was no reason to stop working.

Except all that was left were the two places he didn't want to go.

As he paused outside the door to Mac's room, he wished like hell his older brother would check in. He supposed there was always the option of trying to track Mac down through military channels, but he knew his brother wouldn't appreciate getting red flagged even if it was for a good reason. Besides, given what the guy did, it might not even be possible to find him through regular army contacts.

Sean went inside and worked fast. He needed only four boxes for Mac's stuff and then he was left with nothing but his father's domain.

Gearing up, he headed down the hall with an armful of cardboard and a taping wheel. Inside his dad's room, he flipped on the overhead light and looked around. Pretty much standard-issue, lower-middle-class stuff. The bed was made, but the blankets were old and the pillows thin. On the side table, there was a fake wood alarm clock, a lamp with a yellowed shade and a little thicket of pill bottles.

Sean went over and checked out the labels. He recognized the ones for high blood pressure and cholesterol, but the others didn't mean anything to him. Whatever. They obviously hadn't worked all that well.

He taped up a box to use as a trash bin and tossed the orange vials then emptied the drawer underneath of a bunch of old racing forms.

He was about to start stripping the bed when he saw the slippers on the floor.

The pair were right out of the L.L. Bean catalog,

made of tan leather and lined in sheep's wool. They were old and worn, peeling up off the carpet at the toes. The two were lined up right together, facing out as if his father had kicked them off as he'd gotten into the bed for what had turned out to be the last time.

God... Same kind Eddie O'Banyon had worn twenty years ago. Conceivably the very pair.

Sean picked one up. Inside, as if the soles were made of sand, there was a precise impression of his father's foot registered in relief. The man had clearly spent hours wearing them, shuffling around this apartment, crossing from room to room...until suddenly there were no more trips to be made and the slippers would never be worn again.

Thoroughly creeped out, Sean pushed them under the bed so he didn't have to see them, then took off the sheets and threw them out.

The closet was next. After opening the doors, he stared at what hung from the wooden dowel. It was the same stuff his father had always worn. Low-price button-downs—cotton for spring and summer, flannel for fall and winter—and khakis. Off to one side, there was an old work shirt from the phone company with a patch that read Eddie O'Banyon as well as a suit with a fine layer of dust on the shoulders. Probably the last time that had been worn had been at Sean's mother's funeral.

Looking at the clothes, thinking about the slippers, Sean could picture his father so clearly, it was as if the man's ghost had wandered into the room, all simmering and pissed off at being called from the grave.

To get rid of the Stephen Kings, Sean put his hand into the closet and grabbed the first thing he hit. Going on autopilot, he stripped the hangers bare then picked up the shoes from the floor and cleaned off the top shelf. He hit the dresser after that, whipping through the drawers, throwing out the underwear and socks, putting the sweaters into a box.

Final salvo in the room was the rolltop desk in the corner.

The thing was a rank, ugly, worn piece of crap that had nothing but function to offer the world. Battened down tight, with the top in place, it gave off the illusion of having something precious inside.

But only out of desperation.

As Sean slid up the cover, papers spilled out as if he'd opened some kind of wound and the POS was bleeding white.

What a mess.

Copping a seat in the hard-backed chair, he pulled over the box he was using as a waste bin and started sifting through Medicare notices and doctors' bills and insurance-company correspondence and bank statements. Most of the envelopes were unopened and he felt as if he were on an archaeological dig. The farther he went back, the older things got.

After having turfed the balance of it into some loose organizational piles, he was able to get to the shallow drawers in the back of the desk. He found nothing much important in them, just a couple of old Ticonderoga pencils, some paper clips, a thicket of rubber bands, a bottle of Elmer's glue that had turned into a solid. Everything smelled like the musky wood of the desk and the dry, dusty scent of time's passing.

He moved on to the big drawers underneath...and wasn't prepared for what he found.

He was going through what was just crap, mindlessly pitching copies of *Motor Trend* from the eighties into the trash box, when he ran into the photograph.

He sat up slowly, holding the thing with care.

Black-and-white. Three by five. Torn at the corner.

He and Billy and Mac were all under the age of twelve and standing at rigid attention in ill-fitting suits. They were smiling awkwardly, the pained expressions worn with the same graceless forbearance as their Sunday clothes.

His mother had taken the picture and her handwriting, her beautiful cursive handwriting, was on the back: the date, the place and his and his brothers' names.

Staring at the old ink, it dawned on him that in all the packing he'd done he hadn't found any photographs of her. In fact, there was nothing of hers in the apartment at all. Sure, his father hadn't been sentimental in the slightest, but wouldn't something have survived?

He turned the picture back over and tried to remember what his mother had looked like on the other side of the camera.

When he couldn't call an image to mind, he thought of Lizzie.

He wanted pictures of her. Lots of them. He wanted one at his penthouse by his bed. And one on his desk at his office. And one in his briefcase. And one stored digitally in his BlackBerry.

As if having all that would ensure she didn't disappear when she wasn't with him.

Sean put the shot of him and his brothers facedown on the top of the desk and vowed to go out and buy a camera. Like, tomorrow.

The piles of envelopes got his attention and he figured it was time to find out what kind of mess his father's estate was in. God, he hoped the man's will was in this morass somewhere, but chances were good Eddie had died intestate.

Sean started with the bank statements and got no further.

The first one he went through was from June and there were a number of checks...most of which were written to Lizzie Bond.

In her own hand.

Sean's skin shrank around his skeleton, just tightened up on his body as if he'd been put under a heat lamp and was drying out. As his breath froze in his lungs, he let the hand holding the pale green slips of paper fall to his thigh.

When he could stand it, he looked at the checks again. His father's signature was on the bottom of each one, a messy scrawl that just about screamed feeble and old and coercible.

Except maybe she'd just been writing them out at his request.

Sean quickly ripped open the other statement envelopes. Checks she'd filled out went all the way back for a year and the amounts varied from a hundred to five hundred dollars. There were four that were over a thousand.

When he was finished adding it all up, the total amount was well into the tens of thousands.

With a curse, he tossed a handful of checks onto the desk. As they scattered all around, he reached over to keep them from hitting the floor and caught sight of an envelope postmarked six weeks ago. In the left-hand corner, there was the return address of a local law firm.

As he slipped his finger under the flap, he got a paper cut that bled and he sucked off the sting while unfolding what turned out to be his father's last will and testament.

That left everything to one Miss Elizabeth Bond.

Well…well…well.

What do you know.

Turned out he and his father had something in common after all. Because like Eddie, Sean had been suckered into supporting Lizzie, too.

Man, she was smooth. He hadn't seen this coming.

Sean refolded the will and put it back in the envelope. Rage tickled the edge of his consciousness, making his head buzz, but he wasn't mad at her. He was mad at himself.

He'd been taken for a fool by a woman again and it was his own damned fault.

Chapter Fifteen

Even though it had been a tragically busy night in the emergency department, Lizzie was smiling as she got out of her car and skipped up the front steps to the duplex's porch. When she opened the door, she heard sounds from upstairs so she jogged upward.

One look at Mr. O'Banyon's living room and she stopped dead.

Stacks of U-Haul boxes were as high as her shoulders, each marked with the name of the local Catholic church. The rug that had been under the couch was rolled up and taped. The TV was unplugged and by the door. The few pictures that had hung on the walls were down and so too were the faded lace curtains.

"Good Lord, Sean," she called out. "You've worked yourself to the bone."

As she heard him coming from the back, she smiled. Until he walked in and she saw his face.

The man who had sent her off this morning with a lingering kiss was gone. The man who had poured her cereal and watched her eat and cleaned up her dishes was nowhere to be seen. The lover she had taken into her body and slept beside had been replaced by a hard, cynical stranger.

"Well, I'd better get packing," he said in a clipped tone. "I've got to get out of your way."

"Excuse me?"

He held out a sheath of documents. "Congratulations, your charm worked. Not twice, mind you. But at least you got the house from him plus whatever cash is left in his accounts."

As his words spun around in her brain, Lizzie felt as if she were midway through a car accident. Everything slowed down and she braced herself for imminent impact. What she didn't know was just how bad the injuries were going to be.

"What are you talking about?"

He pushed the papers at her. "Surely you've got your own copy of this?"

Putting her purse down on a box, she took what was in his hand. After she finished reading the will, she looked up in disbelief.

"I didn't ask him to do this. I don't want the house. Or the money."

"Oh, really." The smile that came at her was horrible. Just a baring of teeth. "You know, I have to give you credit. I mean, you had me, you really did."

"Sean, I didn't—"

"I'm sure you're going to get a good price for this place. And soon, too. I'm almost finished here so you can put it on the market right away. Or keep it. Either way, you won't have to worry about rent for a while and not just because some sap is letting you live here for free."

"Why in the world do you think I'd—"

"I saw the checks."

"What?"

"The ones you wrote to yourself and made him sign."

Lizzie was momentarily speechless. But then she had plenty of things to say. "I *beg* your pardon. First of all, your father's hands shook from the meds he was on and it was hard for him to write. Secondly, those checks were to me to reimburse what *I* spent on *him*. He was all but housebound because of his heart and the only way I could get him to let me do his errands was if he paid me up front. And we *still* fought about it all the time. He hated accepting help."

"A plausible denial, but you have no way of proving to me where any of this cash went, do you? Unless you have receipts from the past year, which somehow I doubt you're going to be able to produce. Bottom line? There's a lot more gone from here than can be accounted for through food expenses and miscellaneous purchases. And though I'm sure you're one hell of a cleaning lady, I don't think a good dusting is that expensive."

Lizzie shook her head and thought of all the prescriptions she'd filled and doctor's office co-pays she'd covered and cardiac rehab visits she'd shelled out for. And that was just the tip of the iceberg for what treating his heart had required.

But she wasn't going to justify herself. Sean wouldn't believe anything she told him and she was so angry at him she was likely to fly off the handle.

"You don't trust me at all, do you?" she said.

"Give me one reason, in the face of all this, that I should."

"Wow. Yeah…that's all I've got right now. Just…wow." She picked up her purse and put the will on a box. "You can keep the house, Sean. I wouldn't take it if you paid me to."

"Uh-huh, right. A convenient show, but legally it's already yours."

"I never asked him for this. And I can't believe you find it so easy to doubt me. But you know what? I'd rather know about your lack of faith sooner rather than later." She turned to the door and stared at him over her shoulder. "I've been telling myself you're just slow to trust, but I don't think that's actually true. I think you're broken, Sean…on the inside. So this showdown between us was inevitable, and although it hurts like hell, I'm glad it's out of the way. I'll put your things out in the foyer in a couple of minutes. Don't knock on my door again. Ever."

Chapter Sixteen

Sean spent the night at the Four Seasons and returned to the duplex to let the church folks in the following morning. Lizzie was working another double shift so she wasn't around. Which was good.

His father's place was empty by 11:00 a.m. and he was on his plane going back to Manhattan not long thereafter.

During the flight, he got no work done. Made no phone calls. Ate nothing, drank nothing. He sat alone in the luxurious cabin and tried to convince his brain to shut up. It was a debate he lost. The refrain that he'd been taken as a fool again just kept hammering at him, making him feel stupid and as if he shouldn't ever trust his instincts. God, he'd been so careful. For years. To be taken unawares again challenged his faith in himself.

And the worst of it all? There was a little voice in his head that doubted what he'd seen with his own eyes.... That wanted to believe Lizzie Bond wasn't capable of that kind of cunning… That craved to find out a different truth.

Anytime that whisper got too loud, though, he just reminded himself about all those checks and that will. Also recalled that desperation was no one's friend…and he'd very certainly been desperate for that woman.

God, he was an *idiot*.

As the plane circled Teterboro Airport before landing, his phone went off in his pocket. He frowned at the caller ID on the BlackBerry. Untraceable.

"Hello?"

"Sean O'Banyon?" came a male voice.

"Yeah."

"This is in regard to your brother, Sergeant Major Mark David O'Banyon."

Sean's blood ran cold until it was a solid in his veins. "Yes?"

"I understand you've left a number of messages for him. He's on special assignment right now and will not be able to respond to them for a period of time. This is a courtesy call."

Sean got dizzy from relief. Nearly saw stars. "Any idea when I'll hear from him? There's been a death in the family and I'd prefer not to tell him over the phone."

"I can't answer that in any official manner. But you might think in terms of months, not days. I can, however, try and get a message to him. If this is vital."

"Our father's dead."

There was a pause. "You have my condolences and

I will make sure that he gets the news. Is there anything else?"

God, there were so many other things he wanted to tell Mac, but not through an intermediary. "No. I'll wait to hear from him, but thanks for this."

"He will get the word. You can trust the army."

"I do. Thanks again."

Sean hung up and the plane descended. As the wheels squeaked on the tarmac, he remembered that tonight was the Hall Foundation Gala and he was going as Elena's social shield.

Damn shame he was feeling so transparent.

On Sunday, Lizzie went to the local market and bought the *Boston Globe* for its classifieds section and the *New York Times* for the crossword puzzle. Back at home, she sat on her couch, turned on National Public Radio for company and got out a red pen to circle jobs and apartments.

As she went through the rental section, and looked at addresses and monthly costs, she was nothing but an ache with arms and legs. Her whole body hurt, but the worst of it was in her chest. And she couldn't get her mind to focus. Eventually, she ended up doodling until her pen ate a hole in the newspaper and ink bled through onto her thigh.

She licked her forefinger and rubbed the red mark away.

She was so angry at Sean. Insulted. Hurt. Offended.

Now there was a crossword-puzzle theme. All the emotions you felt when you were grossly misjudged by someone. Probably wouldn't fly though. PISSED OFF was not likely to show up in the *Times* as a clue. And neither was WEEPY AS HELL.

As she started in on another corner with the doodling, part of her wanted to call Sean and yell at him. Part of her wanted to prove she wasn't who he thought she was. And part of her just wanted to crawl into bed and cry.

Determined not to fall into self-pity, she reminded herself that she had three interviews lined up this week and there were a couple of apartments that might work depending on whether their bathrooms were inhabitable. So she wasn't trapped in this apartment and there were prospects for work.

God... the will.

She'd never expected Mr. O'Banyon to leave her anything. They'd never even talked about that kind of thing. And she would have told him no if they had.

Which was maybe why it hadn't come up.

The thing was, even though she was mad at Sean, and even though he had so much money it wasn't as if he needed any cash, she didn't want to take his father's legacy away from him and his brothers. That was inappropriate. And Mr. O'Banyon shouldn't have done it. His children should have come first, no matter what had broken apart the family.

She tossed the *Globe* aside and picked up the *Times*. The massive weight of Manhattan's famous paper was awkward in her hand and the thing spilled out onto the floor.

Which was how she saw Sean on the front page of

the Style section holding a superbly dressed woman in his arms.

For a moment, Lizzie considered running for the bathroom to throw up.

Even eyed the way down the hall.

Sean had said he wasn't seeing anyone else in Manhattan and she believed him. He might be a terrible judge of character, but she knew instinctively he wasn't a liar.

He just hadn't waited long at all to move on.

And what a beautiful woman he'd picked. She looked like a model. Except for her jewelry. Those rubies marked her as a queen.

Lizzie stood and went to her bedroom. Opening up the closet, she pulled out a bag and started to pack for an overnight. It had been a while since she'd been up to see her mother and now was a terrific time to get out of this apartment.

Chapter Seventeen

Six weeks later, Billy O'Banyon sat in a lawyer's office in Southie and wanted to be just about anywhere else on the planet. It wasn't that he didn't want to help Sean out with settling their father's accounts and whatnot. He just hated being around all the books and the paperwork and the kind of people who were confident with writing and reading.

The printed word and him were not friends and anytime he got into situations like this, he always felt like the stupid idiot his father had told him he was.

But whatever. He was going to be out of here and back in the gym within the hour. As their father's will was uncontested and going through probate quickly enough, this wasn't going to be a long meeting. All he had to do was deliver some unpaid bills to the lawyer who was the estate's executor and discuss how the deed transfer and house vacating were going to go.

Actually, being here was his own fault. He could easily have mailed the stuff or dropped it off, but he was a man with a mission. He wanted to run into Lizzie Bond and this was the only acceptable excuse he had.

Sean had been in a bad way for the past month and a half, ever since those two had broken it off. Naturally he wouldn't talk much about what had happened, so Billy wanted to see how the other side was doing. If Lizzie came in looking as if she'd been run over by a John Deere, as well, he was going to get involved. The pair had been good together and sometimes people needed a little nudge to get back on track.

Just call him a romantic. Who happened to be able to bench press five hundred pounds.

"The other party is on their way."

Billy looked up at the voice. The guy who walked into the room was dressed in a gray suit and had a lot of files in his hand. The glasses he wore were more practical than stylish, but they made him look intelligent. Then again, he probably looked that way with contacts, too.

Billy shook the hand that was offered to him and the attorney sat down. With utter nonchalance, the guy started flipping through a file, his eyes scanning text quickly.

Billy watched with envy. Man, what was that like, to easily read what was on a page? To him, words were more like jumbled patterns, abstract shapes without meaning.

The lawyer scribbled something in a margin and looked up. "So you're a football player, I guess."

Billy nodded. "Yeah, I am."

"For the Pats."

"Yeah."

"I've never been into football, but I've heard about you." The tone was vaguely censorious and Billy was used to that. It had been years since he'd grabbed headlines for being a hard-partying playboy, but people didn't forget. At least not in New England.

"I'm really all about the game now," Billy said.

"Which is, of course, why they pay you all that money." The lawyer flushed as if he'd let the words fly without thinking.

"Sorry to keep you waiting," a woman said. "Work emergency."

Billy glanced over. In the doorway, a handsome African American woman dressed in a bloodred suit was standing just outside the conference room. With her kind, smart eyes, she looked like the sort of person who could run the whole country.

Or should be running the country.

Was she Lizzie Bond's attorney?

"Not to worry," the lawyer said. "This won't take long."

The woman came forward and extended her hand to Billy. "Hi, I'm Dr. Denisha Roberts, the executive director of the Roxbury Community Health Initiative."

Billy got to his feet and leaned across the table. "Pleased to meet you."

"Do you have the power of attorney?" the lawyer asked Dr. Roberts.

"Right here." The woman took some papers out of her briefcase and sat down.

"I'm sorry," Billy cut in. "Isn't Lizzie Bond supposed to be here?"

Dr. Roberts smiled as she pushed the documents over to the lawyer. "No reason for her to be. I have to say, this is a really generous thing she's doing."

"What's she doing?"

"Giving the community center the house. It's going to be the basis of our endowment—" Dr. Roberts's eyes popped. "Wait… Are you one of his sons?"

He nodded. "Yeah, but it's okay. We don't want the house."

Which, evidently, Lizzie didn't, either. God, she was just giving the thing away?

The lawyer looked up from reviewing the power of attorney.

"This is all in order." He glanced at Billy. "Do you have the final bill from the hospital stay when he passed?"

Billy blinked. He couldn't believe Lizzie was giving an entire house away.

Dr. Roberts leaned forward and put her hand on his arm. "I want you to know that your father's going to be remembered at our health center. The endowment is going to be called the Edward O'Banyon Fund. At Lizzie's request."

Son of a bitch.

Later that afternoon, Lizzie had all but finished packing up her apartment. As she wasn't officially moving out for another three days, she left her clothes in the dresser and in the closet, but pretty much everything else was in boxes.

She couldn't wait to get out of the duplex.

Her new place was on the dark side of Beacon Hill, a stone's throw from Mass General, where she'd found a job as a floor nurse in the surgical intensive care unit.

Like the studio apartment she'd rented, her new job was going to be fine. She knew a couple of the folks she'd be working with and they were good people. Also, her supervisor had an excellent reputation and had seemed really great throughout the interview process. Of course, she'd much rather have stayed with the community center, but she hadn't lost that connection. She volunteered there on Saturday mornings.

So it had all worked out.

For the most part.

Unfortunately, no amount of positive news got her mind off Sean. Memories of him were shadows that lurked in her thoughts. She remained angry and frustrated, but there were other things she felt, too. Sadness. Loneliness.

Except she had to let it all go, let him go. There was no getting over what he'd said to her or what he'd assumed she'd done. No healing that breach of trust. Besides, he had walked away without looking back. She needed to do the same.

It was so hard, though.

When her phone started ringing, she picked it up. "Hello?"

Her mother's voice was curiously level. "Lizzie?"

"Hi, Mom." When there was just silence on the other end, she frowned. "Mom? Are you okay?"

"Yes, Lizzie-fish. It's just…the oddest thing has happened."

"What?" Oh God. "Mom? You there?"

"Someone likes my pottery."

Lizzie deflated from relief. And exhaustion. "That's great, Mom."

"They really like it."

"I can see why." Unlike a lot of her mother's "work," the pottery was gorgeous, both decorative and functional. The vases were all flowing, organic lines; the mugs wistful and quirky; the plates uneven and charming. When Lizzie had seen some of it during her overnight trip to Essex, the first thing she'd thought was that the objects were just like her mother: beautiful and fey and somehow not of this world.

"Well, the someone wants to sell them, Lizzie."

"Boy, wouldn't that be great." A little extra money was always good. "Is it the little craft store next to the grocery?"

"It's the Mason Gallery in Boston. On Newbury Street."

Lizzie's eyes popped. "What?"

"Mr. Mason was up here buying antiques with his wife and I happened to be taking a stroll with my morning coffee. He saw my mug and when I told him I made it and had others they came back to the house. He liked what I did and wants to send a truck to pick up fifty pieces."

Good…*Lord*. The Mason Gallery specialized in selling one-of-a-kind objets d'art to the high-rent crowd in Boston. Lizzie had only ever walked by the window because she knew the prices inside were way out of her league.

"What should I do, Lizzie?"

"Well, do you want to sell your work?"

"I think so." There was a slight pause and then her mother's voice grew soft, almost ashamed. "But, Lizzie, you know I'm not good with money. Will you take care of all that stuff? I mean, I am not…good with money."

Lizzie closed her eyes, knowing there was so much more in that comment. Her mother was rarely self-aware, but in this moment, she was totally present and obviously clear about her mental deficiency.

The shame was painful to hear. And so very unnecessary.

"Mom, don't worry, I'll take care of everything. I'll tell you what we have to do."

There was sigh of relief. "Thank you. Because you know what? I really like pottery. I could see myself doing this for a long while. I think I'm not just inspired, I think I'm good at it."

Lizzie blinked away the tears that pooled in her eyes. "That's wonderful, Mom. I think that's wonderful."

"You know, Lizzie…you take such good care of me. Except I was thinking last night, I kind of wish someone would take care of you. Or don't you want that?"

Lizzie had to rub her eyes. "I don't know, I'm pretty self-sufficient. I do well on my own."

Like a cheerful bird call, a dinging sound rang out in the background. "Oh, Lizzie…I must go. I have some mugs ready to come out of the kiln now. They're so pretty. Bright blue like a summer sky on the outside, white as clouds on the inside. The rims are sunshine-yellow. I'm calling it my July series."

Lizzie thought back to the morning she and Sean had walked out into the sunlight and both seen the same beauty in the day.

In a raw voice she said, "That sounds lovely, Mom. Just…lovely."

When Lizzie hung up the phone, she replayed the conversation in her head to try and keep herself from thinking of Sean.

She'd only ever heard that serious tone of voice from her mom a couple of times before. The subject had been her love for Lizzie's father—the one constant in the woman's life. So chances were good this interest in pottery was going to stick.

Lizzie put the phone back in the charger and went into her spare bedroom. She'd put the majority of boxes in here to keep them out of her way, and as she looked at her things, she counted the times she'd moved in her life. Out of home to college. Dorm changes. Nursing school. First apartment. Then this one.

She would like a home, she thought. A place to be permanent in…where the front door and the interior rooms were a constant through the seasons of the years.

But she was probably going to be a vagabond for a while yet.

As she glanced at the boxes, she thought, yeah, she and U-Haul were going to be dating for a couple more years. Vagabonds needed to take their stuff with them. And that meant boxes and bubble wrap.

With a long exhale, she went over to the closet and

figured she might as well pack up the winter clothes that were stored there.

As she opened the door, she saw something on the floor inside that brought her to a halt.

It was a tool box. A beaten-up tool box that was painted red, but so scuffed and old it was more like a dull brown. On the side, the telephone company's name was stamped in yellow block letters.

Bending down, she picked it up by the worn black handle and put it on a waist-high stack of cartons.

Mr. O'Banyon's tool box.

He'd given it to her about a month before he'd died, had insisted that she take it with her downstairs after one of their Sunday dinners. When she'd asked him why, he'd told her that he wanted it in safekeeping, that he could only trust her with what was inside. At the time, she hadn't understood why a bunch of tools were in such danger in his apartment, but he'd been agitated from a switch in his meds and a little paranoid, so she'd taken the thing.

Out of curiosity and because the sight of it made her miss her friend, Lizzie flipped free the silver clips in front and opened the lid.

Only to frown.

It was full of papers, not tools. Papers and…photographs.

Which kind of made sense because it wasn't the dead weight it should have been.

Lizzie reached in and took out the picture that was on top of the pile. It was a black-and-white photo of a young, dark-haired woman who was standing in front of what could only be described as a palatial mansion. She was wearing a sundress and staring out at the camera with a lovely, flirtatious smile.

Sean's mother?

Lizzie delved farther into the box and found birth certificates for Mark David, Sean Thomas and William John O'Banyon. As well as a death certificate for Anne Whitney O'Banyon. There were also faded report cards bearing Sean's name. Clippings from the *Globe* featuring Billy on the football field. A commendation from the army for Captain Mark D. O'Banyon.

Way at the bottom, there was a bunch of papers that were folded up and secured with a thin rubber band.

She had no intention of reading them. She truly didn't. In fact, she was feeling bad enough for intruding on things that were Sean's and his brothers'.

But then the old rubber band broke and the documents unfurled.

At the top of the first page she saw three words: *Child Protective Services*.

God help her, she kept reading.

When she was finished, her knees were so weak, she had to sit on the bare floor.

In his office in Manhattan, Sean swiveled his chair around so that he faced the bank of windows behind his desk. Outside, a gorgeous September day was spilling sunshine all over the skyscrapers of Wall Street.

Exhausted, tense, in a nasty-bastard mood, he decided as a public service that he would leave a little early tonight and go for a run in Central Park.

Unfortunately, the plan made him think back to the last time he'd run around outside.

That glorious afternoon with Lizzie at the Esplanade.

Putting his hand under his tie, he felt for his cross through his shirt. As he traced the outline of the crucifix, he pictured her after she'd found it in the grass, a smile on her face, the gold necklace swinging from her fingertips, the holy pendant catching the sunlight.

God, he missed her. Even though he shouldn't.

On some level, he still found it hard to believe she'd done what she had. But as a practical matter, it was difficult to repudiate what he'd seen with his own eyes.

As a finance guy, he knew that cashed checks didn't lie.

"Mr. O'Banyon?"

He swung the chair back around and looked over his paper-riddled desk. Andrew Frick and Freddie Wilcox were standing in the door to his office, the two young guys looking tired, but very pleased with themselves.

"Hey, boys, what's doing?" Sean said.

Andrew came forward and put a four-inch-thick file on the desk, all the while glowing like a kid who was turning an apple in to the teacher. "We're finished with the analysis."

Sean leafed through the documents a little. "Nice. Very nice. Must have kept you two up all night."

"It did, but it's like what you say, you can sleep when you're dead."

Sean closed the file. "Yeah. Right."

Damn... All of a sudden, he wanted to give them a

pep talk about the evils of sinking too much into your work. He wanted to warn them that long hours hardened you and relentless competition drained you and meanwhile life slipped by and you didn't even notice how alone you were.

He wished he could give them a Frisbee and tell them to hit the park and run around barefoot and get dirty and then go home and have a few beers and call up a woman they liked and hang out.

Unfortunately, he had no credibility when it came to R & R. And besides, both of the guys had the glow of the converted in their eyes. They were clearly committed to fighting their way to the top and the over-caffeinated, messianic zeal with which they looked at him suggested he was their poster boy for success.

Man, he remembered having that burn, that drive, that need to win. And he knew what it meant. Nothing was going to derail them.

"Listen, boys, get some shut-eye tonight, if you can," he said because it was the best he could do.

"As long as you don't need anything else from us?"

"No, Andrew, this is what I wanted. I'll check through it tonight, but I have a feeling it's going to be a spotless numbers crunch. Glad you guys are on my team."

The two positively walked on air as they left.

In their wake, Sean felt as old as a stone and just about as lively.

When his BlackBerry went off, he took it out and answered before checking caller ID. He knew who it was going to be. Had been waiting for the call all afternoon.

"What happened at the lawyer's, Billy? Did you see her?"

Except the caller on the other end wasn't his younger brother. "Sean?"

"Mac? Is that you?"

"Yeah." His older brother's voice was thin and raspy, no doubt because he was calling from the other side of the flipping planet. "It's me."

God... What to say? "You heard about Dad? You got my message?"

"You bury him yet?"

"Ashes have been interred."

"Next to Mom?"

"Yeah." There was a pause and the silence made Sean twitchy. Mac was not a big talker under the best of circumstances and it had been a long time since they'd had any contact. But Sean felt as if he had to milk the precious seconds for all they were worth. "So, you sound really far away."

"You okay with him being gone?"

Sean swiveled his chair around so he could see the sky again. He wondered what part of the heavens his brother was under. "Yeah. Fine. Relieved, maybe."

"What about Billy?"

"Same." Sean cleared his throat. Knew he wasn't going to get anything, but asked anyway, "And you?"

"I'm coming home."

Sean sat forward in a rush. "You are?"

"Yeah."

"When?"

"Month or so."

"Are you out?"

"Think I could stay with Billy? In Boston?"

Nicely dodged, that discharge question. "Of course. You want me to tell him?"

"Yeah. When I get closer to my release date, I'll let him know."

"Release date? So you're really getting out?"

"Take care, Sean. Same to Billy. I'll be in touch."

The call ended. And Mac was gone like a ghost.

But at least he was coming home. God, how long had it been since Mac had been to the States for any period of time? Years.

Idly, Sean wondered what his brother looked like now. He'd be forty.

The BlackBerry went off again and this time Sean checked who it was before answering. Billy. Finally.

"Mac just called," he said instead of *hello*.

There was a sharp inhale. "He did?"

"Yeah, he's coming stateside and wants to stay with you in Boston for a little while."

"Whoa. I mean, of course he can bunk at my house here. Thing's big enough for an army." Billy paused, then asked, "What did he sound like?"

"The same. Distant. No idea where he was. Call lasted all of about half a minute."

"At least he's coming home."

"That's what I was thinking." After a brief pause, Sean switched the subject. "So did you see her?"

"No."

"What?" Sean frowned. "Lizzie didn't show?"

"Didn't have to because she's not the one taking

over the house. She gave it to the Roxbury Community Health Initiative. The director came with a power of attorney. Said they're going to use the sale of it to start the center's endowment. And get this, Lizzie asked that the fund be named after Dad."

Sean felt all the blood drain out of his head. A horrible, surreal feeling of doom cloaked him until he was mostly blind and mostly deaf and almost dead in his chair.

Gold diggers most certainly did not give away assets like that.

"I gotta go, Billy. Call you later."

Chapter Eighteen

As night eased over South Boston, a blanket of black heat came in and settled down for the evening.

Lizzie sat in the armchair, right next to the air conditioner, holding her phone in her hands. She tried to dial Sean's number again. And failed.

She just couldn't complete the call to him. One reason was the obvious issue of the way things had been left between them. The other was far more complex.

The tool box had to be returned and it wasn't the kind of thing she felt comfortable just leaving outside the apartment upstairs. As she'd long forgotten how to reach Billy, that left Sean. But what to say?

She collapsed back into the chair and her eyes slid

over to the tool box. For the millionth time, she thought about the papers she'd read.

Mr. O'Banyon, her old friend, was not who she'd thought he was.

Or maybe he'd transformed himself through the years into someone else completely. She couldn't imagine the man she'd known doing what those papers had stated, except it was clear he had.

Things to atone for indeed.

And Sean... Poor Sean. Her heart ached for the little boy he'd been. Ached also for Billy. And for the brother she hadn't met.

The papers had been a report of a domestic abuse complaint and its follow-up. Evidently, the oldest boy, Mac, had missed several days of school. When he'd finally shown up again, he'd gone to gym class, taken off his shirt and one of the teachers had seen the faded marks on his body. Which had triggered the complaint and investigation.

The boys had been taken from the home for two months then returned. All three of them had maintained Mac's contusions had come from street fighting, not their father. Which was, of course, not unusual. Often children protected their parents out of love or fear of retribution or any one of a number of rationales.

Lizzie was willing to bet things hadn't improved when they'd come home. The two months of anger-management counseling Mr. O'Banyon had received back in 1979 likely hadn't turned things around. Especially if he'd continued to drink. Which she was willing to bet he had.

Goddamn it, she would never get answers out of him, would she? She would never be able to confront him. She would never know how long or why or whether what he'd done had eaten him alive as she hoped it had.

Mr. O'Banyon was gone. Dead.

Though the past lived on, didn't it?

As a nurse, she'd seen the tragedies of domestic abuse and she'd talked to some social workers about the wide-ranging effects it had on its victims. One corollary for survivors, which tended to persist through adulthood, was trust issues in relationships. Particularly intimate ones.

So she found it difficult to stay angry with Sean for the conclusions he'd drawn about her character. She didn't appreciate his misconceptions, but at least now she could understand how he'd be predisposed to making them. Especially given the fact that someone had likely once used him for money.

Okay, enough with the thinking. Time to call him.

She started to dial just as she heard a car pull up in front of the house.

On some sixth sense, she leaned forward and looked out the window. Through the blinds, she saw Sean get out of a rental car.

Their eyes met. In the glow of a streetlight, she saw he was wearing another one of his suits and that this time his tie was a brilliant blue. He looked just as she remembered him: handsome, powerful, strong.

A car passed between them. Then with his typical masculine grace, he lifted a hand.

When she raised her palm in response, he started for the house. With long strides, he crossed the street and she heard his footsteps on the front porch.

She opened her door just as he came into the duplex. The cologne she remembered so clearly wafted in, going deep into her nose.

"Hi," he said.

"Hi." All she could think about as she stared at him was what she'd read in that report. She wanted to put her arms around him, hold him tight, ease him. "I was just about to call you."

His brows shot up. "Really?"

"I, ah, found something that belonged to your father." She motioned him in. When he walked into the living room, she shut the door. "It's right here."

She lifted up the tool box and his eyes latched onto the thing.

"God, I can remember him taking that to work all the time." Sean reached out and took it from her. "Guess it's one more donation to the church."

"You need to look inside before you give it away."

Sean's eyes narrowed. Then he put the thing on her couch and opened the lid. As he peered in, his breath left his lips on a long exhale. He picked up the photograph of his mother with reverence.

"So he kept one picture after all," Sean said softly. "I'd wondered. I didn't find any while I was cleaning up."

Lizzie crossed her arms over her chest and covered her mouth with her hand. She hated the strain in his voice, despised its cause.

He rifled through the contents, looking at the birth

certificates and then…the Child Protective Services report.

After he scanned the document, he folded the papers back up. "You read this, didn't you?"

"It was wrong of me, but yes, I did." She sighed. "I'm so sorry, Sean. I had no idea. None. And from what I knew of your father, I wouldn't have guessed him capable of it." When he stayed silent, she said, "I'm very sorry I intruded on your privacy. I'll say nothing, of course. To anyone."

Sean went over to the windows. Against the backdrop of the blinds, his profile was rigid and so were his shoulders.

Lizzie wanted to jump out of her skin as he stood there for the longest time. Was he mad at her? Was he back in the past? What should she do?

His voice drifted over to her. "You know, in retrospect, I'm surprised they let us go back." He tapped the papers against his palm. "Although I guess they really bought the 'we're just rough-and-tumble boys and that's why we have bruises' routine. I wish now that we hadn't been so persuasive."

"Was it the drinking?" she asked quietly. "Your father mentioned to me once he'd struggled with it."

"Yeah, he did what he did only when he was drunk. And hell, even though he got into the sauce every night, it wasn't all the time that he came after us. It was just…you didn't know when it was going to happen so it felt like every day even if there were months of relative quiet." His hazel eyes shifted over to her. "It's okay, though. We're fine now. Everything is fine."

"It's okay if you're not."

"No, it isn't."

Feeling as if she were intruding, but unable to stop because of her concern for him, she said, "Sean, have you ever talked to someone about what happened?"

He frowned. "Talked?"

"Like to a therapist."

"God, no. No need to. Like I said, we're fine." He stared at her. "I wish you didn't know."

"Sean...there's no shame in it. It wasn't your fault."

He looked away. And started to blink a lot.

"You didn't do anything wrong, Sean."

He swallowed with a grimace, as if he had a lump in his throat. "Yeah, I know."

"Do you?"

He swept a quick hand over his face. "Yeah. Yeah, absolutely."

"Sean—"

His tone was hard as he interrupted her. "I really wish you didn't know. Because you were friends with my father and it would have been better for you to remember him without this. Easier."

"I'd rather have the truth. And I am angry at him. I can't *imagine* how anyone could do what he did. Damn it, I want to go back in time and take you three out of that apartment so that you got free of it. I really—" She stopped herself and forced her tone to level out. Her getting fired up was not going to help Sean. He was looking really tense, as if he were about to bolt. "I do want to tell you something, though. As I think back to some of my conversations with your father, I believe he regretted his past. And in the two years I knew him, he never touched a drop of alcohol."

"Did he say when he quit?"

"No, but I think it was a long while ago. Once, when I was cleaning up some detergent that had spilled in a cupboard, I found a stashed bottle way in the back. It was dusty."

"I found a couple of those, too."

As Sean took a deep breath and looked up at the ceiling, she saw him not as he stood before her now, all tall and powerful. She pictured him as a young boy, scared and fragile. "I'm so sorry, Sean."

"Don't say that." His voice cracked and he scrubbed his face again.

"Sean…" She started for him, but he stepped away and she let him go.

"Yeah…" He passed his palm over his eyes again and collected himself. "So, Lizzie, do you want to know why I came tonight?"

She frowned. Why *had* he shown up out of the blue? "Yes…"

"I heard from Billy. Who went to the lawyer's today. He told me that you're giving this house away to the center."

She wrapped her arms around her waist. "Oh… Well… They need the money. And as I told you, I didn't ask for that bequest."

Sean walked over to some of the boxes she'd packed and ran his hand across them. His profile was characteristically handsome, all broad lines and dark hair.

"God…Lizzie…I really wish I could undo what I

said to you. What I thought about you. What I stupidly believed you were capable of. If you'd been after my father's money you wouldn't have let this house go. So those checks... They really were for his expenses, weren't they?"

"Yes."

He cursed. "I swear I've never been wrong so many times about a woman in my whole damn life."

"It's okay."

"How can you say that?"

She took a deep breath. "I guess...because now I understand you a little more, it's easier to forgive."

Sean looked over his shoulder. Lizzie was staring at him with impossibly warm eyes, offering him only absolution and tolerance.

Damn it, he wanted her to yell at him, felt as if he deserved nothing less.

Especially because he was enough of a bastard to want to take advantage of her pity.

"You can forgive me, huh," he murmured. "I'm lucky, then. Because if I were in your shoes, I probably wouldn't be able to."

"We're different, then."

"Yeah, we are." She was a saint. He was a son of a bitch. "I'm truly sorry, Lizzie. More than you'll ever know. We were going in a great direction for a while there. You were the first woman I'd cared about in a long, long time and...hell, I blew my shot at what I've always wanted but didn't think I could have, because I have no faith."

He went back to the window and looked out to the street.

He didn't hear her come up to him, just felt a soft touch on his shoulder. As the contact was made, he whipped his head around, surprised.

"The thing about forgiveness," she said, "is that it means you let things go. You start fresh in a different place."

Sean's heart began to pound with crazy hope. But then he figured she was just talking about resolving the mess he'd created and moving on as friends. Or more likely acquaintances. Still, that was better than nothing.

"I'll take anything you're willing to give me, Lizzie. Knowing I don't deserve it."

She reached up to his face. "But you do. We all deserve good things out of life. Each one of us deserves kindness and warmth…and love."

His arms moved of their own volition and gathered her against him. He had to force himself to hold her loosely because he wanted to crush her to him.

"Thank you," he said roughly into her hair.

Sean closed his eyes and let the world recede until all he knew was the feel of her warmth and the smell of Ivory soap. His eyes stung at the thought that their paths were not going to ever cross again. The idea of leaving her on a friendly note was more tolerable than them parting as they'd been before. But it was still horrible.

She pulled back first and he let her go.

As he scrambled for some excuse to linger, she said, "I want you to go see someone, though."

He blinked. "I'm sorry?"

"If we're going to be together, I need you in therapy. I'm willing to cut you all kinds of emotional slack, but I want you working on what happened, okay? Because the truth is, you're not fine. You've got things you need to talk about that require professional help. And unless you get it, we're just going to end up here again, over something else."

All he could do was stare at her. First, because he wasn't sure he'd heard her right. And then because he figured he had and they might still have something...and how many times in life did a miracle fall in your lap?

"Lizzie, I'm sorry.... Can you be a little clearer? My hearing's fine, but my brain's shorted out."

She laughed a little. "I want to be with you still. If it's something you want."

"Oh...God. Oh, Lizzie...I don't deserve this—"

She cut him off. "I'll be honest with you. If it weren't for your past, I probably wouldn't give things another shot. But because I know what you've been through, I guess I feel as though the not-trusting thing is understandable. I mean, that's hard for you, right? Trusting people."

He found himself nodding. "Yeah...Yeah, it really is."

"Makes sense. If you grew up in a situation where things were out of control and scary, where you never felt safe, of course that would be hard. But relationships require trust. So if we're going to be in one, you need to talk to someone—"

Sean dragged her against him and held her so hard they were one body not two.

He dropped his head to her neck and said, "I'll see someone. I swear to you. I'll do anything to have you in my life. I'm that desperate. I'm that needy for you."

He started kissing her and then she was kissing him back and then they were on the couch in a blaze of passion. Clothes flew and someone had to run down to the bedroom for some protection and they ended up on the floor, but it was utterly glorious.

When the rush was spent and they were in the after-glow, Lizzie glanced over at the tool box.

"Sean…how would you feel about naming the en-dowment after your mother? I think I'd rather have her name on it."

Sean's chest ached at her thoughtfulness, her strength, her kindness.

"I think…I think that would be perfect." He tucked a piece of hair behind her ear. "I think that would be perfect…just like you."

Epilogue

Two months later...

Standing in the bathroom of her studio on Beacon Hill, Lizzie looked at herself in a full-length mirror and didn't recognize who was staring back at her. The woman in the reflection was wearing a black gown and her hair was curled and her makeup was...well, hell, the makeup was fabulous—thanks to help from one of the ladies at the Chanel counter at Macy's.

"You look beautiful," Sean said from behind her.

She glanced at him in the glass. He was dressed in a tuxedo and a crisp white shirt and a black bow tie.

"So do you," she said, smiling.

He slipped his arms around her waist and pulled

her back against his chest. "But I think there's something missing."

She gathered up some of the gown's skirting then let the chiffon run through her fingers. "Are you kidding me? This dress is perfect. Well, maybe it's a little long, but I like the train effect."

Boy, she couldn't believe she was in something like this, a Vera Wang dress. Or that she was going to a gala fund-raiser...for the Roxbury Community Health Initiative. It was going to be an amazing night. The governor, Jack Walker, was going to speak and the money raised would go to the Anne W. O'Banyon endowment for the center.

Sean came around in front of her. "So you think the skirt's too long?"

He eased down on one knee and tugged lightly at the dress. As he did, he had a little half smile on his face, a secret grin that she'd learned he only gave to her.

Over the past two months, they'd seen each other every weekend, either because he flew up or she flew down. They talked on the phone constantly, usually way into the night, and it was safe to say that things were way better than good.

He'd kept his promise and started to see a therapist, even though she knew bringing up the past was hard on him. When he'd call her afterward and talk to her about the sessions, she could hear the emotion in his voice, but he'd made a commitment and he didn't stop going. No matter how difficult it was.

Because her man was like that. Strong.

"I think the length is perfect," he said.

"Still, maybe being in heels is better." She glanced over her shoulder at a shoe box that was next to the sink. Then turned back. "Could you pass me—"

Lizzie's mouth dropped open and her heart stopped beating.

Sean had taken a small leather box out of somewhere and was holding it up to her with the lid closed.

"What is that?" she whispered.

"Like I said, I thought you were missing something." His eyes were warm and grave as he opened the thing.

A diamond the size of a thumb glinted out of a black velvet base.

"Oh…my God…"

"Lizzie, I know it's early, but I love you and I want you to be my wife. And I can't hold on to this ring anymore. It's been burning a hole in my pocket since I bought the damn thing."

He loved her? He *loved* her?

He'd never said that before, though she'd suspected it. What he felt for her had been in his eyes and his voice and his body. But she'd figured he might never actually speak the words just because self-expression was hard for him.

Yeah, well, not only had he let the Big Three fly, he'd backed it up with a serious piece of geology and a proposal.

Sean flushed. "Lizzie, I didn't mean to spring this on you. I just can't not ask. I go for what I want. It's my nature. And I want you—"

She fell to her knees in a rush of chiffon and threw her arms around him, crushing the ring between them. "Yes…yes…I'll be your wife…. I love you, too."

As his big body trembled a little, she got the impression he might have been a bit nervous.

"You know what, Lizzie?" He pulled back, slipped the ring onto her finger and held the diamond in place. "With you in my life, I'll always be out in the sun on a summer day beside the river. No matter where I am or what I'm doing, I'll always be happy."

She smiled through her tears. "It's the same for me."

"Good." He smiled and his South Boston accent came out in full force. "Because I love you there, Lizzie. Got it wicked bad for you."

She laughed and held on to him again. "I wouldn't have it any other way."

* * * * *

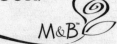

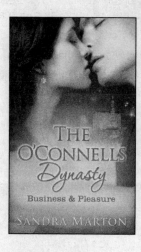
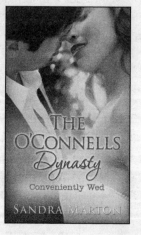

millsandboon.co.uk Community

Join Us!

he Community is the perfect place to meet and chat to
ndred spirits who love books and reading as much as
ou do, but it's also the place to:

Get the inside scoop from authors about their latest books

Learn how to write a romance book with advice from our editors

Help us to continue publishing the best in women's fiction

Share your thoughts on the books we publish

Befriend other users

orums: Interact with each other as well as authors, edi-
ors and a whole host of other users worldwide.

logs: Every registered community member has their
wn blog to tell the world what they're up to and what's
n their mind.

ook Challenge: We're aiming to read 5,000 books and
ave joined forces with The Reading Agency in our
naugural Book Challenge.

rofile Page: Showcase yourself and keep a record of
our recent community activity.

ocial Networking: We've added buttons at the end of
very post to share via digg, Facebook, Google, Yahoo,
echnorati and de.licio.us.

www.millsandboon.co.uk

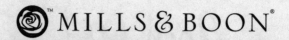